"This wasn't a sudden crash."

"I mean, we saw it coming, right?"

"Yeah, so?"

"So if we saw it coming, how come nobody else on board Magorran did?"

Before I got all the words out, I saw in Uncle Press's face that he knew exactly where I was going with this. The crash happened because the pilot and his crew were dead. But somebody else on Magorran should have seen the crash coming and tried to stop it. That is, if anybody else on Magorran were alive to see it. We both did a quick scan around and saw the same thing—nothing. There was no movement. No life. The sickening truth was setting in. There was a very good chance that everybody on Magorran had met the same fate as its crew.

This may have become a ship of the dead.

I turned away from Uncle Press and puked.

Read what critics and fans have to

"The non-stop plot developments keep the many pages turning and readers wanting more."
—*School Library Journal*, on *The Lost City of Faar*

"A talented world builder, MacHale creates endlessly fascinating landscapes and unique alien characters...the series is shaping up to be a solid addition to the fantasy genre and will keep readers not only busy but also content until the next Harry Potter appears."
—*Voice of Youth Advocates*, on *The Lost City of Faar*

"A fast pace, suspenseful plotting, and cliff-hanger chapter endings...nonstop action, snappy dialogue, pop-culture references, and lots of historical trivia."
—*School Library Journal*, on *The Never War*

"MacHale's inventiveness makes this book the best entry in the series so far...remarkable insight."
—*Voice of Youth Advocates*, on *The Never War*

"Pendragon rules!"—Java

"PLEASE KEEP THEM COMING!!!! And if you need somebody to pre-read your books like I believe you said your nephew and wife do, I'd be right there to do it. THEY ARE THAT GOOD!!!"—Joshua

❖ ❖ ❖

say about the Pendragon series

"I am insanely in love with the Pendragon books. I think that they are even better than the Harry Potter books."—Monique

"I absolutely LOVE your Pendragon books. My two best friends also love them, and whenever I get the next one they fight over who gets to read it first!"—Elisabeth

"Forget the Wands and Rings!! Pendragon All the Way!!"
—A Fan

"I'm pretty sure that I no longer have nails, as I was constantly biting them as I read the fourth Pendragon adventure."—Dan

"Pendragon is the best book series of all time."—Dark

"Nothing compares. I can't read another book without thinking 'Pendragon is better than this.'"—Kelly

"The Pendragon books will blow you away like no other books you have ever read."—Karen

"This series just pulls you into a world filled with suspense, treachery, and danger. Five stars easily; it deserves ten!!!"
—Greg

"Man, I gotta tell ya—these books are fantastic!"—Adam

PENDRAGON

JOURNAL OF AN ADVENTURE THROUGH TIME AND SPACE

FROM ALADDIN PAPERBACKS

PENDRAGON

JOURNAL OF AN ADVENTURE THROUGH
TIME AND SPACE

Book Two:

The Lost City of Faar

D. J. MacHale

Aladdin Paperbacks

New York   London   Toronto   Sydney

This book is a work of fiction. Any references to historical events, real
people, or real locales are used fictitiously. Other names, characters, places,
and incidents are the product of the author's imagination, and
any resemblance to actual events or locales or persons, living or dead,
is entirely coincidental.

First Aladdin Paperbacks edition January 2003
Copyright © 2003 by D. J. MacHale

ALADDIN PAPERBACKS
An imprint of Simon & Schuster
Children's Publishing Division
1230 Avenue of the Americas
New York, NY 10020

Designed by Debra Sfetsios
The text of this book was set in Apollo and Helvetica.

Manufactured in the United States of America
28 30 29 27

Library of Congress Control Number 2002108580

ISBN-13: 978-0-7434-3732-5
ISBN-10: 0-7434-3732-2

This is for my mom,
Ellie

September 2009

To Alex the Great —
My special. Middle
Schooler!
   All my love,
     Nonnie

PENDRAGON

JOURNAL OF AN ADVENTURE THROUGH TIME AND SPACE

Book Two:

The Lost City of Faar

CLORAL

Hi, guys. I gotta apologize for taking so long to write. So much has happened since I left you two, Mark and Courtney. I'm not really sure where to begin. First off, one mystery is solved. Remember the giant shark that nearly ate me down in that mine shaft on Denduron? Well, now I know where it came from. The territory I'm on is called Cloral and it's entirely underwater. No kidding. Underwater. The quigs on Cloral are giant, flesh-eating sharks. Nice, huh?

Now let me tell you about some of the new trouble I've been getting into.

I was almost eaten, again; I came dangerously close to drowning; my arms were nearly yanked out of their sockets; and I think I cracked a couple of ribs—all in the first hour after I got here. Sounds like a fun place, no?

I'm writing this journal now because things have finally calmed down and I need the rest. I think it's best to start my story at the point when I last saw you two. Man, that already seems like years ago. Time sure flies when you're out of your mind.

I still have tons of questions about what's happened to my

life, but two jump to the top of the list. Why is it that I, Bobby Pendragon, have been chosen to become a Traveler? I don't think that's a lot to ask since I've had to risk my butt about a thousand times over while performing my Traveler duties. The second is that I want to know what happened to my family. I keep asking Uncle Press these questions, but getting info out of him is like squeezing blood from a turnip. (Not that I've ever tried squeezing a turnip, but it seems like a tough thing to do.) He keeps saying, "It will all come clear with time." Great. Meanwhile, we keep jumping from one disaster to the next, and the best I can hope for is that I'll stay alive long enough to figure out why the heck I'm in the middle of all this when all I really want to do is go home and hide under my bed with the dog. C'mon! I'm only fourteen! Is that too much to ask?

I guess it is, seeing as my home isn't there anymore. The last time I saw you two, you were standing in front of the empty lot where my house used to be. It's hard to describe the emotions that were banging around inside me back then. I was nervous about going on another adventure with Uncle Press and bummed to be leaving you two guys again. But the worst part was the fear of the unknown.

Uncle Press promised me I would see my family again. Mom, Dad, Shannon, and even my golden retriever, Marley. But he stopped short of telling me where they had gone. He told me that they had raised me and prepared me for the moment when I would leave home to become a Traveler, but he didn't tell me why. Was it planned from the moment I was born? Was my family part of some secret plot? He also told me that he wasn't my real uncle. Meaning, a blood relative. But he hadn't yet answered the single most important question: *Why?* Why are there Travelers who blast through time and space, helping the territories through dangerous times?

Who chooses them? Most important, why me?

To be honest, I've stopped asking these questions because his answers are always so freaking elliptical. It's like he's some kind of Jedi master who only drips out information on a need-to-know basis. Well, I need to know bad. But I guess I'll have to be patient and learn as I go along. I think Uncle Press is afraid if he lays it all out for me in one shot, the truth will make my head explode and I'll end up lying in a corner someplace, drooling. He's probably right.

When I said good-bye to you two, I got into the car with Uncle Press and Loor, my partner from the adventure on Denduron. I was leaving my two best friends to take off with my new friend and partner. At least I considered Loor a friend. We had been through hell together on Denduron and even though I wasn't the warrior she was, I think I had earned her respect. At least I'd hoped I had.

I squeezed into the back compartment behind the two seats of the Porsche without being asked. Obviously Uncle Press was going to drive, and since Loor was bigger than me, there was no way she could fit in the back. She may have been dressed like she belonged on Second Earth, but she looked like no classmate I'd ever seen. I'm guessing she was around sixteen, but with her zero-body-fat, muscular bod, she looked ready for the Olympic decathlon. Her cocoa-dark skin made her look as if she were African, but I knew the truth. She was a warrior from the territory of Zadaa, which exists in an entirely different time and place from here. I think one of the first requirements for the Olympics is that you have to be from Earth. She didn't qualify.

"Comfy?" asked Uncle Press.

"Not even close," I answered.

With a laugh, Uncle Press hit the gas and once again we

screamed away from my hometown of Stony Brook, Connecticut. I didn't even ask him where we were headed, because I knew. We were going back to the abandoned subway station in the Bronx to find the gate that led to the flume that would take us . . . somewhere.

The last time we traveled this route I was on the back of Press's motorcycle, with no clue of what lay ahead. This time I had a clue, but not much more.

We blasted along the turnpike, out of Connecticut, headed for New York City. Within half an hour we had gone from the leafy-green suburbs of Stony Brook to the concrete pavement of the borough of New York called the Bronx. It's the home of Yankee Stadium, the Bronx Zoo, the New York Botanical Garden, and a secret Traveler flume into the unknown.

As Uncle Press maneuvered the quick little sports car through the city streets, people turned to stare. This was a rough neighborhood. They weren't used to seeing a sleek sports car screaming through their 'hood. Or maybe they were staring in wonder at the guy riding in back who was turning blue because his knees were jammed into his throat. That would be me.

With a final spin of the wheel, Uncle Press brought us right up to the curb next to the small green kiosk that was our destination. As I looked at that little building and the peeled paint on the sign above it that said SUBWAY, only one thought came to mind.

Here we go again.

I hadn't expected to see this place again so soon. No, I had expected to *never* see this place again. Uncle Press and I had come through this way only a few hours before, having returned from Denduron. My plan was to get back home, and do my level best to forget about this whole Traveler business. But things changed. I discovered that my family was gone, along with the life I knew. I think Uncle Press brought me back to Stony Brook to see for myself. It was a smart move, because if he hadn't, I never would have believed it. I would always be thinking about how to get home. But there was no home to get back to anymore. The cold, hard reality hit me that my destiny was to go with Uncle Press and learn more about being a Traveler. What a difference a few hours can make.

So there we were again, back in the Bronx, on the verge of starting my new life. I wanted to cry. Yes, I admit it. I wanted to cry. If Loor wasn't there, I probably would have.

Uncle Press hopped out of the car first, leaving the keys in the ignition. Loor and I crawled out after him. Actually, I did most of the crawling. I was so mashed up in the backseat that my legs were now totally asleep, and when I tried to stand, I fell over. Loor caught me and held me up until I got the feeling back. How embarrassing is that?

Uncle Press didn't stop to see if I was okay. He headed right for the stairs that led down into the subway.

"Uh, Uncle Press?" I called. "You sure you want to leave the car here?" I remembered back to our first trip here. We had left the motorcycle and the helmets right where the Porsche was now. I thought for sure that somebody would pinch them, but when we returned that morning, the bike was right where we had left it. The helmets were there too. Unbelievable. Pure luck. But this was really pushing it. A hot sports car sitting alone with the keys in the ignition was too tempting a prize. Worse, it was in a no-parking zone. If thieves didn't get the car, the cops would tow it for sure.

Uncle Press said, "It's okay. The acolytes will take care of it."

Huh? Acolytes? That was a new wrinkle. I looked at Loor to see if she knew what he was talking about. She shrugged. Before I could ask any more, Uncle Press disappeared down into the subway.

I said to Loor, "Yeah, I know—we'll learn more as we go along."

"Don't ask so many questions, Pendragon," she said. "Save them for when it is truly important." She then followed Uncle Press.

Truly important? Wasn't all this bizarro stuff truly important? I wanted to know! But since I was now standing alone and feeling dumb out here all by myself, the only thing I could do was follow. I was getting good at that.

I hurried down the dirty stairs and squeezed through the opening in the wooden boards that were nailed across the entrance. To the rest of the world this was a closed and abandoned subway station that had outlived its usefulness. To us Travelers, it was the crossroads of Second Earth, my home territory, and our jumping-off point to all the other distant territories. Sounds romantic, doesn't it? Well, it isn't. It's scary.

The filthy subway station was all too familiar to me. Subway trains still flew by, but it had been a long time since any had stopped at this forlorn spot. When I hit the platform, I saw something that brought back a chilling memory. It was the pillar that Uncle Press had hidden behind during his gun battle with Saint Dane. It was a battle that had given me the time to escape and find the gate and the flume that sent me to Denduron.

Saint Dane. There's a guy I'd like to forget. Uncle Press says he's a Traveler, like us. But he isn't exactly like us because the guy is wicked. On Denduron he pushed two rival tribes to the brink of annihilation. But we stepped in and messed things up for him.

Unfortunately Denduron was only the beginning. Saint Dane promised to wreak havoc with all the territories in his quest to rule Halla. That's key. He wants to rule Halla. Now, I'm no genius, but since Uncle Press described Halla as "every territory, every person, every living thing, every *time* there ever was," then having a guy like Saint Dane be the ruler is not a very good idea.

What made it all so incredibly creepy was that Saint Dane enjoyed seeing people suffer. I saw that firsthand, too many times. This abandoned subway platform was the first. This was where he hypnotized a homeless guy into jumping to a gruesome death in front of a speeding subway train. It was a cold-blooded trick that Saint Dane said was "to give the boy a taste of what was in store for him."

The boy he referred to was me. Nice guy, huh? I told you before that the worst part about my new life as a Traveler was the fear of the unknown. Well, that's not entirely true. Right up there on my list of fears is knowing that somewhere, sometime, we would cross paths with Saint Dane again. The guy was worse than dangerous, and it was our job to stop him. Standing there on that platform, I was really wanting a different job.

"Pendragon!" called Loor.

I followed her voice to the end of the platform. I knew this route. We had to climb down onto the subway tracks, carefully avoid getting fried by the third rail, and make our way along the grimy, oil-stained wall until we came upon a wooden door. On this door would be a symbol that looked like a carved star identifying it as a gate. That was our destination.

With Uncle Press in the lead, we moved quickly along the tracks. We had to hurry because a subway train could come charging along at any moment. There wasn't much room between the tracks and the wall, and a train speeding past our noses would hurt.

As we got closer to the door, I noticed that the ring on my finger began to grow warm. I looked at it and saw that the slate gray stone was beginning to transform. The dark gray color began to melt away and the stone now sparkled. This was the sign that we were getting near a gate. It was amazing how many things I was taking for granted. Once upon a time, the idea of following a possessed, glowing ring to a mysterious door in an abandoned subway station would seem like an off-the-wall dream. Not anymore. Now it felt natural. Sort of.

Uncle Press found the door, opened it, and hurried us all inside.

The cave inside hadn't changed. I immediately glanced into the dark tunnel that led off into the unknown. This was the flume that would sparkle to life and take us . . . somewhere. Right now it was quiet, waiting for us to tell it where we were going. I'd only traveled through the flume between Second Earth and Denduron. I had to believe that this time we were going someplace else, and now was the time for Uncle Press to tell us where. Loor and I stood together, waiting for him to show us the way.

"We're going to split up," he said.

Whoa. Not a good start. Was he crazy? We shouldn't be broken apart! Uncle Press knew his way around the cosmos and Loor was a fierce warrior. The idea of fluming off to face Saint Dane by myself without any backup was not something I could get psyched up about. A million thoughts and possibilities flashed through my brain—all of them bad. But just as I was about to break into full panic mode, Loor spoke.

"Why?" she asked flatly.

Nothing like keeping it simple. She was good to have around.

"Since your mother died, you are the Traveler from Zadaa," he answered. "They'll need you there soon. I want you to go home and be ready."

"What about me?" I asked, immediately flying into protest mode.

"You and I are going to Cloral," was his answer. "Saint Dane went there for a reason and I want to know what it is."

Good news, bad news. Good news was Uncle Press and I were staying together. Bad news was we were going after Saint Dane. Really bad news.

"But if I'm the Traveler from Second Earth, shouldn't I stay here?" I asked hopefully. "You know, to take care of stuff?"

Uncle Press gave me a smile. He knew I was trying to weasel out.

"No, it's best you come with me," was his simple answer.

Oh well. I wasn't surprised that my lame attempt at getting out of this trip had failed miserably. But hey, it was worth a shot, right?

Loor then stepped up to me and said, "If you need me, I will be there for you, Pendragon."

Wow, that blew me away. I guess I had earned her respect after all. I nodded and said, "I'll be there for you, too."

We held eye contact for a moment. The bond the two of us had created during the war on Denduron was stronger than I realized. I felt safer with her around, but it was more than that. I liked Loor. In spite of her inability to give an inch on anything, Loor's heart was always in the right place. I didn't want to go on without her. And I really believe that if she'd had the choice, she'd have stayed with me. But before I could say another word, she turned and strode into the mouth of the flume. She stared into the dark abyss, took a deep breath, and called out, "*Zadaa!*"

Instantly the tunnel started to breathe. The rocky walls began to writhe like a giant snake slowly coming to life. Then there was the familiar sound—the jumble of sweet musical notes that came from somewhere deep in the tunnel and grew louder as they rushed toward us. The walls transformed from gray stone into brilliant crystalline gems, just as my ring had as we approached the gate. The light that shone from the tunnel was so bright that I needed to shield my eyes. Loor became nothing more than a dark silhouette standing before the brilliant display. She gave one last look back to us and waved good-bye. Then, in a flash of light, she was swept into the tunnel. The retreating light and music carried her away and back to her home, the territory of Zadaa.

In an instant the show was over and the tunnel returned to darkness.

"Your turn," said Uncle Press.

"Tell me about Cloral," I asked, stalling for time. As much as I knew a trip through the flume was kind of fun, I was nervous about what I'd find on the other end. I needed a few seconds to get my act together.

"You'll find out all you need to know once you get there," he answered as he nudged me closer to the mouth of the flume. "Don't worry, I'll be right behind you."

"Why don't you ever give me a straight answer?" I asked.

"I thought you liked surprises?" he answered with a laugh.

"Not anymore I don't!" I shouted back. Uncle Press

used to surprise me all the time with great birthday gifts and helicopter rides and camping trips and—basically all the coolio things a kid could ever want from an amazing uncle. But lately Uncle Press's surprises weren't as fun as they used to be. Especially since they mostly involved me being chased by hungry beasts or shot at or blown up or buried alive or . . . you get the idea.

"C'mon, you're no fun anymore," he teased as he pushed me into the flume. "*Cloral!*" he shouted, and stepped out as the tunnel sprang back to life. I didn't even look into the depths because I knew what was coming.

"Fun?" I shouted. "If you think this is fun, you're crazy!"

"Oh, one thing, Bobby," he said.

"What?"

"Remember the Cannonball."

"What 'cannonball'?" I asked. "What's that supposed to mean?"

The light grew brighter and the musical notes grew louder. I was seconds away from launch.

"Just before you drop into Cloral, hold your breath."

"What!"

The last thing I saw was Uncle Press laughing. Then the light grabbed me and sucked me into the tunnel. I was on my way.

◉ SECOND EARTH ◉

"What are you two doing in here?" shouted Mr. Dorrico, the chief janitor of Stony Brook Junior High. "This ain't a library. You can't sit here reading your—hey, you're a girl! Girls aren't allowed in the boys' washroom!"

Mr. Dorrico had been a janitor at Stony Brook for most of his illustrious fifty-year janitorial career. There wasn't much you could put past him and this time was no different. There was indeed a girl in the boys' lavatory. Mr. Dorrico may have been ancient and terminally cranky, but he could still tell girls from boys. Most of the time.

Courtney Chetwynde and Mark Dimond had been sitting on the floor, reading Bobby's first journal from Cloral. The washroom on the third floor was near the art department. It was rarely used by anyone, boy or girl. It had become Mark's fortress of solitude. When the world got too busy, Mark would come here to escape and think and eat carrots and be alone. If he received one of Bobby's journals at school, this is the place he would come to read it. And since Courtney was now part of the picture, she would join him. The fact that she was a girl never seemed to matter, considering how important the journals were. But now they were faced with an angry chief janitor who looked as if he were going to have a heart attack at the very thought of a girl being in the boys' washroom.

Mark jumped to his feet and quickly grabbed up the pages of Bobby's journal. "It's c-cool. W-We were just leaving," he stammered nervously.

Whenever he got stressed, Mark stuttered. Courtney, on the other hand, was at her best under pressure. She stood slowly, walked up to Mr. Dorrico, and stared him right in the eye.

"The only reason I came in here," she said confidently, "was because there were so many boys in the girls' washroom. It was getting way too crowded in there . . . and they never lift the toilet seats."

"What!" shouted Mr. Dorrico, his face turning three shades of red.

To him this was clearly an offense that threatened to crack the very foundation of etiquette that our society was founded on. He grabbed the mop that he was going to use to swab up the boys' bathroom and charged back out, ready to do battle with the rogue delinquents who mocked the sanctity of the girls' lavatory.

Mark stepped up to Courtney and said, "You are bad."

"Time to go," she replied with a mischievous smile.

They ran from the bathroom and down the hall, careful to avoid the girls' room.

Mark knew that he and Courtney Chetwynde made an odd pair. Mark was an introvert. He lived in a world of books and graphic novels. He didn't have many friends. His hair was always a little too long and a little too unwashed. Sports were a four-letter word to him and his mother still picked out his clothes, which meant he wore a lot of non-name-brand geek outfits that were always about two years out of date. But the thing was, he didn't care. Mark never wanted to be cool. In fact, being comfortable with his noncoolness made Mark feel pretty good about himself. Where everyone else was busy trying to impress their friends with the way they looked or who they hung out with or what parties they went to, Mark couldn't be bothered. So Mark considered himself cooler than cool—in a nerdy kind of way.

Courtney, on the other hand, had it all going on. She was tall and beautiful, with long brown hair that fell to her waist and piercing gray eyes. She got decent grades. Not world-class, but good enough. She also had a ton of friends. But the thing that defined Courtney was sports. Volleyball in particular. Courtney was so tall and strong that it was unfair for her to play against most girls, so she played on the guys' teams at Stony Brook. As it turned out, it was unfair for her to play against most boys, too. She absolutely crushed them. Guys feared her because they didn't want to be embarrassed by a girl, but more because they were afraid when they faced Courtney, they'd lose teeth. At fourteen she was already a legend.

So the differences between Mark Dimond and Courtney Chetwynde were so huge that a friendship wasn't something you'd expect. That is, except for one thing.

Bobby Pendragon.

Both Mark and Courtney had known Bobby since they were little. Mark and Bobby were best buds beginning in kindergarten. Bobby spent so much time at Mark's house that Mrs. Dimond referred to him as her second son. As they grew older their interests changed. Bobby was into sports and was incredibly outgoing. Mark . . . wasn't. But where most people who were so different would drift apart, Mark and Bobby had a friendship that didn't fade. Bobby often said that as different as they seemed, they both laughed at the same things, and that meant they really weren't so different after all.

As for Courtney, Bobby met her in the fourth grade and fell in love. From the very first second he saw her stunning gray eyes, Bobby got slammed with a crush that had yet to fade. Growing up, they were rivals in sports. Bobby was one of the few guys who weren't intimidated by Courtney. Just the opposite. Even though she was a girl, he never cut her any slack. Why should he? She was too good. When they played dodge ball, he'd go after her as hard as she went after him. When they ran the four hundred in gym, he'd make sure the two of them went head-to-head. Sometimes he won; other times Courtney took him. In Little League they were on opposing teams and both were pitchers. When the other came up to bat, they'd each dig down a little deeper to throw heat. Naturally there was the occasional brush-back pitch that sent the other into the dirt. No one ever got hit, though. They may have been rivals, but they were still friends.

The thing was, as strong as Bobby's crush on Courtney was, Courtney felt just as strongly about Bobby. But neither let the other one know until that fateful night when Courtney came to Bobby's house before a basketball game. That's when Courtney admitted to Bobby how great she thought he was. It was also the night the two kissed for the first time. For Bobby, it was one of those incredible moments that actually transcended expectations. It was downright magical.

Unfortunately it was also the night when Bobby's Uncle Press took him away from home to begin their adventure on the troubled territory of Denduron. Bobby's old life ended with that one sweet Courtney kiss.

It was out of concern for Bobby Pendragon that Mark and Courtney got together. Both were terrified that something horrible would happen to him as he flumed through the territories. It was Mark who first started receiving Bobby's journals through the magical ring that was given to him one strange night. It was presented by a kind, strong woman who Mark thought was part of a dream. But in the morning the dream was over, and the ring was still there. This woman turned out to be Osa, Loor's mother, who was doomed to die while protecting Bobby. This ring was the conduit through which Bobby could send the journals of his incredible adventures back to his friends.

Reading about Bobby's adventures was both exciting and frightening for Mark. The perils were more enthralling than any action flick he'd ever seen. But Bobby's stories weren't meant to be entertaining. They were real, and that's why they were so frightening. The idea that there was a group of people called Travelers who voyaged through the universe doing battle against evil was a concept that challenged everything Mark knew about how things worked. Stranger still, knowing that his best friend was one of these Travelers made it all the more tough to deal with.

The fact was he couldn't deal with it. Not alone, anyway. That's why he brought Courtney into his confidence. Together, the two would read Bobby's journals and try to help each other understand what was happening to their friend.

Their meeting place of choice was the basement of Courtney's house. Her dad had a workshop down there, but he never used it. Courtney always laughed at her father, saying how he got all these tools because they looked cool, but then had no idea of what to do with them. So the basement workshop was pretty much a dusty tool-museum, which was perfect for Mark and Courtney. There was a big worn-out couch down there where they would settle in to devour Bobby's journals.

Their run-in with Mr. Dorrico came toward the end of the school day, so the two didn't go back to class. Instead, they headed right to Courtney's house. Courtney even skipped volleyball practice. She never missed practice unless there was an emergency. The arrival of a journal from Bobby definitely qualified.

Courtney ran down the basement steps ahead of Mark and leaped into the old couch sending up a cloud of dust. "C'mon!" she shouted impatiently at Mark. "I'm dying! I want to know what happened on Cloral!"

Mark had Bobby's journal in his backpack. But rather than dig it out and sit next to Courtney so they could continue reading, he stood over her, looking nervous.

"What's the matter?" she asked, trying to sound as impatient as she felt.

"C-Courtney, I-I'm scared," he said softly.

Normally Courtney would bulldoze over guys like Mark if she wasn't getting what she wanted. But this was different. They were a team. They shared a secret. If one of them was having a problem, the other one had to respect that. So as eager as she was to rip the pack off of Mark's back and grab Bobby's journal, she took a breath and tried to relax.

"I am too," she said softly. "But I want to know if he's okay."

"I'm not talking about Bobby," Mark whined. "I'm scared for us."

Courtney sat back in surprise. Mark now had her full attention.

"Why?"

Mark paced. "Ever since he left a few months ago, I've been giving this a lot of thought."

"Yeah, no kidding. Me too," Courtney said. But obviously Mark's thoughts were more troubling than Courtney's because he was the only one worried just then.

"Think about what's at stake here," Mark continued. "Saint Dane is trying to rule Halla. That's everything. Every time and every place there ever was. Don't you think that's a little scary?"

"Well, yeah," she answered. "Until a few months ago the biggest thing I had to worry about was passing algebra. Going from that to sweating over the future of all space and time is kind of a leap for me."

Mark nodded. A problem this huge was kind of hard to get your mind around.

"Okay," he said while continuing to pace. "It's hard for me to understand too, but there's more. Uncle Press told Bobby that all the territories were about to reach a turning point. It was the job of the Travelers to help them get through the crises so they could continue to exist in peace. If they failed, the territory would fall into chaos, and that's when Saint Dane would step in."

"Okay, so?" Courtney said impatiently. She wanted to know where this was going.

"So think about it," Mark said, getting worked up. "Bobby and Press went to Denduron because that territory was on the verge of a civil war. We just read that Press told Loor she had to go back to her home territory of Zadaa because they would need her there soon."

Courtney listened carefully. Mark was leading to a point and she wanted to make sure she fully understood what it was.

"Saint Dane went to Cloral," he continued. "Bobby and Press followed him there. Cloral must be reaching its critical time too."

"I get all this. But why are you so scared?" Courtney asked.

"Think," he said quickly. "We're reading these journals like they're stories happening far away from our safe little town. Sure, Bobby is right in the middle of things, but nothing is touching us. Not here. Not in the safe suburbs."

Courtney was starting to catch on. "You're saying something big might happen here, too?" asked Courtney soberly.

"Exactly!" shouted Mark. "We're a territory too. Second Earth. We're not immune. We're part of Halla or whatever it's called."

Courtney turned away from Mark to let this sink in. If all the territories were about to reach a turning point, that had to include their own territory as well. This was definitely bad news.

"I'll tell you something else," Mark said. "We've been trying to figure out why Bobby is a Traveler. I have no idea why, but I'll bet I know *when*."

"Huh?" said Courtney. "When what?"

"It seems like Travelers only go where they are needed, *when* they're needed," reasoned Mark. "I'll bet the time has come for Second Earth to need a Traveler, and that's why we now have one. Bobby."

Courtney didn't ask another question. She didn't need to. What Mark said made all sorts of sense. Up until now, everything that Bobby had written was true. He wrote that Uncle Press warned him that all the territories were nearing a critical time. *All* the territories. That included this one. Second Earth. Home.

"You want to hear more?"

"Not really," answered Courtney nervously.

"I think we're part of it, you and I," he said. "Bobby is sending us his journals. Besides him, we're the only ones here who know what's going on."

"You think we're being prepared for a battle on Second Earth?" Courtney asked softly, as if she could hardly get the words out.

"I think that's exactly what's happening," answered Mark.

Suddenly Courtney was just as scared as Mark. He had finally made his point, but she wished he hadn't.

"So what do we do?"

Mark took off his pack and sat down next to her.

"That part I haven't figured out," he answered. He dug inside the pack and pulled out Bobby's journal. Unlike the first journal that was written on crude, yellowed parchment paper, these pages were light green and supple. Each page was roughly the size of standard printer paper, but the edges weren't square. These pages were oddly shaped, as if they had been hand-made. The green pages were like a light, thin rubber. The writing looked pretty much the same as the other journals though. The words were written in black ink, and the handwriting was definitely Bobby's.

"Until we get more of an idea of what to expect," continued Mark. "All we can do is read Bobby's journals and learn as much as we can so when the time comes . . . we're ready."

Courtney stared into Mark's eyes. His last comment sounded ominous. This wasn't a game happening to someone else. This was real. Common sense told them that sometime, somehow they were going to get sucked into this nightmare. Courtney was beginning to hate common sense. The question was, when would it happen? Those questions could only be answered by the words in Bobby's journal, so without any more conversation, Mark and Courtney looked down at the strange green pages and continued to read.

CLORAL

The flume.

It was my fifth time flying through this magical tunnel into the unknown, but I still wasn't used to it. Heck, I could travel like this a thousand times and I wouldn't get used to it. As I told you guys before, it's kind of like sailing down a huge water slide. But it's not as violent as a water-park ride. It's really more like floating on a cushion of warm air. The tunnel walls that were surrounding me looked like transparent crystal. But I knew this only happened when the flume was activated. Why does it do this? Haven't got a clue.

Beyond the walls I saw stars. Billions of them. I was in the middle of the universe traveling through space and time. At least that's how it was explained to me. I wondered if the flumes were actually solid. Was it possible to damage a flume? Could an orbiting satellite accidentally smash into one? What about a meteor? Or an asteroid? I figured I had enough to worry about without thinking about that kind of potential disaster, so I tried to think of something else.

Up ahead I could see the twists and turns of the tunnel. The first time I had done this I was afraid to bounce off the walls, so I tried to lean into the turns like one of those maniacs on a luge run, but as it turns out I didn't have to bother. Whatever force was speeding me along also prevented me from slamming into the walls. All I had to do was kick back and enjoy the ride.

Until now, I had only taken the flume between Second Earth and Denduron. This was the first time I was headed to somewhere else. I wondered if I was going to hit some kind of intersection and get shot in the new direction. The answer came pretty quick. There were no turns. There were no junctures. I was on the express line to Cloral.

How did I know that? I heard a sound. I was used to hearing the jumble of sweet musical notes as I shot along, so this new sound jumped out at me. It kept getting louder, which meant I was getting closer to it. It wasn't until I was almost to the end when I realized what it was.

It was water.

Suddenly the warning Uncle Press had given me before I got sucked into the flume made sense. He told me to remember the Cannonball and to hold my breath. In that instant I remembered the Cannonball. Do you remember, Mark? It was a ride at the water park in New Jersey that Uncle Press took us to a few years ago. It was a short, fast water slide that went underground, then shot you out for a fifteen-foot drop into an icy cold pool of snowmelt mountain water. I think the word you used to describe it was "rude." Well, if I was right, then Uncle Press's warning meant that I was about to be shot out of the flume into a pool of water. I quickly folded my arms in front of my chest, crossed my legs, and waited for the end.

It came quickly. I was fired out of the flume like a torpedo, feet first. One moment I was floating comfortably in the flume, the next moment gravity took control and I was falling through the air toward . . . what? Everything was a blur. I couldn't get my bearings or my balance. All I could do was hope to land on something soft. Or wet.

It was wet. With a graceless splashdown, I hit water. But thanks to Uncle Press's warning, I was ready. I hit feet first and plunged below. I even remembered to hold my nose so I wouldn't get a sudden brain-flush of water shooting up my nostrils.

The water was tropical warm, like swimming in Florida. As soon as I stopped driving downward, I kicked my legs to push back to the surface. I wanted to know where I was and what the territory of Cloral had going on. When I broke the surface I took a quick look around to check the place out. I was treading water in a large pool in an underground cavern. Not a big surprise. So far all the flumes were underground. But unlike the other flumes that I walked into, the opening to this flume was cut into the cavern wall about twenty feet above the water. That's where I had just been shot out like, well, like a cannonball. Thanks for the warning, Uncle Press.

A quick scan around told me that the cavern was completely sealed and the only light came from the water where I was floating. I figured the sun was shining outside and it reflected off the sandy bottom to create a luminous green pool that was bright enough to light up the entire cavern.

The place was about the size of two tennis courts, with a high arching ceiling that reached a peak far above. It kind of reminded me of being in a small church. The walls were craggy, sand-colored stone that looked to have been carved by centuries of erosion. There were also thousands of green, leafy vines that grew right out of the stone and draped down over the rocks like a curtain.

But the thing that really jumped out at me were the

thousands of colorful flowers that grew from the vines. The light from the pool of water must have been enough to let them grow, or maybe flowers didn't need light on Cloral. Whatever the case, they were like a spectacular tapestry of color all over the walls. There were vivid reds, deep blues and vibrant yellows. The flowers were all different shapes and sizes and looked nothing like Earth flowers. Some were trumpet shaped, others looked more like small helicopter blades. Stranger still, they seemed alive. No kidding, all the blossoms were slowly opening and closing like they were breathing oxygen. Seeing these thousands of moving flowers made the cavern itself seem alive. It was magical and creepy at the same time.

I had calmed down by now and floated lazily in the green pool. It was actually kind of cool. I also think I was mesmerized by this wondrous place. I probably would have kept floating there for a long time if I hadn't heard the familiar sound of musical notes coming from the flume overhead. It took a second for me to register what was happening. Uncle Press was about to arrive. That was good. But I was treading water on the very spot where he was going to land. That was bad. I instantly kicked and lunged for the side of the pool to get out of the way. No sooner did I touch the rocky edge when I heard, "Eeeehaaaa!"

Uncle Press shot out of the flume headfirst. The force of it sent him sailing out into the center of the cavern. He seemed to hang there for an impossible second until gravity kicked in. As he began his arc down, he thrust his arms out to form a perfect swan dive. Then just before splashdown, he brought his arms together and entered the water almost vertically. He barely even made a splash. A perfect ten all the way around.

I pulled myself up and sat on the edge of the pool as Uncle Press resurfaced. He had a huge, exhilarated smile on his face as he shook his head to throw his wet hair out of his eyes.

"Yeah! I love this place!" he shouted with joy. "Headfirst is the only way to go."

I was beginning to think that Uncle Press liked being a Traveler. At least he enjoyed it more than I did, that was for sure. With two quick strokes he swam to the side of the pool and hauled himself out. He was a little out of breath from his dramatic arrival, so he sat on the edge and looked at me with eyes that were alive with excitement.

"Welcome to Cloral," he said with glee. "This is my favorite territory. No contest."

He sounded like some kind of tour guide whose job it was to make sure I was enjoying my vacation. But this was no vacation. Not even close.

"So what's the deal here?" I asked, not really wanting to hear the answer. "Is there a war? Some impending disaster? Some evildoings that Saint Dane cooked up to make our lives miserable?"

Uncle Press gave a shrug. "I don't know," was his casual response.

Huh? Up until now Uncle Press had all the answers. He didn't always share them with me, but it was good to know that at least one of us wasn't totally clueless.

"Don't know?" I shot back. "Why do you keep stuff from me? If we're headed for trouble, I want to know."

"I'm not trying to hide things from you, Bobby," he said sincerely. "I really don't know what's happening here. On Denduron, I'd been living with the Milago and knew that there was civil war brewing. But I've only been to Cloral a couple of times. As far as I know, everything here is fine and dandy."

"So then why are we here?" I asked with frustration.

Uncle Press looked me right in the eye, suddenly all business.

"We're here because Saint Dane is here," he said soberly. "He hasn't tipped his hand yet, but he will."

Right. Saint Dane. Back on Denduron, moments before Loor and I had made our death-defying escape from the mine shaft, Saint Dane had jumped into a flume and shouted, "*Cloral!*" Since the mine was seconds away from blowing up, Loor and I would have gladly followed him, except that he sent a killer shark riding a wave of water back through the flume to stop us. We had two choices: death by shark-lunch, or flee deeper into the doomed mine. We chose to run and luckily escaped through a ventilation shaft before the entire place exploded.

It suddenly dawned on me that the reason we were here on Cloral was because of me. I was the one who knew Saint Dane came here. I guess I was playing more of a part in this whole saga than I really cared to.

"Tell me about Cloral," I asked. I figured I should at least know what to expect from this new territory.

Uncle Press stood up and glanced around the colorful, living, underground cavern.

"The whole planet is covered by water," he began. "As far as I know there isn't an inch of dry land anywhere. This cave is part of a coral reef that's about sixty feet underwater."

"You're kidding?" I interrupted. "Who lives on this territory? Fish?"

Uncle Press laughed and reached toward one of the vines that clung to the rocks. Behind the colorful flowers, attached to the same vine, were dark lumpy-looking things. He plucked one off like an apple from a tree and tossed it to me. I caught it awkwardly and saw that it looked like a small, dark green cucumber. It was kind of rubbery, so I guess it was really more like a pickle than a cucumber.

"Break it in half," he said.

I held both ends and snapped the strange tube in half easily. The green skin on the outside was so dark that it was nearly black, but the inside was bright red.

"Try it," he said while plucking another one for himself. He took a big bite and chewed. I figured if it didn't kill him, it wouldn't kill me, so I took a bite and it was delicious! It was like the sweetest little watermelon I had ever eaten. Even the skin was good, though chewier and a bit more salty than the sweet pulp inside. No seeds, either.

"I think there may have been a time when the people of Cloral lived on dry land," he continued. "But that was centuries ago. There aren't any records of it. Whatever happened to the planet, no one knows. But the land is long gone."

"So how do they live in water?" I asked while wiping the sweet juice from my chin.

"They don't," he answered. "They live on floating cities called 'habitats.' Whole communities are built on these monster barges. Some are so big you'd swear you were on an island."

"That sounds impossible," I said. "Where do they get food? And building materials? And—"

"Why don't I just show you?" Uncle Press interrupted.

Good point. We could sit here talking about it, or I could see for myself. I hated to admit it, but I was kind of interested by a world that was always floating.

Uncle Press wiped fruit juice from his mouth and walked carefully across the rocky ledge until he came to a thick mound of vines near the base of the wall. He pulled them away and I saw that the vines had been covering a pile of clothing and equipment. I immediately remembered the cave on top of the mountain on Denduron where Uncle Press gave me the leather clothes of that territory. It was against the rules to wear anything from other territories, so we needed some Cloral clothes.

"I don't get it," I said quizzically. "If you didn't know we were coming here, how did you know enough to have this little stash of stuff ready?"

"We aren't alone, Bobby," he said while picking up and checking out something that looked like a clear-plastic bubble the size of a basketball. "There are acolytes who support us on every territory. They brought this gear here."

Acolytes. That's who supposedly took care of the motorcycle back in the Bronx.

"Who are they?" I asked. "How come I've never seen one?"

"You won't," he answered. "At least not often. But they're around."

"If they're so helpful," I added suspiciously, "how come they didn't help us out a little more on Denduron?"

"It's not like that," he said. "They aren't Travelers. They can't play a direct role in our mission. All they can do is help us blend into the territory. Here!"

He tossed the plastic bubble to me. It was light, but solid. One section of the globe was open so it looked kind of like a big, round fishbowl. There was also a small gizmo attached to it that looked like a silver harmonica.

"Put your head in it."

Yeah, right. Sticking my head into that alien object is not something I'd do by choice.

"Just put it on," he said with a smile.

Why couldn't he just tell me what was about to happen for a change? Why did I always have to experience it myself? Oh well. Why argue? I reluctantly lifted the clear globe and slowly lowered it down over my head—until a freaky thing happened. As soon as the top of my head touched the inside of the globe, the clear dome started to change shape! I instantly yanked the cursed thing off. It immediately stopped moving and returned to its original round shape.

"What the hell was that?" I exclaimed, totally freaked out.

Uncle Press laughed and reached toward the pile of stuff to get another clear globe.

"The Clorans are pretty advanced," he explained. "They've got some pretty incredible toys."

"Like torture devices that clamp on your head and suck out your brain?"

"No, like anything to do with water. Water is their life. They've learned how to use it in ways you can't even imagine."

He put the second globe over his head. Instantly the clear dome began to writhe and change shape. In a few seconds the sphere went from totally round, to a perfect formfitting shell around his head. It was unbelievable. The thing had taken on the shape of Uncle Press's head. He smiled at me from inside the clear mask.

"They've figured out how to create solid material from water," he said while tapping the shell that had formed around his face. It was hard again. Amazing. I could even hear him clearly, though his head was encased in . . . whatever it was encased in.

"And this thing here"—he pointed to the silver harmonica thing attached at the back of his head—"this is a filter that takes in water, breaks it down atomically, and feeds oxygen into the mask so you can breathe. Cool, aye?"

Now I got it. This strange living mask was some kind of scuba gizmo. You could breathe underwater with this thing.

And the clear plastic would act as a mask to keep water out of your eyes so you could see. How cool is that?

Uncle Press pulled the clear mask up off his head, and by the time he placed it in his lap it had already become round again.

"Centuries of living on water makes you resourceful," he said.

"Absolutely," I added. "What else you got there?"

There were two gizmos on the pile that I can best describe as looking like the plastic floats lifeguards use when they make rescues. Uncle Press picked one up and held it out for me to see. It was roughly football shaped, bright purple, and had handle grips on each side. It was about a foot and a half long. One end had a round, open mouth. The other end came to a point. There were also rows of slits that ran across the top and bottom.

"Okay, I give up," I said.

"It's a water sled. When you're in the water, grab the handles, hold it out in front of you and pull the trigger."

I could see that hidden inside each of the handles was a trigger.

"The open end goes in front," he explained. "Point it where you want to go. Water gets sucked in through these slits for power and the whole thing pulls you along. The harder you squeeze the trigger, the faster you go. Easy peazy."

This was getting good. I was beginning to see why Uncle Press liked Cloral so much. He then threw me a pair of rubbery swim fins that needed no explanation.

"Get changed," he added.

It was time to dress like a Cloran. I had been through this drill before. So I walked across the stone ledge and began to dig through the pile of Cloral clothes. Uncle Press did the same. There were shirts and pants and even shorts that I guess were supposed to be used as underwear. Good thing. I didn't get to wear any underwear on Denduron and the rough leather clothes gave me a raging rash that was only now starting to calm down.

The material was soft and kind of rubbery. Cloral was all about water, so I guessed these clothes would be perfect for swimming and would dry fast. The colors were bright, too. All were on the cool end of the spectrum, blue, green, and purple. I knew from the times that Uncle Press had taken me scuba diving that the best colors to use underwater were in the blue family—they showed up best. Colors like red and yellow were quickly filtered away underwater so they ended up looking gray, but blue still looked like blue underwater. So did purple and green.

I had the feeling that there would be more opportunities for my scuba diving experience to come in handy here on this water territory. Uncle Press had taken me to diving classes last year and I got my open-water diver's certification. Uncle Press then took me on a great trip to Florida where we dove in the ocean and explored some of the fresh water springs. That was fantastic. We swam with schools of fish and hitched rides on turtles.

Uncle Press and I had done a lot of great things like that. I was beginning to think that maybe those adventures weren't so much about having fun as they were about preparing me for some of the challenges I would face as a Traveler. I guess I should be grateful—except maybe for the time he took me sky diving. It was a blast, but I really didn't want to think about what he may have been preparing me for with that little episode. Yikes.

I grabbed a light blue shirt and pair of pants that looked

sort of like the same color. Nobody knew me here, but I didn't want to look like a clashing, colorblind geek. I picked out some blue shorts, too. I wasn't sure if they were the right size, but when I put them on, it was like they were made for me! There weren't any zippers or buttons, either. I dumped my Second Earth clothes and stepped into the shorts and pants, then pulled the shirt down over my head. The stretchy clothes molded to my body perfectly. They weren't too tight, but were still formfitting enough that nothing would twist and get in the way in the water. There were even soft boots with hard rubber souls that slipped on easily and fit like they were custom-made. It was all very Star Trek.

"Put on a belt, too," said Uncle Press, and handed me a thin, soft strap.

"That's okay," I replied. "I'm not a belt kind of guy."

"It's not about fashion," he said. "It's a BC."

Cool. Going back to my scuba experience, I knew that BC stood for buoyancy compensator. Scuba divers have to wear a weight belt underwater or they'd float back to the surface. A BC is a vest that you fill with air from your scuba tank to help you adjust your buoyancy so you won't sink to the bottom, or shoot up to the surface. When everything is perfect, it's called "neutrally buoyant." It makes swimming feel like flying. But I wasn't sure how this little belt was going to keep anybody neutrally buoyant.

"It's automatic," Uncle Press explained. I think he was reading my mind again. "It takes on water for weight, or creates oxygen for lift, depending on what you need. I told you, these guys are pretty advanced."

I took his word for it and threaded the strap through the belt loops on my new pants. I was really eager to get in the water and try out these new toys. This was like old times with

Uncle Press, only better. Yes, so far I really liked Cloral. It was a major improvement over Denduron. It was warm, the clothes didn't suck, the local fruit was pretty tasty, and from what Uncle Press told me, this was a territory that wasn't at war with anybody and had advanced enough to create some pretty nifty gadgets. I was actually jazzed about getting out of the cavern and starting to explore.

That is, until I saw Uncle Press doing something odd. As soon as he finished dressing in his local outfit, he took one of the extra pairs of Cloral pants and tied a knot on the end of each leg.

"Grab a bunch of fruit," he ordered.

I started grabbing off pieces of fruit from the vines. Uncle Press took the pieces and stuffed them into the pant legs he had just tied off. I figured maybe he was using the pants as a makeshift bag to carry some fruit to the surface. That was cool. I liked the stuff. He filled the pants up until they looked like a lumpy pair of legs, then yanked down a piece of vine from the wall and used it as a rope to thread through the belt loops and tie off the waist.

"Hand me one of the water sleds," he asked.

Okay, now he lost me. What was he doing? I gave him one of the two purple sleds and he tied the other end of the vine that was holding the pants together to the handles. There was now about a three-foot length of vine between the water sled and the pants full of fruit.

"You gonna tell me what you're doing?"

"We've got to swim out of here," he explained. "Put on fins. We'll use the air globes to breathe. We're only about sixty feet down. There should be a skimmer waiting for us on the surface."

"A skimmer?"

"It's like a speedboat. Very fast. Easy to maneuver. You'll love it."

"Courtesy of the acolytes?"

"Exactly."

"What's with the fruity pants?"

"No big deal. Just a little quig bait."

Uh-oh. That was it. Fun time was over. He punctuated this last comment by digging down under the rest of the Cloral clothes and pulling out a nasty-looking speargun. I knew this was going too well. There were quigs lurking outside. If you remember, quigs were the nasty beasties that Saint Dane used to guard the gates to the flumes. On Second Earth they were wild dogs. On Denduron they were prehistoric, cannibal bears with spiny backs. On Cloral they could only be . . .

"Sharks," I said flatly. "You're saying there are giant sharks swimming around out there waiting for us to pop out in our spiffy new rubber outfits?"

"You saw one yourself, on Denduron."

I did. In the mine shaft flume on Denduron. I still remember its demonic, yellow quig-eyes as it rode the wave of water toward us. The memory made my knees buckle. The tropical vacation was over.

"Don't worry," said Uncle Press. "I'll send the water sled out first. Our smell is already on these pants. If there are any quigs around, and I'm not saying there *are*, mind you, they'll chase the smell."

"You think they'll be dumb enough to go for it?"

"They're vicious, not bright," he answered with confidence. "We'll have plenty of time to get to the surface and find the skimmer."

He handed me the speargun, which I took gingerly.

"You don't expect me to use this, do you?"

"Just hold it," he said. He then took another small piece of vine and looped it through the handle of the water sled. With a quick tug, he tightened it down so that it pulled the trigger, then tied a knot to keep it in place. The trigger supposedly kicked over the engine, but it wasn't making any noise.

"Why didn't it turn on?" I asked.

"I told you, it needs water for power."

Uncle Press knelt down next to the pool. He first placed the loaded pants into the water. They floated off to the length of the vine that was attached to the sled. Then with both hands on the sled, he lowered the purple engine underwater as well. As soon as the slits were underwater, I could hear the low whine of its motor kick to life. The trigger was pulled all the way so it was on full power. The little sled nearly yanked Uncle Press off the ledge. He had to struggle just to hang on to it.

"Told you," he said with a laugh. "This thing has some giddyap."

He was enjoying this way too much. He then released his grip and the sled jumped out of his hands. The vine attached to the pants snapped tight, and it was gone in an instant, dragging the pants o' fruit after it.

Uncle Press then sat down to put on his swim fins. I put the speargun down and did the same, quickly. I wanted to be up and out of the water before any quigs realized they were on a wild-fruit chase and came back looking for meat. Uncle Press then picked up one of the clear globes and tossed it to me.

"Let's go," he said with a smile.

I think he was actually looking forward to this. He was crazy. I put the globe over my head and it immediately began changing into the shape of my face. I developed instant claustrophobia and had to tell myself that it was going to be okay.

It worked for Uncle Press. It'll work for me. Either that or it will smother me and I'll die right here in this fruit-filled underwater cavern. Maybe that wouldn't be such a bad thing. It would definitely be better than getting chomped on by Jaws.

"Breathe normally," instructed Uncle Press. "It's easier than using a regulator from a scuba tank."

Breathe normally. Yeah, right. We were about to dip into shark-infested waters and he wanted me to breathe normally. Maybe I should try and stop my heart from pounding out 180 beats a minute while I was at it.

"I'll use the water sled," he said. "It'll be faster than swimming. When we go under, get on my back and hold on to my belt with your left hand, tight."

"What do I do with my right hand?"

"That's for the speargun."

"Oh, no," I said. "I'm not taking that responsibility. No way."

"Just hang on to it," he said, trying to reassure me. "Nothing's going to happen. But on the off chance it does, we'll stop and you can give the gun to me. Okay?"

I guess that made sense. If the choice was between having a speargun and not having it, I'd certainly rather have it. So I reluctantly reached down and picked up the weapon. The gun was made of what looked like bright green plastic. The spear that was loaded in the gun was actually clear, like glass. But it looked pretty lethal just the same. I'm guessing it was made from the same hard material as our air-globe helmets. I felt the tip. Oh, yeah, it was sharp. I had held a speargun once before, in Florida. So I knew how to be safe with it. But to be honest, I never shot anything. I couldn't bring myself to do it. I never even liked fishing with a rod and reel, let alone a high-powered weapon. Okay, so I'm a wuss.

"Once we submerge," Uncle Press instructed, "we have to swim under the rock ledge for about thirty yards. We won't use the water sled until we get out from under the ledge. Then we've got to travel about a hundred yards along the reef to where the skimmer is anchored. Understand?"

I understood all right. I understood that I didn't like Cloral anymore, no matter how nice and warm the water was. But I didn't say that. Time was wasting. Uncle Press grabbed the other water sled and slipped into the pool. I jumped in too and immediately felt the belt tighten around my waist. This thing really did work automatically. I found that I didn't have to tread water to stay afloat. The belt had compensated for my weight and kept me hovering in the water comfortably. I would have been really impressed, if I wasn't ready to puke out of fear.

"Is that decoy really going to lure the quigs away?" I asked hopefully.

"In theory."

"Theory! Don't give me theory! I want guarantees!"

"The sooner we go, the sooner we'll be safe," he replied calmly.

"Then let's get out of here!" I shouted.

With a wink and a quick swing of his arms, Uncle Press sank underwater. I took one last look around the cavern and spotted the mouth of the flume far overhead. I was sorely tempted to shout out *"Second Earth!"* so the flume would suck me up and bring me home. But I didn't. I was here now and I had to go forward, not back. Actually, I had to go down. Underwater. With a sweep of my arms and a kick of my legs, I thrust up out of the water, then sank back down below the surface. We were on our way. Hopefully it wouldn't be a short and painful trip.

CLORAL

Swimming underwater is a very cool thing.

My parents taught me how to snorkel in Long Island Sound when I was a kid and Uncle Press, as I told you, took me to get my diving certification. I never liked regular old swimming much. To me, doing laps in a pool was like jogging on a treadmill. There was nothing interesting to look at. But diving below the surface was a whole other story. That was like dropping in to a different world.

Of course, I had been dropping in to a few too many different worlds lately, so I wasn't as psyched about this dive as usual.

Once I sank below the surface, I was afraid to take a breath. I was used to breathing through a mouthpiece connected to a hose that was connected to a scuba tank. But there was no mouthpiece in this weird head-bubble thing. And there was no tank of compressed air strapped to my back either. All I had was a stupid little harmonica-looking doo-dad stuck near the back of my head that was supposed to take oxygen out of water. Suddenly the whole thing sounded pretty impossible. Even though I knew I was underwater and my head was still completely dry, I couldn't bring myself to let go and . . .

"Breathe!" commanded Uncle Press.

I spun around and saw that he was floating right next to me. How weird was that? I could hear him even though we were underwater with our heads encased in clear plastic. His voice sounded kind of high and thin, like the treble knob on my stereo was cranked all the way to ten and the bass was backed off to zero, but I could hear him as plain as if, well, as if we weren't underwater.

"Trust me, Bobby," he said. "Look at me. I'm breathing. It works."

I wanted to trust him. I also wanted to shoot back to the surface and breathe real air. But my lungs were starting to hurt. I didn't have any choice. I had to breathe. I exhaled what little air I had left in my lungs, then took in a tentative breath, to discover it worked. I had no idea how, but that little harmonica gizmo was letting me breathe. It was even better than using a mouthpiece and a scuba tank because there were no hoses to deal with. And because there was no mouthpiece, I could talk. We could communicate underwater!

"That's better," Uncle Press said reassuringly. "You okay?"

"Yeah," I answered. "How come we can talk?"

"It's the re-breather," he said, tapping the silver device on the back of his globe. "It carries sound waves, too. Cool, aye?"

Cool was the word.

"Let's go," he ordered.

With a kick of his fins Uncle Press took off swimming. He left a trail of carbon dioxide bubbles that came from the re-breathing device as he exhaled. Now that I was getting used to breathing in the air globe, I took a quick look around to get oriented. The pool of water we had flumed into turned out to be the opening to a passageway underneath a huge overhang of rock. Uncle Press was now slowly swimming toward a ribbon of light about thirty yards away that I could tell was the end of the rock ceiling, just as he had described. Behind me I saw that the ceiling only went back a few more feet before ending at a craggy wall. This was a pretty out-of-the-way place for a gate to be hidden. But I guess that was the idea. The gates were *all* hidden in remote places so ordinary people from the territories wouldn't accidentally find them.

Uncle Press was already several yards ahead of me and I didn't want to be left here alone, so I kicked off and started after him. The BC belt was doing a perfect job of keeping me neutrally buoyant. I kicked easily and swam perfectly level. I didn't have to worry about banging my head on the rock ceiling above or crashing into the sand below. Excellent. If only I weren't so worried about a quig sneaking up on us, it would have been perfect. I gripped the speargun and did a quick look right and left to make sure no bogey had wandered under the rock shelf to join us. The water was incredibly clear. I'm guessing I had about a hundred feet of visibility, which is amazing. If there were any quigs headed for us, at least we'd have a little bit of warning before we got chewed on.

Uncle Press stopped when he got to the end of the overhang. The ceiling was lower there, so the distance from the rock overhead down to the sandy bottom was now about five feet. Uncle Press swam a few yards out into open water then motioned for me to look at something. I joined him outside and saw that he was pointing back to the lip of the rock where we had just come out. There, carved into the stone, was the familiar star symbol that designated this as a gate to the flumes. I gave him an okay sign, which is the universal signal you use underwater that means you understand.

Uncle Press returned the okay sign, which is custom, then smiled and said, "We can talk, remember?"

Oh, right. We didn't have to use hand signals. I'd forgotten. Habit, I guess. I looked up and saw a wall of rock we'd been swimming under that extended straight up. This was the formation that housed the cavern and the flume.

"Now check this out," he added, and pointed behind me.

I turned around and was confronted with one of the most breathtaking sights I had ever seen. Beyond us was open, green-blue sea. The sandy bottom turned into a coral reef that spread out before us like a colorful blanket. It was awesome. I had been on tropical reefs before and seen all sorts of tropical fish and unique coral formations, but I had never seen anything like this. The colors of this reef were nearly as vibrant as the flowers in the cavern we had just left. There were intense blue fans the size of umbrellas that waved lazily in the soft current. Dotted around them were giant chunks of brain coral, which are called that because they look like, well, like brains. At home brain coral is kind of brownish and dull. Here on Cloral, it was bright yellow. Yellow! I told you before that water filters out red and yellow at this depth, but not here on Cloral. Every color of the spectrum could be seen. There was vibrant green vegetation growing all over the reef. Off to our left was a thick forest of kelp. The vines started on the reef and floated all the way to the surface like leafy ropes—and they were bright red! Other coral had grown up out of the rock bed and formed shapes that looked like a green topiary garden. If you used your imagination, they seemed like a herd of small animals grazing on the rocks. But they weren't; they were coral. Amazing.

Swimming among all this splendor were the most incredible fish I had ever seen. They traveled in schools, each seeming to know exactly what the others were thinking as they all changed direction at the exact same time. It always amazed me how there could be a hundred fish in a school, but none of them ever made a wrong turn or bumped into one another. One school looked like silver flutes with long delicate fins that fluttered quickly like the wings of a hummingbird. Another school of fish were perfectly round and thin, like a CD. Only they were bright pink! Still another school looked exactly like small bluebirds with beaks and feathers. I know they were swimming, but with each flap of their fins it sure seemed like they were flying. It was all a perfectly orchestrated ballet, and it was beautiful to watch them swim about the colorful reef, lazily enjoying their day.

I was totally in awe of the spectacular scene. The water was as clear as air. It was even more special because the air globes allowed me to look all around. Unlike diving goggles where you pretty much had to look straight ahead, the air globe gave me a perfect view of everything—and, man, it was worth it!

That is, until something happened that caught my eye.

"Uh-oh," said Uncle Press.

He had seen it too. One second there were hundreds of these weird fish gently dancing through the currents. The very next moment they all scattered. It happened so fast that if I had blinked I would have missed it. Every single last fish in my view had suddenly darted off in a different direction. There's a better word for it. They had fled. Something had scared them. And if they were scared, I was too.

"What's going on?" I asked, not really wanting to hear the answer.

"Something just spooked the fish."

"Yeah, no kidding," I said. "What do you think—"

"Look out!"

Uncle Press grabbed my arm and pulled me back down under the rock ledge. A second later I saw what caused the fish panic. Yup, it was a shark. A quig shark. It wasn't in a hurry though. The big beast drifted past us as we cowered back in the shadow of the ledge. It used no effort to propel itself along.

It was beautiful and horrifying at the same time. Most of its body was battleship gray, but its underbelly was jet black. And it was big. We're talking *Jaws* big. It was way bigger than the shark Saint Dane had sent back at us through the flume. One thing was the same though. Its eyes. The beast had the cold, yellow eyes that told me it was no ordinary shark. It was a quig, no doubt about it. The monster glided past, turned away from the rock, and started swimming directly away from us.

"Maybe it didn't see us," I said hopefully.

"It saw us," came the flat response. "It's just taking its time to—here we go!"

I quickly looked back outside and saw in horror that the shark had done a complete 180 and was now swimming directly at us! It had moved away from the rock overhang so it could get up a good head of steam to make its kill run at us. There was nowhere to run, or should I say, swim. We were trapped and this thing had us in its sights.

Uncle Press grabbed the speargun away from me, planted his feet, and took aim. The quig kept coming. It was almost on us. Its jaws were already open in anticipation of the big bad bite.

"Shoot!" I yelled. "Get him!"

Uncle Press waited to make sure he wouldn't miss. I hoped he was as good with this speargun as he was with the spears on Denduron. His finger tightened on the trigger, but he didn't fire.

Believe it or not, the shark being so big turned out to be a good thing. Its head slid underneath the ledge, but its dorsal fin hit the rock above. Yes! It was too big to fit under the ledge. It couldn't get to us! Uncle Press lowered the speargun because the immediate danger was gone. That is, unless the quig could figure out how to squeeze in sideways. I didn't think that would happen. Fish don't swim sideways.

"So much for your decoy theory," I said.

"It worked," replied Uncle Press. "But this bad boy was quicker than I thought. Look."

I saw that stuck in the shark's teeth was the decoy water sled, completely tangled up in pants and vines. The quig went for the bait all right, but it was just an appetizer. It now wanted the main course. Us.

The huge quig wriggled and squirmed, trying to force its way under the rock shelf. If it's possible for a fish to look angry, this thing looked major-league ticked. It writhed its body, swung its tail and gnashed its jaws, desperately trying to get at us. We were just out of its reach by a few yards. Too close, in my book, but no matter how furiously the quig pushed, its body was too big to squeeze any closer. Phew!

"If you've got a plan B, now's the time to tell me," I said nervously.

"I've always got a plan B," came the confident reply. "I'm going to swim over to the left and come out from under the ledge. When it sees me, I guarantee it'll come after me. As soon as I get a clear shot at it, I'll take it. Its skull is thin. One shot and he's gone."

"Why wait?" I shouted. "Do it here!"

"I can't get a good shot through the sand. I don't want to miss."

He was right. The quig's violent thrashing had kicked up a storm of sand and it was hard to tell which end was up.

"As soon as it follows me, swim out as fast as you can, and keep swimming straight ahead along the reef. About a hundred yards dead ahead you'll see an anchor line that'll lead you up to the skimmer. I'll catch up with the water sled. Got it?"

"No, I don't," I said with rising panic. "What if you miss? What if the spear misses the skull and all you end up doing is pissing him off more? I want a plan C."

"There is only a plan B." Then he added with a confident smile, "And I never miss."

"Uncle Press I—"

He didn't stay to listen. He kicked off forward, coming dangerously close to the snapping jaws of the quig, then shot off to the left using the speedy water sled to pull him along. He did a great job of tempting the quig, because it pulled its body back out from under the ledge and started to shadow him.

Now was the time. The quig was busy, and if I was going to get out of here, it had to be now. Unfortunately, I couldn't move. Panic had set in and I was frozen. The idea of swimming out into open water where that quig could turn around and chomp me like a Slim Jim had shut down all of my systems. I was absolutely, totally incapable of moving.

Then I spotted something. The billowing sand was starting to settle and I saw it lying on the bottom near the edge of the rock outcropping. It was the water sled Uncle Press had used as a decoy! The quig must have dropped it out of its mouth when it backed out. It gave me a flash of hope. If I could use the speed of that water sled, then maybe I had a chance of getting to the skimmer before Moby Dick came a-nibbling. That was it. I had to do it.

My legs worked again. I pushed forward and quickly swam to the tangle of pants and vines that engulfed the water sled. I picked it up to find that the pants were totally wrapped around the thing. The fruit stuffing was gone though. The quig had gotten a treat out of this after all. But there was a problem. I quickly saw that the sled wasn't going to work because the pants were totally wrapped around it. The pants kept water from entering the slits, and that's where it got its power. I had to get rid of the pants, or the sled would be useless. So I frantically began tugging at them.

While I worked I glanced up to where Uncle Press had gone, but there was no sign of him, or the quig. Had he speared it already? I had absolute confidence in Uncle Press. If he said he was going to shoot the quig, then the quig would be shot. But what if the quig had his *own* plan B and decided not to follow him? Then all bets were off. I had to think less and work faster. Finally I figured out how the pants had gotten twisted around the sled and with a final yank, I pulled them free.

Big, big mistake.

You know what it's like when you're walking in bare feet and stub your toe really hard? A weird thing happens. There's about a half-second delay between the time you crunch your toe and when the pain registers in your brain. That's just enough time to think "Uh-oh!" before you feel the hurt. I don't know why that happens, but it does. Well, that's kind of what happened to me right then and there. The instant I pulled the pants off the water sled, I realized I had made a huge mistake.

What hit me was that the little piece of vine Uncle Press

had used to tie the trigger down was still in place. The sled was still turned on. The only reason it wasn't moving was because the pants had prevented water from entering the slits. But as soon as I pulled the pants away, the slits were cleared and water could rush in to power the engine and— like when you stub your toe—I had about a half-second to think "Uh-oh!"

Oh, yeah. The sled was on and ready to go. I wasn't. Too bad.

Things happened fast. The powerful little engine sprang to life and jumped out of my hand. It only got worse. While trying to get the pants away from the sled, I had gotten the vine twisted around my wrist. It was the vine that had tied the pants to the water sled. It was the vine that was *still* tied to the water sled, and the other end was now wrapped around my wrist. Yeah, you guessed it. The vine snapped taut and an instant later I was yanked sideways and dragged through the water by the runaway sled, full throttle.

Worse still, it pulled me out from under the rock ledge, into open water and right in the same direction that Uncle Press had lured the quig. That was the *last* place I wanted to go, but I had no way of steering because the sled was out of my reach. I desperately tried to pull the vine off my wrist, but it was so twisted I couldn't free it. I was absolutely, totally out of control. I tried to look ahead, but I was moving so fast the force of the water kept spinning me around. No matter what I did to kick my fins or twist my body, I kept spinning helplessly. I felt like the tail on an out-of-control kite. I wasn't the one in charge, it was the runaway water sled that was calling all the shots, and right now it was pulling me toward an angry quig.

I twisted my neck to look up ahead and sure enough, there

it was. I saw the immense gray shape of the quig, lurking just outside the rock ledge, peering in at what I guessed was Uncle Press. I was traveling parallel to the rock ledge, further out than the quig. In a few seconds I would pass by the monster and unless it was deaf and blind, I would get its attention. I could only hope that between now and then Uncle Press would nail it with the speargun. But he would have to shoot fast because I was almost at the quig.

Then two things happened. When I flew by the quig, it heard me coming and it made a sudden, surprised turn to see me. It was a small turn, but enough to let something else happen that made me want to scream. I saw the glint of a spear come shooting out from under the rock ledge—and miss its mark. The missile sliced through the water just over the quig's head. Uncle Press assured me that he wouldn't miss, but he hadn't figured that I'd be flying by like an idiot to distract his prey.

The quig had dodged eternity, and now the prey was me.

I was traveling on my back now. My arm felt like it was going to rip out of the socket, that's how powerful the pull from the water sled was. But when I looked back, I realized the pain in my shoulder was the least of my problems. The quig was after me. As fast as this sled was pulling me, the quig was faster.

It took only a few seconds for the huge beast to swim right up beside me. We were traveling at the same speed with ten yards between us. I can't begin to tell you how helpless and vulnerable I felt. I knew that soon this bad boy would turn into me and clamp its jaws on my midsection. I saw its yellow eye staring at me. There was no emotion there, just calculation. It was measuring the perfect moment to turn and strike. This was going to be a bad way to die. I'm not exactly

48 ~ PENDRAGON ~

sure if there's a *good* way to die, but if so, this isn't it.

The quig didn't come any closer. It didn't need to. When it struck, it would need a little bit of distance to get a good run at me. In fact, it started to pull a little bit ahead. It made a few quick little head turns toward me, as if judging the exact right distance and speed for its attack. This was torture. I was at the point that I wanted to get it over with.

Finally it struck.

The shark opened its jaws and made a sharp turn toward me. I gritted my teeth, waiting for the pain.

But then I saw a flash of light just over the shark's head. Was it a flash of light? No, it was another spear! I thought for an instant that Uncle Press had reloaded, but that was impossible. There was no way he could have reloaded and got up above fast enough to be shooting from that angle. No, the spear had come from someone else.

Whoever the archer was, he was good. The spear flew directly down at the shark and struck it on top of the head, burrowing into its skull. The instant the spear found its mark the quig started to thrash. It was still headed toward me though, and as it spun I got slammed in the ribs by its tail. Yeow. It hurt, too. Bad. But I didn't care. It didn't hurt like its teeth would have.

The quig continued thrashing and sank down beneath me. A moment later it crashed into the reef. The sled kept pulling me away, but I looked back and saw that the monster was writhing uncontrollably. It was a horrifying sight. This fish was history. It wasn't going to eat me or anybody else.

I was saved from the quig, but I was still traveling out of control. I wondered how long this little engine would go before burning out. Now my arm was starting to hurt bad. Not to mention my ribs, which had taken a healthy whack of shark tail. I wasn't sure how much longer I could take this.

Then something caught my eye. It was a gray shape moving up alongside me. Uh-oh. Was there another quig? I spun around to get a better look and saw that it wasn't a quig at all. It was a guy being pulled by another water sled. But it wasn't Uncle Press. This guy wore black pants with a black top that had no sleeves. Through the clear air globe on his head I saw that his hair was kind of long and black. He had an empty speargun strapped to his leg, which meant he was probably the shooter who saved my life. I had no idea who this guy was, but I liked him already.

He knew how to handle a water sled, too. He eased over close to me until we were traveling side by side. He held on to his sled with one hand and let go with the other to reach back to his leg. What was he doing? He brought his hand forward again and I saw that he was now holding a very large, very nasty-looking silver knife. For a second I freaked. Was he going to stab me? But that didn't make sense. He wouldn't have gone through the trouble of killing the quig just to kill me himself. At least I didn't think so.

He reached forward with the knife and with one quick move he lashed out at me. Not knowing what he was doing, I closed my eyes. But what he did with that one strong swipe was cut the vine that attached me to the runaway water sled. The pull on my arm stopped instantly. The force of the water slowed me down. I looked ahead to see the runaway water sled continue forward on its crazed trip to nowhere. Good riddance!

I was dazed and hurt. I tried to move my legs to get some sort of control, but I was floundering. That's when I felt something grab the back of my shirt. It was the guy in black. He had come around and was now right next to me.

Without a word he grabbed the back of my collar and began towing me to the surface. I totally relaxed. Whoever this guy was, he was in charge now and I didn't care. All I could think about was breathing fresh air again.

The trip to the surface took about twenty seconds. The closer we got, the brighter the water became. I couldn't wait to get on top. Then just before we surfaced, the guy in black let go of my collar and let me float up on my own.

It was a great feeling. My head broke the surface and the BC belt kept me floating. That was a good thing because I didn't think I could tread water just then. I yanked the air globe off my head and took a deep breath of fresh air. The sun was warm, the air smelled sweet, and I was alive.

"Friend of Press's, are you?" came a voice from behind me.

I spun around to see the guy in black floating next to me. He had taken off his air globe and I now saw that he was a little older than me, and had a slight Asian look with almond-shaped eyes. He had deep, sun-colored skin and long black hair. He also had the biggest, friendliest smile I thought I'd ever seen in my life.

"Told me he was bringing somebody to visit," the guy said cheerfully. "Sorry 'bout the rude welcome. Them sharks can stir up a real natty-do sometimes. Easy enough to handle 'em though. Just gotta know the soft spots," he said, tapping his head.

"Who are you?" was all I could think of saying.

"Name's Spader. Vo Spader. Pleased to meet you."

"I'm Bobby Pendragon. You saved my life." I wasn't sure what else to add but, "Thanks."

"No big stuff. It happens. Never saw anyone caught up by a sled like that though. No sir, that was a real tum-tigger."

"Yeah, a real tum-tigger," I said. Whatever *that* was.

"Took us a might off course though," he added, looking around.

I looked around too and what I saw made my heart start to race again. Because what I saw was . . . nothing. Oh, there was plenty of water all right. But that was it. We were in the middle of the ocean with no landmass in sight.

If a tum-tigger was bad, this was definitely a tum-tigger.

CLORAL

Talk about feeling helpless. Here we were, two guys floating like corks in an endless ocean. A quick three-sixty scan showed no land, no boat, and no rescue of any kind in sight.

"Beautiful day, isn't it?" asked Spader.

Beautiful day? We were lost at sea and he was talking about nice weather? Either he was in strong denial, or he was crazy. Either way, he was starting to make me nervous.

That's when I felt a tug on my foot.

I screamed. The quig was back. Or he had a brother. Or he had *two* brothers. And they were both after me and they . . .

The water to my right began to boil and an instant later a bubble-covered head surfaced. It was Uncle Press. He yanked off his air globe and smiled at me.

"Have a nice trip, Bobby?" he asked. "That wasn't exactly plan B."

"You think I *tried* to get dragged like that?" I shot back, all indignant.

"Whoa. Relax. I was kidding."

"And I thought you never missed?"

I couldn't help but add that last dig. I knew it was my fault he missed hitting the quig with the spear, but still, he did say he *never* missed. No qualifications.

"Then it's a good thing Spader came along," he said calmly.

"Hello, Press!" exclaimed Spader. "Good to see your face again."

"Yours, too," said Uncle Press. "Lucky for us you were in the area."

"I was out doing a bit of fishin' and spotted your skimmer anchored a ways back," said Spader. "I have to say I was a might surprised. You know this is shark territory."

"Yeah, tell me about it," I threw in. "Maybe we shouldn't be here anymore."

"Right!" shouted Spader. "No sense in waiting for another nibbler to come a-callin'."

Spader looked at his big, black diver-style watch. I think it must have been some kind of compass because he checked it, looked up, changed position, then announced, "Off we go."

He popped the air globe back on his head, pointed his water sled, then shot off across the surface.

I looked at Uncle Press thinking that this guy must be crazy. There was nothing out here. Where was he going?

"I love that guy," he said.

"Where is he going? We're in the middle of an ocean."

Uncle Press put his air globe back on and swam close to me. "He'll bring us to our skimmer. You okay?"

"I feel like I was stretched on a medieval rack and beaten with a club. Other than that, I'm cool. But I don't think I can swim."

"You don't have to. Put your globe on and grab my belt."

I did as I was told. I put the air globe back on and it instantly conformed to my head. I then reached out for Uncle

Press's belt. I made sure to use my left hand. My right arm had taken a bit too much abuse. It was probably two inches longer now, too.

Uncle Press gently squeezed the throttle on his water sled and we started our journey toward the skimmer that would take us . . . somewhere. Luckily the water was calm so the trip was easy. Good thing, too. I needed to catch my breath. As Uncle Press pulled me through the gentle swells, I floated on my back and looked up at the sun. Yes, the sun. There was only one, unlike Denduron where there were three. It was a hot sun, too. So far everything about Cloral gave me the feeling of being someplace tropical. Both the water and the air were warm, but not so hot as to be uncomfortable. Of course, the whole quig thing made the place feel a little less like paradise, but you can't have everything.

We had only traveled for a few minutes when Uncle Press slowed to a stop. I let go of his belt and saw that bobbing on the water in front of us were two water vehicles—skimmers. Spader had actually found his way here with the help of his watch. Talk about finding a needle in a haystack. I was impressed.

Spader had already climbed aboard one of the vehicles. They looked kind of like Jet Skis. But these sleek vehicles weren't toys. They were way too high-tech for that. Each frame was about the size of a very shallow bathtub. They were pure white and looked to be made out of plastic. The bow was pointed and the stern was straight across. To control it, the driver stood at a column that looked like motorcycle handlebars. Behind the driver's space was a molded seat for a second passenger. The sides only came up a few inches. I guess water getting inside wasn't a problem.

You'd think they'd be unstable, but that was taken care

of. The skimmers had wings. If you've ever seen an outrigger canoe with beams that project out to the side, with pontoons on the end, you'll know what I'm talking about. The skimmers had outriggers on either side. Right now they were lifted up out of the water, which gave them the look of a bird frozen in midflap. On the ends of each outrigger were torpedo-shaped pontoons. My guess was that when under way, the outriggers would be lowered into the water to make the skimmer stable.

Spader's skimmer was identical to Uncle Press's, except that he had a float thing that was attached to the back like a caboose. It was some kind of equipment carrier that floated behind the main skimmer.

No, these skimmers weren't toys. They looked more like those sleek, high-end corporate jets that big shots fly around in. I have to admit, they were way cool.

As Uncle Press climbed up on his skimmer, I watched this Spader guy. Who was he? Was he the Traveler from Cloral? Whoever he was, he was pretty confident in the water. But I guess you have to be if you come from Cloral. His skin was really dark, but I don't know if that was natural or because he was out in the sun so much. Probably a little of both. He was about six feet tall and looked pretty strong. Not a muscle guy, but definitely lean and mean. His black hair was long and shaggy and nearly came to his shoulders.

But the thing that stood out most about him was his personality. I know that sounds weird, especially since I had just met him and all, but right from the start I knew this guy had it all going on. He was concerned enough about Uncle Press that he went looking for him when he saw that his skimmer was anchored in quig waters, then risked himself to save my life. But he shrugged the whole thing off like it was no big deal. That was pretty cool. And the guy always looked like he was having fun. Whether it was flying underwater with his sled, or getting his skimmer ready to run, the little smile on his face made it look as if he always enjoyed whatever he was doing. You gotta like a guy like that. Bottom line, from what I had seen so far, I thought Spader was pretty cool.

"C'mon, Bobby," said Uncle Press.

I kicked my fins and slid over toward the skimmer. Uncle Press had to pull me out of the water because I had no strength left in my arms. I laid down on the deck of the skimmer, happy to be on something solid again, even if it was just a small high-powered boat.

"You okay, Pendragon?" called Spader from his skimmer.

I struggled to sit up and pretend that I wasn't totally out of my league here, which I was.

"I'm good," I shouted, not convincingly. Then added, "Real good!" as if that would make me sound better off than I was. I'm sure I didn't fool anybody.

Spader let out a big, warm laugh. For a second I thought he was laughing at me, but he wasn't.

"Don't you worry, mate, been there myself. Many times," he said. "We'll fix you up spiff soon as we get back, don't you worry."

"Get back where?" I asked.

Spader now stood at the controls of his skimmer, as did Uncle Press. I saw that they each began flipping toggle switches. As they did, the skimmers came to life. I heard a slight whine of engines, then in turn, each of the outriggers that had been sticking up in the air began their descent into the water.

I also saw that Spader and Uncle Press had both grown tense. They each stood stiffly at their control columns while throwing quick, furtive glances at each other. Something was up. I didn't like this.

"It's a wonderful place," continued Spader. "You're going to love it."

"I'll second that," added Uncle Press. "Spader lives on the most beautiful habitat on Cloral."

The two were speaking calmly, but their body language said they were anything but calm. What was going on? Was there another quig zeroing in on us? Each of the four outriggers was now underwater and I could hear the low hum of the skimmer's engines waiting to be told what to do.

"Nice of you to say, Press," replied Spader. "Last one to Grallion buys the sniggers?"

"Snickers?" I said. "They have candy bars here?"

"Sniggers, Bobby. It's a drink," answered Uncle Press. Then to Spader, "But I don't know the way."

"No worries," laughed Spader. "Follow me!"

With that Spader gunned his skimmer and shot forward.

"Hang on!" shouted Uncle Press and hit the throttle.

Our skimmer took off and I got rocked back on my butt. I wished he had given me a little more warning. Now it all made sense. These guys were playing with each other. They wanted to race. Okay, I could deal with that. I scrambled to my knees and got into the seat behind Uncle Press. Our two air globes were rolling around on the deck so before I could look to see where we were going, I grabbed them to make sure they wouldn't go flying overboard.

We were moving fast—faster than I've ever traveled over the water. I looked down at the pontoons and saw that they weren't just for balance. They were below the water and I saw a jet of water coming out of each one. They were the skimmer's engines. The skimmer didn't have a rudder or anything, so when Uncle

Press turned the control bars, it would send more or less power to either pontoon. That's how the thing was directed. Very cool.

I looked up ahead and saw that Spader had a pretty decent head start. Uncle Press was intense at the controls, but I could tell by the look on his face that he was enjoying this. I didn't blame him. I was too.

"What is Grallion?" I asked.

Oddly enough, I didn't have to shout. The engines of the skimmer weren't loud like a powerboat. Instead they gave off a steady, solid hum. Rather than the loud drone of an engine, most of what I heard was the hull flashing across the water. The water was amazingly smooth too, so we shot across it like ice skates on glass.

"Grallion is the habitat where Spader lives," said Uncle Press without taking his eyes off our adversary.

"What's his deal?" I asked.

"He's what they call an aquaneer. All the habitats have a crew that keeps them moving safely over the water. It's an important job. Spader's good at it. He's a good guy, too."

"Yeah, but is he the Traveler from Cloral?"

"Look!" he shouted.

He pointed ahead of us and there on the horizon I saw our destination. At first it was just a hazy gray smudge that could have been an island. But the closer we got, the more I saw that the outline was too regular to be an island. No, this thing was man-made. And it was big. This was Grallion.

Uncle Press gunned the throttle and easily caught up to Spader. I then realized what his strategy was. We had to lay back until we saw Grallion. But now that we knew where it was, the race was really on.

"You've got too much drag!" taunted Uncle Press at Spader. "We'll beat you at three-quarters!"

"But you've got the extra weight, mate!" Spader shot back. "Even up!"

Both guys gunned the throttle and the skimmers charged forward even faster. We hadn't been at full speed up till now. Unbelievable.

To be honest, I was less concerned about our race to decide who was going to buy sniggers than I was about our destination. Mark, remember the time we went to Manhattan on that school trip to visit the aircraft carrier *Intrepid*? It was pretty impressive, right? Well, imagine approaching the *Intrepid* on the water in a rowboat. Can you picture that? Takes your breath away, doesn't it? Well, now multiply the size of that aircraft carrier by about four hundred and you'd have Grallion.

I kid you not, this was a floating island. As we sped toward it, I kept thinking that we'd be there any second. But we weren't. With each passing moment this monster barge kept on getting bigger and bigger. It was about four stories high, but that's not where the size was. This thing they called a habitat spread out before us for what seemed like a couple of miles. Because we were approaching head-on, I couldn't tell how far back it went, but if the front end was any indication, this thing was the size of Stony Brook.

"We've got him now!" exclaimed Uncle Press with glee.

I looked over to Spader's skimmer to see we had pulled ahead by a few feet. Apparently the drag from his equipment caboose was a little bit more than the extra weight that I added to our skimmer.

"There's the marker buoy!" Uncle Press said, pointing ahead.

I looked to see there was a buoy floating about twenty yards off from the habitat. Beyond the buoy I saw that at the water line there was some kind of seagoing entrance to the barge. The opening was large enough to pilot small crafts inside. I could even make out other skimmers in there, along with a few small boats of various shape and design.

"The buoy marks the safety zone," added Uncle Press. "Once you pass it, you've got to slow down. That's our finish line."

We were only a few yards away from victory. I didn't know which excited me more, knowing that we were about to win or looking up at Grallion as it loomed over us. Spader wasn't giving up though. He coaxed a little more power out of his skimmer and pulled to within a few feet of us. This was going right down to the finish line. And . . .

We won! We passed the marker buoy first. With an exuberant "Yes!" Uncle Press killed the engine.

But Spader didn't stop. He kept on full throttle, headed toward the water dock. All we could do was watch him in wonder.

"Maybe he *is* crazy," I said.

Uncle Press gunned the engine and followed him in, though at a safer speed. What I saw in the next few seconds was amazing. As I told you before, Spader jammed into Grallion at full throttle and full speed for these skimmers were *fast*. I saw a handful of dock workers go wide-eyed and scramble out of the way in anticipation of the nasty crash that was sure to follow.

Spader didn't flinch. He drove his skimmer right toward the dock. In seconds he would be mush. But with only a few yards to spare he hit the water brakes and spun the skimmer— later he called it autorotating—into a complete 360 that killed all his speed. With a rush of water caused by his turn, he slid sideways and barely kissed the dock. Without missing a beat, he jumped out, turned back to us, made a deep bow and said, "You lose, mates."

We pulled up slowly in our skimmer. All I could do was applaud. Forget anything they've ever shown on those network stunt shows, this was hands down the most amazing thing I had ever seen.

"Oh, no," Uncle Press called out to him. He was trying to sound angry though I know he wasn't. "We all play by the same rules. We passed the buoy first."

"But the race was to Grallion!" answered Spader. "That buoy isn't Grallion. Almost doesn't count."

Spader was laughing. So was Uncle Press. Maybe this trip to Cloral was going to be fun after all.

"Spader!" came an annoyed voice from above the dock.

We all looked up to see a woman wearing what looked like some kind of uniform standing on a catwalk above the dock. She looked ticked.

"Wu Yenza," Uncle Press whispered to me. "Chief aquaneer."

"Spader's boss?" I asked.

"Yeah, Spader's boss."

"Uh-oh."

Yenza looked to be in her thirties. She had short black hair and was in pretty good shape. I guess all aquaneers had to be in good shape. She wore a black outfit that was similar to Spader's, but it had long sleeves with yellow stripes near the cuff that gave it a kind of military feel. I'd go so far as to say she was kind of hot, in an older woman way.

"Now, Spader!" shouted Yenza. She then stormed off.

Spader turned to us and gave a little shrug. He didn't look all that nervous about the slamming he was sure to get.

"Let's call it a tie, right, mates?" he said with a smile. "Sniggers on me at Grolo's, soon as I can make it!"

With that he turned and bounded up the stairs that led off

the dock and into the bowels of Grallion—and to deep trouble for him.

"He's doomed," I said.

"Nah. He'll get yelled at and told never to be so reckless again. But they won't do anything to him. Everyone likes Spader. He's the best aquaneer they've got."

We maneuvered the skimmer to the dock, tied it up, and stepped onto the floating platform.

"You didn't answer my question," I said.

"What question was that, Bobby? You've got so many."

"Is Spader the Traveler from Cloral?"

Uncle Press didn't answer right away. He busied himself getting our air globes and fins out of the skimmer. I knew he wasn't ignoring me, but the fact that I didn't get a simple yes or no made me nervous.

"Yes," he finally answered. "Spader is the Traveler from Cloral."

"I *knew* it!" I shouted.

"There's just one thing. Spader doesn't know it yet. He has no idea that he's a Traveler. We're going to have to tell him."

Uncle Press grabbed our gear and walked toward the stairs. I stayed there a moment, letting those words sink in. Here I had just met a guy who seemed to love everything there was about life—about *his* life—and we now had the job of telling him that it was all going to change. In my short time of being a Traveler, that was the hardest thing I had to deal with—finding out that my life wasn't what I thought it was, and having to leave it behind.

I didn't look forward to being the one who had to bring someone else's world crashing down around them.

CLORAL

From the moment I first left my home in Stony Brook, I'd been jumping from one disaster to the next. It seemed like I was always scared, or confused, or scared *and* confused. There were a few times when things didn't totally suck, but for the most part I was getting slammed every time I turned around.

But after spending some time on Cloral, I am very happy to write that the next few weeks were actually pretty great, for a change. From the second we stepped onto the habitat of Grallion, I felt safe. But it was more than that. As I learned about Grallion and how the floating habitats worked on Cloral, I felt as if I had found a place that had gotten it right. The Clorans had a society and a way of life that was like a perfect machine, where every piece and every person played an important part. Everyone relied on everyone else, and they respected each other for the roles they played.

That's not to say there weren't problems. The Clorans weren't mindless Disney animatrons who lived only to serve or anything like that. Far from it. They had their own opinions, and they didn't always agree with one another. It was the big picture that they kept in perspective. There were no wars and no tension between people of different races. There didn't seem to be any class distinction either. Meaning, though some people had more responsibility than others and got paid more salary, no one treated anyone like a second-class citizen. It was amazing.

I tried to figure out how such an ideal society could exist, when supposedly evolved societies like ours on Second Earth always seemed to be at one another's throats. The best theory I could come up with is that it was because each and every person on Cloral faced the same big challenge—they had to deal with living on the water. Yes, they had created these amazing boat cities that made you feel as if you were on dry land, but you weren't. You were floating. That meant anything could happen. A rogue storm could wipe out an entire city. Growing enough food to feed the entire world was an ever present worry. A simple virus could endanger an entire habitat. This was not an easy life. These people were united by a common cause—survival. Any other disputes were trivial compared to the larger challenges facing them every day.

But I'm getting way ahead of myself. Let me tell you what happened right after Uncle Press and I arrived on Grallion.

Since Uncle Press had been there before, he gave me a tour. As we climbed up from the depths of the docks, I noticed two things. One was that the inside of this barge was a labyrinth of machinery, pipes, engines, and pumps. I looked down long catwalks where workers busied themselves keeping the giant floating habitat running.

The second thing I noticed was that nothing seemed to be made out of metal. I'm not sure what the material was, I guess you would call it plastic or fiberglass or something. But all the walkways, pipes, supports, girders, and even the machines looked to be made out of the same kind of lightweight material.

When we walked on the stairs, rather than the sharp clanging sound of metal, our footfalls were almost silent, as if we were walking on carpet. I guess it made sense. You have to use lightweight stuff when everything has to float. And here's a weird thing: Even though the underbelly of Grallion looked like a vast factory, it wasn't all that loud. You could tell the place was alive, but it wasn't much noisier than Stony Brook Library on a busy Saturday. Pretty cool.

"What do they do here?" I asked Uncle Press as we climbed the stairs. "Do they just float around fishing and racing skimmers?"

"Every habitat has a specific purpose," was his answer. "Some manufacture materials, others process food, some are financial centers, others mine raw materials."

"And what about Grallion?" I asked.

"See for yourself."

We had reached the top of the stairs, where a door opened onto the main surface. We quickly stepped out into the sun and I got my first look at Grallion. Mark, Courtney, I'm not sure I can find the right words to describe it, that's how awesome a sight it was.

First, did I say Grallion was big? Well, big doesn't cover it. It was enormous. I felt as if I had reached dry land. But after having been below, I knew this wasn't dry land at all. This was a vehicle, but unlike any vehicle I had ever seen. Now, are you ready for this? Stretching out in front of me for as far as I could see . . . was farmland. I swear. I saw acre upon acre of flowering plants, fruit trees, and vines heavy with colorful vegetables.

Yes, Grallion was a giant, floating farm!

"This way," said Uncle Press, and walked off.

I didn't move at first. I couldn't. I wanted to get my mind around what I was seeing.

"You'll get a better view over here," called Uncle Press, laughing.

He knew I was blown away and he was enjoying it. I ran after him. I wanted to see more. He led me up the stairs of a tower, and from this higher vantage point I got a great view of the farms of Grallion. I saw that there were very distinct sections, broken up by walkways where farm workers could travel. There were even small electric vehicles that moved quickly and silently along roads that criss-crossed each other. To our far left I saw row after row of fruit trees. Many of them bore fruit that looked like apples and oranges, but there were trees with clusters of unfamiliar fruit as well. Some were bright green tubes that looked like balloons hanging from the branches. Other trees had great purple orbs the size of grapefruits. Others were covered with pure white fat berries. They all looked ripe and ready for picking.

Directly in front of us were rows of thousands of individual plants that grew out of the dirt. Yes, dirt. At least I think it was dirt. It was brown and looked soft, so if it wasn't dirt, it was a good imitation. Some plants bore small fruits and vegetables, others looked as if the whole thing would be picked like lettuce, or pulled out of the ground like a carrot or a potato.

To our right were aisles of fences where viney plants grew. This section held the same dark green, pickle-looking fruit that we had found in the cavern underwater. Another area of vines was covered with fruit that looked like round white disks. This odd fruit looked fragile and fluttered when the wind blew.

There was another whole section that grew beneath the shade of a gauzy tarp. These must have been plants that do better with indirect light. I'm guessing that the covered area took up a square mile. Another whole area looked to be planted with some kind of wheat. Unbelievable.

I watched as workers went busily about their jobs, tending to the crops. Some were pickers, others took water and soil samples. Still others did pruning.

The best word I can use to describe this vast farm full of lush fruits and vegetables is . . . perfect.

"This habitat feeds around thirty thousand people, give or take," Uncle Press explained. "The crating is done below and it's all transported forward. There's another dock near the bow where boats from other habitats arrive to transport the produce back to their homes. It's all very efficient."

"How many people work here?" I asked.

"I think about two hundred," he answered. "Only about fifty live here full-time: the habitat pilot and crew, some support people, the farm supervisors, and the agronomers."

"Agronomers?"

"Scientists. The guys who figure out what gets planted where. They're always experimenting with fertilizers and crop rotation and whatnot."

"Then there are about sixty aquaneers like Spader who keep the habitat running smoothly and coordinate the comings and goings of all the small boats. They live here in short shifts—maybe three months at a time. The rest of the people are like migrant farm workers. They come and go depending on the needs of the crops. That's where all the short-timers live."

He pointed far off to the left, where I saw a row of low houses running along the length of one side of the habitat. The houses looked like small, two-level homes.

"The homes on the other side are for the long-timers—the pilot and agronomers and whatnot."

I looked far to my right and saw another row of houses

along the opposite side that seemed to be a bit larger than the others. And why not? If these people were here permanently, they *should* have bigger homes.

"We're at the stern," he pointed out. "This is where most of the farm equipment is kept and where the agronomers work. In the bow there's a big wheelhouse where the habitat is controlled, but there are smaller control sheds on each side."

"This is a weird thing to say about a farm but, it's beautiful," I said.

"It's not weird at all. It *is* beautiful. Let's hope it stays that way."

Leaving that ominous thought hanging, Uncle Press started climbing back down the stairs to the main deck.

"What do you mean? What could happen?" I asked while following.

"Did you forget why we're here?" said Uncle Press tersely.

Oh, right. Saint Dane. The turning point. For a few seconds I actually stopped worrying about him. It was hard to imagine this place facing any kind of huge turmoil. Not like Denduron. That territory was a mess from the get-go. This place seemed more like, I don't know, Eden.

"So what do we do?" I asked, feeling kind of dumb for asking my previous question.

"I think we should live here for a while," he answered. "If Saint Dane is here, he'll be planning something. The best thing we can do is blend in, get to know the territory, and be ready if something strange happens."

"Which leads me to another question," I said.

"Of course it does," he replied. Wise guy.

"What do you tell people when you flume to a new territory? Don't they wonder who you are? Where you came from? Why you just happened to drop out of nowhere?"

"Ahhh," said Uncle Press knowingly. "Good question. Obviously you can't go telling people you're a Traveler from a distant territory and you're here to prevent their world from crumbling into chaos. That would be bad."

"Yes, that would be bad," I agreed.

"But there's another way of saying it," he went on. "I have told Spader that I'm from a distant habitat and my goal is to see all of Cloral. So I'm traveling around, going where my mood takes me and picking up work to help pay for my journey."

We had reached the bottom of the tower and Uncle Press stopped and looked at me.

"The thing is," he said with a sly smile, "that's not far from the truth. I just leave out the part about trying to prevent the collapse of their civilization. That would be hard to explain."

"Tell me about it," I said.

We continued walking along the perimeter of the farm.

"So we'll take jobs here. It's not difficult work. They're always looking for help. And we'll stay vigilant. The more you know about a territory, the better chance you'll have of helping them. That's what I did on Denduron."

"And when do we tell Spader that he's a Traveler?" I asked.

"When we need to," came the quick reply.

Uncle Press picked up the pace and I had to keep up with him. He suddenly seemed to be in a hurry to get somewhere.

"Where are we going now?"

"You heard Spader!" he answered, suddenly sounding all enthusiastic. "Sniggers are on him at Grolo's. You don't pass up an offer like that."

Sniggers at Grolo's. I guessed that would be a good thing.

We walked to the far side of the habitat where the temporary housing quarters were. Close-up they looked like small apartments. Nothing fancy, but nice enough. Men and women were hanging out, some were reading, others played with their kids. Two guys were playing catch with a curved tube that looked like a boomerang. I watched as they threw it far off to the side, only to have it circle back and land right in the catcher's hands. It was the Cloran version of playing Frisbee.

All these people wore the same lightweight, colorful clothing that Uncle Press and I now had on. We fit right in. Many smiled and waved a friendly greeting as we passed by. Uncle Press made sure to return every wave and I did the same. These people didn't know who we were, but it didn't seem to matter. They looked like a friendly bunch and that was okay with me.

After walking for what seemed like a mile, we came upon another row of low buildings that ran parallel to the homes along the edge. I didn't have to ask what they were. It was a minimall Grallion-style. There was a clothing store and a place to get haircuts. A small grocery store was next to a small library and that was next to a shop that carried a little bit of everything from tools to toys to cookware. On Second Earth we had a name for this kind of store. Target.

I wondered if there was a video arcade hidden somewhere, but then figured that was probably something unique to Second Earth. Oh, well. We got to the far end of the shops and finally arrived at our destination. A carved sign over the door welcomed all who came this way. It said simply: GROLO'S.

"Center of the Grallion universe," said Uncle Press. "And the finest sniggers ever pulled on any habitat this side of center."

"If you say so," I said, humoring him.

"Actually I have no idea," he said softly. "I haven't had sniggers anywhere else, but that's what they tell me."

He winked and entered the pub. I was right after him, excited about finally discovering the wonders of the much-talked-about sniggers.

As we walked inside, I saw that Grolo's was pretty much your standard tavern. I guess it doesn't matter what territory you're on, people like to meet and drink and swap stories and laugh too loud, because that's exactly what was going on here. There was odd music playing, though I'm sure to the good people of Cloral it wasn't odd at all. If I were to liken the music to something at home, I'd say it was kind of a New Age, techno, Japanese, string thing. How's *that* for a description? I know, it makes no sense, but if you heard it, you'd agree. I have to admit, I didn't hate it. It had kind of a dance beat and added a strong helping of feel-good to the place.

The pub was jammed. It was a mix of men and women of all ages, though I think I was the youngest there. I suddenly wondered if they would card me. That would have been embarrassing. Not only was I underage (at least by Second Earth standards), I didn't have any ID on me at all. If anyone asked, it would have gotten tricky. But they didn't, I'm glad to report.

Everyone seemed to be having a good time while drinking, or laughing, or telling stories, or doing all three at once. I noticed one table of people who weren't swept up in all the revelry though. There were four people, two men and two women, who were having an intense debate. The table they sat around was covered with large pieces of paper that looked like plans of some sort. They each kept jabbing their fingers at the plans while trying to make their point.

"Agronomers," Uncle Press said. "I think they're the only people around here who ever get stressed."

"How come?" I asked.

"It's their show. Grallion is about farming and if Grallion doesn't produce, then they're not doing their job."

I looked again at the agronomers, but now with respect. That's got to be some kind of serious pressure. If they fail, people don't eat.

"Press!" someone called out above the din. "What kept you? I thought you got into another natty-do with the sharkies!"

It was Spader. He had beaten us there. He sat on the bar, surrounded by a few other people who were laughing and drinking with him.

Uncle Press strode right up to the group.

"I thought you were in for a tum-tigger with Yenza!" exclaimed Press.

Sheesh, we'd just gotten here and Uncle Press was already picking up on the local jargon. I figured I'd better keep on my toes.

"Me?" laughed Spader with huge bravado. "Now why would dear Yenza have a row with me? I fill her life with happiness and joy!" He then added slyly, "And besides, I think she fancies me. If she were to kick me off Grallion, she'd die of a broken heart."

Everyone laughed at Spader's high praise of himself, but it was a friendly laugh. They knew Spader was joking. It was all just a goof.

"The chances of Wu Yenza dying of heartache over the sorry likes of you," shouted one guy jovially, "is about the same as old Grolo running out of sniggers."

Everyone hooted in mock horror. A quick look around showed me that everyone was drinking from clear mugs that were filled with a deep red liquid that I figured was the legendary sniggers. Spader leaned back over the bar and grabbed the handle of the tap that I assumed was where they drew the sniggers. He pretended to pull it, and his eyes went wide with shock.

"Empty!" he shouted in overblown horror. "Hobey-ho, he's run out of sniggers! Yenza *does* fancy me!"

Everybody laughed. A heavyset guy behind the bar, who must have been Grolo, playfully shoved Spader away from the tap.

"Don't go startin' rumors," he said, laughing, "or it'll be up to you to stop the riot!"

Spader laughed and rolled away. Grolo grabbed the tap and drew another mug of the frothy red liquid. Everyone was having a great time and Spader was the reason. He was the center of attention and he didn't disappoint those who wanted him to keep the party rolling. He grabbed a mug of sniggers and exclaimed, "So where is he, Press?"

"Standing right here, watching the show," answered Uncle Press.

Who were they talking about? Spader handed Press the mug of sniggers and quickly glanced around. In a second his eyes settled on me. Uh-oh. He was talking about me. I was sure that he had already told the story about how I got tangled up in the water sled and had to be rescued. I wanted to crawl away and hide. If I was going to live on Grallion, I didn't want people to think that I was a total loser. For a second I thought of turning and running, but that would have made it worse. No, I was going to have to face the ridicule. I could only hope that it would be fast.

"That's the guy!" shouted Spader.

All eyes turned to me. The best I could do was stand there and take it. I thought that maybe I could come up with something clever to make it all a joke. But my mind locked. I couldn't come up with anything funny about what had happened. My sore ribs and aching shoulder were a painful reminder of that.

"If it weren't for him," began Spader, "Press would be shark meat."

Huh? I looked to Uncle Press. He raised his mug of sniggers at me and winked.

"Press was trapped under the shelf," said Spader, spinning a dramatic tale that had everyone enthralled. "The nasty wogglie was nosing in on him. He was a big 'un, mind you. But then Pendragon here came flying by with the water sled. With no fear for himself, he distracted the beggar and gave Press the chance to slip away. Bravest thing I ever saw. Of course, I was lucky enough to be in the right place to put the finishing touches on the big wogglie myself."

He added this last bit with false modesty and everyone responded with hoots, like they didn't think he deserved any credit at all. No, in their minds, the real hero was me! I couldn't believe it. Suddenly, a mug of sniggers was thrust into my hand.

"To Pendragon!" shouted Spader. He raised his mug in a toast. Everyone else around the bar raised their mugs toward me as well. Uncle Press did too, with a huge smile on his face.

"Welcome to Grallion!" added Spader.

"Hobey-ho ho!" chimed everyone else as they raised their mugs to drink in my honor.

I couldn't believe it. Talk about snatching victory from the jaws of defeat, no pun intended. Of course, I felt a little guilty. It didn't exactly happen the way Spader described it. But still, it was sort of the truth. I looked to Spader and he gave me a little smile that told me he knew it was only sort of the truth too. But it didn't matter to him. He motioned for me to take a drink of sniggers, and I did.

I wasn't sure what to expect. I had tasted beer once before and I guess that's what I thought it would be like, but it wasn't. That was a good thing because I hated the taste of beer. To be honest, the first taste of sniggers that hit my tongue was totally nasty. It was like drinking carbonated cabbage juice. But in an instant the sour taste went away and what I was left with was an incredibly sweet sensation that actually left my mouth tingling. I once had this soda in Maine called Moxie. When Moxie first hits your tongue it tastes sweet, but after you swallow it leaves a nasty, bitter taste. This sniggers stuff was like reverse-Moxie. The first taste was foul, but it immediately went away and left a wonderful memory that lingered until your next sip. I liked this stuff! Hobey-ho ho!

"Put these on my tab, Grolo!" announced Spader as he jumped off the bar. "I've got business with my friends."

"You don't have a tab, Spader," barked Grolo.

"Then start one for me!" Spader shot back with bravura.

Grolo waved him off with a mock disgusted gesture. I didn't think he minded giving away a few pints of sniggers to Spader. The aquaneer was the life of the party here at the tavern. The more stories he told, the more everyone else drank sniggers. Spader was good for business. He put an arm around Uncle Press, his other arm around me, and led us away from the group toward the front door.

But when we reached the table of agronomers, he suddenly stopped and turned us to them. The scientists stopped their work and looked up to us expectantly.

"We just want you mates to know," said Spader, "we think you are doing a bang-up job. Really."

The scientists didn't know how to react. They just sat there and stared at us.

"Now get back to work!" snapped Spader and led us

toward the door. As we walked he whispered to us, "Scientists. They're brilliant but easily confused."

We blasted out of Grolo's into the sunlight, laughing.

I really liked this guy. But even though I was grateful for his story back there, I couldn't let it go without saying something.

"That story you told about me," I said. "You know that wasn't really how it happened."

"Says who?" Spader shot back. "That's how I saw it. There's always two ways of looking at things, Pendragon. In my few short years I learned that seeing what's positive about a situation is a lot more fun and gets you a lot further than looking for what might be wrong with it. That's my philosophy, for what it's worth."

Spader may not have been a wise old soul, but what he said made a whole lot of sense. I didn't think I had ever met anyone who was as full of energy and fun as this guy was. Without trying all that hard, he made you feel good. I could tell Spader had even gotten to Uncle Press. He said that Cloral was his favorite territory. I'm sure there were a lot of reasons for that, but I'm guessing Spader was a big one. It was fun to be around him. Over the next few weeks I learned a lot more about Vo Spader, and all of it was good.

He was the kind of guy who knew the right people to go to in order to get things done. He got Uncle Press and me set up in a small house near his. It was on the side of Grallion where the temporary workers lived, and since we had become temporary workers, we were right at home. The place was small, but comfortable enough. There were bunk beds (I got the top) and a small kitchen and some simple furniture. The best part about it though, was that the back window looked right out on the ocean. How great was that?

He got us jobs working on the farm. I was afraid this was going to be torture, but it wasn't. Not all of it, anyway. At home on Second Earth the big farms employ pickers who show up during harvest time, pick whatever needs to be picked, and move on to another. That seemed like pretty hard work, and not all that rewarding.

But that's not how it worked on Grallion. Rather than simply going out to pick whatever is ripe, the farm workers on Grallion are assigned to a quadrant. That's an area roughly the size of an acre. The workers are called "vators" and they have the responsibility of taking complete care of their quadrant, from feeding the plants to pruning, and yes, to picking the fruit. But the vators' responsibility doesn't end with the picking. They follow their crops all the way through the washing, sorting, and packing process right up until their crops are shipped out. It's very cool and gives you a real sense of accomplishment. I guess it's the difference between working on an auto assembly line where your whole job is to put the wheels on cars as they pass by you, versus staying with the same car from the very beginning and proudly watching it roll off the line.

Now, you may be thinking that I have no business running a farm, and you'd be right. Before coming to Grallion I didn't know the difference between weeds and worms. I didn't think Uncle Press did either. But it didn't matter because we weren't the only vators assigned to our quadrant. There were six other workers with us and each was pretty experienced. They showed us how to check plants for signs of disease and how to treat them with natural compounds brought up from the ocean floor. All the fertilizer was natural too. It seemed like even though Cloral was covered with water, much of what they used on the surface was brought up from below and processed for use on the habitats.

The fruit grew quickly on Grallion, so there was a harvest of some sort every few days. You would think this was the hardest part, and maybe it was, but it wasn't all that bad. It wasn't like we had to go out into the fields with baskets and fill them up with heavy fruit and lug them back to a central area or anything. It was way more civilized than that. Beneath every narrow walking path was an underground conveyor belt. All we had to do was pick the fruit and drop it on the ground, then lift the doors and drop the fruit down below. The conveyor belt would take it all to a central area where another of the vators from our quadrant would be waiting to wash, sort, and pack them up. It was all so simple.

Uncle Press and I went below several times to receive the harvested fruit from our quadrant and ensure that it was all cleaned and packed properly. We then used a forklift to bring the boxes of fruit all the way forward to the loading docks.

This is where we saw Spader at work. It was a busy place. There were all sorts of transport boats coming and going, bringing shipments of fresh fruits and vegetables back to their habitats. The habitats themselves were never allowed closer than a half mile to Grallion. That would have been dangerous. Instead they would send in small boats that would safely enter the docking area. Spader's job was that of traffic cop. He'd travel just in front of the incoming boats on his skimmer, calling back instructions to get them safely docked. He'd then jump on the dock, tie up the boat and signal the dockworkers to begin the loading process. Once a cargo boat was loaded, he'd reverse the process and guide the boats safely out of the docking area and send them on their way back to their habitats.

But that's not all Spader did. He was also on the pilot's crew. The pilot was like the captain of a ship. He was in charge of the vessel and its safety. Spader was still kind of a junior crew member, so most of his duties were of the lookout variety. At any given time there were ten lookouts stationed around the habitat to warn of any impending problems. It was a boring job, but an important one. It was probably pretty boring being a lookout on the *Titanic*, too. For a while, anyway. That will give you an idea of how important that job was.

I can guess what you're thinking. I made working on Grallion sound as if it were actually fun. Well, fun isn't exactly the word. It was work and some of it was hard, but I didn't mind it. I felt like I was an important part in keeping the wheels turning.

No, working the farm wasn't exactly fun, but there were plenty of other things to do that were *definitely* fun.

Spader took me on adventures. You know how much I like to dive, and on Grallion, hanging out *below* the water was a pretty normal thing. I already described how easy it was to swim underwater using the air globes. These gizmos made swimming underwater almost as natural as walking on the deck of Grallion. Actually, it was better. This is the closest to flying that I think a human will ever come. Spader and I would have races underneath Grallion. I really got the knack of using the water sleds. I found that by subtly shifting my body position, I could turn faster and move quicker. It was all about becoming aqua-dynamic. It didn't take long before I was almost as fast as Spader.

Spader took me fishing, too. I'm not much of a hunter, so he did most of the spearing. I acted more like a scout who found the larger fish and alerted Spader. I guess that makes me kind of like a hunting dog. Oh, well, that was my choice. But I have to tell you, I didn't mind eating the fish afterward. (Spader was a pretty decent cook, too.)

At first I was nervous about quigs, but Spader assured me that the sharks never came near Grallion. I knew that was because quigs only patrolled near gates and flumes, but I wasn't about to tell Spader that—yet.

Spader also showed me something that was really bizarre. Near where Grallion was anchored was another farm. An underwater farm! The people of Grallion didn't just farm on the habitat, they had crops growing on the ocean floor, too! This submerged farm had its own vators who tended the place wearing air globes. They grew everything from fruit, to long leafy vines that were cut at the base and brought up whole. Spader explained to me that these underwater farms were even more important to Cloral than farms like Grallion. He said there were farms all over the planet on the ocean's floor that had fed the Clorans for centuries. Growing food on habitats was a relatively new practice. The most important farms were underwater.

There was another underwater sport that Spader introduced me to, and once I got the guts to try it, I was hooked. Spader called it spinney-do and this is how it worked: A spinney was a kind of fish that traveled in small schools of maybe four or five and they looked like really skinny dolphins. I'm serious. Imagine a regular old dolphin, then imagine it being only about six inches in diameter and you'd have a spinney. At the backs of their heads they had these bizarro ridges. I had no idea what the spinneys needed them for, but they were crucial to playing spinney-do.

Spader motioned for me to be quiet and to watch. He then left me and swam cautiously up behind the spinneys, who were busily feeding on some kelp. They had no clue that he was there. They may have looked like skinny dolphins, but they were nowhere near as smart. Spader was able to sneak up right behind them. With one quick move, he jumped on the back of one and grabbed the ridge behind its head! Well, the spinney didn't like that at all and it started to bloat! It was like one of those puffer fishes that get all fat when you touch them. Only the spinney was so big, when it puffed up it got *huge*! It was strong, too! It had suddenly transformed from this sleepy, dopey fish into a water-going bucking bronco! Spader held on to the back ridge with both hands and wrapped his legs around its body as the fish started thrashing and bucking.

"Eeeyahhhaaa!" shouted Spader. You'd think he knew about Westerns and bronco busting, but I guess shouting like that comes naturally when your adrenaline spikes and you're holding on to an animal for all you're worth. Spader then got cocky and let one hand go, just to show off. The spinney twisted and spun and did its best to launch Spader, but Spader wasn't letting go. Finally, the big fish shot upward. Spader wasn't ready for that move because he did a somersault right off the fish's back. The real beauty of spinney-do was that even when you got thrown, you were still underwater so it wasn't like you were going to hit the ground and break a rib or anything.

"Next one's yours, mate!" exclaimed Spader, still flush with excitement.

I wasn't so sure I wanted to try, but it looked like fun. Two spinneys were poking around the kelp and Spader motioned for me to give it a go. To be honest, I was scared. But I wasn't going to let Spader see me chicken out, so I did my best.

My best was bad. I actually got as far as grabbing the spinney's back ridge and wrapping my legs around its body. But I hadn't expected it to be so strong. The thing bloated, bolted, and was gone. I just floated there, my hand still out, not sure of what happened. Spader swam up to me and patted me on the back.

"Gotta be faster than that, mate," he said, laughing. "You're on their turf down here."

Good advice. I'd remember it next time.

While Spader and I were having these adventures under the sea, Uncle Press was spending his off time learning more about Grallion and about Cloral. After all, we were here on a mission and the more we learned about this territory, the better prepared we'd be when Saint Dane made his move. I felt kind of guilty about having so much fun while Uncle Press was playing Sherlock. But he assured me that it was just as important for me to get to know Spader—he was the Traveler from Cloral, even though he didn't know it yet. At some point we were going to have to work together, so Uncle Press figured it would be a good idea for the two of us to bond.

That was okay by me. Spader and I were having a blast. The thought of battling Saint Dane was the furthest thing from my mind, most of the time. So after having spent a bunch of weeks on Grallion with Spader, I decided that my first impression of him still stood. He was a guy with a big personality and an even bigger sense of fun. He was a truly good guy who listened as much as he spoke. He also cared. He was quick to help out a friend, or even a stranger. He wasn't a slacker, either. He may have liked to have a good time, but he worked hard and he loved his job. This was a good guy to know. I'll remember those first few weeks on Grallion for the rest of my life. It was a great time.

But it was soon going to end.

One evening Spader made me dinner at his house. Uncle Press chose to hang at Grolo's instead. Spader had speared a couple of particularly tasty Kooloo fish that day and grilled them over hot coals in his backyard. Sounds like home, no?

The fish was golden and delicious. After dinner I cleaned up the dishes and Spader went to work cleaning up the rest of his house. There were clothes and pieces of equipment scattered everywhere. To be honest, it looked more like a garage than an apartment. Spader wasn't big on being neat, but tonight was different. He went around picking things up and putting things away and basically making the place look like someone actually lived there.

"What's the occasion?" I asked. "Got a date?"

I then noticed that Spader had more energy than usual. Believe me, for Spader that's really saying something. He was pretty much bouncing off the walls as he worked. It was like somebody took his power dial and notched it up a few amps.

"Big day tomorrow, mate," he said with excitement. "My father is coming by. Can't let 'im think I live like a dirty old crocker fish!"

This was the first I heard about Spader's family.

"Where does he live?" I asked.

"He's an aquaneer on Magorran," he said while continuing to clean up. "It's a manu habitat. Schedule has it swinging by tomorrow for supplies."

"Manu habitat?"

"They build things. Pieces for machinery and skinners and whatnot."

"Is that your home?"

"Home? No, mate. Home is Panger City. Lived there my whole life until I went to the Aquaneer Academy. My mum's still there. Haven't seen either of 'em for . . . hobey, can't remember. It's been a while."

I was beginning to get the bigger picture about what life was like on Cloral. These habitats were like cities and people left home to work, just like back on Second Earth.

"Dad's a real spiffer," Spader continued. "Gave me the aquaneer bug. Had me around skimmers my whole life. They wanted to make him an officer but he turned 'em down—didn't want to leave the docks. His tour's up soon so he can get back to Mum. Hobey, I can't wait to see his face again. Give me a hand here mate, would you?"

I helped him lift a couple of large water sleds he had been working on and put them into a closet.

"You never told me about your parents," said Spader.

Uh-oh. Up until now I'd been able to dodge questions about home. I'm not a good liar. Uncle Press and I made up a story about how we came from a distant habitat that was a university. We said it was full of intellectuals and professors, which explained why I needed to learn so much about working in the water and how the "real world" worked. Whenever Spader couldn't believe how little I knew about Cloral, I'd shrug and say: "I didn't get out much."

I hated lying to Spader, but I knew the truth would come out soon enough and hoped that when it did, he'd understand. But now he was putting me on the spot again by asking about my parents. I was going to have to come up with some version of the truth, because the whole truth would have blown Spader's head off.

"Dad's a writer," I said. "Mom works in a library."

That was the absolute truth, and it made my heart sink. This was the first time I had spoken about my parents in a long time. What made it worse was I had to pretend as if nothing was wrong. I couldn't tell Spader that they had disappeared, along with my sister and my dog. I think Spader must have sensed my anguish, because he didn't ask any more questions. That was good for all sorts of reasons.

"It's tough being away from loved ones," he said softly.

"Yeah, tell me about it."

"Tell you what, come with me to meet Dad tomorrow! You'll get a knock out of him, you will!"

"Sounds good," I said, but with a touch of sadness. I missed my family.

Uncle Press said that Spader was the Traveler from Cloral. I wondered if his parents had raised him to be a Traveler the same way Uncle Press said my family did for me. If so, did that mean they would disappear the same way my family had? Spader obviously cared about his parents. As we worked to make his house a little neater, I hoped that when the habitat of Magorran arrived the next day, his father would be on it.

The next day Uncle Press and I made the long walk forward to the transport docks to be there when Spader's father arrived. I could tell that Uncle Press was disturbed about something. As I told him of my previous day's adventures under the waters near Grallion, he stared straight down at his feet and didn't say a word. His mind was definitely somewhere else.

"What's up?" I asked.

"I don't know," came his thoughtful answer. "I'm feeling . . . uneasy, and I can't put my finger on it."

"What? Now you're psychic?"

"It's just a feeling. Don't you sense it?"

I thought. I felt. I looked around. Nothing.

"Uhh . . . no. Should I?"

"Maybe," he answered. "It's a Traveler thing."

"You mean we can predict the future, too?"

"No, but you'll start to realize you can pick up on things. It's like walking into a room and knowing right away that there's an argument going on, even though you haven't heard a word spoken. It's just picking up on the signals that people send out. No big deal."

"And you're picking up bad signals right now?" I asked, not really wanting to know the answer.

"I'm not sure. I just have this sense of . . . dread."

"I don't like dread," I shot back. "Dread is bad. Could this have anything to do with Spader's parents?"

"We'll find out soon enough," he said while pointing forward.

I looked to where he was pointing and saw it.

Magorran.

The manu habitat had appeared on the horizon and was steaming toward Grallion. Though it was still far away, I could tell that it was a different type of habitat than Grallion. It didn't seem as big. It might have been a third of the size. But the buildings on deck were taller. I guessed that these were some of the factories that Spader told me about. The closer it got, the larger these buildings loomed. It was pretty impressive. Uncle Press and I picked up the pace and hurried to the forward dock area to be there when the first advance boats arrived.

When we got there, we saw that several aquaneers stood on their skimmers, ready to shoot out to meet the advance boats. Uncle Press saw something down on the dock and pointed it out to me. I looked, and couldn't help but smile.

It was Spader. It wasn't weird for him to be down there or anything. It was the way he was dressed. Spader wasn't much for wearing his aquaneer uniform: the black long-sleeved out-fit with the yellow stripes on the cuff. He normally wore his sleeveless shirt that was cut off at the shoulders. But today was different. Today Spader was here to greet his father and he was decked out in his best uniform. It was clean, too. I even think he took the time to comb his hair. To use one of his sayings, he looked pretty spiff.

As we stood above the docks, waiting for the first boat from Magorran to arrive, I began to have the same sense of dread that Uncle Press was feeling. I wasn't being overly insightful or anything, it was because I sensed a stirring among the aquaneers who were gathered below on the floating dock. Up until now they had been casually chatting and laughing. Suddenly their body language grew more tense. All eyes were focused out on the water and at Magorran.

I then looked up at Magorran. The habitat was drawing nearer. Most of the habitats that came to Grallion for supplies stayed far away. Grallion was anchored and stayed in place while the other habitats hovered about a half mile away. It was a safety thing. The habitats were so big that they didn't exactly turn on a dime and you never knew when the current would change. So all things considered, it was smart to keep the habitats far apart and send smaller boats between them.

But now something was wrong. There was confusion. It looked as if the aquaneers weren't sure of what to do. I didn't know what was going on, but whatever it was, it was bad. The answer came quickly. Wu Yenza, the chief aquaneer, ran out onto the upper platform near us. Her eyes were wild with excitement—and fear.

"Perimeter breach!" she barked out. "Warn them off!"

The aquaneers scattered. A moment later a piercing horn sounded long and loud.

"What's going on?" I asked Uncle Press.

Uncle Press didn't look at me. His eyes were focused on Magorran. When he spoke his voice was soft and calm. It was the voice of someone describing the inevitable.

"It's not stopping," was all he said.

I looked out onto the water and saw what he meant. Magorran, this giant habitat, was headed right for us. It had already passed the half-mile safety border and was showing no signs of slowing down. Even if it threw its engines into reverse, it was already too late. There was going to be a crash.

A second alarm sounded that was even louder and more piercing than the first. Where the first alarm sounded like a warning to Magorran, this new alarm sounded more like a warning to Grallion. Impact was inevitable. The only thing that could be done was to prepare for it.

The habitat of Magorran was looming closer. I could now look onto the deck and was surprised to see that there were no people. Wherever they were, I hoped they were doing whatever they could to slow themselves down.

The aquaneers below us began to stream up the stairs to get on deck. That is, all but Spader. Spader just stood there, staring at the oncoming habitat. It looked as if he were mesmerized by the behemoth that would soon crash into Grallion.

"Cast off lines!" shouted Yenza. "Everyone on deck! Move!"

Spader didn't move. Somebody had to kick him into gear. I started for the stairs to go down to him, but Uncle Press put a firm hand on my shoulder. I looked up to my uncle and saw that he was calm. He shook his head no, telling me not to go. But something had to be done.

"Spader!" Uncle Press called out to him.

Thankfully, Spader heard him. He turned around and looked up to us. On his face was a look of confusion. Not fear, just concern.

"Time to go, son," Uncle Press called to him. His voice was firm but unpanicked. It cut through the frenzied energy around us louder than any siren. Spader gave one quick glance back at Magorran to see that it was nearly on us, and then he broke for the stairs. He was the last one up.

"Let's get out of here," commanded Uncle Press. "We'll be safest on deck."

Spader joined the other aquaneers while Uncle Press and I ran for our lives. We climbed up the stairs as quickly as possible until we got on deck. I didn't dare look back. I didn't want to see what was about to happen. All around us was panic. Several different alarms were sounding. Aquaneers were everywhere, desperately trying to cast off the heavy lines that kept Grallion in place. Those who didn't have specific jobs in an emergency were doing the same thing we were—running back to get as far away from the impact zone as possible.

It was going to be ugly. I briefly wondered if both these giant habitats could withstand a collision without sinking. The thought of these huge vessels both going to the bottom was too horrible to even imagine, especially since I was on one of them. I tried to get that out of my mind. One thing at a time, and right now, the best thing we could do was keep running away from the impact zone.

On the deck in front of us I saw a frightening sight. The shadows cast by the buildings on Magorran were chasing us across the deck. It was right behind us. Impact was imminent. I finally couldn't stand it anymore and had to turn and look. What I saw made me gasp. The sheer size of Magorran was mind-boggling. The buildings on its bow must have been seven or eight stories tall, and they were headed right for us. Seeing something so big took my breath away. Knowing that it was going to hit us made me think I'd never take another breath again.

"Keep moving!" ordered Uncle Press.

I turned to continue running with him, and that's when it happened.

Magorran collided with Grallion, full steam ahead into a world that would never be the same.

END OF JOURNAL #5

◎ SECOND EARTH ◎

"How can he end a journal here?" shouted Courtney in dismay. "That's not fair. He can't leave us hanging like that!"

Courtney looked to Mark, expecting him to be just as outraged as she was. But Mark had other things on his mind. He had finished reading the journal several minutes before Courtney and was now busily leafing back through the pages of Bobby's Journal #5 and rummaging in his backpack. The frown on his face said that something was bothering him.

"He's messing with us," added Courtney. "He knows we pore over every word of his journals and he gave us a cliffhanger. That's just . . . wrong. This isn't a game. Why did he . . . What are you doing?"

Mark kept reading through the earlier pages, looking for something. Courtney was suddenly intrigued.

"You saw something, didn't you?" she asked. "Did you figure out who caused the habitats to crash? Was it Saint Dane?"

Mark didn't answer. The scowl of tension didn't leave his face either.

"*Mark!*" Courtney shouted with frustration.

This rocked Mark back into the room. His look of worry was replaced by the look of a small boy who just got caught doing something wrong.

"I-I'm an idiot. A total idiot, th-that's all I can say."

He was on the verge of tears. He held up the pages of Bobby's latest journal. "It's missing. The first page is missing."

Courtney jumped to her feet and grabbed the light green pages from him. She shuffled through them quickly, looking for the missing page.

"That's impossible. We read it together, in the bathroom at school. It's got to be here."

She flipped through the pages once, twice, a third time and then looked to Mark and shouted, "It's not here!"

"I know!" cried Mark.

"Don't panic. When was the last time we saw it for sure?"

"In the boys' room," whined Mark. "We were reading when Mr. Dorrico burst in yelling and I jammed all the pages in my pack and—"

Courtney dove at Mark's pack and frantically dug through it.

"Don't you think I already looked there?" said Mark with frustration. "Like five times already?"

Courtney threw the pack down and clicked into a different gear. She knew that being all frantic and pointing fingers of blame wouldn't help get the page back. They had to think clearly.

"We had it in the bathroom," she began, thinking out loud. "That's for definite. But we came right here. That means we lost it somewhere between the bathroom and here. It's gotta be here!"

Courtney started tossing the cushions on the sofa, desperate to find the lost page. Mark didn't help. His mind was already jumping ahead.

"There's another possibility," said Mark softly. "M-maybe it never left the bathroom."

"What?"

"I-I mean, everything happened fast with Mr. Dorrico and all. Maybe I didn't grab all the pages."

Courtney stared at Mark. For a moment Mark was afraid she would lunge at him and tear out his adenoids. But she didn't. Instead she glanced at her watch.

"School's closed," she said, all business. "If Mr. Dorrico found that page, he probably tossed it in the trash. That means it's either still in that trash can, or outside in the Dumpster."

The two stared at each other for a solid thirty seconds. Neither wanted to admit what the next step might be. Mark broke first.

"We're going through that Dumpster tonight, aren't we?" he said, sounding sick.

"Do you want someone to find that page and start asking questions? Like the police?"

That was a no-brainer. There would be way too many questions to answer if Captain Hirsch of the Stony Brook Police saw that page. Mark and Courtney hadn't been entirely honest with him about their knowledge of Bobby's disappearance, so if someone else found that page, they would look really bad.

"I'll meet you there after dinner," said Mark. "Bring rubber gloves. This is gonna be gross."

And it *was* gross.

Mark and Courtney met as planned, right after dinner. Both used the excuse that they were going to the library on the Ave. Instead they spent a solid two hours digging through the Dumpsters of Stony Brook Junior High. Neither could have imagined that one school could create so much disgusting ick in one day. Going through piles of discarded paper wasn't so bad. Paper was dry. Where it got tough was when they had to search through the stuff that *wasn't* dry. Their journey through garbageland couldn't have happened at a worse time. On that very day, the cafeteria had served spaghetti creole, the furnace had been cleaned and overhauled, and Miss Britton's biology class had the pleasure of dissecting frogs. That meant that the Dumpsters were loaded with sticky tomato sauce, greasy rags, and putrid frog guts.

It was not a happy two hours. Finally, after having wiped sloppy red sauce off yet another page for what seemed like the one zillionth time, Courtney had had enough.

"It's not here," she announced.

"It's gotta be," said Mark while wiping a smudge of grease from his chin. "Keep looking."

Courtney hauled herself out of the Dumpster. She was done.

"Look," she said. "If it's in here and we can't find it, then nobody else will either. It'll just end up at the dump and nobody will ever see it again."

"That's just it!" cried Mark. "Bobby trusted me with his journals. I could never face him again if I lost even one page."

He began digging again with even more energy. A tear grew in his eye. Not because the Dumpster smelled rank, which it did, but because he felt horrible for having let his best friend down. Courtney leaned into the Dumpster and put a hand on his shoulder. Mark stopped digging and looked at her.

"We're not going to find it here," she said softly, trying to calm Mark down. "The more I think about it the more I think it's gotta still be in the garbage can in the boys' bathroom."

Mark felt a spark of hope.

"You think?"

"We were in there just before last period, right? I always see the janitors emptying the garbage cans early in the day. I think there's a good chance Mr. Dorrico saw the page and stuck it in the can and it's still sitting there, waiting to get emptied tomorrow."

"I think you're right," he exclaimed, his spirits rising. "All I've got to do is get there first thing, before it gets emptied."

Mark felt much better. There was still hope, and a plan. Both were cautiously optimistic that they'd find the stray page the next day. The only thing they had to worry about for now was getting home and dumping their clothes before their parents caught a whiff of them. They both *really* needed a shower. It would be tough to explain why they smelled like rotten tomatoes, grease, and formaldehyde.

The next morning Mark was waiting at the front door of school as the janitors arrived for the day. He usually got to school early because he liked to hang out in the library and get some work done before classes, so the janitors didn't think it was odd that he was there. Mr. Dorrico was with the group. Mark knew that this was his chance to find out about the paper, but after what happened in the bathroom with Courtney the day before, he was totally embarrassed about approaching the man. Still, he didn't have any choice.

"Excuse me, Mr. Dorrico?" called Mark.

Mr. Dorrico stopped and looked at him suspiciously. The kids at Stony Brook almost never spoke to the custodians. It wasn't a law or anything, but the two groups didn't have much in common. Until today, that is. Mr. Dorrico stared at Mark. Mark could tell that he was trying to remember where he had seen him recently. Unfortunately Mark was going to have to remind him.

"My name's Mark Dimond," he said tentatively. "R-Remember yesterday? I was in the third-floor bathroom with Courtney and we were reading and—"

"*That's* how I know you!" exclaimed Mr. Dorrico.

At first he seemed happy for having solved the mystery of who this kid was, but his joy quickly turned sour as he remembered the scene from the day before.

"You kids think you're funny, don't you," he scolded.

Mark didn't feel like being lectured, but he figured it would be better to let Mr. Dorrico blow off steam. He might have a better chance of getting the information he needed if Mr. Dorrico felt like he had done a good job of telling him off. So Mark didn't interrupt him. He stood there and took it.

"I've been working at this school for the better part of fifty years," Dorrico went on. "There's nothing I haven't seen and nothing I haven't cleaned up."

Mark thought that was a particularly disgusting thought, but he let the guy ramble.

"So if you think you're being clever or original by trying to make me look foolish, then you've got another think coming!"

"You are absolutely right, sir," said Mark in the most respectful tone he could manage. "We both felt really bad about what happened. A girl should *never* be in the boys' lavatory. To make light of that rule is an insult to everything this school stands for. We felt so bad about it, we decided the best thing to do would be to apologize to you."

He ended his speech with a big, sincere smile. He was afraid he was laying it on a little thick, but he was on a roll and couldn't stop. Mr. Dorrico was thrown. He wasn't expecting a total apology.

"Uh, well," he fumfered. "You're right. Where's the girl? Shouldn't she apologize too?"

"She will," answered Mark quickly. "As soon as she gets to school."

"Okay then," said Mr. Dorrico with finality. "I'm glad we agree."

He started to walk off, satisfied with the knowledge that he had been shown the respect he deserved. But Mark couldn't let him go. He ran quickly in front of him.

"Uhh, there's one thing though," he said tentatively. "When we were in there, we were doing homework. I know, bad place to do homework. But I'm afraid I might have left one of my papers behind. You didn't see it, did you?"

Mr. Dorrico kept walking.

"I saw something," he answered thoughtfully. "It was a green piece of paper with writing on it. Didn't look like a normal piece of paper though. It was more like a piece of plant or something."

"Yes! That's it!" shouted Mark jubilantly. "Did you throw it in the trash?"

"I got a policy. Things get misplaced. If I find something that looks like schoolwork I'll leave it where I found it for a day in case the kid comes back to fetch it. If it's still there after a day then . . ."

Mr. Dorrico continued talking, but nobody was listening. Mark was already gone. As soon as he heard that the paper was left out in the open in the bathroom, he beat feet for the third floor.

Mark flew up the stairs, sprinted down the hall, skidded around the corner, and blasted through the swinging door that led into the lavatory. When he got inside he did a quick look around to discover there was no journal page to be seen. He dropped to his knees and looked on the floor. He checked all the stalls. He looked on the window ledges and under the sinks. No page. He then grabbed the wastebasket and turned it over. It was empty. Mark felt sick. Could one of the other custodians have thrown it away and then emptied the wastebasket last night? That wouldn't be fair. Courtney said they didn't empty them until the morning. But then where was Bobby's page?

Mark sat down on the floor of the lavatory, totally beaten. His last hope was gone. He dropped his head into his knees and closed his eyes. He knew he had to clear his head and think. What would he tell Bobby? He had let his best friend down. Bobby was able to flume all over Halla and stop wars but he couldn't even be trusted to hold on to a sheet of paper.

"'Hi, guys. I gotta apologize for taking so long to write. So much has happened since I left you two, I'm not really sure where to begin.'"

Mark heard those words being read aloud. They were the first words from Bobby's Journal #5—the first words on the missing page.

Mark raised his eyes from his arms. When he did, his heart sank even deeper than it had been a few moments before. Standing inside the door to the boys' lavatory, holding the missing page, was Andy Mitchell. Mark stared up at the kid with greasy dark-blond hair and a bad case of acne . . . and wanted to retch.

If it was possible to have a true archenemy in junior high, then Andy Mitchell was Mark's archenemy. Mitchell was the kind of guy who loved to pick on guys like Mark. The word "bully" always jumped into Mark's mind, but he was a little old to be afraid of bullies. Still, Mitchell loved to harass Mark. He'd cheat off of him in class—when Mitchell decided to show up for class, that is. He'd make fun of Mark's stutter for the amusement of his equally idiotic band of friends, and he never passed Mark in the hallway without giving him a quick punch in the arm. Mark always had to be looking over his shoulder for Mitchell because he never knew where the next bomb was coming from.

The only time Mark was completely safe was when he was with Bobby or Courtney. Mitchell never messed with those guys. Like all good bullies, he was also a coward. Of course, since Bobby left on his adventure, Mark found himself alone more often and at the mercy of the ever present Mitchell. Mark knew he was a classic creep whose power came from the fact that he wasn't afraid to intimidate and belittle. But he was also the kind of guy who would find that power ebbing as his peers grew up and stopped taking him seriously. Unfortunately that time wouldn't come for a while yet. For now, Mitchell was in charge.

Mitchell stood inside the lavatory door with Bobby's journal page in one hand and a burning cigarette in the other.

"There's two possibilities here, Dimond," said Mitchell as he gave a quick, juicy snort. Mitchell always seemed to have a cold. It added to his hideous mystique. "Either this is some lame story you're writing, or you know exactly what happened to Pendragon and you're not telling anybody."

Mark slowly stood up. His mind was in overdrive. What would he tell this guy to get him to give up the page and leave him alone? There weren't a whole lot of options open.

"Y-You g-got me, Mitchell," Mark said tentatively. "It's a s-story. For English. Where did you get it?"

"I found it in here after school yesterday," answered Mitchell. "What's the deal? You miss your buddy Pendragon so bad you gotta make up stupid stories about him?"

"I-I know. It's really s-stupid," said Mark.

This was going pretty well. Mitchell was making up all the answers. Mark didn't have to do anything. Now all he had to do was get Mitchell to give him the page.

"Thanks for finding it."

He held his hand out for the page. This was the moment of truth. Was Mitchell going to give it back?

"What'll you give me for it?" Mitchell asked.

"What do you want?"

Mitchell gave this some thought. This was tough for him. He usually didn't think much.

"Forget it," he answered. "Just take it. It's no fun messing with you anymore. It's too easy."

Mark had to try to stop from smiling. This was amazing. He was going to get the page back, no harm, no foul. He didn't want Mitchell to think he was too happy about it, so he just shrugged and held his hand out. However . . .

It was at that exact instant that his ring started to twitch. Mark felt the telltale movement, but it was such a surprise that he could only stand there, frozen. Then the gray stone started to turn clear and glow. Bobby's next journal was about to show up, and it couldn't be happening at a worse time.

Mark clamped his other hand over the ring to hide it. He made eye contact with Mitchell, hoping against hope that he hadn't seen the ring move. But one look into Mitchell's wide eyes told him the truth. Mitchell had seen it, all right. They stood there for a moment, staring at each other. Finally . . .

"Gotta go!" Mark put his head down and headed for the door. But he had to go past Mitchell, and there was no way Mitchell was going to let him get past. He caught Mark and shoved him back into the bathroom.

"What's going on?" shouted Mitchell, with a touch of fear.

"N-Nothing. I-I'm sick is all."

Mark tried to get by again, but Mitchell wouldn't let him pass.

"Show me that ring!" Mitchell demanded.

By this point the ring was starting to expand on Mark's finger. He couldn't keep his hand on it any longer. Though it killed him to do it, he had to take the ring off and lay it on the ground. As soon as it hit the floor, the dazzling flash from the stone lit up the dark bathroom with a sparkling spray of light.

Mitchell stood over the ring in wonder. He started to bend down to touch it.

"Don't!" commanded Mark.

His voice was so forceful, Mitchell backed off. It was the only time Mitchell had ever done anything Mark wanted him to. Mark didn't feel any victory though; his dominance would be short-lived.

The ring was now expanded to its full size and Mark saw the familiar black hole in its center. The two then heard some odd musical notes coming from deep within.

"Dimond?" yelled Mitchell nervously. "What is this?"

Mark didn't answer. He knew it would be over soon. If he were lucky, Mitchell would run in terror.

But Mark wasn't lucky.

Mitchell stayed. The light from the stone blasted out so brightly that both guys had to shield their eyes. The musical notes grew louder, and then a second later, it was over. The lights stopped flashing. The ring was back to its normal size. Sitting next to it on the floor was another roll of pages that Mark knew was Bobby's next journal. It had arrived the exact same way all the others had, only this time it couldn't have happened at a worse time.

Mark bent down and picked up the roll and the ring. He put the ring back on his finger, and hoping to keep whatever power he had over Mitchell going, he held out his hand.

"Give me the page," he said as forcefully as possible.

Mitchell was numb. He actually started to do what he was told. He held the lost page out for Mark. Mark reached for it, and just as he was about to grab it, Mitchell snatched it back. He was slowly getting his balance back.

"What just happened here?" he asked shakily.

"You wouldn't understand," said Mark, still trying to hold on to whatever leverage the bizarre episode had given him. "J-Just give me the p-page." Mark was losing it.

"I ain't giving you nothing!" declared Mitchell.

The power had shifted again. Mitchell was back in charge.

"I'm starting to think you didn't write this. I'm starting to think Pendragon's been writing about where he is, and he's sending letters to you, special delivery."

Mark didn't know what to say. Mitchell had hit the nail right on the head. How was he going to explain this? Mitchell looked at the page again, then smiled a sly little smile. Mark's heart sank.

"I'll bet there are a lot of people who'd like to know about these," he said.

"Andy, you can't," Mark pleaded. "This isn't stupid kid stuff at school. There are things going on here you can't even imagine. If you told anybody about it, you'd be starting something that I guarantee you'd regret."

This seemed to hit home with Mitchell. Mark realized it might be his one chance to gain some real leverage over the bully.

"There are only three people who know about these pages," Mark continued. "Me, Courtney Chetwynde . . . and now you."

"Chetwynde knows?" shouted Mitchell in disappointment.

This was good for Mark. Mitchell was just as afraid of Courtney as Mark was of Mitchell. Mark was beginning to realize he had more tools to work with than he thought.

"Yes, Courtney knows everything," continued Mark. "This is a serious thing. If you start telling people about it, then you might get in just as much trouble as we will. There's a lot at stake here. You want to go public with it? Go ahead. But your life will never be the same."

Mark felt as if he had laid that on pretty thick. He wasn't at all sure whether Mitchell would get in trouble if he revealed the journals, but he counted on the fact that Mitchell was dumb enough to *think* he could get in trouble. Mark knew that was the one weapon guys like Mark had over guys like Mitchell. They were smarter.

"Don't be an idiot, Mitchell," said Mark. "Give me the page, forget you saw anything, and I promise never to tell anyone that you know."

Mitchell stared at the ground, thinking about the offer. Mark knew that Mitchell was over his head. This was way too much for his brain to process.

"I'll make you a deal, Dimond," said Mitchell tentatively. "I'll give you the page, and I'll shut up about what I saw. But you gotta do something for me too."

"I asked you before, *what*?"

"This isn't before," said Mitchell. "This is now. Before I didn't see the hocus-pocus stuff. My offer is this: I'll keep quiet as long as you let me read what Pendragon sends you."

"What?"

This was probably the worst thing Mark could imagine. He didn't want to share Bobby's journals with anybody, let alone lame-wad Andy Mitchell. What was he going to say to Courtney? He didn't know what to do.

"That's my offer, Dimond," said Mitchell, suddenly sounding more confident. "Either you start showing me those letters, or I start blabbing to everybody about what's going on. I might get in a little trouble, but nothing like what you and Chetwynde will catch."

Uh-oh. Mitchell was being smarter than Mark thought possible.

"Okay," said Mark, though it killed him to do it. "But I can't let you read it before me and Courtney. The letters are being sent to us, not you. After we read 'em, I'll let you have a look. But the letters stay with me, and if you tell anybody and I mean *anybody* about what's going on, I'll make sure you get in every bit as much trouble as we do."

Mitchell thought a second, then handed the lost page to Mark. Mark grabbed it like it was his most valuable possession in the world. And at that moment, it was.

"Deal," he said. "When do I get to read what you got?"

Mark started for the door. He was feeling bold and lost at the same time. He no longer cared about Mitchell's bully tactics. Their relationship had just been kicked into a higher gear. It was a dangerous gear that was way beyond petty bully stuff.

"I'll let you know," declared Mark, and opened the door.

"You better, Dimond," threatened Mitchell. "We're partners now."

Mark stopped and looked back at the creepy Andy Mitchell. He was right. They *were* partners now, sort of. The thought made Mark's stomach roll.

A short while later Mark met Courtney near the gym, just as they had arranged the night before. Courtney was all sorts of excited to know if Mark had found the missing page.

"Well?" she asked impatiently.

Mark's mind raced. What was he going to tell her? He knew he was going to have to tell her the truth, but right now he felt as if he had failed her, and failed Bobby. It started when he left the page in the bathroom and continued when he didn't have the guts to stand up to Andy Mitchell. He felt like such a loser. Yes, he was going to have to tell Courtney the truth, but he couldn't bring himself to do it just then.

"I got the page," he said. "And this."

He pulled Bobby's newest journal from his pack. Courtney's eyes lit up.

"Double score! Excellent! See, I told you it was going to work out."

"You were right," said Mark with absolutely no enthusiasm.

Courtney didn't sense this. She had enough enthusiasm going for the both of them.

"That's weird," said Courtney.

"What?" Mark shot back, hoping that she hadn't sensed something had gone terribly wrong.

Courtney took the newest journal from Mark and looked at it.

"This isn't like the last one," she said with curiosity. "The last journal was written on that green, waterproof paper. This is . . . different."

She was right. Mark had been so nervous about Andy Mitchell, he hadn't even noticed it himself. This new journal was much more like Bobby's first journals that he wrote on Denduron. The pages were brown and crusty looking like parchment.

"You're right," was all Mark could say.

"Okay, we gotta wait till after school to read," she said, handing him back the pages. "Meet me out front after last period and we'll get back to my basement. Okay?"

"Sure. Sounds good."

"Man, I hope I can wait that long. I'm dying! Don't peek, all right?"

"No problem. I won't peek," said Mark, wondering how he was going to keep Andy Mitchell from peeking all day.

Mark and Courtney then separated and went about their normal school day. Mark did his best to immerse himself in schoolwork to get his mind off his dilemma. A few times while classes were passing, he caught sight of Andy Mitchell. Mitchell wouldn't say a word. He'd just give Mark this exaggerated wink as if to say: "We've got a secret, right, pal?" Mark would just turn away and cringe.

After school Mark and Courtney met up just as planned. They barely said anything to each other as they walked to Courtney's house. A dozen times Mark started to tell her about Andy Mitchell, but couldn't find the right words. He saw how excited Courtney was about reading the new journal, and didn't want to crash her mood.

When they got to the house, Mark decided that he wouldn't say anything about Mitchell until after they read Bobby's journal. In spite of all the extra stuff that was going on, Mark was excited to find out what happened to their friend. So without Courtney realizing that a momentous decision had been reached, the two sat down on the dusty couch to jump once again into the world that had become Bobby's.

"I'm shaking," said Courtney as she held the pages.

"Yeah, tell me about it," countered Mark, though he was shaking for a whole bunch more reasons than Courtney.

Luckily for him, the time for talking was over. It was time to read.

CLORAL

Oh, man, I gotta apologize to you guys. I didn't mean to leave you hanging like that. It's just that things are happening fast now and I haven't had many chances to write. That last journal was getting pretty long and I wanted to send it before something happened to it, or to me. I wasn't thinking. Sorry.

I'm writing this new journal from a place where I finally feel safe. At least for now, anyway. I won't tell you where it is yet because the events that led me here were pretty wild. I'd rather recount things as they happened and not jump ahead. It's easier that way. But I'll tease you a little by saying you're not going to believe where I am. Now let's get back to where I left you hanging.

When Magorran hit Grallion, I felt it rather than saw it. The impact sent a giant shockwave throughout the habitat that knocked most people off their feet, including me and Uncle Press. The habitat shuddered and shook and a horrible grinding sound filled the air as the two giant ships collided. I couldn't see it, but I could imagine the destruction that was happening at the point of impact. I could only hope that it wouldn't be so devastating as to send both habitats to the bottom.

Moments before the collision the aquaneers had thrown off most of the lines that secured Grallion, so that when the habitats hit, we would be pushed back instead of holding firm. If not for that move, there would have been way more damage. Also, the pilot of Grallion threw the engines into full reverse, which helped to soften the blow. Still, that wasn't enough to avoid the crash. Even after the collision, Magorran kept coming. The big habitat was powerful and moving fast. It pushed Grallion across the surface of the ocean like a toy. A really big toy. The only way to stop it was to stop Magorran.

Once we realized we weren't going to sink, Uncle Press helped me to my feet. There was a strong vibration from the force of the charging habitat and it was difficult to stand. Up till now I never even felt like I was on a ship. Now I felt like I was on the *Titanic*, and it was banging against the iceberg.

But there was one other thought that made me even more nervous. When something this huge and bad happened it could only mean one thing: Saint Dane was in the house. The look on Uncle Press's face told me he was thinking the same thing. This accident was classic Saint Dane. I could almost hear the wheels turning in Uncle Press's head as he calculated what the crash might mean to Grallion, to Cloral, to Halla, and to us. Finally he announced, "We're on the wrong habitat."

"You're kidding, right?"

He wasn't. Uncle Press took off running toward the impact point. This was insane. The safest place to be was far away from where the two habitats had collided. But being safe wasn't usually high on Uncle Press's To Do list. He was headed right for the most dangerous place on board, and I was right after him. We ran past several vators who were fleeing from the bow to a safer part of the habitat. There was a name for those guys. Smart. We weren't being smart; we were headed toward disaster.

The closer we got to the bow, the more damage there was. The deck had buckled and split. I could look down through jagged tears and see below to the pipes and struts that held Grallion together. It got tricky dodging around these open fissures. One wrong step and we could have fallen a few stories into the guts of Grallion. It was like running over a rickety old footbridge where the bottom could fall out at any moment. Still, Uncle Press wouldn't stop.

When we got near the bow, we saw the full extent of the devastation. Each of the two habitats were crushed where they impacted. It was a twisted mess of beams, girders, and decking. This no longer looked like a habitat. It looked like a vast, floating junkyard.

"Now what?" I asked.

Uncle Press pointed to several aquaneers who were leaping on board Magorran. They were led by Wu Yenza, the chief aquaneer. It was a daring jump because even though the decks of the two habitats were only a few feet apart, they were both still moving and grinding against each other.

"Follow them," said Uncle Press, which was the last thing I wanted to hear. But he didn't give me time to think. He ran to the edge of the deck, hesitated only a second, then leaped from Grallion onto Magorran.

"Let's go, Bobby!" he yelled.

Imagine standing on an ice floe as it hurtled down a river and you had to jump onto another ice floe that was going just as fast. That's pretty much what this felt like. The gap between the two decks was only a few feet, but it felt like a mile. I looked down. Big mistake. I could see through four stories down of twisted wreckage to the frothing white water. Falling would really, really hurt.

"It's cake, Bobby!" shouted Uncle Press. "C'mon!"

Cake. Yeah, right. I inched as close as I could to the edge without getting dizzy. The deck lurched under my feet. This was definitely *not* cake! I waited until Grallion settled, took a breath—and jumped.

I cleared the chasm by a good five feet. Okay, maybe it *was* cake.

"Now what?" I asked, trying to sound as if I were more in control of myself than I really was.

"The pilot house," answered Uncle Press. "Let's find out who's driving this bus."

The pilot house where the habitat was controlled wasn't far from which we boarded. Like the pilot house on Grallion, this was an enclosed structure where the pilot, the first mate, and a few other aquaneers would send the commands that controlled the habitat. Whatever the problem was with Magorran, the logical place to start looking for it was the pilot house.

We took off running, but it wasn't any easier over here than it was on Grallion. This deck was torn up from the impact as well. The whole habitat shuddered and heaved as it bounced against Grallion. It was like trying to run across a minefield during an earthquake.

The goal was to stop Magorran. I feared that when we got to the pilot house, we'd find none other than Saint Dane standing at the wheel wearing an aquaneer uniform and an evil, leering smile. But that would have been too easy. Saint Dane may have been responsible for this, but he wouldn't have done something as obvious as piloting the habitat himself. No, Saint Dane didn't work that way. He was a manipulator. This was an epic disaster that was worthy of him, but the cause of it would be far more diabolical. This was only the beginning. It wasn't just about two habitats colliding. There had to be something grander at stake. So as much as I feared seeing Saint Dane at the wheel, it was his overall scheme that I feared more.

Before we got to the pilot house, the habitat suddenly stopped shuddering. The aquaneers who boarded ahead of us must have reached the controls and shut down the engines. There was a strange calm. The horrible cracking sound of the two habitats grinding against each other stopped. The drone of the engines stopped. The rush of the water crashing between the two wrecked habitats stopped. The aquaneers must have slowed Magorran because after one last loud, twisting crunch, I saw Grallion pull away. The two habitats were once again separate.

As Grallion drifted away, I saw the extent of the damage, and it was pretty nasty. The entire bow end of the farm barge looked like a car after a head-on collision. Decking was bent and cracked. Geysers of water shot from burst pipes. Pieces of beams and struts floated in the water. The dock area was destroyed along with most of the small boats that were kept there. In a word, it was mangled. I'm sure that Magorran looked the same, though I couldn't tell because I was standing on it. The big question now was, why had the aquaneers on Magorran lost control? If our aquaneers could stop it so easily, what prevented the Magorran crew from doing the same?

Uncle Press and I reached the pilot house that was about a hundred yards back from the damaged bow. I was glad to see the collision hadn't destroyed it. It was a solid structure that was probably built that way in case something hairy like this happened. This was the first good news we saw. Magorran could still be controlled from here. The question was, why did it go out of control in the first place? The moment we opened the door, we had the answer. There were two aquaneers from Grallion at the controls. Yenza was at the wheel, the other worked the array of toggle switches for the many water-powered engines that controlled the habitat.

The aquaneer crew from Magorran was there as well. There was the pilot, the first mate, and three other aquaneers. I recognized their rank because they wore the same uniforms as the crew from Grallion. But there was one big difference between this crew and our crew.

These guys were all dead.

It was a creepy scene for obvious reasons, but it was made all the more so because the crew looked so . . . natural. It wasn't like there was a violent fight or anything. Just the opposite. The pilot sat in his chair, still looking forward with sightless eyes. The first mate was hunched over a map with a pen still in his hand as if he were in the middle of plotting a course, probably to rendezvous with Grallion. The other aquaneers were sitting on the deck near their stations as if they had simply fallen asleep. But these guys were definitely not asleep. Their eyes were wide open. There was something else. Uncle Press saw it first and pointed it out to me. Each of the poor dead aquaneers had a trace of something on the corners of their mouths. It was dry now, but it looked to have been a trickle of green liquid that had dribbled out of the corners of their mouths and crusted there.

They were dead all right. The mystery of the collision was solved. These guys died at their posts under full power. But the idea of five guys suddenly dying was tough to comprehend. It was then that I was hit with a thought that was even more horrific than the sight in front of me. It was like an alarm rang in my head. I reached out to Uncle Press, grabbed his sleeve and pulled him out of the pilot house.

"This wasn't a sudden crash," I croaked out through my dry mouth. "I mean, we saw it coming, right?"

"Yeah, so?"

"So if we saw it coming, how come nobody else on board Magorran did?"

Before I got all the words out, I saw in Uncle Press's face that he knew exactly where I was going with this. The crash happened because the pilot and his crew were dead. But somebody else on Magorran should have seen the crash coming and tried to stop it. That is, if anybody else on Magorran were alive to see it. The horrible realization hit Uncle Press just as it hit me. If nobody else tried to stop the crash, did that mean more people were dead? We both did a quick scan around and saw the same thing—nothing. There was no movement. No life. The sickening truth was setting in. There was a very good chance that everybody on Magorran had met the same fate as its crew.

This may have become a ship of the dead.

I turned away from Uncle Press and puked.

CLORAL

"Spader!" shouted Uncle Press.

I had my hands on my knees while tossing my lunch. I looked up to see Spader booking across the deck several yards away. He was headed deeper onto Magorran and I knew why. He was going to find his father.

Behind us Wu Yenza came from the pilot house and saw him too.

"Stop right there!" she commanded. "Do *not* go onto this habitat!"

Spader didn't even glance at her. There was nothing stopping him.

"We'll stay with him," said Uncle Press to Yenza.

"You are not authorized to be here," she said sternly.

"We're civilians," countered Uncle Press. "You can't stop us."

"We can't protect you either."

I didn't like the sound of that. Whatever caused this horrible disaster could still be out there. On the other hand, chances are it was Saint Dane, and that bad boy was our department.

"Understood," said Uncle Press. "We'll bring him back."

Yenza wanted to argue, but Uncle Press had already started to jog after Spader. I looked to the chief aquaneer and shrugged. She scowled at me and I turned and ran after Uncle Press.

Spader had a head start on us and it was tough keeping up with him. It didn't help that he knew exactly where he was going. We had to keep him in sight or he'd be gone. As we ran across the deck of Magorran I tried to keep an eye on him while taking in the new surroundings. This was a manu habitat, but the factories must have been toward the stern because the area we were running through seemed more residential. There were several tall structures that looked like apartment buildings surrounding a big park. This could have been a normal, downtown neighborhood back on Second Earth. It was strange to think that we were floating. Stranger still was the fact that the place was deserted. There wasn't a soul to be seen—living or dead. It gave me hope that everyone had evacuated Magorran before they met the same deadly fate as the crew.

Up ahead Spader hurried into one of the apartment buildings. When we entered after him, all my hopes that the habitat had been abandoned came crashing down. Sitting in the lobby were three more bodies. Like in the pilot house, it looked as if death touched them quickly and with complete surprise. They were three men who must have been factory workers because they all wore the same bright blue coveralls. They sat around a table that was covered with multicolored tiles. My guess was they were playing some kind of game when they met their fate. One still held a tile as if ready to make a play. He never got the chance. The whole scene was creepy and I didn't want to look too closely, but I did see that all three men had the same trace of dried green liquid on their chins. Whatever it was, it must have had something to do with the way they died.

I didn't want to be there anymore. This was getting dangerously gross. I was all set to turn and bolt back for Grallion, when we heard a crash coming from deeper in the building that sounded like breaking glass. Either it was Spader or somebody was still alive. Uncle Press took off toward the sound and as much as I wanted to run the other way, I stayed with him.

As we ran down a long corridor I tried not to think about what horrors lay behind each of the closed doors we passed. It was like running through a tomb. We finally came to a door that was open slightly.

"You ready for this?" Uncle Press asked.

"No, but we gotta do it," I answered.

So he pushed the door open and we both entered.

We saw right away that this was an apartment very much like Spader's on Grallion. It was small and simple, with molded furniture and windows that looked out on the ocean. Nobody was here, so we had to move on into the bedroom.

That's where we found him. Spader stood in the middle of the room. At his feet was a shattered vase. That was the sound we heard. Spader must have broken it himself, probably in anger. When we entered, he didn't turn to look at us. That was because he was focused on his father. The man was sitting at a desk with his head resting on the surface. Yes, he was dead. Like the others, it looked as if he had died peacefully. He wore his full aquaneer uniform. My guess was he wanted to look as good for his son as Spader wanted to look for him. My heart went out to my friend. I had expected Spader to discover that his father had disappeared, just as mine had. But this was worse. Much worse.

I think Spader was in shock. His eyes were focused on his father as if he thought he could change the sight before him by sheer willpower.

I had no idea of what to say or do. Uncle Press walked over to the fallen aquaneer and gently closed his eyes. He then looked to Spader and said in a gentle voice, "Don't be sad, this is the way it was meant to be."

Though he didn't know it yet, Spader was a Traveler. As I was told many times before, everything happens for a reason. I didn't quite buy it yet, but that's what I was told.

Spader looked into Uncle Press's eyes and I saw how bad he was hurting.

"This is the way it was meant to be?" he asked with a shaky voice. "I don't understand."

"You will," Uncle Press said gently.

"We're going to help you."

I knew what Uncle Press meant. Pretty soon we were going to have to tell Spader about being a Traveler. But I didn't think it was going to help him understand anything. I've known about being a Traveler for some time now, and I'm still pretty clueless.

Uncle Press looked down at the dead man, and saw something. Clutched in his right hand was a small folded piece of paper. Uncle Press gently took it from his hand and read it. He then looked at Spader, and handed the note to him. When Spader took it, I thought he was going to burst out in tears. That's because the letter was for him.

Scribbled on the sheet was one word: "Spader." In his dying moments Spader's father had written a note to his son. It was odd to see "Spader" written out in normal letters. Since Travelers understood all languages, I suppose we could also understand all *written* language as well.

As Spader took the note I saw Uncle Press put something quickly into his pocket. Spader didn't see it because he was looking at the note. But I did. Uncle Press had taken something else from the dead man's hand and didn't want Spader to see it. He looked at me and gave me a stern look which clearly said: "Don't say anything."

"What does the note say?" asked Uncle Press.

Spader showed the note to Uncle Press and I looked over his shoulder to see it too. It wasn't a written message; it was a drawing. It was a circular symbol about the size of an Oreo cookie. It looked to me like two interlocking letters from an Asian alphabet. I had no idea what it meant or what it represented.

"Do you know what this means?" asked Uncle Press.

Spader shook his head. Uncle Press handed it back to him and said, "If your father wanted you to have it, it's more important than we realize right now."

Spader nodded, folded the paper and put it in his pocket. He then looked to my uncle and I saw a change in the aquaneer's eyes. He was no longer in shock. He was totally in control.

"I'm going to find out what happened here," he said with certainty.

"Good. We're going to help you," Uncle Press answered.

The moment was broken by the sound of hurried footsteps. A group was headed down the hallway toward us, fast. Seconds later they entered the apartment and I saw it was a group of five aquaneers, headed by Wu Yenza. These guys looked as if they were on a mission. They were all business, and they carried guns. This was the first time I had seen weapons of any sort on Cloral, other than spearguns for fishing. These weapons were sleek, silver rifles with wide barrels.

I would have thought they were kind of cool, if I hadn't been so worried they might be used on us. Yenza had a gun as well, but hers was a silver pistol in a holster on her hip.

She strode purposefully into the bedroom and scanned the scene. When her eyes fell on Spader's father, she cringed with surprise and sorrow.

"I'm sorry, Spader," she said kindly. "I knew your father. There is much of him in you."

Spader acknowledged this with a nod.

"Magorran is being evacuated," she then said, clicking into business mode. "All nonessential personnel must return to Grallion."

"What's the point?" asked Uncle Press.

"We're sending in a medical team," she answered quickly. "The habitat will be quarantined until we determine what caused these deaths."

Good point. If a virus had done this, it could still be hanging around. It was best to leave this to the experts.

"When you get back to Grallion," she continued, "you will be disinfected. Do not take anything from here. Understand?"

I was sure that the same thought shot through all of our heads. What about the piece of paper with the round symbol on it? Was Spader going to leave it? The answer was *no*. He walked out of the room, past Yenza, without giving up the paper. Uncle Press and I shared glances, then followed him out.

We were escorted back toward the bow of Magorran by two armed aquaneers. We weren't under arrest or anything, they just wanted to make sure we got back quickly. Spader didn't say a word. He walked stiffly, looking straight ahead.

When we got near the crushed bow, I saw there was a

flurry of activity going on. Several more aquaneers had arrived and were putting on bulky suits that made them look as if they were getting ready to handle plutonium. I figured they wanted protection against any nasty microbe that might be on Magorran. I really hoped those suits weren't necessary, because if they were, it would have meant Uncle Press and Spader and I were already infected. Suddenly the idea of being disinfected was sounding pretty good. We had to get back to Grallion, fast.

One of the aquaneers stopped us and said, "We'll get you on a boat for Grallion. Wait here." He took off, leaving the other aquaneer to make sure we stayed put.

As we stood there I glanced over at the pilot house and saw something strange. Two agronomers were standing outside, away from everyone else. They were arguing. It was the man and woman whom I recognized from Grolo's. The man seemed to be pleading with the woman. He was angry and waved his arms to make his point, but the woman didn't want to listen and kept turning away from him. I had no idea what they were saying because we were too far away, but I wanted to remember what I saw.

A transfer boat brought the three of us back to Grallion. But we weren't allowed to go home right away. They first brought us to a medical building and made us give up our clothes. I think they burned them, because I never saw them again. We were given replacements though. We also had to empty our pockets. This was going to be tricky. It meant giving up my Traveler ring, not to mention Uncle Press's ring and whatever it was he took from Spader's father. I also wondered what Spader was going to do with the note. It could be a vital clue as to what happened on Magorran and I feared it would be destroyed.

The rings proved easy. They were sent through a sterilizer and given back to us. As for the other stuff, I wasn't sure. Before we got dressed we had to shower with some foul-smelling soap that stung my skin. Some medical personnel watched us the whole time to make sure we washed all the nooks and crannies. Nice, huh? To be honest, I didn't mind. I would have scrubbed myself with acid in Yankee Stadium if I thought I might be carrying a microbe that was deadly enough to do the damage I saw on Magorran.

Once we were released, all freshly scrubbed and stinging, we walked back toward Spader's house. Spader wasn't saying much and I figured it was because his thoughts were with his dad. Well, his thoughts may have been with his dad, but that's not why he was so quiet. As soon as we got away from the medical unit, I saw the real reason. He opened his mouth . . . and pulled out the note from his father. He had folded it and got it through without anyone knowing. Smart guy. We asked him to come for dinner, but he wasn't in the mood. He wanted to be alone. Can't say I blame him. Uncle Press and I went back to our apartment and I finally got the chance to talk with him in private.

"What happened over there?" I asked right away. "Was it Saint Dane?"

"It could have been," answered Uncle Press. "Or it could just have been a horrible accident."

"Accident?" I shouted. "How many people died on Magorran? Two, three hundred? That was no accident."

"You might be right, but we've got to look beyond the tragedy here. Saint Dane doesn't wreak havoc just for the sake of it. He always has a plan. If he caused those people to die, it's because it served some overall scheme. Remember, he's about pushing a territory toward chaos. If we're going to find his hand in this, we've got to figure out what his overall plan is."

"What about Spader?" I asked. "He's in bad shape. It's going to be hard to tell him about the whole Traveler thing."

"But he's got to learn soon. He's the only Traveler from Cloral now."

"You mean he wasn't before?"

"Up until he died, Spader's father was the Traveler. Now it's Spader."

"Oh, man!" I blurted out. "Spader's father was a Traveler too?"

"Yes," said Uncle Press softly. "And he was a friend."

He reached into his pocket and said, "I took this from him, but it belongs to Spader now." He held up the item he secretly took from Spader's dad and I instantly recognized what it was. It was a Traveler's ring just like mine. The band was made of heavy silver; the stone in the center was slate gray and there was some kind of bizarro engraving around it.

"I want you to give this to him. You'll know when the time is right," said Uncle Press, as he dropped it in my hand.

I nodded and put the ring in my pocket. I wasn't sure I wanted this responsibility, but Spader was my friend. How could I not do it?

Uncle Press then said, "Spader's father must have known something was going to happen."

"What makes you say that?"

"The paper he left for Spader. His last act was to get that symbol to his son, the Traveler. It's why I think the deaths on Magorran weren't an accident. There's something bigger going on."

"What do you think the symbol means?"

"I don't know, but I'll make you a bet: When we find that out, we'll find Saint Dane."

It was official. The game was on. It looked like Saint Dane had made his first move. But this wasn't like Denduron. There were no obvious good guys and bad guys here. At least not yet, anyway. There was nothing we could do but keep our eyes and ears open—and wait.

The next few days slipped by in a weird haze. Uncle Press and I went back to work, but our hearts weren't in it. It didn't seem like anybody else cared to be working either. Everyone wanted to know what the medical team would find on Magorran. I found myself stopping and staring out at the manu habitat that was anchored a mile away. It looked like a dark storm cloud looming on the horizon. The only signs of life were the several boats that would travel back and forth from Grallion to ferry medical personnel and repair crews.

Repairs were also under way on Grallion. The pilot brought us back to our original position and anchored us there. I heard that the collision with Magorran pushed us nearly ten miles over the ocean. It was important that Grallion return to its home because that's where the underwater farm was.

I tried talking to Spader a few times, but he didn't want company or conversation. I understood, but I also knew he shouldn't be totally alone. It was sad. The loss of his father changed him. He went from being a total extrovert to spending all of his time alone. This wasn't good, so one night I got two bottles of sniggers from Grolo's and paid him a visit.

When I knocked on his door, Spader didn't answer. But I knew he was in there so I let myself in. I found him lying on the floor, staring up at the ceiling. By the rank smell in there, I guessed he hadn't showered much in the past few days. I didn't say anything though, I just walked in and pressed the bottle of sniggers into his hands.

"Hobey-ho," I said.

Spader looked up at me and for a moment I didn't think he recognized me. His mind was miles away. But then he focused and smiled. He took the sniggers, too.

"Strange days, Pendragon, my friend," he said as he sat up.

"Yeah, strange days," I answered, and we both took a drink of sniggers. It tasted good. I don't think sniggers had alcohol in it, like beer. But it definitely had a sparkle, and that was good.

"What were you thinking about?" I asked.

Of course I knew he was thinking about his dad, but it was as good a way as any to start a conversation. Spader lifted his other hand and I saw that he was holding the piece of green paper with the round symbol. He waved it at me as if to say: "I'm thinking about this."

"Any idea what it means?" I asked.

"Not a clue," he answered. "But I know who might."

"Who?"

"My mum. She's a teacher. Sweetest lady in the world and twice as bright. I gotta get back there . . . tell her about Dad."

Spader closed his eyes. I wasn't sure if he was going to cry, but I looked away just in case. Things were about to get even worse for him. Here he was faced with the horrible task of telling his mother that her husband, his father, was dead. But there was more. There was the whole Traveler thing. When Spader went back to Panger City to find his mother, was she going to be there? Now that he had become the Traveler from Cloral, was she going to disappear the same as my family? Was he going to lose *both* of his parents? I felt like I had to say something to start getting his mind around the Traveler concept.

"Spader," I said cautiously. "There's something you should know."

Spader looked at me. His eyes were red. He wanted words of comfort from me, but I had none to give. As I sat there looking at him, I realized I had no idea of what to say. I needed to explain something that I didn't fully understand myself. Talk about the blind leading the blind.

"What, Pendragon?" he asked.

As I opened my mouth to say . . . I don't know what, Uncle Press entered the apartment. Whoa, big relief. He had bailed me out big time.

"I have news," he said. "About Magorran."

Spader and I both sat up in anticipation. We had been waiting for information for days. But one look at Uncle Press told me that it wasn't going to be good news. He looked nervous, and maybe even a little bit angry.

"Let's have it then," prodded Spader.

Uncle Press took a chair and sat opposite us. He spoke softly and clearly so we understood completely.

"The medical team made their report," he began. "They examined and tested every one of the victims."

"How many?" I asked.

"Two hundred and twenty."

Though I knew the number was going to be high, it was still a shock to hear it. Uncle Press let that information sink in, then continued.

"The test results came back exactly the same on each and every one of them." He took a breath and said, "They were all poisoned."

The news hit me like a hammer to the head.

"H-How?" I blurted out. "How can that many people be poisoned?"

"They aren't sure, but they think it may have had something to do with a shipment of rice. It was bad, and they all ate it."

"What do you mean *bad*?" demanded Spader.

"They don't know," answered Uncle Press, trying to stay calm. "They can't tell. They said it was unlike anything they'd seen before."

Spader jumped to his feet and started to pace. "Bad rice? How can people die because of bad rice?"

"It gets worse," added Uncle Press. "The agronomers are afraid it may not be the only case. If there's a problem with the food supply, then what happened on Magorran is just the tip of the iceberg."

My thoughts immediately went back to the argument I witnessed between the two agronomers on Grallion. They knew something was wrong. The horrible reality was slowly beginning to sink in. Cloral was a territory covered by water. People relied on farmers to grow food both on the habitats and underwater. If something was poisoning the food supply, it would be beyond disaster. Compared to this, bubonic plague would seem like a nasty cold going around.

There could be only one reason for this . . .

Saint Dane. This had his stamp all over it. If the food supply went bad, there would be chaos throughout the territory, no question about it.

"We don't know the extent of the problem. Maybe it was a one-time thing and they caught it," Uncle Press said calmly.

"Not in time to save my father," snapped Spader. There was anger in his eyes. He wanted someone to blame for his father's death. Uncle Press and I knew who it might be, but now was not the time to share it.

It was late, so we left Spader alone. Uncle Press and I went home to form a plan. The next day was the memorial service for the victims on Magorran. We decided that after the ceremony we would join with Spader, get a boat, and travel to

Panger City to find Spader's mom. The only clue we had to go on to start tracking down Saint Dane was the strange symbol that Spader's dad left him, and Panger City was as good a place to start looking as any. With that plan in place, we tried to get some sleep.

I barely slept all night. The thought of territorywide famine made it a little hard to have sweet dreams. There were too many thoughts banging around in my head, so I decided to finish my journal to you. Writing always makes me sleepy, and this time was no different. I got as far as telling you that Magorran and Grallion had collided, and couldn't keep my eyes open anymore. So I rolled up the pages and sent them on to you. It wasn't until the next morning that I realized what a cliffhanger I had written. Again, sorry.

I laid back down on my bunk and finally got a few z's. But soon the sun was brightening the sky on a new day, the day we would leave Grallion.

The memorial service was scheduled for shortly after sunrise. I didn't know what to expect, but it turned out to be a pretty emotional moment. It took place on the stern of the habitat, away from the destruction up front. Everyone on Grallion was there. We stayed with the farm workers, the vators, who pretty much kept together in one large group. The aquaneers were lined up along the stern, shoulder to shoulder, in full dress uniform. Spader was among them. It had to be tough for him to stand there, but he did it. Good man.

The pilot of Grallion, a leathery-looking gray-haired guy named Quinnick, led the ceremony. I won't write down all that was said, but as you can imagine, it was pretty intense. He spoke about the dedication of those who serve others, and the harsh reality that all life must one day come to an end. He spoke glowingly of the crew and workers of Magorran, and about how they would never be forgotten.

Then an aquaneer stepped forward and began to play an instrument that looked to be made from a large piece of coral. It was a wind instrument, and though it seemed pretty crude, the sound it made was sweet, like an oboe. The tune he played was haunting and sad. It was a fitting send-off to the poor people of Magorran.

But it was short-lived because suddenly, without warning . . . *boom!*

An explosion rocked Grallion only a few yards from where we stood. The crowd didn't react immediately. Everyone just sort of looked around, stunned, not knowing what was happening.

Boom! Boom!

Two more explosions rocked the habitat, chewing up pieces of deck and dirt. People started to scatter and run for cover. We were under attack, but from where?

The answer came from Wu Yenza. She stood on the stern and yelled out, *"Raiders!"*

Raiders? What were raiders? The only raiders I knew were from Oakland. I looked off the stern and had my answer. There was a ship powering toward us. It wasn't a habitat, it was a battleship, and its giant guns were trained on us. These guys weren't from Oakland.

Things were turning very sour, very fast here on Cloral.

CLORAL

We were under attack.

Most people on deck scrambled for cover and I was one of them. Uncle Press and I stuck with a group of vators who fled to the building that held most of the farming equipment. That wouldn't give much protection, but it was better than standing out in the open with bombs raining down!

As we ran more missiles pounded the deck and blasted dirt and water everywhere. Yes, water. These weren't your everyday, ordinary cannonballs. Remember, this was Cloral. Everything here had to do with water. I soon found out that the giant guns on the battleship were actually huge water cannons that fired big, dense balls of water. But when these water missiles hit, they were every bit as destructive as a steel shell. And they could fire round after round without fear of running out of ammunition. After all, their ammunition was water, and there was an infinite supply around these parts. What made it even more frightening was that there was no sound. The guns didn't let out a giant roar when they fired, so it was impossible to prepare for a strike. The first clue that a water missile was about to hit was a faint whistling sound, and then it hit.

About a dozen of us crowded into the equipment shed and scrambled to the windows to look out on the action.

I looked to Uncle Press and said, "Raiders? What's the deal?"

Uncle Press didn't know. This was a wrinkle he wasn't prepared for.

"I have never seen them attack a habitat this large," one vator said with more than a touch of fear. "They usually prey on small vessels."

"What do they want?" I asked.

"Whatever we have," came the simple answer. "And they're not afraid to kill for it."

Gulp. I looked out the window to see that the aquaneers were scrambling to defend the habitat. These guys weren't just sailors, they were trained in using weapons as well. They moved fast and efficiently as they took up defensive positions facing the incoming cruiser. But the only weapons they had were the silver rifles I saw back on Magorran. They didn't have big cannons or missile launchers or firepower of any kind that could stand up to the barrage from the raiders' huge water guns. Their rifles seemed like, well, they seemed like water pistols compared to the mighty arsenal they faced.

"Why isn't Grallion armed?" I asked the vator.

"I told you," he answered. "The raiders have never been so bold. There was never a reason to be armed. Until now," added Uncle Press soberly.

All my romantic notions about pirates were just blown away, no pun intended. To me pirates were charming rogues who drank grog and chased wenches and shivered me timbers and were basically comical characters in search of treasure. But these weren't Disney pirates. The guys firing on us were killers. *Bold* killers. They were attacking an unarmed farming habitat with over two hundred people on board. But for what? There were no riches on Grallion. What could they possibly want?

Then the barrage of missiles stopped. We took a look at the battle cruiser and saw that it had pulled to within a few hundred yards of Grallion. Its guns were still aimed at us, but they were no longer firing for the time being.

The ship looked very much like a battleship from home, though of course there were no military markings. It was a light green color that made it blend in with the green water. I counted eight water cannons in all. Four front and four back. I wondered what their next step was. Were they going to board us? That wouldn't make sense because any advantage they had with their big guns would be lost once they set foot onboard. There were plenty of aquaneers with rifles to give them a hard time if they set foot on our deck. No, the advantage these bad guys had was from a distance.

Then, a booming, amplified voice came from the battle cruiser.

"Good morning, Grallion! I trust we have your attention."

It was a man's voice and he actually sounded cheery. He could have been calling to a neighbor over the backyard fence to talk about the Yankees.

"My name is Zy Roder, pilot and chief of the good ship *Pursuit*. Perhaps you've heard of me?"

The more I listened to this guy's booming voice, the more my stomach twisted. I looked to Uncle Press and his grim expression told me he was feeling the same way. Near us, a vator had been watching the cruiser through a spyglass. The moment we heard the voice coming from the raiders' ship, Uncle Press approached the man and asked if he could borrow the telescope. The worker obliged and Uncle Press took a closer look at our new nemesis.

"If you have heard of me," the voice continued, "then you know I am a fair man. I wish no harm on anyone."

Uncle Press saw what he needed to see, then handed me the spyglass. I took it and looked out at the cruiser. The crew of the ship he called *Pursuit* were all on deck. There was a mix of men and women, which meant that at least raiders weren't sexist. They weren't all torn up and scuzy looking the way you think of movie pirates either. No, just the opposite. These guys looked like an organized, buttoned-up crew. But the way they stared at Grallion made me think of a pack of hungry wolves, patiently waiting to strike. Their stares were blank and lacked any human emotion, except for maybe greed.

I moved the spyglass until I found the man called Zy Roder. He stood on the uppermost deck, holding something dark that I could only guess was a microphone. Like all the raiders, Zy Roder wore the same kind of lightweight clothing that everyone wore here on Grallion. He was a tall guy, with shoulder-length blond hair that blew around in the sea breeze. You might even call him handsome. He stood with his legs apart defiantly, with one hand on his hip. Pretty cocky. This was a guy who was used to getting what he wanted. I wondered what it was he wanted from us.

But the thing that struck me most about him was his eyes. Even though I was looking through a spyglass, I could see they were the same, icy blue eyes that I had grown to fear. There was no mistake.

It was Saint Dane.

He had arrived on Cloral and taken up with a band of out-law marauders. The question now became, what was his next move? I handed the spyglass back to the vator. I didn't want to watch anymore.

"By now you must know of the horrible disease that is

spreading throughout Cloral," he continued. "Our food is being poisoned. Why? I have no idea. But I do know that safe food will soon grow scarce."

This was Saint Dane all right. He was doing what he did best, spreading fear.

"Our request is simple. The food on Grallion is safe . . . so far. You have so much, and we so little. These are my terms. Load ten of your largest transfer barges with grain, fruit, and vegetables. Send each barge out to us with a single aquaneer. We will take the barges and leave you in peace."

The farm workers around us erupted in protest. They complained that ten barges of food would wipe Grallion out for weeks. Worse, if they gave up all their supply of safe food, then what would be left for them to eat? Already, the fear of tainted food coming in from the outside was suspect. Who could blame them, after what happened on Magorran?

"If you refuse us," Zy Roder continued, "then we will resume our attack." The man now grew more intense. Gone was the pleasant voice of a fellow sailor. Saint Dane or Zy Roder—whatever he called himself here—wanted the people of Grallion to understand what he was capable of.

"We cannot sink Grallion, but that is not our intent. We will begin with your pilot house. It will be obliterated so that you will have no control of your habitat. Then we will destroy your docks so you will be trapped. We will target your engine rooms so you will have no power. You will be prisoners on your own habitat, with no means of escape. Trust me, friends, we know where you are most vulnerable and we will not leave until our demands are met."

This was pure Saint Dane. He probably didn't even care about getting the food. What he wanted was to cause panic. The word would spread quickly among the habitats that the food supply on Cloral was suspect, and that would create chaos as normally peaceful people would start to fight over the dwindling supply of fresh food. My guess is that Saint Dane probably had something to do with poisoning the food supply as well. His plan for toppling Cloral was beginning to become clear.

"I will give you one peck of time to begin the transfer," his voice boomed. "If I see no sign of your compliance, we will open fire. So until then, enjoy your day!"

What was a peck? Was that an hour? A minute? A second? Uncle Press read my mind and said, "Twenty minutes, in case you were wondering."

Saint Dane had one more thought. "Oh, one last thing," his voice boomed. "Welcome to Cloral . . . Pendragon."

Yikes. My knees buckled, which I'm sure was the exact reaction Saint Dane wanted. He knew we were here. Luckily, the other vators had more to worry about than why this pirate had given me a personal greeting. That would have been hard to explain. So instead of questioning me, they all started chattering at once. Half argued to give him the food, the other half wanted to fight. Neither choice was a good one.

"At least we know a little about his plan now," said Uncle Press, trying to sound positive.

"Yeah, big deal," I shot back. "What are we going to do about it?"

At that moment Spader burst into the shack. He looked around quickly until he saw us. "Press, Pendragon, come!" he shouted.

Neither of us knew what else to do, so we followed. Once outside we saw that Spader was off and running. He led us down to the same floating docks where we first arrived on Grallion. The area was deserted because all the other aquaneers were up on deck, ready to defend their habitat.

He ran to the end of one dock and jumped onto his skimmer. We finally caught up to him. I shouted, "What are you doing?"

While he spoke Spader busily prepared the skimmer for a trip.

"My father taught me everything there is to know about every ship on the sea," he said quickly. "I know about that raider cruiser, the *Pursuit*. There were only a few built, back when the aquaneers feared there might be a war between the habitats. They even built warships that traveled underwater. But the war never happened and the cruisers and submarines were never used—except for a few that got hijacked by raiders."

"What's the point, Spader?" asked Uncle Press.

Spader stopped working and looked up at us. "I know where she's vulnerable. I can scuttle the guns."

"How?" I asked in disbelief.

"Simple. There are two intake ports below the waterline. That's where they bring in water for power and ammunition. If I drive a skimmer into an intake port, it'll jam up the works. No water, no guns. It'll be dead in the water and we can take her!"

"Did you tell Yenza about this?" asked Uncle Press.

"She wouldn't listen. She thinks I'm off my cake."

"Are you off your cake?" I asked.

Spader jumped off his skimmer and back onto the dock. He stood across from us and spoke with sincerity.

"Ever since you turned up here, I've had a feeling," he said. "First you, Press, then later when you came back with Pendragon. I feel like you two mates are here for more than just picking fruit. Am I right? Are the three of us in for a natty-do, or am I just shooting fish?"

It seemed Spader had some rumblings about his future as

a Traveler after all. He didn't know much, he could only sense it, but it was there just the same. His father probably taught him many things to prepare him for this moment, just as Uncle Press did for me. Whatever it is that makes one a Traveler, it was starting to kick in.

"Are you with me?" Spader asked.

"More than you know," answered Uncle Press. "What's your plan?"

Spader jumped back down onto his skimmer.

"Press, stay here. Get to Yenza. Tell her what we're doing. When the intake ports are jammed up, I'll send up a signal with this flare."

He held up a small pistol that was probably a flare gun.

"This flare won't go up until the *Pursuit* is crippled," he added. "Then Yenza can take a crew and board her before the raiders figure out what happened."

"What about me?" I asked.

"You're getting pretty good under the water, mate," he said.

"Whoa! You want me to go with you? Under that cruiser?"

"I told you, there are *two* intake ports. I can't hit 'em both at the same time."

I looked to Uncle Press, hoping he'd bail me out of this suicide mission. He didn't.

"Are you up to this, Bobby?" he asked.

No! I wasn't!

"It'll be easy, mate," said Spader. "They won't be looking underwater. All we have to do is sneak up from below, wrench off the intake covers and send in a couple of skimmers. Snappy-do!"

It did sound easy. I spent a lot of time underwater with Spader and I was pretty confident down there. Maybe I could do this after all.

"I don't suppose there's a plan B?" I asked Uncle Press.

"Not this time," he answered. "Unless you've got one."

I didn't. I was going underwater.

"Wait for the flare!" shouted Spader.

"Be careful!" Uncle Press shouted back as he ran back up the stairs toward the deck.

Yeah, careful. That was a joke, right?

Spader opened the cargo carrier that was behind his skimmer and pulled out two water sleds and two air globes. He threw one air globe to me and stowed the two water sleds in the floor compartment of his skimmer. He then unhooked the cargo carrier so he wouldn't have to drag it along.

"Are those water sleds big enough to do the job?" I asked.

"Nah, those are for our getaway," said Spader.

"Then what are we going to use to jam the intake ports?"

Spader jumped from his skimmer onto another that was right next to it. He threw a few toggle switches and the engines whined to life.

"You take my skimmer," he said.

This didn't make a whole lot of sense. If we were going to sneak up on the raiders' cruiser from underwater, then why were we each taking a skimmer? They may be fast, but Saint Dane and his crew would see us coming for sure.

Spader put his air globe over his head and it instantly conformed to him. I did the same. I jumped onto the skimmer and started to power it up. Finally I couldn't take it anymore and asked, "Won't they see us coming?"

Spader pointed to a black toggle switch that was under the steering column.

"They would—if we were on top of the water."

He flipped the black toggle and a rush of air bubbles blew out from under his skimmer. Then it started to sink. Spader looked at me and smiled. I found the same switch on my skimmer, and threw it. The same thing happened. Slowly my skimmer submerged. As it turned out, these babies didn't just fly over the water, they traveled underwater, too!

Just before his head went under, Spader asked, "How do you know Zy Roder?"

"Long story," I answered. "I'll tell you later."

"You'd better. Hobey-ho!"

With that, my head sank below and we were under way. Spader had given me skimmer lessons before, so I was familiar with how it operated. But this was way different. Rather than stand up, I held on to the steering handles and my body floated parallel to the deck.

"You okay?" asked Spader.

"I think," was my answer.

"Then let's hit it!"

He cranked his throttle, dipped the nose of his skimmer, and immediately shot down to the ocean floor. I did the same, and we were off. This was a lot like using the water sleds, except they were much more powerful. I was too heavy on the throttle at first and the skimmer nearly pulled out of my grasp. I followed behind Spader but made sure to stay out of his wake because when I got too close, the jets from his skimmer's pontoons hit me like turbulence. It took me a few minutes, but I eventually got the knack of controlling the vehicle and staying clear of Spader. Now all I had to do was worry about the killers we were sneaking up on.

Spader hugged the sandy bottom. That was smart. The deeper we were, the less chance there was of us being spotted. Remember, the water was very clear on Cloral. Visibility had to be at least a hundred feet. I really hoped that from the deck of the *Pursuit*, we just looked like big fish.

In no time I could look up and see the dark shape of the cruiser floating above us. Everything looks bigger underwater, but even accounting for that, this ship looked immense. It was like a giant black cloud that blocked out the sun. Spader set his skimmer down in the sand directly beneath the massive ship, right in its shadow.

"I'll go up first," he said while taking out a wrench-looking tool from his back pocket. I'll pull off the intake covers, then come back for you. Get the water sleds ready to go."

I nodded and gave the "okay" sign. I still wasn't used to talking underwater. Spader took off swimming up to the *Pursuit,* and I swam to his skimmer to get the water sleds. So far so good, but time was running out. I didn't have my watch (since I wasn't allowed to have a Second Earth watch on another territory), but I guessed that we were getting close to the end of the twenty-minute time limit.

I got both water sleds and rested them down in the sand between our skimmers. A few moments later, Spader joined me.

"It was snappy-do," he announced. "Covers came right off. All that's left is for us to drop off our gifts."

"Tell me exactly what to do," I said.

Spader pointed up at the hull. "Right near the stern you'll see a big round opening. I left the cover hanging from it so you wouldn't miss. There's two of 'em. I'll take the one on the far side of the keel. All you have to do is bring the skimmer right up to the mouth, hit the throttle, and let her go. Soon as it's on the way, meet me right back here. I'll set off the flare, and we'll have a leisurely water sled ride back to Grallion while Press and Yenza start the natty-do topside."

"Got it," I said. It didn't sound all that hard.

"Then let's be heroes," said Spader, and hit the throttle of his skimmer.

He didn't speed to the surface; he traveled with more caution. Now was not the time to get cocky and make a mistake. I powered up and ascended just as cautiously. I kept looking up at the dark hull as I grew closer, expecting some alarm to sound and to have the raiders start firing their water cannons down at us. As long as we stayed directly under, we stood a good chance of pulling this off.

It only took a few seconds for us to reach the ship. A steady hum came from its engines. I glanced to Spader. He pointed up at the hull. I looked, and sure enough, there it was. There was a round opening about six feet in diameter with a metal cover hanging below it. The intake port wasn't flush with the hull, it was perpendicular to it. The metal cover that hung from the opening had narrow slits to let water in and debris out. Now that the cover was off, anything could get stuck inside and we were riding two very big pieces of debris. I was beginning to think this would work.

Spader and I now had to separate. He gave me a thumbs up sign—a Second Earth gesture he picked up from me—and glided his skimmer across the keel to the far side of the ship and the other intake port.

Now came the most critical part of the operation. I carefully guided my skimmer up toward the open port. The opening wasn't much bigger than the width of the skimmer, pontoon to pontoon, so I had to make sure the whole vehicle got inside. I also didn't want to bang the skimmer against the hull because that might alert someone that predators were lurking below. I carefully used the throttle to maneuver the craft into position. I had to bring it right up under the hull, then move parallel with the hull into the intake port. It was tricky, but I soon had the entire skimmer resting inside the port. The hard part was over. I was almost there. All I had to do was hit the throttle.

But I never got the chance.

That's because the ship came to life. The engines that had been idling quietly suddenly roared. I guessed the twenty minutes were over. The raiders were getting ready to fire on Grallion. The noise grew deafening, but worse than that, I felt a rush of water and realized with horror that I was being sucked into the intake port! The *Pursuit* was drawing in water for power and ammunition—and I was well within sucking range! The force of the intake pulled me into the opening. In seconds I would be splatter. There was nothing to grab on to. I was going in.

That's when a strange thing happened that I still can't explain. Even as I think back to what happened, it doesn't make sense. It felt like someone seized me by the hand and pulled me out far enough to grab on to the edge of the intake port. I wrapped my fingers around the lip then struggled to bring my other hand forward and grab on as well. I looked up, expecting to see Spader there, but he wasn't there. Whoever had saved me was gone.

Did I say saved? I wasn't saved yet. I held on to the lip of the intake port with the tips of my fingers. My entire body was still inside the tube leading into the ship. The force of the water grew stronger. I didn't have the strength to pull myself forward. I tried to find something with my feet to push off of, but the inside of the tube was smooth. I wasn't going to last much longer.

That's when I realized that the force of the intake pump wasn't just pulling on me, it was pulling at my skimmer, too. There was still hope! If I could hold on long enough, the skimmer would be sucked into the engine and jam it up just as if I had sent it in myself. All I had to do was hang on. But I didn't know how long I would last. It was torture. The only thing keeping me from being hamburger were the tips of my fingers. I watched as the skimmer slowly moved past me, headed deeper into the ship. It was taking too long. I wasn't going to be able to hang on much longer. The force of the water grew stronger, and the skimmer moved faster. But that meant it was even tougher to hold on. I screamed. Why not? Nobody could hear me over the roar of the engines.

My fingers had gone numb. I was done. Like a fiendish hungry beast, the intake pump finally won the battle. I lost my grip. I flew in toward the engine, knowing I was seconds away from death. I could only hope that it wouldn't hurt too much.

But an instant later I heard a horrifying grinding sound, and the pull of water stopped. The skimmer had been sucked into the engine! Spader's plan worked. Yes! I instantly kicked my fins and swam out of that hole as fast as I possibly could. I blasted out into open water and shot down toward the bottom, kicking for all I was worth.

Spader was already there, waiting for me. I was totally out of breath and probably looked as terrified as I felt.

"What kept you?" asked Spader calmly.

I wanted to scream that I was nearly sucked into the engine, but figured it could wait until later.

"Did you do it?" I yelled.

"Of course," was Spader's confident answer.

"Then shoot the flare!" I ordered.

He pointed the gun topside and fired. A screaming bright arc of light blasted from the pistol and shot toward the surface leaving a bright trail of light behind it. I looked up to see that the missile broke the surface and continued on into the sky. We had done it. We had crippled Saint Dane and the *Pursuit* and opened the door for Yenza and the aquaneers to defend Grallion.

But we had done something else, too.

A few seconds later I saw four splashes next to the ship. Four divers had just hit the water, and they were coming after us. Yeah, you guessed it. The raiders saw our flare.

"Uh-oh," said Spader. "Hadn't thought of that."

"We can't get back to Grallion," I said. "They'll get us for sure."

"Then let's give 'em a chase," said Spader as he grabbed his water sled.

We both powered up and sped off along the ocean floor headed for . . . I didn't know where. We flew over the bottom, inches from the coral, looking for a place to hide. It was a good thing that Spader and I had played all those games underwater, because my skills at handling the water sled were pretty good. Without slowing down, I looked back and saw the four raiders were right after us. They had water sleds too. I wondered if one of them was Saint Dane.

As we flew along the ocean bottom something caught my eye off to our right. Something was swimming alongside us, shadowing us. I only caught a quick glimpse because whatever it was, it darted below the coral. But what I saw didn't make sense. It couldn't have been a person because it was moving too fast. It might have been a big fish, maybe even a quig, but quigs were gray and black. This thing was green, like the water. Weird.

"The kelp!" shouted Spader.

I forgot about my strange vision and looked ahead to see the beginnings of the tangle of red sea kelp that grew from the coral reef and stretched up to the surface. If we could get into that dense jungle, we might have a chance of losing the raiders.

"Stay close," commanded Spader. "Don't want to get separated in there."

We hit the dense kelp but didn't slow down. The slimy leaves whipped at us as we sped by. Imagine running full tilt through a wet field of corn. That's what it was like. For a moment I thought we were home free, but it didn't last long because a second later, we popped out of the far side. Bad news. The kelp forest wasn't anywhere big enough to hide us. We had to keep going.

And that's when it happened. It was just a slight movement. I wasn't even sure what it was at first, but a moment later it hit me. It was my ring. It was getting warm and the gray stone was starting to glow. That meant that we were getting near the gate. I looked up ahead and saw the shelf of rock where the quig had nearly gotten us. It was the rock formation that held the gate to the flume. I knew instantly that it was our best and only hope. Spader was going to have to learn about being a Traveler sometime. I couldn't think of a better way to do it and save our butts at the same time.

"Follow me!" I shouted to Spader and changed my direction toward the rock overhang. Spader didn't question. He followed. The thought of running into a quig flashed through my head, but right now it was the least of our worries. When we were just about to shoot under the rock ledge, Spader yelled, "Stop!"

I did. He glided up to me and said, "Don't want to get trapped under there, mate. They'll have us for sure."

I looked back toward the kelp forest in time to see the four raiders break out of the vegetation and spot us.

"Do you trust me?" I asked.

"Well sure, mate, but—"

"Then c'mon!"

I hit the throttle and shot under the rock ledge. I did a quick look back to see if Spader was following. He was. For a change I could take the lead and he believed in me enough to follow. Now all I had to do was deliver.

The rock ceiling looked different, but only because the last time I was here I was going the other way. But that wasn't a good excuse for being lost. I had to find the gate. The raiders had already gotten to the rock ledge and were still coming fast. All they had to do was follow our bubbles and they'd have us. I could only hope that I'd find the gate before I hit the dead end of rock.

I started to panic. I was lost. I didn't know where the gate was. This rock ledge was huge. We could swim around here for hours without finding it. What was I thinking? I had led us into a trap. I had to calm down and think. Where was it?

The answer hit me instantly. I had been in such a rush to get in here that I wasn't thinking straight. There was an easy way to find the gate. It was my ring. I swept my hand out in front of me and saw that the stone would dim or grow brighter, depending on the direction I pointed. I carefully judged when the ring was shining brightest and that told me our course. It was like following a compass. I took off in that direction and seconds later, I saw it. The round hole in the ceiling was only yards ahead. I aimed my water sled toward it and gunned the engine.

A quick thought went through my mind. Maybe I shouldn't be leading the raiders to the gate and the flume. But I reasoned that it didn't make a difference. If it was Saint Dane behind us, he already knew about the gate. If it wasn't Saint Dane, then it wouldn't matter if the raiders found it. The flume didn't work for non-Travelers. No, this was the right move for all sorts of reasons.

I broke the surface inside the cavern and looked around quickly. It was exactly the same as we had left it. A moment later, Spader broke the surface next to me and looked around in wonder.

"Hobey, mate! How did you know about this?"

I pulled off my air globe and tossed it onto the ledge. I threw my water sled there too. There was no time to explain things to Spader. The raiders would be here in a second. So I yanked off his air globe and threw it and his water sled to the side. The two of us floated in the middle of the pool, treading water.

"I hope there's another way out of here," he said.

I laughed at that. I actually laughed.

"Spader," I said. "You have no idea . . . but you soon will."

I glanced up at the opening to the flume. I counted on the fact that we didn't have to climb up the sheer rock face to get there. We didn't have time.

"I'll ask you again," I said. "Do you trust me?"

"Of course, mate, but you better come up with something quick or we're going to have our own natty-do right here and—"

"*Zadaa!*" I shouted.

The flume came to life. The familiar bright light shot from the opening. The jumble of musical notes grew closer. Spader looked up in awe.

"Hobey, Pendragon," he said softly. "Where did you say you were from again?"

The water around us started to swirl. The light from the flume grew bright and the two of us were pulled up, together, out of the waters of Cloral.

A second later, we were on our way to see Loor.

END OF JOURNAL #6

◉ SECOND EARTH ◉

"Why did he go to Zadaa?" huffed Courtney. "Why didn't he bring Spader here to Second Earth? This is his home!"

Mark knew the answer. Loor was a Traveler. She would be able to help Bobby explain things to Spader. Things were getting hairy on Cloral and Loor was the kind of person you went to when things got hairy. Mark felt that Courtney should have realized this, but her jealousy toward Loor was clouding her thinking. Not that he'd point that out to her. No way.

Courtney stood up angrily and shoved the pages back at Mark.

"Well, if Bobby Pendragon thinks his new friend can help him better than we can, then *good luck* is all I have to say!"

"C'mon, Courtney," said Mark softly. "You know he did the right thing."

Courtney looked as if she wanted to argue, but backed off. She knew.

"Yeah, well, whatever," she said with a pout.

Mark now faced a dilemma. He had to tell Courtney about Andy Mitchell. He made a dumb mistake by leaving the page in the boys' bathroom and because of it, Mitchell knew about the journals.

"I'm sorry, Mark," added Courtney. She had calmed down. "You're right. You've been right about everything from the beginning. It's good that one of us thinks straight. At least now we know why these pages are different than the last ones. He wrote this journal on Zadaa, not Cloral, right?"

Mark wanted to scream. Courtney Chetwynde relied on him to be the brains of this duo and right now he was feeling like anything but. She trusted him and listened to his advice, which is more than anybody else ever did, except for Bobby sometimes. It killed him to have to admit he had screwed up royally.

"You okay?" asked Courtney, sensing that something was wrong.

"Yeah, sure, I'm f-fine," answered Mark quickly. "Just worried about Bobby is all."

"You'd better get those pages back to your house before anything else happens."

Mark looked at Courtney, saw the trust in her amazing gray eyes and made a decision. He couldn't tell her about Andy Mitchell. At least not yet. He wanted to work this out on his own rather than risk losing Courtney's faith. This was his problem and he was going to have to deal with it.

So he gathered the pages of Journal #6 together, put them in his pack, and left for home. Normally, once they finished reading a journal, Mark would stash it in the safest place he knew— an ancient rolltop desk in his attic. His parents hadn't gone up there in years and Mark had the only key. He wore it on a chain around his neck just to be safe. Every precaution had been taken. As soon as a journal was finished, it went into the desk.

Tonight was a little different though. Mark crept up to the attic and unlocked the desk drawer. He placed Journal #6 inside next to the brown rolls of parchment that were Bobby's journals from Denduron. But rather than lock them up, he took out Journal #5—the journal Andy Mitchell had seen the first page of. This was the journal he would show Mitchell. He hoped that maybe this would be enough. Maybe Mitchell would think it was all a crazy joke and get bored after reading these pages. It was the best Mark could hope for.

He spent a sleepless night, wondering how he was going to get out of this predicament. Sharing the journals with Courtney made sense. Courtney was Bobby's friend. Courtney could be trusted. But Andy Mitchell was different. He was an idiot. Worse, he was a bully-idiot. There was no telling what Mitchell would do with the information about Bobby once he got it. But as hard as he tried to figure a way out, he just couldn't find it. He had no choice but to show Mitchell the pages tomorrow.

At school the next day Mark did his best to avoid Mitchell. He held out the desperate hope that Mitchell had forgotten all about the journal page he'd found in the boys' bathroom. Mark got through the entire day without even seeing his nemesis. His hopes started to rise. He told himself that Mitchell didn't care enough to even show up for school! Maybe this would all blow over.

Wrong. No sooner had Mark stepped out of his last class than he felt a hand clamp down on his shoulder.

"Time for a little homework, aye, Dimond?" chuckled Andy Mitchell.

Mark's heart sank. The guy hadn't forgotten at all. It was time to deal with the devil. Mark shrugged Mitchell's hand off his shoulder and said, "Let's go."

Mitchell snorted and chuckled. He made Mark's skin crawl, but there was no way out of this. So Mark led him up to the boys' bathroom on the third floor. No one would bother them there, especially not Courtney. After her run-in with Mr. Dorrico, they decided not to read the journals there anymore. This was the best place Mark could think of to get some privacy, and to avoid Courtney. He felt guilty as hell about it, but there was no other way.

When they got inside Mitchell stood with his hand out. Mark stared at him. Mitchell snorted back a good one and hawked a lougie into a urinal. Mark nearly retched. He had a fleeting thought of barging past Mitchell and running away, but that would have been useless. No, this was the only way. So reluctantly he reached into his pack and pulled out the roll of green, slick paper that was Journal #5.

Mitchell reached out to grab it, but Mark pulled it away.

"You gotta read it here and you gotta give it right back when you're done," Mark said. Mitchell wasn't used to being ordered around like this, especially not from a geek like Mark Dimond. But Mark was intense. He was not fooling around. Mitchell snorted and chuckled, again.

"Whatever," he said, and swiped the pages away from Mark. He walked over to one of the stalls saying, "I'll read it in here."

"You will read it right here, where I can see you!" commanded Mark.

Whoa. If Mitchell wasn't sure about how important those pages were to Mark, he sure was now. Mark was not going to allow Andy Mitchell to control this situation any more than he had to. He already had too much control as it was. If Mitchell didn't do exactly as he said, Mark was ready to grab the pages away and take his chances with the police.

Mitchell chose to back off and gave another signature snort.

"All right, be cool," he said with a shrug. "I'll read 'em wherever you want."

Mitchell then walked to the far wall, turned his back to it, and slid down to the floor. With one last snort, he began to read the journal.

Mark didn't move. He stood by the sinks, staring at Mitchell. This was killing him. With each passing second he felt as if he were betraying Bobby a little bit more.

Mitchell took forever to read the journal. He wasn't exactly a rocket scientist and he constantly had to ask Mark the meanings of words. Mark would roll his eyes and explain to him what words like "submerge" and "erosion" meant. Worse, when Mitchell got to words that were specific to Cloral like vators or pecks, his total cluelessness made Mark want to scream. Mark felt bad for any teacher who was saddled with the likes of Andy Mitchell. He wondered who had the patience to teach him how to tie his shoelaces.

Finally, mercifully, Mitchell finished the journal and looked up to Mark. This was the critical moment. Mitchell's first reaction was going to tell Mark how much trouble he was going to cause from here on in. Mitchell stared at Mark for a moment, as if trying to pull his thoughts together. Mark figured that pulling those slim thoughts together couldn't take more than a nanosecond. It didn't. Mitchell snorted and laughed again.

"Who are you kidding?" he said with a sneer. "You made this up!"

Mark didn't react. He just stared at Mitchell. The truth was, he didn't care if Mitchell believed the journals were real or not. But Mark realized instantly that not reacting was the exact wrong move. He saw it in Mitchell's eyes. Mark realized that if he had argued with Mitchell and said something like "I didn't make it up! It's all true! I swear!" then Mitchell would have figured he was just some loser geek with a wild imagination and that would have been the end of it. But he didn't. By not arguing, he had done the exact opposite. His silence convinced Mitchell that everything in the journal *was* true. Mark wished he had a second chance to react, but it was too late.

Mitchell began to stand up. Before he got his balance, Mark swiped the journal pages out of his hand.

"Easy!" complained Mitchell.

"Are we done now?" asked Mark as he rolled up the journal.

"Done?" laughed Mitchell. "We're just starting! I want to read the other journals. The ones from that Denduroni place."

"Denduron. I can't let you—"

"And I want to read the journal that showed up here yester-day. I'm not stupid, Dimond. I saw it. It was brown, not green like this one. You already got another delivery from Pendragon and I want to see it."

"N-No way! I agreed to let you read the rest of—"

Mitchell lunged at Mark, grabbed him by the shirt, spun him around, and slammed him against the hard tile wall of the bath-room. He knocked the air out of his lungs and Mark nearly passed out. Mitchell wouldn't let him go though. He stuck his nose right in Mark's face and hissed, "Stop tellin' me what to do, you little freak. You wanna mess with me? I'll hit you so hard you'll be eatin' and fartin' out of the same hole."

Mark didn't believe that was possible, but he didn't want to risk it.

"Now listen to me. Do not tell Courtney Chetwynde I know about this. If you do, I'll go right to the police and fry both of your butts. Understand?"

"But—"

Mitchell slammed Mark against the wall again. This time Mark hit his head on the tiles.

"*Understand?*"

"Yeah, I understand."

"And I want to see the rest of them journals. We are sitting on a very big thing here. Someday we are gonna be famous, thanks to that weez Pendragon."

Mark was horrified. Mitchell, the village idiot, was already planning on how to release the journals to the world. This could not get worse.

"I want to see another one of them journals," he commanded, then threw Mark out of the way, and strode toward the bathroom door.

With one final snort, he then kicked the door open and left.

Mark sunk down to the floor, hurting in more ways than one. He had messed up worse than he could imagine. Mitchell now had complete control over him. Worse, if he told Courtney about it then Mitchell would make sure that the police knew everything. There was no one he could go to for help. He wanted to handle this on his own, but he was doing a truly bad job. He had let Bobby down, he had let Courtney down, and he had let himself down.

And then, just to add to his confusion, the ring on his finger started to twitch. In the past this had always been a moment of excitement because it meant he was going to hear from his best friend again. But now the idea of another journal arriving meant that it was going to be one more journal he would have to share with Andy Mitchell. One more journal that he would have to explain to the dimwit. One more journal that marked his total failure as a friend.

Mark took off the ring and put it on the floor. He then rolled over and turned his back to it. He knew what was going to happen. He didn't have to see. He closed his eyes and softly whispered, "I'm sorry, Bobby. I'm going to fix everything, I swear."

When he turned back around, the ring was lying right here he had left it. Next to it was another journal.

ZADAA

I have seen things that I never thought possible and most of it isn't good.

Since I wrote you last, things here have been pushed to the hairy edge of catastrophe and I feel as if it's up to me to bring it back. The worst part is I don't know how. Not a clue. I'm frustrated, freaked out, and most of all . . . scared. Definitely scared. Not only for me, but for the whole territory of Cloral. Whoever had the bright idea of making me a Traveler should be re-thinking that decision right about now. Did I mention how scared I was?

I'm writing this journal from a place that is both wondrous and frightening. As I think back on the events that led me here, I can't help but wonder where it's going to end. Every time I think I've got a handle on things, something new happens that turns me upside down. I thought I couldn't be surprised anymore, but I am. I guess that's why they call it surprise.

Once again we are on the verge of a battle. I don't want to sound overly dramatic or anything, but if things go south, this may be the last journal I write. I'm not trying to freak you out but, well, okay maybe I'm trying to freak you out a little. Why not? The whole point of writing this is for you to know what I'm going through, right?

I'm getting way ahead of myself. There's a lot to write about and I don't have a ton of time. I finished the last journal where Spader and I had hit the flume for Zadaa. There wasn't anything unusual about the trip, except for the fact I wasn't alone this time. Spader and I flew side by side. This was Spader's first flume ride and I wasn't sure how he would react. He was pretty tense at first, as you can imagine, but once I assured him everything was fine and that he could enjoy the ride, he simply looked forward and folded his arms. We flew along like that for a few minutes and I could tell he was starting to relax. He had been through a lot hairier situations than this under the sea. Maybe not as bizarre as this, but definitely not as hairy.

"What is this, Pendragon?" he finally asked. I could tell he was working really hard to stay calm.

"It's called a flume," I answered. "It's taking us to meet a friend of mine."

"And where is that?" he asked. "Your home habitat?"

"No, it's a place called Zadaa. She'll help me explain to you what's going on."

He nodded as if to say, "Okay. I'll wait until we get there to ask the eight hundred million other questions I have." He did ask one more question though.

"Pendragon, are we safe?"

Wow. How could I answer that one? I felt totally unsafe every second of every day. But I couldn't tell him that. I decided to play dumb to the more cosmic issue and only deal with the here and now.

"Yeah," I answered. "The flume is safe. I promise."

Moments later we arrived. The flume deposited us into an

underground cavern. Big surprise, right? Spader looked back into the flume that had now gone dark, his eyes wide with wonder.

"Don't worry," I said. "It works both ways. We can take it right back to Cloral."

"You mean we're not on Cloral anymore?" he asked in shock.

Oh man, this guy had a lot to learn and I didn't know where to start explaining.

"Let's find my friend," I said. "Then we'll try to answer your questions."

Try was the right word. There was only so much I was going to be able to explain to Spader. Once he started asking the big questions as to what all of this meant, I'd be just as lost as he was. I needed to find Loor as soon as possible.

I looked around the cavern and saw a pile of clothes. A quick exam showed me they were lightweight white robes, like those long togas they wore in movies about ancient Rome.

"We gotta wear these," I said. "It's what people wear around here."

Spader didn't question. We took off most of our Cloral clothes, but left on our shorts. Technically that was against the rules, but I wasn't going commando here. No way. There were also leather sandals and we each put on a pair. As we dressed, I hoped that Spader wouldn't ask me how these clothes got here because I wouldn't have a good answer. I supposed they came from the mysterious acolytes that Uncle Press had told me about, but that's all I could say. Luckily Spader didn't ask.

As I placed our Cloral clothes on the ground, I saw something that made me smile. There was another pile of clothing there. It was a pair of denim overalls and a pink shirt and a pair of Dr. Marten's boots—the clothes Loor wore when she came to Second Earth. Seeing these gave me confidence. Loor was definitely here. Of course the trick now was to find her. Up until now Uncle Press had been my tour guide. Now I was on my own. Gulp. I glanced around the cavern but saw no way out. We were surrounded by walls made of brown, sandy stone. A complete 360 showed no entrance, no door, no passageway, no nothing. But that was impossible. There had to be a way out. Then, just before I began to hyperventilate in panic, I saw it. There were footholds and handholds chiseled into the rock that led up toward the ceiling. I walked to the wall and looked up to see. Sure enough, the cutouts led up into a dark crevice. This was the way out.

I wanted to shout "Woo hoo!" but decided I should be cool. Like it or not, I was in charge and I wanted to show Spader I had total confidence, even though I didn't. So without a word, I began to climb. The cutouts led up into the dark crevice. In seconds, I was totally surrounded by rock. I knew this had to be the way out, so I didn't panic. After climbing for another few seconds, I hit a dead end—with my head. Ouch. That hurt. My first thought was that we were trapped, but then I realized my head didn't hurt as much as it should if I had just bashed it into hard rock. I carefully reached up and found that I was right. The ceiling wasn't rock, it was wood. A quick push up revealed that it was a trapdoor. We were out!

I scrambled up and out, followed right behind by Spader. Once he was out, I threw the trapdoor shut and saw that carved on the top of it was the star that showed this was a gate.

So far, so familiar.

We found ourselves in what looked to be a storage room. The walls were made of the same sandy stone as below, but there were large wooden storage bins that were filled with what looked like metal machine parts. The floor was covered with sand, which made me realize the trapdoor was normally buried. So I quickly covered it over with a few inches of sand.

Spader watched me but didn't say anything. I'm sure he was trying to process all this new information. His questions would come later.

"Okay," I said. "Let's find Loor."

A wooden door led out of this storage room and as soon as I reached to open it, it hit me that I had no clue what to expect on Zadaa. All I knew was that Loor was a warrior. Obviously that meant that Zadaa wasn't exactly a futuristic society. I could only hope that it wasn't like the Wild West and that we wouldn't have to fight for our lives every step of the way. That would suck.

As soon as we opened the door we heard a loud, steady sound. It was a constant, unwavering roar.

"It's water," Spader said.

That's exactly what it sounded like. Rushing water. But the sound was huge, so if it were rushing water, then there was a lot of it. We left the storage room and made our way through a labyrinth of tunnels cut into the rock. It reminded me of the mines of Denduron, but these passageways were more like corridors than wide mine shafts. Every few feet was another wooden door. We didn't bother to look inside any of them. This wasn't about exploration, this was about getting out and finding Loor.

The farther along the rocky corridor we walked, the louder the roaring water became. Finally we reached the mouth of the tunnel and stepped out into an awesome scene. We found ourselves on the bank of an underground river. It was about twenty yards across and moving fast. The cavern we were in was huge, with a high ceiling. To our left, about fifty yards downstream, the river split into three smaller rivers. Each new river disappeared into its own separate tunnel.

Upriver to our right was a waterfall. The water shot into the fast-moving river from a tunnel in the rock face about four stories above us. Mental note to self: Do *not* fall into this river. Swimming would be impossible because the water was moving so fast. There was no telling where the split rivers led.

"What are you doing here?" came a stern voice.

We both spun around to see a man wearing a similar white robe to the ones we wore. He was a small guy who wore a round gray hat that looked like a baseball cap without the brim. It looked hard, like it was for protection. In his arms were a bunch of rolled-up papers that could have been plans. He had come from the same tunnel we had, which meant he must have been behind one of the doors we passed. He was light skinned, which surprised me because both Loor and her mother, Osa, were very dark.

"I've never seen you two here," he said suspiciously. "What do you want?"

He seemed to be in a hurry and was all sorts of agitated as if our surprise appearance had thrown off his schedule. This was going to be tricky. I had no idea what kind of explanation to give the guy except to tell him the truth—sort of.

"We, uh, we're looking for a friend," I said. "Her name is Loor."

The guy's eyes widened further. Uh-oh. I must have said the wrong thing.

"Loor?" he said in surprise. "That is a Batu name. Why would you be looking for a Batu down here?"

Good question. Too bad I didn't have a good answer. Forget the truth. It was time to start lying.

"She, uh, she told me she might be coming down here," I said.

"Ridiculous!" the guy snapped. "No Batu would miss that barbaric tournament of theirs. If she told you she was coming here, she was lying. But they are all liars, no?"

With that the man hurried off, clutching his rolls of paper. Spader touched me on the shoulder and I saw that he had a look of total confusion on his face. Welcome to the club.

"What did he say?" he asked.

"You heard him," I answered. "Loor isn't down here."

"But how did you understand him? He was talking all gibberish."

At first I didn't know what Spader meant, but then it hit me: He was new to the Traveler game. He hadn't gotten to the point where he could understand all languages, yet.

"Long story," I said, and ran after the man with the scrolls. Spader followed dutifully. I caught up to the guy and walked alongside him.

"I'm embarrassed to say this, but my friend and I are lost. You know, all these tunnels and whatnot. Could you show us the way to the surface?"

The man stared at me suspiciously. This was a critical moment. If he started questioning me on who we were, we'd be sunk.

"You work in the manufacturing sector, don't you?" he asked.

"Uhhh, yes! Manufacturing. That's where we work."

"Let me give you a piece of advice," he said. "Do not make friends with a Batu. They cannot be trusted."

"Yes, good advice," I shot back. I figured I'd better agree with whatever this guy said if we wanted to get his help. "When I see Loor I'm going to just . . . call off our friendship.

No more lies! But I have to find her first, so how do we get out of here?"

"Follow me," he said, and walked off quickly.

Yes! We were on our way out. He led us along the riverbank and right up to the waterfall. As we got closer I saw that it was possible to walk behind the falling water. We climbed a few stone steps and passed right behind the wall of water. Very cool. We then saw that cut into the stone wall behind the falling water, was a tunnel. The man led us inside and after a few steps we came upon a room that had the coolest, strangest gizmo I think I had ever seen.

The best thing I can liken it to is one of those big pipe organs you see in church, but it was ten times the size. One whole wall was covered with pipes of every different size, ranging from about an inch in diameter to as wide as about ten inches. They ran from the ground, all the way up to the stone ceiling.

The guy put his rolls of paper down and stepped up onto a stone platform that faced a vast array of levers, switches, valves, and knobs. There must have been a couple hundred of these controls. I had no clue how he could tell one from another because none seemed to be marked. He walked back and forth on the platform, expertly flipping switches, tightening valves and loosening others. At one point he picked up one of the scrolls, unrolled it to check something, then tossed it down again and went right for a few more valves and opened them up. Whatever he was doing, it seemed very important. At least to him anyway.

Spader gave me a questioning look. I could only shrug. I had no idea what the guy was doing. I didn't want to ask him either or it would give away the fact that we didn't belong here.

"Uhhh," I interrupted. "Excuse me but, you were going to show us the way out?"

The guy kept working on his levers, but looked back over his shoulder at us. I could tell we were bothering him, but too bad.

"That way," he said, nodding toward an opening cut into the rock on the far side of the room. "Keep making rights, and remember what I said. Do not trust the Batu. Stay with the Rokador."

Ohhh-kay, whatever *that* meant. I didn't ask. "Thank you!" I said, and motioned for Spader to follow me. The man went right back to his work and we got the heck out of there.

We walked quickly through the doorway and, as instructed, kept making rights until we found a spiraling ramp that led up. We climbed and every so often we'd reach a new level and saw corridors that led off to places unknown. But, we didn't need to explore any more of this underground world. We needed to climb out.

After climbing for several minutes we finally leveled off and found ourselves in a room that was full of light. The walls were made of brown stone, but they were smooth, not like the rock below. It was clear that we were on the surface and the room we were in was man-made, not man-dug. A quick look around showed a doorway that led to the light. It was time to take our first look at Zadaa. I had no idea what to expect, but I was getting anxious to see the territory where Loor came from. I led Spader across the room, stepped out into the warm sun, and stopped short because the sight in front of us was absolutely breathtaking.

It was a sprawling city made entirely out of sand-colored stone. Imagine ancient Egypt before wind and time destroyed it and you'd have Zadaa. We stood on a rise that gave us a pretty great overview. There were soaring temples with sculpted figures that towered over the streets below. There were pyramids and tiered buildings with lush hanging plants draped over balconies. In the distance, beyond the boundaries of the city, there was nothing but desert. But the city within was alive with vegetation. It was like a vast oasis in a sea of sand. Running parallel to many of the streets were stone troughs that carried fresh water throughout the city. There were also ornate fountains everywhere. After having seen the river below, I knew what the source was. I wondered if the system of valves and switches that the guy down below was so busily working on had something to do with controlling the water flow.

This was a beautiful city, and I could easily imagine Loor walking the streets. Yes, this was Loor's home. It made absolute sense to me.

"Where is the ocean?" asked Spader.

His voice was shaky. After all of the bizarro experiences I had put him through, the sight of this city was the first thing that really rattled him.

"Where is the ocean?" he asked again, more nervously.

It suddenly made sense to me. Cloral was a hundred percent water. There was no dry land. Seeing a place that was just the opposite must have been pretty freaky.

"It's okay," I said, trying to calm him. "There is no ocean here. At least not one that I can see. These people live on dry land."

"That's impossible! How can you live on dry land? There isn't enough water for power or food!"

Okay, how weird was that? But I guess if you live in a place where everything comes from the ocean, having no ocean would be pretty scary.

"It's cool, I swear," I said. "It's just a different way of living. You'll see."

Spader didn't look so sure, but I wasn't worried about him. He'd get it soon enough. It was then that I realized something strange. I glanced back out on the city and realized that there was something very important missing. There were no people! This was a huge city, yet the streets were empty.

"Let's take a look around," I said, and started to walk. Spader didn't follow me this time. He was rooted to his spot. I had to go back to him and say, "C'mon! We have to find Loor."

Reluctantly he followed. We walked along one of the streets that was paved with stone. Towering statues loomed over us as we made our way through this strange and wonderful place.

"I'm having trouble walking," Spader said.

I didn't get what he meant until I saw that he looked kind of unsteady. He seemed almost dizzy and had trouble keeping his balance. I realized that he was going through the reverse process of getting used to being on a boat. My father called it "getting your sea legs." Spader had lived his entire life floating. This was the first time he was walking on solid ground and it was a strange sensation. Spader was trying to get his "land legs."

I tried not to laugh and said, "You'll get used to it pretty quick. But if you're going to barf, let me know." I didn't know how far this landsickness might go.

We continued on a little more slowly and started to see some people, but not as many as you'd think. The people up here on the surface had much darker skin than the guy we saw below. These people looked more like Loor and Osa. Their skin was dark, and they wore multicolored robes that were pretty spectacular.

"I wonder where everybody is?" I said. "Maybe it's some kind of holiday and—" That's when it hit me. The guy in the cavern below had said that the Batu would all be at the tournament! Maybe that was why the streets were deserted. Maybe everybody was at this tournament.

The very next person we saw, I stopped and asked, "Excuse me, which way to the tournament?"

It was a woman. She was tall and stern looking. She stared at me as if not sure why I would be asking such a simple question.

"Not many Rokador are interested in the tournament," she said coldly. "They do not have the stomach."

Rokador. That's what the guy down below had said. Maybe the guys who lived below were called Rokador and the people on the surface were Batu. We must look like Rokador. I wasn't sure if it was because of our white gowns, or the fact that we were pretty pale compared to the people on the surface.

"I think we can handle it," I said.

The woman chuckled, but I'm not sure if she was laughing with us or at us. She directed us to stay on this street and it would take us right to the tournament. Excellent. We were happening. Spader and I picked up the pace. I felt certain this would bring us to Loor.

As we continued walking Spader got stronger. He was adapting pretty quickly, so I figured it was a good time to start getting him up to speed on things. I began by telling him about the territories and about how they were all connected by flumes. I explained how Uncle Press and I came from a territory called Second Earth and that we were both Travelers who journeyed to the territories to help out in times of trouble. I explained how Loor was a Traveler as well, which is why I wanted her help. I didn't go into much more detail. It was better for him to get his mind around things a little at a time. For the first time I understood how Uncle Press felt when he explained things to me and I had so many questions. It really was easier to learn things as you went along.

Besides, the cheering up ahead told me that we had arrived at the tournament. Spader and I came to a building that looked like a coliseum. It wasn't as big though. I guess it was closer to a high school stadium than a pro ballpark. It didn't look as if we needed tickets either, because we walked right in.

The place was indeed a small stadium. As it turned out, my theory about why the streets were empty was correct. There were a couple of thousand people filling the stands. A quick look around told me that most of the spectators were Batu. They were dark skinned and wearing those colorful robes. But there were also a number of Rokador scattered throughout the crowd. They really stood out with their white robes and lighter skin.

There was a dirt playing field, and for an instant my thoughts went back to the Bedoowan stadium on Denduron and the gruesome quig battles where innocent miners were fed to beasts. I really hoped that they weren't doing anything nasty like that here.

Spader and I walked up to the railing and looked onto the field in time to see two teams marching in from opposite sides of the arena. They were all Batu—not a Rokador among them. They looked like warriors. Each and every one of these players was lean and buff. They weren't just men, either. It was half and half, men and women. They all wore these short leather tunics that showed a lot of skin, which is how I could tell they were all cut like athletes. They also wore lightweight protection on sensitive areas like elbows, knees, and the ever important groin. There were ten warriors to a side, and they marched in single file, carrying leather helmets under one arm while holding thin wooden clubs in the other.

"What's the do here?" asked Spader.

"I'm guessing there's going to be some kind of contest," I answered. "My friend Loor is—" That's when I saw her. The last warrior to march in was Loor. Though she was younger than the rest, she looked every bit as formidable.

"That's her," I said to Spader while pointing to Loor.

"That's your friend?" Spader asked with a mixture of surprise and awe. "She's . . . she's . . . amazing."

Spader stood staring at Loor, unable to take his eyes off her. I finally had to give him a shove to bring him back to reality.

"Don't even think about it," I said. "She's not your type."

"What type is she?" Spader asked.

"The type who has no interest in anything but kicking ass. If you think I'm kidding, watch."

The warrior teams stood on opposite sides of the arena and began the final act of suiting up. Here was the odd part. Each of them had these things that looked like wooden stakes that stuck out to the sides from their elbows and their knees. The stakes were about six inches long. One team had red stakes, the other had green. When they put their helmets on I saw that they also had a wooden stake that stuck straight up like those World War I German helmets. In all, each warrior had five wooden stakes sticking out of them. I had no clue what those things were for but I have to tell you, they looked pretty goofy.

Each team stood in a line, shoulder to shoulder, facing their opponents across the arena. A Batu guy wearing a bright yellow robe walked to the center, where he planted a stick in the ground. On the end of the stick he hung what looked like a necklace made of large, golden teeth. He then silently walked back and entered the grandstand. From the safety of the stands, he turned back to the playing field, raised a golden horn to his lips, and let out one short note.

Instantly everyone in the stands fell silent and focused their attention on the warriors below. I had a moment of fear for Loor. I had no idea how dangerous this was going to be. I knew she could handle herself, but what was the point of this game? I knew nothing of Zadaa and their customs and feared this would be one of those "fight to the death" type spectacles. There was nothing I could do but watch and hope she'd be okay.

The Batu in the yellow robe then gave one long, sustained blast from the horn. All the warriors raised their wooden clubs toward him in salute. Then Yellow Robe stopped blowing his horn, and the battle began. Instantly both teams of warriors let out war whoops and charged toward each other. Loor was right there with them. I wanted to close my eyes, but that would be disrespectful. Whatever was going to happen, I needed to see it.

The opposing teams clashed, swinging their clubs. I quickly saw the purpose of the wooden stakes that protruded from their bodies. They were the targets. This wasn't about knocking each other's heads off, it was about trying to knock their opponents' wooden stakes off. It was all about speed, and balance and blocking shots and returning shots that were well aimed. Of course, as good as they were, many shots missed their mark and there were a lot of painful body shots and whacks to the head. But this was not a blood feud. This was sport. I'm sure the shots stung and there would be dozens of black and blue marks the next day, but nobody was going to die here. Once I realized this I relaxed and tried to enjoy the spectacle.

Loor was on the red team. The green team was bigger and brawnier, but the red team seemed faster and more agile. I wasn't sure which was more important in a battle like this, speed or power.

It looked like it was going to be power. One red-team warrior had all five of his stakes knocked off in about five seconds. He dropped his club and ran off the field. Now I was starting to get the rules. You could keep fighting until all five of your stakes got knocked off. Then you were out.

Loor was brilliant. She kept to the perimeter of the fighting and took on all comers. She was being more defensive than aggressive, which really wasn't her style. But it seemed to be working because most warriors had at least one stake knocked off and she still had all five. She jumped and spun and knocked away attack after attack like some kind of fevered Jackie Chan clone.

"She's the smartest one out there," said Spader. "And quite beautiful, too."

I was beginning to think that Spader was really happy about coming to meet Loor.

Then one of the green warriors dove for the golden necklace and began to run off with it. Instantly three red warriors attacked him. The guy didn't have a chance. His stakes were knocked off immediately and he dropped the necklace. Now I understood the end game. This wasn't just about being the last one standing. My guess was that if someone grabbed the necklace and made it back to his area, then his team would win. It was like capture the flag. A really scary, painful version of capture the flag.

I then began to see that this wasn't just a wild clash. There actually was some strategy going on. Loor's red team took more of the defensive role and assigned a few warriors to guard the necklace. The green team, on the other hand, was all about attacking. It was every man for himself, and so far their strategy was winning. The red team had lost three warriors and several others had only three stakes or fewer. The green team had lost only one warrior and were pressing the attack. It looked as if the way to win this game was to attack with reckless abandon and overpower your adversary.

But that's when things changed. The remaining red team warriors had gradually worked themselves into a ring around the golden necklace. The green team was too busy slashing and hitting to realize they were being outmaneuvered. Also, the green team had been attacking so hard that they were beginning to get tired. Their swings weren't as forceful as they had been moments before. I guessed it took more energy to attack than to defend, and the red team still looked fresh.

The red now had formed a tight circle around the necklace and were able to fend off the attacking green warriors with much less effort. Every red-team member was in the circle except for Loor. She was still on the perimeter, playing it safe. Then one of the red-team warriors let out a loud yelp. It must have been a signal, because that's when Loor made her move.

She dodged around the green warrior she had been battling and sprinted for the circle. At the same time the red team broke open the circle just long enough for her to run inside. Loor scooped up the necklace and then the entire red team formed a wedge to protect her as they dashed toward their side of the arena. It was like a kickoff return right up the middle where the blockers formed the perfect wedge. They bowled over the green team, who were now so exhausted they could barely lift their clubs. In seconds the red juggernaut, with Loor in the center, rolled into their area, the winners.

Loor held up the necklace in victory.

I went nuts. I screamed, I shouted, I jumped up and down and cheered like my team had just won the Super Bowl with a touchdown in OT. It was awesome. Loor was awesome. Agility and skill had triumphed over brawn and might. It was a victory for the little guy and I was loving every minute of it.

Unfortunately nobody else in the stadium was as excited as I was. Here I was jumping up and down like some crazed fan from the Cleveland Browns Dog Pound, and everyone else just sat there, watching me, wondering who this idiot was who had lost control. Every eye in the stadium was on me, including the warriors down on the field. I felt like a total imbecile.

"Is this a custom where you come from?" asked Spader, who was just as surprised at my enthusiasm as everyone else in the stadium.

In fact it was, but that didn't make this nightmare any easier. I stopped yelling, looked down on to the field and made eye contact with Loor. She too was looking up to see where all the screaming was coming from. She saw me, but at first it didn't click for her. She was exhausted and still flush from the battle and the victory. Seeing me didn't compute. It made me feel even worse. She didn't even know who I was. I felt horrible. Then, a moment later, I saw it in her eyes. She finally recognized me; that's when something happened that I never would have expected. It was so shocking that I no longer cared about being embarrassed. It just didn't matter anymore, because as she stood there breathing hard, Loor looked up at me and smiled.

ZADAA

"It was a training exercise," Loor explained. "All warriors must take part. It is good experience to teach fighting as one, and as a team." For all of the mayhem she just went through, Loor came out fairly intact. Nothing broken, only a few bruises.

"Seemed more like football with weapons to me," I countered.

Both Loor and Spader gave me blank stares. They had no idea what I meant. That was okay. It didn't matter.

The three of us walked along the streets of the desert city, which Loor told us was called Xhaxhu (pronounced Zha-ZHOO). It was the capital city of Zadaa.

Spader walked behind us with his head down, listening to everything we said. Unlike the other people of Zadaa, he was able to understand her because she was a Traveler. Understanding everyone else would come in time, just as it did for me. I wished that Loor could have seen him the way he was when I first got to Cloral. She would have loved that guy. But as I wrote before, Spader had changed. Okay, he was pretty freaked out about our trip to Zadaa; can't blame him for that. The death of his father had turned him inside out. I could only hope that at some point he would deal with his anger and become his old self again.

"Why did you come to Zadaa, Pendragon?" asked Loor.

"Two reasons," I said. "Uncle Press and I think we know what Saint Dane is up to on Cloral and we could use your help, big time. The other reason is . . ."

I looked back at Spader, debating about how much I should blurt out in front of him. I decided it was time to jump in with both feet.

"The other reason is that Spader's father was the Traveler from Cloral. He's dead. Now Spader is the Traveler. The problem is, he has no clue . . . about anything. I've got to get him up to speed and I need your help to do it."

I looked back to Spader. He had stopped walking and was now staring right at me with confusion and what I thought might be a little bit of fear. I had just hit him with a boatload of information that didn't compute. Nothing I had just said made any sense to him. That was pretty obvious. Loor turned to him and said, "Tell me what you will remember most about your father."

Spader shot her a look. The question surprised him, but he wanted to answer. He looked down, remembering. He then looked back to Loor and said, "He was a great man, a great teacher, and I loved him." I think he was holding back a ton of emotion.

Loor touched him on the shoulder and said, "Then you will make a great Traveler. Come with me."

She turned and continued walking. Spader looked to me and I saw that the confusion was still there, but the fear was gone. I knew at that moment that coming to see Loor was the best move I could have made.

Loor took us to her home. The large building was made of

the same brown sandstone that all the structures were made of here on Zadaa. It was all on one level, with wooden floors and a thatched roof. The place was big, too. There were many rooms where others lived, like some big, sandy apartment building. Judging from the other muscle-types who were hanging out, I figured this must have been some kind of warrior dormitory. Loor's space had two rooms—one main room where the cooking was done and another that was a bedroom. The furniture was woven, like wicker. There were a few low chairs and a bed that were plain and simple. A community bathroom outside the apartment had a trough of running water for drinking and washing. Another trough of water that was the sewer ran underground. The place was crude, but efficient.

The three of us sat in the main room and Loor actually cooked for us. She baked three loaves of very tasty bread and we had crunchy fresh vegetables to go with it. She also gave us a sweet drink that was made from the sap of a tree. It reminded me of coconut. Uncle Press would have loved this. I wondered what he was doing just then, and if he was safe from the raiders on Cloral. But there was nothing I could do about that now, so I tried not to worry.

As we ate, Loor told us about her life as a warrior in training. She was part of the military here on Zadaa. The apartment she lived in was given to her by the military and she could live there for as long as she served. Because she was so young, she was pretty much a low-level soldier. But she hoped to someday become a leader. I had no doubt she would.

When we finished eating and cleaning up, we all sat there staring at one another. There was a very big issue hanging in the room and I had no idea how to attack it. Spader did it for me. He had been listening silently to our conversation and finally decided it was time to speak.

"You called me a Traveler," he said, breaking the ice. "What does that mean?"

Loor took the lead. She calmly explained to Spader how every territory had a Traveler who could fly through the flumes. She told him how each territory was about to reach a critical turning point and how it was the job of the Travelers to do all they could to make sure the outcome would keep the territory peaceful. To fail would mean the territory would fall into chaos. She also told him of Saint Dane, the evil Traveler who was working to do the opposite. His goal was to push the territories into bedlam.

This is where I jumped in. I told Spader that Saint Dane could change the way he looked. On Cloral, he was the pirate Zy Roder. Uncle Press and I felt sure that he was responsible for poisoning the crops. I said how a bad food supply on Cloral would cause a civil war when people fought over the food that was still safe—just the kind of thing Saint Dane would love.

Loor finished by saying how she and I still didn't understand why we had been selected to be Travelers, or who it was that chose us. But the job we were given was an important one. She said how the battles with Saint Dane weren't only about each territory, they were about all of Halla. She explained that Halla was everything—all territories, all people, and all time. Saint Dane's ultimate goal was to control Halla. The only thing standing in his way were the Travelers. That would be us.

Spader listened intently. This was some serious stuff we were laying on him. I had no idea how he would react.

"So?" I asked. "What are you thinking?"

I could tell he was trying to put this puzzle together in his head but was having trouble getting all the pieces to fit.

"This is . . . this is a lot," he said.

Yeah, no kidding.

"I'm sorry, mates," he added. "I'm an aquaneer. I know boats, I know water, I know how to fix them and have some fun along the way. That's pretty much what my life's about. But now you're telling me I've got to be responsible for the future of everything? Hobey, I'm not the best choice for that particular job."

"Tell me about it," I threw in. "Neither am I!"

Loor stood up and took something out of a wicker basket near the fireplace.

"Do you think your father was someone worthy of being a Traveler?" she asked Spader.

"Absolutely," Spader shot back without hesitation.

Loor handed Spader the item she pulled from the basket. I saw that it was a piece of green paper that was folded in two. It looked like the same kind of paper I was used to writing my Cloral journals on. Spader opened it up to reveal that it was a drawing. Actually, it was *half* of a drawing. It looked as if it had been ripped in two and this was the left half.

The drawing was in black ink. There was a solid, horizontal line about a third of the way up from the bottom. Below this line there was another line that started at the bottom near the lower left-hand side and curved up until it hit the right edge of the page, making a quarter of a circle. Above the horizontal line were a bunch of dots sprayed around in no particular pattern. In the upper right-hand corner were a series of five symbols. It looked like they continued on to the right half of the page that had been torn away.

I had no idea what this half drawing meant, until I noticed something that rocked me. In the upper left-hand corner of the page was a round symbol. It was the exact same symbol with the interlocking letters that was on the note Spader's father had left for him. I looked to Spader in shock. Spader's eyes were fixed on the paper. Finally, after an eternity, he whispered,

"Faar."

"Far?" I shot back, my pulse rate spiking through the roof. "Far what?" I looked to Loor and demanded, "Where did you get this?"

"My mother was a Traveler," she said calmly. "She knew Spader's father."

Whoa! Major twist.

"Before I knew of my destiny," Loor continued, "she returned from one of her travels with this drawing. She told me of a man whom she admired greatly. She said he knew answers when most did not yet know the questions. He had risked his life many times over to find the information on this page. He said it was important to the future of Cloral. But he feared it might be found by those with evil intent. That is why he tore it in two and gave half to my mother. Your father said that his time was growing short, and that his son would carry on his work. He asked my mother to pass this on to his son when he came looking for it. My mother is now dead, Spader. It is my duty to give this to you."

This was incredible. The web of Travelers was truly inter-connected.

"This is the same symbol your father left you," I said to Spader. "If you know what it means, you gotta tell us!"

Spader stood up and paced. Things were happening too fast for him.

"It's a tall tale," he said nervously. "A children's story."

"What is?" I insisted.

"Faar!" he snapped back. "It's a legend. Everybody knows it."

"We don't," I said.

"Then I'll tell you," he continued. "The symbol represents

a mythical city called Faar that was built on the only dry land that existed on Cloral. It was supposed to be this amazing place full of scholars and music and scientists and art, like some kind of perfect place. But there was a tum-tigger of a disaster and this perfect place sank into the sea. The elders of the city saw the disaster coming and prepared for it. Somehow they saved the city, even though it sank into the ocean. The legend says the people of Faar will always live down below the water, secretly protecting all those who live on the habitats above."

"It was destroyed?" asked Loor.

"It sank, I didn't say it was destroyed," Spader said.

"Why didn't you tell us this when you saw the symbol on Magorran?" I asked.

"Because it's a fable. It was a bedtime story my father used to tell me. I thought he was giving me the symbol so I'd remember our time together. I didn't think it meant anything more than that! I still don't!"

"But, what if your father was trying to tell you something?" I said, attempting to keep my mouth from running ahead of my brain. "What if this is more than a children's story? What if your father discovered that Faar really exists?"

"That's impossible!" scoffed Spader.

"But if it isn't," I continued while holding up the half page. "This could be a map. Or *half* a map. Your father might have discovered Faar."

"But Faar isn't real!" he shouted back at me.

"But if it is," added Loor, "it would be just the kind of thing Saint Dane would want to destroy especially if it is important to the people of Cloral."

"Saint Dane!" shouted Spader. He was really worked up now. All the input over the last few days had finally gotten to him. "I don't know about territories or Travelers or Halla or flumes or any of that scutty-do magic, but there's one thing you've said that makes sense. If this Saint Dane is responsible for poisoning the people of Magorran, then I don't care *why* he did it. He killed my father and I'm going to pay for that. Pendragon, take me back to Cloral, now!"

This was going badly. After all we told Spader about being a Traveler and the mission we were on, there was only one thing he took away from it. He wanted revenge on Saint Dane.

I jumped up and said, "You don't get it. Saint Dane isn't just some *guy* you get even with. The dude is like . . . evil. And he has powers—more than you can imagine. He'd kill you before you even know you're in trouble."

"He couldn't be tougher than Loor!" countered Spader. "She's a warrior. She could come with us and use some of those natty weapons on him."

"It doesn't work like that," I said, trying not to get too frustrated. "You can't bring things from one territory to the next. We learned that the hard way."

"Fine!" he shouted. "There are plenty of weapons on Cloral. Let's just go after him!"

"You can't go after him!" I shouted back. "One on one, you'll be dead meat!"

"Then I'll be dead meat," said Spader with finality. "But I can't let my father's death go unavenged—no matter how big and bad this guy is. Take me back *now*!"

I had to think fast. Spader was out of control. I had to diffuse this situation, fast, before he did something dumb.

"No," I said with as much force as I could generate. "I'm tired and I'll never find the gate in the dark. If you want to go back on your own, knock yourself out. I'm not going back until tomorrow."

I sat down, picked up my coconut drink, and tried to act casual. It was a major-league bluff and I could only hope that Spader wouldn't go looking for the gate by himself. I didn't think he could find it, but you never knew. He stood with his feet firmly planted and his fists balled, weighing his options. Finally he said, "All right. We go back tomorrow. But then I'm going after Saint Dane whether you're with me or not."

With that he stormed out. I started to go after him but Loor put a hand on my shoulder.

"Let him walk alone," she said. "He needs to calm down."

I sat back down and dropped my coconut drink. I *hated* coconut.

"Well, that couldn't have gone any worse," I said with a false laugh.

"He has spirit," said Loor.

"Yeah, tell me about it. But if he goes after Saint Dane—"

"You must control him, Pendragon. You know as well as I that Saint Dane will kill him. I do not mean to sound uncaring, but he is no help to us dead."

"I get it. Between the two of us we can—"

"No," she said firmly. "I cannot go to Cloral with you."

That was *not* what I wanted to hear.

"What do you mean?" I asked incredulously. "We're Travelers. We help each other. You know 'the way it was meant to be,' and all that stuff. Don't bail on me now!"

"I have not yet found the turning point on Zadaa. But there is growing tension between the Batu and the Rokador. I want to try and stop the trouble before it grows worse. If I am successful then it will be one less battle we have to worry about in the future."

"Yeah, but what about the battle I'm fighting right now?"

"Your mission now is to control a passionate new Traveler and to solve the mystery of Faar. Think, Pendragon. You are better suited to that task than I. I would simply batter Spader senseless until he was unable to chase Saint Dane."

Good point. Diplomacy wasn't high on Loor's skill list.

"When you need a warrior," she added, "I will be there. You know that."

Of course she was right. Loor was always ready to fight, even if fighting wasn't the smartest way to go. I didn't need the responsibility of controlling *two* hotheads. Putting it another way, if she was the brawn of this team, then I was the brains. It was time to start using them.

"Is it possible?" I asked. "Could Spader's father have found a lost city?"

"After what we have been through," said Loor, "do you still think anything is impossible?"

The two of us looked to each other and shared a moment of unspoken understanding. We had been through a lot together and we knew there was much more to come. No, nothing was impossible in this new life of ours. The easiest thing to do was accept it.

Loor slept in her bedroom that night and I stretched out on the floor of the main room. She gave me a rough blanket and left an extra in case Spader came back. I'm happy to write that a few hours later, he did. He entered the apartment and lay down in front of the fire. I didn't say anything because I had no idea what kind of mood he was in. The last thing I wanted was to set him off again.

"Pendragon, you awake?" Spader whispered.

"Yeah."

"You're right, mate. I don't know all the rules of this game yet. Hobey, I don't even know what the game is. I'm willing to listen to what you think is best."

Whew, that was a relief. Now I could sleep.

"But you have to know something," he added. "I will learn from you. I will try and understand what it means to be a Traveler. But if I have a chance to hurt Saint Dane, I'm going to take it."

"That's the whole point, Spader," I said. "We all want to put Saint Dane out of business. But we've got to be smart about it. This might sound cold, but there is more at stake here than getting revenge for your father."

"But he was my *father*, Pendragon!" he said with emotion. "How can I look past that?"

I didn't sit up. I didn't raise my voice. I answered Spader as calmly as possible.

"You're not the only one who's been hurt here. Both my parents and my sister are gone. Loor's mother was killed. We both watched as Saint Dane's men shot her full of arrows. It hadn't been easy but we've been able to look past it. You'd better have the guts to do it too."

Spader didn't respond. I think I nailed him right between the eyes. Yes, we had all lost loved ones. Spader didn't have a monopoly on that particular horror. I could only hope that he now understood that the only hope we had of defeating Saint Dane was by fighting the larger battle, together.

I was too exhausted to think anymore. It had been an incredibly long day. I needed to sleep, so that's what I did.

We all got up before the sun. Loor started a fire and cooked us more of that incredible bread, along with a half dozen eggs. At least I thought they were eggs. They were green and looked more like something you would see in a Dr. Seuss book than on a menu at Denny's. Still, they were good and I was starving. We needed to eat every chance we had because we couldn't be sure where our next meal would come from.

It was now time to get going. Spader stood before Loor and said, "Thank you for helping me understand, and for holding my father's note. I guess we'll see each other again."

"We will," she said. Then added, "Trust Pendragon. He is the light we all need to follow."

That caught me by surprise. What did she mean by that? It sounded like a compliment, but it also sounded like she was expecting way too much from me. Spader looked to me and I'll bet he was wondering the same thing. He then nodded and left us alone.

"What was that about the light and the following?" I asked her.

She scoffed, saying, "I wanted to make sure Spader listened to you. That is all."

Oh. Okay. That was cool. I guess.

"When you need me," she added, "I will be there."

"Thanks for helping with Spader," I said. "I was lost there for a while."

"Your instincts are good, Pendragon," she said. "Someday you will realize that."

I nodded and backed out of the room. This was the second time I had to say good-bye to Loor, and it wasn't any easier. Still, I knew where to find her if need be.

Spader and I walked back toward the gate without saying much. I had to concentrate in order to retrace our steps through the city. It helped that my ring was doing a hot-cold thing to help guide us. With only a few wrong turns, we finally found the building with the ramp that led down to the underground river.

I really wanted to avoid running into that guy who worked the knob-and-lever gizmo. I didn't want to have to answer any more questions. But as luck would have it, the guy was there again, still checking his plans, still spinning his controls. What a boring job. We tried to sneak by without being noticed but—

"Are you lost again?" he said without looking at us.

"No," I said with authority. "Just passing through."

"Do you believe me now?" he asked.

"Uh . . . about what?"

"About the Batu. They are liars and barbarians. I hope you found that so-called friend of yours and told them I said so."

Loor was right. There was definitely bad blood between the Rokador and the Batu. I hoped she had luck in diffusing it.

"Yeah," I lied. "Thanks for the advice."

The man didn't say another word. I motioned to Spader and we continued on through the tunnel that led to the waterfall. Once we had gotten away from the roar of the water, Spader said, "I understood."

"What do you mean?"

"The guy back there. When he first started talking it sounded like: 'Shshaa shashaaa shashaaa' or something. But then all of a sudden he started making sense. I understood what he said about the Rokador and the Batu. What happened?"

I had to smile. "What happened is that you're becoming a Traveler."

Next stop, Cloral.

◈ SECOND EARTH ◈

The telephone rang, making both Mark and Courtney jump. When they were reading Bobby's journals they both became so immersed in the adventure that there own world seemed to slip away. But a jangling telephone is a surefire way to bring anyone back to the here and now.

Unfortunately for Courtney, they were reading the journal in Mark's bedroom. Though Mark did his best to excavate all of his crusty sweat socks and half-eaten cheddar cheese (extra sharp) sandwiches, the room was still in need of professional fumigation. The good news was that Courtney's gag reflex stopped when she got used to the putrid smell. The bad news was that she was afraid there were noxious gases eating away at her brain. Her goal was to read quick and get out fast.

They had been displaced from Courtney's basement because Courtney's father was actually going to attempt to make something in his workshop. That was always cause for worry in the Chetwynde house. Nothing good ever happened when Mr. Chetwynde decided to swing a hammer. Things usually got broken. When the telephone rang, Courtney's first thought was: "Dad hurt himself! He's headed for the emergency room." She had absolutely no faith in her father's handyman abilities.

Mark had to answer the phone because nobody else was home.

"Hello?"

"What's the deal, Dimond?" snarled a familiar voice.

The call wasn't about Courtney's father, it was Andy Mitchell. He was actually calling Mark's house. Mark wondered how Mitchell got his telephone number. Not that it was tough to get, but he couldn't picture Mitchell figuring out how to do something as complex as using a telephone book.

"Hey!" answered Mark with false friendliness. "How's it going?"

Mark was trapped. He didn't want to say anything that would make Courtney suspicious about what was going on with Mitchell. He knew she wouldn't continue reading the journal without Mark, so she had nothing to do but listen to his conversation. Mark fought his rising panic and pressed the phone closer to his ear so Courtney couldn't hear the other end of the conversation.

"You tell *me,*" answered Mitchell. Mark could hear him snort and spit. "We have a deal, remember?"

"Uhhh, of course I do," answered Mark, trying to sound all innocent.

"So what's the problem?" asked Mitchell.

"No problem, everything's cool." He looked to Courtney and held up a finger as if to say: "I'll be off in a second."

Courtney shrugged. No biggie.

"So when am I gonna see the other journals?"

"Uhhh, let's see. How about . . . tomorrow?"

"How about in an hour?"

Mark's stomach twisted. "Okay, that's good too. Tell you what,

I'm kinda doing my homework now. But I should be done in an hour. Why don't you call me back then?"

Mitchell hung up abruptly. Mark didn't know what to do. If he just put the phone down, Courtney would wonder what happened. So he pretended to still be on the call.

"Uh-huh. Yeah. Sounds good. Okay, talk to you later. Bye."

Mark hung up the phone and hoped that Courtney only cared about getting back to reading the journal.

She didn't.

"Who was that?" she asked. Of course she did.

Mark hated lying. He wasn't good at it. He now had to get very good, very fast.

"Friend of mine," he answered, trying to sound casual. "He needs some help with homework. A-Algebra."

The instant Mark said that, he wished he hadn't. Up to that point he'd been cool, but when he made the full-on lie, when he said "algebra," he stuttered. Courtney caught it, too. He saw it in her eyes. Was she going to bust him on it? Courtney stared at him for a moment, then shrugged.

"Whatever," she said. "Can we get back to the journal?"

"Sure, yeah, of course."

Mark sat back down on the bed. He felt horrible. He hated lying to her, but was too embarrassed to tell her the truth. He was being blackmailed and had no idea how he was going to get out of it. If Courtney found out now, he was certain she'd lose all faith in him. It was a horrible position to be in. But for now at least, he could forget his own problem and lose himself in Bobby's problems.

"What do you think of this Faar place?" Courtney asked.

"If it's real, then destroying it would be the perfect, evil thing for Saint Dane to do. From what Spader said it's a legend that everybody on Cloral knows. It's part of their culture. If Saint Dane finds it and destroys it, it would be like pulling the rug out from under an entire territory. If the place is already a mess because of the food shortage, then the whole territory could crumble."

"Which is what Saint Dane wants," added Courtney.

"Exactly."

"Let's read," said Mark.

"Yeah, you've got an algebra lesson to get to."

This stung Mark, but he couldn't let it show. It was time to focus on Bobby.

CLORAL

We found the gate easily enough by following the signals
sent from my ring. I opened the trapdoor and let Spader go
down first into the crevice that led to the flume, then followed right behind.

When I was halfway down, I heard something off to my
right. Remember, we were climbing down using footholds that
were dug into the rock walls. It was like descending through
a black cave. The crevice was only wide enough for one person, but it stretched off to either side for I don't know how far.
It was too dark to tell. So when I heard something move off to
my right, I froze. It wasn't a loud sound, it was more like a
small pebble had been knocked into the crevice. Though it
was a small sound, something had caused it. Something was
out there in the darkness.

I cautiously looked to where I'd heard the sound, and was
faced with two yellow eyes staring right back at me. Yikes!
They were small, but that didn't matter. We were near a flume
and that could mean only one thing: quigs. I had no idea what
kind of beastie was behind those nasty eyes, but it wasn't
going to be some harmless teddy bear.

190 ~ PENDRAGON ~

My fear was that the slightest movement would push it into attack mode. My brain locked. I didn't know what to do.

Luckily Spader did. I felt him shoot up from below and reach out toward the yellow eyes. Before I could warn him, the yellow eyes were gone! I heard a loud *crack,* and that was it.

"W-What just happened?" I asked shakily.

"I got it, mate," answered Spader.

We both hurried down the rest of the way until we reached the cavern. There, lying at the foot of the rock wall, was the quig. It was the nastiest looking *snake* I had ever seen. It was about four feet long with a hooded head. All along its back were smaller versions of the sharp spines that the bear quigs had on Denduron. But most important, it was dead. Spader had snapped it like a whip.

"I'm used to those wogglies," he said casually. "They end up on the habitats every so often. All you gotta do is crack 'em good." He took a closer look at the fiendish thingy and frowned. "Never saw a sea snake looking like that before though."

And he never would either. Except here on Zadaa. The gruesome truth was that the quigs on Zadaa were snakes. I'd bet they were poisonous, too. I hated snakes more than anything. More than cannibal bears or wild dogs or even monster sharks. Snakes did something to me. Maybe because they were so quiet and sneaky. As I stared down at that creepy reptile, I hoped that Loor would do a really good job in keeping the Batu and the Rokador apart, because I did *not* want to come back to Zadaa.

Spader and I then changed back into our Cloral clothes and hit the flume. He went by himself this time. I showed him how to call out the name of the territory he was headed for, and just before the sparkling lights took him away, I warned him that the drop into Cloral was going to be wet.

Believe it or not, I was beginning to enjoy my trips through the flume because while I was flying I felt completely safe. Nothing to do but kick back and enjoy the ride. When I got to the end of this trip, I even spun around and tried to imitate Uncle Press's headfirst swan dive into the pool. But I timed it wrong and ended up landing on my back with a huge splash. It hurt, too. Hello, Cloral. So much for a cool entrance.

Spader was already standing on the edge of the pool.

"I'll lead from here," he said.

We were on his turf again, or should I say, in his water. He was back in charge. That was okay with me so long as we both agreed on the plan.

"What about the sharks?" I asked.

Spader grabbed his air globe and water sled.

"No worries there," he said. "Stay close to the bottom. Those beasties don't attack down. The only time you get into a natty-do is if you're on their level."

"Yeah? What if they come down to our level?"

Spader reached behind his back and pulled out his large, silver knife.

"Let 'em," he said with confidence.

"Whoa, did you bring that knife to Zadaa?"

"Didn't think I'd go someplace strange without my trusty, did you?"

"You gotta understand something, Spader," I said nervously. "Maybe I didn't explain this and if I didn't, it's my fault. But you can't bring things from one territory to the next. It's like . . . like . . . an infection. Believe me, I made that mistake and it was a disaster."

"It's just a knife, Pendragon," he said dismissively. "Couldn't do no harm."

With that he popped on his air globe and dove into the water. This was bad. Spader said he would learn from me, but the first thing I tried to tell him, he blew off. This was going to be tough.

But there was nothing I could do about it now, so I popped on my air globe and followed him under. I didn't want him to get too far ahead of me. After all, he had the knife. We both skimmed the bottom, traveling side by side with our water sleds. I kept glancing around, looking in the distance for the shadowy killers. And it wasn't just quigs that worried me. When we left for Zadaa there were four raiders after us. I had a brief hope that maybe the quigs ate the raiders, but that would have been hoping for too much. When we broke out into open water from under the rock overhang, I felt even more vulnerable. I kept glancing around, checking our backs. At one point I thought I saw a shadow moving several yards off to our right. I was about to tell Spader, when the shadow suddenly twisted and shot away. There was definitely something there all right. But if it was a quig, or a raider, it had decided to leave us alone.

Once we had traveled a few minutes I began to relax. As Spader said, the sharks only hung around that reef. I stopped worrying about getting eaten and began to worry about what we might find back on Grallion. When we left, we had just jammed up the raiders' battle cruiser and signaled to the aquaneers that the big guns wouldn't fire. The question now was, what had happened after that? Had the aquaneers boarded the cruiser? Had the raiders boarded Grallion? Had there been a battle between the good guys and the bad guys? Most important, was Uncle Press okay?

At least one answer came to us quickly. As the water sleds sped us closer to Grallion I saw something in the distance that wasn't there when we left. At first I didn't know what it was because we were so far away. It just looked like a dark mass. But as we got closer it began to take shape, and it was big. Really big. Spader recognized it for what it was first.

"Hobey-ho!" he exclaimed. "They had a natty-do all right!"

We sped closer, and that's when I saw the eight long tubes sticking out from the huge mass. Though the proof was right before my eyes, I could barely believe it. The long tubes were cannons. The dark mass . . . was a sunken ship! It was the raiders' battle cruiser. A minute later we glided and slipped right by the immense hulk. It was lying on its keel, tipped to one side. Being that close to something so big always took my breath away. It reminded me of the video footage I'd seen from the wreck of the *Titanic*. But this ship had only been on the bottom for a short time. It hadn't rusted out yet.

Whatever happened topside after we jammed up its guns, it was pretty clear that the raiders had gotten their butts whipped. Now I wanted to get to Grallion as soon as possible to hear the victory story.

We drove our water sleds past the huge sunken ship and continued on to Grallion. We stayed underwater the whole way and didn't surface until we had slipped into the dock area where we had launched the skimmers.

An aquaneer was on the dock, tinkering with an engine. He saw the two of us surface and his eyes grew wide.

"Spader?" he said with awe. "Spader!" The guy jumped up and started yelling for joy. "They're back! They're alive! Hobey-ho, Yenza, they're back!"

We were greeted with a hero's welcome. The aquaneers mobbed us on the docks and all but carried us topside. I got smacked on the back so much, I ended up with black and blue marks. No kidding. But I didn't care. This was great. When we got up into the sun, I took a quick look around to see there was absolutely no hint that a battle had taken place here. That's because it all happened on the water, and on the raiders' cruiser. The aquaneers took turns telling us what happened.

Just before the deadline that Zy Roder had given them for firing his guns again, Yenza quickly passed an order to every aquaneer. She said they were to attack soon as they saw a flare fire from beneath the water. The aquaneers thought she was crazy, but they followed orders. Sure enough, they saw our flare and went after the raiders with everything they had. They sent several boats loaded with aquaneers to swarm the cruiser and caught the bad guys completely by surprise. The *Pursuit*'s big guns were useless and the raiders weren't prepared for close-in fighting. Before they could rally to defend themselves, the aquaneers had boarded the cruiser and had little trouble taking command.

The only bad thing was that so many of the raiders escaped on small speedboats. Worse, their pilot, Zy Roder, had escaped as well. Yeah, Saint Dane got away. When I heard this, I glanced to Spader. I could tell that this news had tweaked him. He knew that Roder was really Saint Dane, and I'm sure he hoped to hear he had been captured. No such luck.

The aquaneers then scuttled the battle cruiser so no one could use it in anger again. While listening to them recount their victory, I split my attention between the aquaneers and Spader. I wanted to see Spader's reaction to what had happened. What I saw, I didn't like. This wasn't like the time at Grolo's where he was the center of attention, telling tales and buying everyone sniggers. No, if Spader was happy about the victory over the raiders, he didn't show it. He listened to the group intently, then after they finished their story he gave them polite congratulations. The old Spader would have jumped up and shouted: "Hobey-ho! Nobody challenges Grallion! Sniggers are on me!" But not this new Spader. This was a darker Spader, and it had me worried.

That's when I saw a welcome sight behind the group of ecstatic aquaneers. It was Uncle Press. He smiled and waved me over. I ran to him and the two of us hugged.

"You're becoming a legend around here," he said with a chuckle. "Next they'll be writing songs about you."

"Trust me, I wasn't all that heroic," I said. "I almost bought it down there." It sounded modest, but I meant it.

"Where have you been?" he asked.

I gave him a quick rundown on our trip to Zadaa and our meeting with Loor. I explained how Spader was getting up to speed on being a Traveler, but he wasn't handling it well. I said how his one and only concern was to get revenge on Saint Dane, and it was going to be hard to hold him back. I also told Uncle Press about the most important discovery of our trip: the symbol and the half of a map that might lead to the Lost City of Faar, as the legend referred to it. Uncle Press agreed that Faar, if it indeed existed, would be a perfect target for Saint Dane.

Spader then broke away from the celebration and joined us.

"Saint Dane got away," he said with no emotion, though I knew he was burning up inside.

"Don't worry," said Uncle Press. "We'll see him again."

I had been thinking a lot about what our next move should be, and it was as good a time as any to throw it out there.

"I think we should go to Panger City," I said.

Spader shot me a surprised look and said, "No. Leave my mum out of this."

"I'm afraid your mum may already be in it," I said, trying not to sound too harsh.

"Why? How?" Spader demanded.

"Spader's dad gave half of the map to Osa to give to Spader. That means the other half is still out there somewhere. We didn't find it with Spader's dad, so I'll bet you anything it's with Spader's mum."

Spader reached into his pocket and pulled out the half map. Uncle Press took it and examined it.

"These numbers on top," he said. "They could be partial coordinates."

Spader grabbed the map back angrily.

"I don't care about your fantasy games. Leave my mum alone."

"You don't get it," I said urgently. "Maybe this whole Faar thing is a fable and we've got nothing to worry about, but if it isn't and Saint Dane is trying to find that lost city, then he'll want this map. If your mum has the other half, she's in trouble."

This hit Spader hard. I couldn't have shocked him more if I had thrown ice water in his face. I hated to do it, but he had to understand what was at stake here. He looked at the half map, then jammed it into his pocket.

"Yenza," he said. "She'll give us a boat. We can be in Panger City by nightfall."

He took off running toward the aquaneer barracks. Uncle Press watched him run off and then said, "He's hurting."

"This is bad. When he finally comes face to face with Saint Dane—"

"We'll worry about that when it happens. Right now let's get ready for a treasure hunt."

CLORAL

Uncle Press and I followed Spader to the far side of the aquaneer barracks. As we got closer, we heard yelling coming from the building. "I warned her, yes I did! I saw this coming but no one believed me!"

It was coming from Wu Yenza's office. When we peeked in the door, we saw Yenza behind a desk, looking stern, as usual. Spader stood to the back of the room, listening. All the hubba was coming from two agronomers who stood in front of Yenza's desk. They were the same man and woman I had seen outside the pilot house on Magorran shortly after the crash. They were arguing then, and they were still arguing now. At least now I had the chance to hear what it was all about. The man was a short, balding guy with an elflike face named Ty Manoo. In another life, he could have easily gotten a gig in Santa's workshop. The guy paced, flailed his arms for emphasis, and spit when he talked.

"We set something in motion that must be stopped!" he shouted.

The woman didn't seem all that worried. Her name was Po Nassi. She was tall and slim with sharp features that reminded me of a sly cat. She stood with her arms folded, looking bored, as if Manoo were nothing more than an annoying kid.

"You are overreacting again," she said while rolling her eyes.

"Overreacting!" Manoo shot back. "There are hundreds dead on Magorran! We were attacked by raiders! What kind of reaction would you suggest?"

"What is the problem?" asked Spader.

"The problem is we caused the poisoning on Magorran," Manoo spit out.

Whoa. New development. Uncle Press and I looked at each other and entered the office. It was time to get involved. Yenza saw us and stood up. She looked kind of flustered, like she was losing control of the situation and from what I saw of Yenza, she did not like to lose control.

"Spader, get your friends out of here," she ordered.

"No," Spader shot back. "They're here to help us."

"I don't want to cause a panic," Yenza argued. "Until we find out exactly what happened, we don't need rumors circulating."

Uncle Press spoke to Yenza in a calm, controlled voice. "If I may, Commander. Pendragon and I have come from a long way off because we heard there might be some . . . difficulty here. We won't spread rumors; we won't cause a panic. Our only goal is to help see you through this crisis."

Yenza looked into Uncle Press's eyes, and I could see her relax. It was kind of creepy, actually. Uncle Press's soothing words had taken the fight out of her. It reminded me of the quiet way that Loor's mother, Osa, had a calming effect on people. It was almost hypnotic. I wondered if this were some kind of Traveler trick and made a mental note to ask about it later.

"They already helped save Grallion once," Spader added. "They're friends."

Yenza looked us over. Finally she sat back down and said to the agronomers, "Tell them what you told me."

Immediately the little guy, Manoo, took over.

"It was an experiment," he started. "The population of Cloral is growing. The demand for food is always getting greater."

Nassi didn't want to be left out and added, "We calculated that at the present rate, there was a good possibility the day would come when the demand for food would be greater than the supply. So we set out to perform an important service."

"We started looking for ways to increase plant growth," Manoo continued. "We figured if we could get crops to grow bigger and faster, we'd never have to worry about having enough food. We experimented with fertilizers and crossbreeding and found ways to change the very cell structure of plants. But it was wrong!"

"It wasn't wrong!" countered Nassi. "It's a work in progress!"

"But we were changing nature!" cried Manoo. "I tried to tell them we were headed for disaster, but no one listened."

"That's because we were successful!" Nassi argued.

"Successful?" shouted Manoo. "We changed nature! We created plants that grew faster but turned poisonous!"

Manoo was a mess. He wiped his sweaty forehead with his sleeve and continued.

"It was the fertilizer," he said. "We created a fertilizer that affected the normal growth cycle of plants and changed their genetic structure. It was incredible. Plants grew seven times faster and yielded twice as much fruit. We were all so excited that we wanted to share the discovery with everyone. But we moved too fast. We didn't test the results."

"It was only recently that we discovered an unfortunate . . . side effect," Nassi said, trying to sound casual, as if it were no big deal. "Some of the mutated crops became poisonous. We never actually used the fertilizer on Grallion's crops. We're safe here."

"But, we had already sent a sample of the fertilizer to the Agronomy Society. We only wanted them to study it, but they were so impressed they immediately began manufacturing it and sending it all over Cloral!" shouted Manoo.

Yenza jumped to her feet. "You're telling me that a fertilizer is being used all over Cloral that turns crops deadly?" she screamed, trying to control her horror.

"Yes!" shouted Manoo. "What happened on Magorran is just the beginning!"

This put a whole new spin on things. Could it be that Saint Dane wasn't responsible for the poison crops after all? Was he simply taking advantage of the situation? The creation of this killer fertilizer seemed to be the turning point on this territory, but it looked to be the people of Cloral who brought it on themselves.

"The Agronomy Society is on Panger City," Spader said. "We've got to get there and stop them from sending out more fertilizer."

"That's *exactly* what we have to do!" squealed Manoo.

"Give us a speeder craft," added Spader. "We can be in Panger City before nightfall." Spader was being very clever. Stopping the fertilizer was critical, but the main reason he wanted to get to Panger City was to protect his mum. There was a whole "two birds with one stone" thing happening.

"I'm going too!" added Manoo. He then turned to Nassi,

stuck a finger in her face and spit out, "You are too. I'm not going to take full blame for this."

Nassi shrugged and said, "Fine, whatever you want. I don't mind taking the credit. Once we perfect the process, we'll be heroes."

"But right now, we're killers," Manoo said angrily.

This got a reaction from Nassi. Up until then she was only looking at the problem as a science experiment. Being called a killer was a whole 'nother ballgame. She actually looked shaken.

"I'll go," she said, cowed.

Yenza came around from behind her desk heading for the door.

"Meet me at the stern dock in two pecks," she ordered. "I'll prepare a speeder. We're *all* going to Panger City." Then just before she left the office she turned back and lifted a finger.

"Do not mention this to anyone," she commanded sternly. "Any of you. If Grallion is safe, there's no need to cause panic."

She then left. Nassi and Manoo followed after her, leaving us alone with Spader.

"Is it possible?" he asked. "Could Saint Dane have nothing to do with this?"

"It's possible, but it doesn't matter," answered Uncle Press. "He may not have started it, but he'll take advantage of it."

"And there's still the stuff about Faar," I added. "How does that fit in?"

"Hopefully we'll find out on Panger City," answered Uncle Press.

Forty minutes later, or two pecks, depending on where you come from, the six of us were at the dock, ready to leave for Panger City. I stood with Uncle Press, Spader, and the two agronomers, Nassi and Manoo. The speeder we were going to take was a coolio-looking powerboat that looked about forty feet long. It was painted the same sea-green color as the raiders' battle cruiser. It had a cabin up front that was big enough to hold a galley and some bunks. The wheelhouse was on top of the cabin. Wu Yenza was already there, powering up. The deck was large, with seats along the rails. It kind of reminded me of the dive boats Uncle Press used to take me on. But unlike dive boats, this baby looked like it could do some serious haul ass.

We all boarded and Spader cast off the lines. Yenza powered up the engines, which as usual weren't all that loud. These water-powered engines were great! Yenza then expertly guided the boat away from the docks of Grallion and out into open water. Moments later, once we had passed the marker buoy, Yenza hit the throttle and this boat showed us why it was called a speeder. I was nearly thrown over by the sudden surge of power, in seconds we were flying over the water like a seagoing jet.

Like the skimmers, the ride was smooth and pretty quiet. The only way I could tell we were moving so fast was from the wind whipping at my face. When I stood up I had to lean forward or it would have knocked me back down.

The two agronomers kept to themselves during most of the trip. They stayed in the cabin up front and argued. What else was new? They had pads of paper where they scribbled out equations and formulas. I assumed they were trying to figure out how to undo the harm done by their mutant fertilizer.

Yenza stayed at the controls. Spader acted as navigator. He had charts and plotted a course to Panger City. Uncle Press and I had nothing to do except worry. Would it be too late to recall

all the fertilizer? How far had it spread? Had it already started a chain reaction that would infect all the crops of Cloral? Stranger still was the mystery of Faar. What was so important about this mythical city that the dying wish of Spader's father was to tell his son about it? How did this all tie in with Saint Dane? Hopefully, all of these questions would be answered on Panger City.

"This makes perfect sense," said Uncle Press softly. He was looking out onto the water, thinking.

"What does?" I asked. I wasn't used to hearing that things were making sense.

"The agronomers went too far," he said thoughtfully. "Their intentions may have been noble, but they created a monster. It's just the kind of thing that Saint Dane would take advantage of. He'll do everything in his power to keep the poison spreading and turn Cloral upside down. This is the turning point. This is why we're here."

"Then what about this lost city of Faar?" I asked.

"I don't know where it fits into this puzzle, but if Spader's father was concerned, then I'm concerned too."

I looked up to the wheelhouse and saw that Spader was staring at the horizon. I wanted to know what was going through his mind. He was a great guy. A friend. But I was afraid his anger over the death of his father was going to get him into some serious trouble and make things worse for all of us. Hopefully his mother was safe. But then Spader would have the tough job of telling her that his father was dead. But as rough as this would be, what I really feared was that something might have already happened to his mother, like it happened to my family. If Spader lost his mother, then I was sure he'd go off the deep end.

The trip took most of the day. I tried to get some sleep but my mind was racing with worry. I watched the sun as it traveled across the sky on its way to the ocean. Then, just as I was finally nodding off—

"There!" shouted Yenza.

I quickly climbed the ladder to the wheelhouse and looked forward to where she was pointing. I didn't see it at first because it was only a gray speck on the horizon. But as we drew closer and the speck grew bigger, I saw it for what it was.

Panger City.

Even though we were flying over the water at an incredible speed, it must have taken us another two hours to get there. That's how big this city habitat was. The closer we got, the larger the buildings grew. It soon became clear to me that this habitat was every bit as big as Grallion, but unlike Grallion, it was covered with buildings. It really was a city! I was staring at skyscrapers! Some of them must have been over forty stories high. This looked every bit like a big city from home, but cities at home weren't floating on the ocean. It was incredible!

As we got closer I saw more detail in the buildings. Like I told you before, there was no steel on Cloral. Everything was made from some kind of hard plastic compound. Rather than familiar building colors of gray concrete and silver steel, these buildings were white and light blue or green. But other than that they looked very much like office buildings at home.

When we got inside the safety buoy and slowed down, I had to strain my neck back to look up at the huge buildings that towered over me. Only one thought came to mind: How can this thing possibly stay afloat?

Yenza carefully drove our speeder into the dock area, which was very much like Grallion's. Two aquaneers to guide us in and tie us up. They immediately stood at attention and saluted Yenza as she jumped off the boat.

"We may be leaving at any time," she said with authority.

"Yes, sir!" responded both aquaneers professionally.

Yenza then turned back to us and barked to Manoo and Nassi, "Where is the Agronomy Society?"

Manoo scrambled over the rail of the boat, nearly fell in the water, but caught himself and stood up straight as if nothing were wrong. Nassi rolled her eyes and gracefully got off the boat.

"We'll take you there," he said sharply.

The little man waddled past Yenza and headed up the stairs toward the surface. The rest of us got off the boat and followed. I walked with Spader and asked, "When was the last time you were home?"

He didn't answer. He kept looking ahead and picked up the pace to get away from me. So much for small talk. Spader's mind was somewhere else.

When we arrived on the surface, we stepped out of a building and onto a scene that looked pretty much like any busy city street. The sidewalks were full of people hurrying to wherever they were hurrying; small vehicles traveled on the streets; and vendors sold food from wheeled carts. It was like being back in New York City, except everything looked more colorful, and *way* cleaner.

There was one other detail that made it very different from home. There were water canals that ran parallel to every street. They were around twenty feet across, which was about the same width as the streets, but that was plenty big enough for the many small water-powered boats that traveled quickly along, speeding people on their way. I'd never been to Venice, Italy, but from the pictures and movies I'd seen, this was kind of like that. One quick look around showed me that these canals crisscrossed the entire city habitat. Every so often there were footbridges that stood like half circles over the waterways so that boats could glide under them. At each bridge was a beautiful fountain that sent up sprays of water in various patterns. The fountains had no function except to look good.

I have to say, Panger City was a beautiful place.

But I didn't have much time to hang out and appreciate it. When we all regrouped on the street, Spader didn't stop. Without a word of explanation he kept walking toward one of the canals.

"Spader!" called Yenza. "Spader, get back here. That is an order."

Spader wasn't listening. I knew where he was going and nobody was going to stop him.

Yenza was about to run after him, but Uncle Press stepped in front of her saying, "He's going to see his mother."

This made Yenza soften for a moment, but just as quickly her hard look returned.

"I understand, but that's not why we're here," she said angrily. "He knows that."

"He does," said Uncle Press calmly. "We'll stay with him. It's more important that you get to the Agronomy Society."

Yenza looked at Nassi and Manoo. Nassi was getting impatient. Manoo just looked like he wanted to pee.

"We can't waste any more time!" Manoo squealed.

Yenza looked back to Uncle Press and said, "Let him talk to his mother, then bring him back to the speeder."

"Understood," replied Uncle Press.

Yenza definitely had a soft spot for Spader. I think he got away with a lot of things Yenza would never allow from her other aquaneers. On top of that, Spader had saved Grallion, with our help of course. So I guess he deserved a little slack.

I saw that Spader had already jumped onto a skimmer and was powering it up.

"Uhhh, Uncle Press," I said. "We're going to lose him."

"Go!" shouted Yenza.

Uncle Press and I took off on a run toward the canal. It seemed as if all the skimmers were community property because people were getting on and off randomly and just leaving them, kind of like bicycles in China.

Spader kicked his skimmer into gear and sped off. We were losing him.

"Uncle Press!"

"There! Got one," he announced, pointing. He saw an empty skimmer and we both jumped on. Uncle Press quickly powered up, hit the throttle, and we were off.

Luckily there was a speed limit on the canals. It was pretty crowded and to go too fast meant a guaranteed accident. Spader was already far ahead of us, but I could tell he was having trouble going as fast as he wanted to because it looked like rush hour had hit Panger City. Uncle Press maneuvered our skimmer around the slower traffic and only managed to tick off a few people by cutting them off.

We traveled quite a ways through the canyons of towering buildings. We couldn't stop to appreciate the tour though; we had to keep up with Spader. Spader knew exactly where he was going and made several turns down different canals. I kept watching him and directed Uncle Press who was busy avoiding other skimmers.

Finally Spader turned off into a narrow canal that ran between two smaller buildings. I saw where he dumped the skimmer and kept watching to see which building he was going toward. I had a strange sense of déjà vu. This is exactly what happened when we followed Spader to his father's apartment on Magorran. I could only hope that we wouldn't find the same kind of horror here on Panger City.

We landed our skimmer and quickly jumped off. When we ran up onto the street, Spader was standing there, waiting for us.

"I just saw you," he said, sounding a little embarrassed. "I didn't know you were following me."

"Yeah, well, we're sort of in this together whether you like it or not," I said.

"I'm sorry," he said. "I'm glad you're here. I'm a little . . ."

He didn't finish his sentence. I could tell he was afraid of what he might find.

"It's okay, Spader. We're with you," said Uncle Press.

Spader nodded, then turned and led us into the apartment building where his mother lived. This place looked like any apartment building at home, except for the fact it was light yellow. It was five stories high with around ten apartments to a floor. Spader knew exactly where he was going. We climbed the stairs to the top floor and walked to the door on the far end of the corridor. That's where Spader stopped, caught in the moment. Soon he would find what he came for, and I could tell that as much as he wanted to go inside, he was afraid to. He looked up to us. Uncle Press gave him an encouraging nod.

Spader knocked on the door. "Hobey-ho!" he called happily.

There was no answer. He knocked again.

"Mum?"

There was no sound of footsteps coming to the door. No one called from inside to ask who it was. I hoped that his mother was out shopping or taking a nap or visiting friends.

Spader glanced at us again and tried the doorknob. It was open. His heart must have been racing because mine sure was. He then took a deep breath and stepped inside. Uncle Press and I followed him, stepping into his mother's home.

I have to tell you guys, I never thought I'd have this feeling even *once* in my life, but to go through it twice was, well, it wasn't fair.

The apartment was totally empty. Not a piece of furniture or picture or any other sign that anyone had ever lived there. It was just like the feeling I had when we all went back to 2 Linden Place in Stony Brook and I saw that my house was gone. Well, it wasn't exactly as bad as that because what I saw back on Second Earth with you was that my own family had disappeared. I knew exactly what Spader was going through.

He stood near the door, staring at the empty home, unbelieving. Uncle Press walked up to him, put a hand on his shoulder and softly said the magic words, "Try not to be sad. This is the way it was supposed to be."

Spader pulled away from him angrily.

"How can that be?" he shouted. "Where is she?"

"She's not dead, Spader," said Uncle Press. "You're a Traveler now. That meant it was time for her to move on too."

Spader shot a look of total confusion to Uncle Press. I have to admit, I was still confused about this whole family-disappearance part of being a Traveler myself.

"So then where is she?" I asked. "And while we're at it, where's *my* family?"

Uncle Press looked uncomfortable. I think he knew exactly where they were, but for some reason he didn't want to say.

"Spader, I'll tell you the same thing I told Bobby when he found out his own family was gone," he said calmly. "You were always destined to become a Traveler. Your family was here to raise you and teach you and help you become the person you are today so that you could begin your journey. But they've begun a journey of their own now. Someday you'll see them again, I promise."

"What about my father?" demanded Spader. "He didn't go anywhere. He was killed!"

"He was a Traveler," answered Uncle Press. "He had other duties. I promise you both, as time goes on you will understand everything, but for right now, you must know that nothing horrible happened to your mother."

This was bringing up all sorts of old, horrible feelings in me. I was getting frustrated over not knowing all there was to know about being a Traveler. I could only imagine what Spader was feeling. This was still very new to him. We stood in the room for a few moments, then Spader suddenly ran farther into the apartment. We followed him as he ran through the empty home, into what was probably once a bedroom at one time.

He stood in the middle of the room and said, "This was my room. I lived here from the time I was born until I left to become an aquaneer. I don't believe that my entire childhood can be wiped away as if it never existed."

He went into a closet. "Pendragon, help me," he said. I shrugged and followed.

"Help me up?" he asked.

I clasped my hands together and held them out. Spader put his foot in and I hoisted him up.

"I had a hiding place nobody knew about," he said while running his hands along the wall over the closet door. "It is where I kept the things that were most important to me."

I felt bad for him. Spader was doing the same thing I did when I walked onto the empty lot at 2 Linden Place. I looked over every inch of that empty space, desperate for any sign that proved I had lived there. But there was nothing. Even the scar on the tree that had been made by our swing was gone. I knew that Spader's secret hiding place would be empty.

Over the closet door was a piece of wall that had been neatly cut out and replaced. Spader knew exactly where it was. He pulled away the piece and reached into the compartment. Of course it was empty. I could tell by the pained look on his face.

But then, just as he was about to climb down, his face changed. He had found something after all.

"Let me down," he ordered.

I awkwardly bent down and dropped his foot. He banged his shoulder against the door frame as he came down, but he was okay.

"What did you find?" I asked. I couldn't believe that some hint of his past life had actually been left behind.

Spader held the treasure in his hand.

I knew instantly that it wasn't something he put there himself. It was a piece of green paper, folded in half. Written on the outside in black letters was: "For Spader. I'm proud of you and I love you. Hobey-ho!" I could only guess that it was his mum's handwriting.

Spader unfolded the paper and I saw his mum's final gift to him. It was the other half of the map that led to the lost city of Faar.

"She may be gone," he said softly. "But I guess her job wasn't finished until I got this."

"Hello? Anyone home?"

The bright voice came from the entrance to the apartment. It was a woman's voice. For a moment I thought Spader's mother had returned. Spader did too. He ran for the entrance. Uncle Press and I were right behind.

But when we got there, we saw that it wasn't Spader's mother after all. It was Po Nassi, the agronomer. What was she doing here?

"Here you boys are! Why did you run off like that?" she asked like a scolding but jovial schoolteacher.

"Why aren't you with Yenza and Manoo?" asked Uncle Press.

"Those two are on a futile quest," she answered with a huff. "My time is better spent elsewhere."

This was weird. Had she followed us?

"Now," she said. "Young Spader. Did you find what you came for?"

Spader answered her with a confused look. Uncle Press and I did the same. What was she talking about?

"I didn't think it was possible, myself," she explained. "Like all you wet little Clorans, I thought the lost city of Faar was a myth. That is, until I saw the symbol your father had drawn for you. He was a resourceful Traveler. I'm guessing he discovered the city was real and knew its location. Now I think you know it too."

Uh-oh. Uncle Press stiffened beside me. The hair began to stand up on my neck. I was afraid I knew exactly where this was going and it was a very, very bad place.

"How could you know?" Spader asked, dumbfounded. He had no clue what was going on, but he was about to find out.

Nassi looked to Uncle Press and gave him a catlike grin.

"Ahh, Press. Don't you just love them when they're young?" she asked. "Such . . . innocence."

And then it happened. The agronomer Nassi began to transform before our eyes. Her face contorted, her body shifted, her whole figure grew watery and unformed. It only took about five seconds, but I guarantee they were five seconds that Spader would replay in his mind for the rest of his life. I probably would too, but I had seen it before. Her hair grew long and gray. Her body rose to a solid seven feet tall. Her clothes changed from Cloral blue to the black suit that was all too familiar. And again, what stood out most were the eyes. They became icy blue and charged with an evil fire.

"Does it make more sense to you now, water boy?" snarled the tall, ominous figure.

Spader looked at me with total confusion.

"It's Saint Dane," I said with no emotion. "He's been playing with us all along."

CLORAL

"**Y**ou naughty boys, you sank my battleship," Saint Dane said playfully, as if he really didn't care.

Spader looked to me and to Uncle Press. I think he was in shock. Nothing had prepared him for seeing Saint Dane transform the way he did. I wasn't exactly comfortable with it either, but at least I had seen it before so I didn't go into total mind lock.

"The poison fertilizer?" asked Uncle Press. "Was it your doing?"

Saint Dane let out an evil laugh. Here we go again. I hate it when the bad guys laugh. It always means they know more than you do.

"You give me too much credit, Press, my friend," Saint Dane said. "You know I don't initiate anything."

"But you don't mind helping it along," Uncle Press added.

"Of that, I am guilty. That weasel Manoo and his agronomers would have abandoned their experiments years ago if I hadn't convinced them otherwise. It was so easy to feed their egos. I told them they would be heroes for saving Cloral from starvation for generations to come!" He laughed ironically.

"They were too blinded by visions of glory to realize they were brewing up the means to kill every living soul on the territory. Surprise!"

"So you *did* kill my father," Spader spat at Saint Dane.

"Indirectly, I suppose," Saint Dane said, beginning to sound bored. "But we're all much better off with one less Traveler, don't you think?"

This pushed Spader over the edge. He lunged at Saint Dane, ready to grab his throat. But Saint Dane pulled a quick draw from under his coat and jammed a silver pistol into Spader's chest, stopping him cold. Spader's eyes were wild with hatred, but there was nothing he could do.

"Talk to Pendragon," Saint Dane said calmly. "He knows you can't defeat me."

"No?" I jumped in. "What about Denduron?"

Saint Dane turned to look at me for the first time. His cold blue eyes gave me a chill.

"A minor inconvenience," he said. "This game has only begun, Pendragon."

"Game?" shouted Spader. "You killed hundreds of people. This isn't a game!"

"But of course it is," answered Saint Dane. And with that he began to transform again. His body grew liquid, he shrank slightly, and when the change was complete, standing before us was Zy Roder, the raider pilot.

"This is very much a game," he said with a different, raspier voice. "And the stakes are high indeed!"

At that moment the door flew open from the hallway and several more raiders entered the apartment. They all held silver guns like the one Roder/Saint Dane had. Any thoughts we had about escaping had just gotten very dim.

"Now," said Roder/Saint Dane. "I have a question for you.

Tell me what you know about this place called 'Faar.'"

We all did our best not to look at each other.

"Faar is a children's story," Spader finally answered. "What is it you want to know?"

Roder/Saint Dane jammed his silver gun into Spader's chest, making him wince in pain.

"Please don't waste my time trying to be coy," Roder/Saint Dane said. "I saw the symbol of Faar on your father's desk."

"I knew that he'd been searching for Faar," he continued. "But when I saw the symbol, I knew he'd been successful."

"You were there?" I said, stunned. "On Magorran?"

"To be precise, Po Nassi was there," he chuckled. "Only seconds before you three arrived."

I got the feeling that Saint Dane loved fooling people with his little charades.

I really hated this guy.

He then looked directly into Spader's eyes and said, "Your father discovered Faar and passed the information to you, didn't he?"

Spader didn't move. He wasn't about to give Roder/Saint Dane the two pieces of map. No way. But Roder/Saint Dane flashed forward with his free hand and grabbed Spader around the neck. Both Uncle Press and I made a move to stop him, but the other raiders jumped between us, holding us back.

"Tell me," Roder/Saint Dane seethed. His strength was incredible because he lifted Spader off the ground with only one hand. "Tell me what you know, or I'll first kill Pendragon, then Press, and then I'll go back to Grallion and see what mischief we can get into there. The only one I won't kill is you. You'll have to live knowing they died because you wouldn't tell me what I will find out soon enough anyway."

Spader was turning blue. Both Uncle Press and I struggled

to get away from the raiders, but it was no use. There was nothing we could do to help Spader.

Then, slowly, Spader reached into his pocket for the map.

"Don't!" I shouted. But it was too late. Spader pulled out the two map halves and tossed them on the ground. Instantly Roder/Saint Dane threw him down and Spader collapsed on the floor, gasping for breath. Another raider picked up the two pieces of paper and handed them to Roder/Saint Dane. The evil Traveler held the two pieces together and studied them for a few seconds.

He then let out a smile and said, "It's so simple. Thank you, Spader. Now Cloral has absolutely no hope of fighting off the plague I've nurtured for so long."

Huh? What did a mythical lost city have to do with the killer fertilizer that was spreading across the territory?

Boom! A gunshot sounded from out in the hallway that sent the raiders scrambling for cover. I can't believe I acted as fast as I did, but in the one second of confusion, I lunged forward and grabbed the two pieces of the map from Roder/Saint Dane.

Boom! Boom! Two more gunshots. Though they weren't exactly gunshots. Remember how I described the way the water cannons on the battleship fired compact missiles of water? As it turned out, that's exactly what *all* the guns on Cloral fired. And right now, standing out in the hallway was Wu Yenza and two aquaneers. I wasn't sure how they knew we were in trouble, but I didn't care.

The water bullets they fired hit the walls and exploded, doing more damage than any bullet could.

"Drop your weapons!" shouted Yenza.

While Roder/Saint Dane and the other raiders ducked for cover, Uncle Press grabbed Spader and me and pulled us into the back room. The raiders were too busy defending themselves to come after us.

"Is there another way out?" Uncle Press shouted.

"There's a ledge, all the way around the building," gasped Spader, still trying to get his breath back from nearly being strangled.

"Show us!"

From the other room I heard the booming sounds of more water missiles hitting the walls. One shot blasted right through a wall and into the room we were in, missing me by a foot. These weren't like any water pistols I'd ever played with!

Spader threw open a window and leaped out. Uncle Press pushed me toward the window to go next. I hesitated. I was never good with heights and we were on the fifth floor. Yikes. But there was no other choice. There were more raiders than aquaneers outside. As soon as the bad guys realized that, they'd be coming after us. So I put my fear aside and climbed out the window.

There was a two-foot-wide ledge that went all around the building. Normally two feet would be plenty wide enough to walk on. But when you're five stories in the air, it feels more like two inches. I looked down and started getting dizzy.

"Go!" shouted Uncle Press. "He was already out behind me and pushing me to follow Spader.

Spader was moving quickly ahead of me, approaching the corner of the building. I took two steps and—

Boom! A piece of wall blasted out in front of me, spewing splintered bits of building everywhere. Suddenly I wasn't worried about the height anymore and started to run. More blasts of water missile blew out chunks of building just behind Uncle Press. If we stopped, we'd get blasted off the ledge.

Spader reached the corner and made the turn. I was right

behind him. We were now on the far side of the building from where the battle was taking place. Spader found a window and jumped inside. For a moment I thought we were going to drop in on some unsuspecting guy taking a nap or something, but luckily we found ourselves in a stairwell.

"Go down the stairs!" Spader ordered. But rather than lead us down, he headed back toward the corridor where the fight was going on. Uncle Press grabbed him.

"What are you doing?" he shouted.

"Going after Saint Dane!"

He tried to pull away from Uncle Press, but my uncle held him firm.

"Listen, Spader," Uncle Press said. "You just had a taste of what we've been telling you about. Saint Dane has powers that you are no match for."

"Not to mention the gunfight going on," I added. "You go back there, you're history."

Spader was torn. His blood was boiling and he wanted a piece of Saint Dane—bad.

"We told you before," Uncle Press continued with a calm voice, trying to talk Spader down. "There's a bigger battle to be fought here. You heard what he said about Faar. It could be the last piece in the puzzle for destroying Cloral. Which do you think is more important? Going back in there and getting killed, or doing what your father wanted you to do?"

Spader looked up at my uncle with questioning eyes.

Uncle Press then said, "Let's go find the Lost City of Faar."

Boom! Like an exclamation point on his sentence, a water missile ripped through the door to the corridor. The raiders were coming after us. But Spader was with the program now. He knew what we had to do.

"C'mon!" he yelled, and bolted down the stairs. We all flew down, taking three stairs at a time. I thought I was going to take a tumble and break my neck, which would have been a really stupid thing to do at this point. But speed was everything now, so I kept going.

We blasted out a side door to the apartment building and went on a dead run for the canal and the skimmers. As we rounded the building, I saw that Yenza and the two aquaneers were backing out of the front door, still firing their water guns at the raiders. I really hoped there were no innocent bystanders in the way.

"Yenza!" yelled Uncle Press.

The chief aquaneer looked up and saw that we were out of the building. She immediately gave a command to the other aquaneers. They gave up on the fight and joined the sprint for the skimmers. As we ran across the grass toward the canal, small water bombs kicked up the dirt at our feet. I didn't have to turn around to know the raiders were now out of the building and after us. I could only hope that we were far enough away that their guns wouldn't be accurate enough to do any damage.

We all hit the canal at about the same time and jumped on the skimmers to make our escape. Nobody had to say a word. Uncle Press and I were on one, Spader and Yenza on another, the two aquaneers on a third.

The skimmers all whined to life. We were seconds away from blasting off. Then Spader turned around and actually gave me a smile.

"Last one back to the speeder buys the sniggers." For a second, the old Spader had returned. He gunned the engine and took off. Uncle Press gunned ours, too, and the aquaneers were right behind. With the water around boiling from the incoming rain of water missiles, all three skimmers blasted off and away from the raiders.

The dash back to the dock was hairy, but not because of the raiders. As I wrote before, the canals were busy. But this time nobody cared. With Spader in the lead, we all flew over the water, dodging other skimmers like gates in a ski race. I wondered if there was a Panger City highway patrol that would pull us over for reckless skimming. Luckily, there weren't any accidents, though we had a ton of close calls.

It wasn't until we made it back to the canal near the docks that we could all finally take a breath. Or at least a half breath because this race was only just beginning. We tied up the skimmers and headed for the dock.

"How did you know to follow us?" Uncle Press asked Yenza as we ran.

"It was Nassi," she answered. "I never trusted that woman. As soon as you left to follow Spader, she went after you."

"You saved our lives, Yenza," he said. "Thank you."

Yenza then stopped on the side of the busy street and faced the three of us. The aquaneers stood behind her, ready for anything. Yenza was used to calling all the shots and I didn't think she liked being out of the loop, especially when it meant having to battle raiders. "You were talking to Zy Roder like you knew him. What is going on?"

The three of us exchanged looks. How could we possibly explain any of this to her? It was Uncle Press who took a shot at it.

"Po Nassi was working with Zy Roder," he explained.

Technically, Po Nassi *was* Zy Roder, but Uncle Press made the wise decision not to go down that road. Good thinking.

"She knew exactly what she was doing," he continued.

"She knew the fertilizer was poison. Spader's father was work-ing with me to investigate this horror . . . until he died."

"Po Nassi was deliberately trying to poison Cloral?" she asked in shock. "Why?"

"That's tougher to answer, but it's true. We've got to leave Panger City right away. Where is Manoo?"

"I'm right here!"

The little elf-man hurried to us from the building that led to the docks. He looked all sorts of angry and upset.

"Where have you been?" he demanded.

"Did you get to the Agronomy Society?" Yenza asked, ignoring his question.

"Yes," Manoo answered nervously. "But it's too late!"

"What do you mean?" Yenza demanded.

"The fertilizer," whined Manoo. "It's been sent all over Cloral. Almost every underwater farm is using it right now. Our entire food supply is going to be poisoned! It's a total dis-aster!"

How's *that* for a horrifying news item? Saint Dane's plan had kicked into high gear and Manoo was out of his mind with worry.

Welcome to the party, Manoo and I've been out of my mind for a while now.

"Get back to the Agronomy Society," Uncle Press ordered Manoo. "Make sure they track down and stop every shipment. Can you do that?"

"I suppose," answered Manoo. "But who are you to tell me—"

"Just do it, Manoo!" barked Yenza.

She called to the two aquaneers, "Make sure this man gets back to the Agronomy Society safely."

The aquaneers both offered a crisp salute and stood ready

to go with Manoo. Yenza took Manoo by both arms in a warm gesture of trust and friendship.

"Do what you can, Manoo. Hobey-ho."

Manoo stood up straight as if the entire fate of Cloral were now resting on his shoulders. He was now on a mission, and he took it seriously.

"Let's go!" he shouted to the aquaneers, and the three took off.

Yenza then turned back to Uncle Press and said, "And why must we leave Panger City?"

Uncle Press looked to me and held out his hand. I knew exactly what he wanted and handed him the two pieces of map.

"Ever hear of the Lost City of Faar?"

In minutes we were back on the speeder boat, blasting away from Panger City, bound for, well, the plan was to head for the Lost City of Faar, but at the time it seemed like we were chasing a fairy tale.

When we put the two pieces of the map together, this is what we saw: The horizontal solid line that was a third of the way up from the bottom on the left half of the map continued on to the right half of the map all the way to the far side. The curved line that began at the lower left corner formed a complete semicircle with another curved line on the other half. It was now a wide, upside-down smile beneath the horizontal line. The spray of dots that was above the horizontal line on the left half of the map was also on the right half. Finally, the series of numbers from the left half continued on to the right.

We had no idea what the horizontal line or the semicircle beneath it or all the dots meant, but Spader and Yenza knew what the numbers meant. They were map coordinates that marked a very specific point in the ocean. We now had a location, but it was a long way off from Panger City. Their best guess was that it would take us all night to get there, even with the speeder boat throttled up to the maximum. Spader set the course and locked it into the speeder's automatic pilot to make sure we wouldn't stray. When traveling that long of a distance, even a minor error could have sent us way off course. Unless something bizarro happened, by morning we would be at the exact spot where the map said we would find the Lost City of Faar.

I was excited, but also pretty doubtful. The idea of finding a lost, sunken city seemed pretty far-fetched. But as Loor said, after all we'd seen, nothing was impossible.

I also hoped that Saint Dane had a lousy memory. He had only looked at the map for a few seconds before Yenza and the aquaneers came in with their water-guns blazing. Hopefully he'd forget a number in the coordinates, or switch two, or mess up something else that would send him in the wrong direction. That's what I hoped for, but I didn't think for a second that it would happen. I knew that Saint Dane now had the same information we did. The real question was how quickly he could catch up. It was going to be a race, but a race to what?

It was a beautiful night and the water was so calm that the stars were reflected in the water in front of us. I was standing on the bow looking out on this awesome sight, when I sensed that someone was behind me.

It was Spader.

"Tell me about where you come from," he asked.

"That's a lot of ground to cover," I answered.

"It's called Second Earth. Don't ask me if there's a First Earth or a Third Earth because I don't know. I live in a town called Stony Brook. We have big cities and farms and small towns just like Cloral, the only difference is they don't float on the water. I think something like four-fifths of the planet is covered with water; the rest is dry land."

"So how do you get around if you can't use skimmers and speeders?" he asked.

"Well, we have cars . . . vehicles that can go long distances on land, and big trains that travel on rails. And, oh yeah . . . we can fly."

"What?" he asked in shock. "You can fly?"

I laughed. "Sort of. We have vehicles that fly. Some are small and hold only two people, others are big enough to carry four hundred."

"Hobey, that's magic!" Spader said in awe.

I guess to someone from another territory that didn't have airplanes, the power of flight was pretty amazing. It was almost as amazing as being able to breathe underwater with plastic globes that molded to your head. Every territory was unique in its own way and believe it or not, I was beginning to like the idea that I was going to see more of them.

"And you have a family?" he asked me.

"Yeah. Mom, Dad, and a little sister named Shannon."

We both fell silent for a while. We knew what we were both thinking. What had happened to our families?

"You know something, Pendragon?"

"What?"

"I believe Press," he said with confidence. "We're going to see them again. But not before some amazing adventures come our way."

I had to smile. Maybe he was beginning to accept our fate.

For the rest of the night Spader and Yenza took turns at the controls and keeping watch. We all tried to get some sleep, but

226 ~ PENDRAGON ~

it wasn't easy. We went below to the cabin, where there were some bunks. As excited as I was, I really needed some sleep, and konked out as soon as my head hit the pillow. I planned to sack out for only an hour or two, but as it turns out I slept through the entire night!

What finally woke me up was the sound of the engines slowing. I immediately sat up in the hammock, banged my head on a beam of course, swore to myself, then headed topside.

Uncle Press, Spader, and Yenza were already standing on deck. We must have made some pretty good time because the sun hadn't come up yet. It was still pitch dark and the stars still shone off the water. It was very quiet, especially now that the engines were killed and we weren't moving. I did a complete three-sixty and saw nothing but water.

"Are we here?" I asked.

"Right on the spot," answered Spader.

"It's strange," Yenza said. "According to the charts we're over a huge trench, one of the deepest on Cloral. But my instruments show it to be fairly shallow. I don't understand."

"Could we be in the wrong spot?" I asked.

Spader answered the question. "Not a chance."

I walked up to the bow of the speeder and looked out onto the water. It was so calm that it was tricky to find where the horizon stopped and the water began. Especially since the stars reflected off the water.

The stars. The stars reflected off the water. That's when it hit me.

I ran to the others and shouted, "Give me the map!"

Spader had it. He had glued it together using some kind of, well, glue. I held it up toward the horizon. Then I slowly turned, still holding the map out in front of me until everything lined up and—

"That's it!" I exclaimed.

"What's it?" asked Uncle Press.

"Look," I said, pointing to the map. "The horizontal line represents the horizon. And all these dots above it are—"

"Stars!" shouted Spader. "Hobey-ho, look!"

It was incredible. The dots on the map lined up perfectly with the constellations in the night sky. There was no mistaking it. We were in the right spot.

"Good thing we got here at night," Uncle Press added.

"So then what's this big half circle below the line?" I asked.

I think it hit all four of us at the same time because we all looked at one another cautiously. We knew exactly what that semicircle was supposed to be. If the straight line was the horizon, then anything below it was water. And there was only one thing that was supposed to be below the water in these parts.

"Could it be?" Spader asked in awe.

"I've heard about Faar since I was a girl," said Yenza with reverence. "It's supposed to be the most wonderful place that ever was. It's where Cloral was born. To think that it could be real . . ." She couldn't finish the sentence. The idea was too incredible to her.

"One way or another, we're going to find out," said Uncle Press.

I could tell from his tone of voice that he wanted to treat this as any other expedition. He probably wanted Spader and Yenza to get rid of any childhood fantasies and fears that might get in the way of our solving this mystery.

"Let's all eat something," he said. "Then get ready to dive. As soon as it's light enough to see, we'll have a look at what's down there."

There was a stock of dried fruits and vegetables on board. The thought crossed my mind that these might be poisoned like the rest of the food on Cloral. But since they were dried, they had probably been here for a long time and were safe. So we all sat on deck and ate breakfast. To be honest, it was disgusting. That stuff tasted like shoes. Not that I've ever eaten shoes before, but if I had, I'm sure they would taste like this. But we had to eat something so I pretended like they were Pop-Tarts. Shoe-flavor Pop-Tarts.

Gradually, the sky grew brighter and then the sun began to peek up on the horizon. Soon we were bathed in its warmth and light.

It was time to start our mission. Since this was an aquaneer speeder boat, it was well equipped. There were air globes and spearguns and water sleds. It was decided that Yenza would stay on board while the three of us went sunken city hunting. So Uncle Press, Spader, and I got geared up. We each popped on an air globe and strapped on spearguns.

I didn't have my watch, but I was pretty sure we were past the twenty minutes that you're supposed to wait to go swimming after you eat. I had to laugh to myself. Here I was about to search for a mythological underwater lost city on the other side of the universe, and all I could think about was some old wives' tale my mother told me about getting cramps at a picnic. It was times like this that I really missed her.

"If we see something, we'll surface and let you know," Uncle Press said to Yenza. "But understand one thing. Zy Roder has the same information we do and I guarantee he'll be headed this way. Whatever you do, do not take him on yourself, understand?"

"You're talking to a chief aquaneer, Press," said Yenza with a little bit of an attitude. "I can handle things."

Uncle Press smiled in apology. "Sorry, my bad. Just be careful. Please."

"I'll say the same to you," she said with a little smile.

I was beginning to think that Yenza was developing a "thing" for Uncle Press. Bad idea for her. He wasn't the kind of guy you'd want to start a relationship with. He was on the road a little too much.

"Spader, take the lead," Uncle Press said. "We'll follow on either side of you." He then smiled and said, "Look for a really big city."

"Hobey-ho," said Spader with a laugh.

"Hobey-ho," I echoed.

We all grabbed our water sleds, gave a quick wave to Yenza, and did a giant stride into the water. A few seconds later we were all settled and floating next to each other on the surface.

"Everybody set?" asked Spader.

We were. He dove underwater and Uncle Press and I followed right behind him. We descended in V formation for several feet, then took a look around. Yenza was right. The water wasn't all that deep here. I'm guessing it was maybe sixty feet to the bottom. That isn't very deep at all and certainly no place to hide an entire city. The bottom was fairly barren. For as far as I could see there was nothing but blue-green water and a huge field of low, brown coral. No city. No nothing.

"Let's head this way," said Spader. "It's the way Pendragon lined the map up with the stars."

As we sped along with our water sleds, I saw that this area of the ocean was much less interesting than the ocean bottom around Grallion. There were no plants or kelp fields. There were no farms. There didn't even seem to be any fish. This was the Cloral equivalent of our moon. We traveled for a long way with nothing to see but more nothing. I hated to be the killjoy and say that we should give up, but I was beginning to think we were wasting our time.

I was just about to say something when I saw movement out of the corner of my eye. Quick movement. I looked to my right, but nothing was there. I figured it must have been an eyelash or something . . . until I saw it again. Something moved out there. I saw it a little better this time and thought it was a fish. It made me think back to the big fish that was shadowing Spader and me when we were making our escape from the raiders under Grallion. It was the same kind of thing.

Then I saw it again, and again.

"Did you see that?" I asked.

Spader slowed to a stop and we pulled up.

"What was that?" he asked.

"I saw it too," said Uncle Press.

Phew. I wasn't crazy and hallucinating. But that meant there were strange fish out there who were smart enough to be shadowing us. They were fast, too. And big. Not Moby Dick big, but at least as big as a man.

"There!" shouted Uncle Press.

We all looked to see a green shape moving off to our right. It was far enough away that we couldn't make out exactly what it was, but it was moving a little more slowly than the others so we could at least confirm that it was real.

"I say we follow, mates," said Spader.

"Hobey-ho," answered Uncle Press.

Oh, swell. I really hoped this wasn't a bad idea. We all gunned the water sleds and took off in the direction of this strange green fish. We were at full throttle, but the fish far enough ahead of us that we really couldn't get a good look at it. I felt like it was teasing us and luring us forward. But that was impossible. Fish don't lure people—people lure fish.

"Are you seeing this?" Spader asked.

We all looked ahead to see that the bottom was beginning to fall away. It was getting deeper.

"Stay near the bottom," said Uncle Press. "Don't lose that thing."

I felt the water pressure build around me. At home it wasn't smart to dive any deeper than, say, sixty feet. Going deeper caused all sorts of problems with water pressure and decompression sickness and a nasty thing called "the bends" that you got if you stayed down too deep for too long. But that wasn't a problem on Cloral. I guessed it had something to do with the rebreathing devices in the air globes that kept the right mix of gases in your system. But still, this was deeper than I had ever gone before. It was getting dark, and the bottom kept falling away. We were chasing a big, smart fish into the dark unknown and I was getting scared.

"There's a ridge up ahead," announced Spader.

About thirty yards ahead of us it looked like there was going to be a drop-off. Yenza had said this was the deepest trench on all of Cloral, and I had the feeling we were about to see it. But I was sure this was the end of the line for us. There was no way we were going to go any deeper. We didn't have lights, the water was getting cold, and who knew what was down there?

I also saw that the fish thing we were chasing reached the edge and shot down over the side. I had no plans to follow it.

"Take us to the edge," said Uncle Press. "We'll stop there."

Phew. It was official. The edge was as far as we were going. Uncle Press and I pulled up even with Spader so that the three of us were now traveling shoulder to shoulder. Whatever we were going to see over the edge, we would see it together. A few seconds later we reached the end and looked down into the abyss.

Mark, Courtney, yeah, I'll say it again. What we saw was impossible. It was a vision like I had never encountered in my life and I can't imagine I ever will again. There are unique things in every territory. Some are evil, some are beautiful, and some are just plain spectacular. What we saw fell into the spectacular category. The three of us could only hang in the water and stare in wonder.

"Hobey," said Spader dumbly. "This is a dream, right?"

"If it is," said Uncle Press with the same dumb feeling, "we're all having it."

The bottom fell off into black. We were on the edge of a trench that rivaled the Grand Canyon. As clear as the water was, we couldn't see the bottom or the far side of this trench—its expanse was breathtaking. But what we saw before us made the immense size of the trench seem inconsequential. For what we were seeing was a magical water ballet.

The water below the edge was full of *hundreds* of the same green fish like the one we were just following. But now that we were closer, we saw that they weren't fish at all. They were people. At least I thought they were people. They were certainly people-shaped, but they were covered in a green skin that made them look like they were also part fish. Though they had arms and legs, these looked as much like webbed fins as they did regular old human appendages. Their faces were also covered by the same green skin. I know that sounds gross, but it wasn't.

It was an incredibly graceful sight. They were all twisting and swimming and diving and generally looking as if they were having a great time. It was like watching an amazing aquarium with scores of twirling fish dancing in the water.

Several lights shone up on them from somewhere below. These beams swept back and forth as the fish-people swam in and out of their light. I was totally mesmerized. I felt as if I could watch them forever. It was just plain beautiful.

But then three of these fish-people left the larger group and swam over toward us.

"Uh-oh," I said. "Time to get scared."

"Don't move," commanded Uncle Press.

I didn't, but instantly switched from rapture into near-panic mode. What did these fishies want with us?

Each of the fish-people swam gently up to one of us and motioned for us to follow. Whoa, these things really could think. Maybe they were more "people" than "fish" after all.

"What do we do?" I asked nervously.

"I say we follow," said Uncle Press, already swimming forward.

Gulp. I didn't have time to argue. Spader and I followed. I had no idea what these creatures wanted. Did they expect us to join in their dance? Would it be some kind of insult if we didn't?

I then saw that we weren't joining the main group. These guides were actually leading us deeper into the trench. I had a moment of panic, but Uncle Press said in a calm voice, "It's okay. Just go slow."

Then, below us, something caught my eye. It was the wall of the trench. I first heard a small rumble, and then I saw a crack of light beginning to appear out of the rock face.

"What is that?" asked Spader, his voice cracking with tension. Good. I wasn't the only one who was chicken.

The crack of light grew larger and larger and we soon saw

that it was actually some kind of rock door that was opening up. Then, as if on cue, all of the dancing fish-people gathered together like, well, like a school of fish, and all swam together *into* the light! They dove as a group, sped down, and disappeared into the rock wall.

Our three guides were still with us. They motioned for us to follow, and then they, too, dove down toward the light.

The three of us stayed where we were. Even Uncle Press seemed a little reluctant.

"What do you think?" I asked.

Uncle Press looked down at the three guides who had stopped again and were gently motioning for us to follow. He then looked up to us and said, "I think the Lost City of Faar . . . isn't lost anymore."

CLORAL

If I had only one sentence to describe what it was like to be a Traveler, it would be this: "Just when you think you've seen it all . . . you haven't."

As if fluming from one bizarre territory to another wasn't enough, within each of these territories I kept finding new and different places that had my head swimming—no Cloral analogy intended. I guess I shouldn't be so surprised. It would be the same thing for a first-time Traveler coming to Second Earth. To go from a city like Chicago to the rainforests of South America to a tundra village in Siberia would be just as rattling. Still, what we found under the ocean of Cloral went way beyond my imagination.

As strange and exciting as it was for me, it must have been a hundred times more bizarre for Spader. To him the Lost City of Faar was a fable. Could you imagine walking through the forest and finding a hut where seven dwarves lived with a beautiful princess? Or stumbling upon Noah's Ark? Or finding the Garden of Eden? Every culture has its myths and legends. I can't imagine what it would be like to discover that one of them was true. But that is exactly what Spader experienced when we swam through the rocky entrance to the Lost City of Faar.

I wasn't totally convinced it was a good idea to follow these fish-people into the opening in the wall of rock. So far they hadn't done anything but frolick, like playful sea lions. But still, they could have been luring us to our deaths. Did these strange creatures feed on excited divers who followed them without a question, convinced they were about to discover the truth behind a myth, only to be served up like reverse-sushi? As always, my mind went to the worst possible outcome.

What changed my thinking was something I saw just below the opening. It was partially hidden by a tangle of seaweed, but there was no missing it because it was about five feet across. It was an ancient carving. Some of the detail had been eroded away by time, but there was no mistaking the strange, interlocking letters. Spader saw it too and smiled at me. It was the symbol his father had left for him. It was the symbol of Faar. We were in the right place.

With a glance and a nod to each other to show we were all prepared to go to the next step, the three of us swam together, shoulder to shoulder, into the light that blasted from the large opening.

We found ourselves in an underwater tunnel that was big enough to drive a car through, if you happened to have a car that could drive underwater. We passed by the big lights that were shining out into the open sea. Once past them, my eyes adjusted to the dark and I saw that the tunnel led far back into the rock. Every few feet were small marker-lights that showed the way. That was a relief because I wasn't so sure I would have had the guts to swim into a pitch-dark tunnel. I then heard a loud, scraping sound that made me quickly look back. The rock door was shutting behind us. A loud *crunch* told us the door was locked into place and we were closed in. Gulp. We had to go forward whether we liked it or not.

"Everybody cool?" asked Uncle Press.

"I guess," was my shaky answer.

Spader just floated there with wide eyes.

"Spader, you okay?" Uncle Press asked.

"Just a little nervous," he answered.

Good. I'm glad he said it first. Truth be told, nervous didn't quite cover it for me. My heart was thumping so hard I was surprised the others didn't hear it. Then something touched my shoulder.

"Ahhh!" I screamed, and spun around.

It was one of the fish-people. Man, those guys were quiet. Like snakes. That's why I hate snakes—too quiet. Did I tell you that?

The fish-guy motioned for us to follow and swam into the tunnel. The three of us had no choice but to follow. We swam close together. It felt safer that way. The tunnel was pretty long and not all that interesting. It gave my mind time to wander and I started to think about what this lost city was going to be like. I wondered if it was completely underwater. That would be weird, like living in one of those fish tanks that people decorated with little castles and sunken ships.

So far the fish-people hadn't tried to communicate with us other than with hand signals. I wondered if that meant they couldn't speak. I hoped that a Traveler's ability to understand all languages included sign language.

These questions, and a whole bunch more I hadn't thought of yet, would soon be answered, for I saw that the tunnel was growing brighter.

A few moments later the water level began to drop. We were soon able to raise our heads above the waterline. The farther we traveled, the lower the water got. We went from swimming underwater, to swimming on the surface, to walking along the bottom. That answered my first question. Faar may have been underwater, but it was dry. That was cool. I didn't like the idea of hanging out in a fish tank.

The water got low enough so we felt comfortable taking off our air globes. We were now standing in the tunnel with only a few inches of water lapping at our feet. I looked forward and saw that the tunnel was about to make a right turn. The bright light that came from around the bend up ahead told me that we were soon going to see the Lost City of Faar.

We took off our fins and our spearguns, placing them in a safe pile along with our water sleds.

The fish-man we had been following then walked back to us. Yes, I said walked. On two legs. I had a brief memory of *The Creature from the Black Lagoon,* that goofy old black-and-white horror movie. But if this guy wanted to do us any harm, he would have done it back in the water so I wasn't scared. Much. He reached up to his head and began to peel away the green layer of skin that covered his whole body. It made a wet, sucking sound as he tugged on it. For a second I thought I would puke. If this were some kind of snakelike skin-shedding ritual, I'd rather not have to see it, thank you very much.

But after a few seconds I realized what was really happening. As the light green layer of skin came off, it revealed a guy who was very much human. The green stuff wasn't skin after all; it was some kind of fish suit. It reminded me of those tight suits that speed skaters wore in the Olympics. It was absolutely formfitting. But unlike speed skaters, this suit also gave the swimmer webbed feet and hands. Once the suit was pulled off, I saw that the guy's hands were normal too. No webs, no scales. Underneath the fish suit he wore a blue, also formfitting, suit that went from his neck to almost his knees. It wasn't all that different from the clothes we had on ourselves.

As it turned out, there was nothing unusual about the guy at all. He was short, not much over five feet. But he looked strong. Not a lot of fat on those bones. I couldn't tell for sure how old he was, but I'd guess he was around thirty, in Second Earth years. He was also completely bald. Michael Jordan bald. That wasn't all that weird, but something about his face wasn't quite right. I couldn't figure it out at first, but then it struck me: He didn't have eyebrows. You never think about eyebrows until somebody doesn't have them. It's kind of freaky-looking. Not horrible, just freaky. Adding to the freaky quotient was the fact that his eyes were the lightest color blue I had ever seen. I actually had to look close to see that there was any color in them at all. His skin was also very white, which didn't surprise me since he lived underwater.

In all, he was a fairly normal-looking guy, with a few strange characteristics. But nothing that would give me nightmares or anything. Things were looking up.

The guy finished pulling off his suit—it was all in one piece—and walked up to us. "My name is Kalaloo," he said with a warm smile.

"Are we in . . . ?" Spader asked, a little dumbfounded.

"Faar?" the guy said. "Yes. This is Faar."

We all exchanged quick glances that said, "We made it!"

Uncle Press said, "My name is—"

"Press, yes, I know," said Kalaloo. "And you're Pendragon," he said to me. "And you're Spader. You look like your father."

Whoa! Underwater-guy knew who we were?

"You knew my father?" Spader asked in wonder.

"I was sorry to hear of his death," the guy said with sympathy. "He was a friend."

"Time out," I said. "How do you know us?"

"Spader's father told us there would be others. We have been expecting you for some time, and watching you as well."

"I knew it!" I blurted out. "I saw one of you under Grallion when we were escaping from the raiders!"

"Yes, that was me," he answered. "I wanted to make sure nothing happened to you. I almost failed when you were being pulled into the engine of their ship."

"That was you?" I said in shock.

He smiled and nodded. "It was very close."

"Well, uh, thanks," I said.

"Thanks" didn't cover it.

The guy had saved my life. My head was spinning. It felt like we were three steps behind, again.

"How do you breathe underwater?" I asked. "You don't have gills or anything, do you?"

Kalaloo let out a warm laugh and said, "No, but sometimes I wish we did."

He lifted up the green suit and showed us that built into the fabric was a small, shiny silver mouthpiece.

"This pulls oxygen from the water; it's very efficient."

This looked like a smaller version of the harmonica thing on the back of the air globes.

"I was hoping that Osa would be with you," Kalaloo said. "Will she be joining us soon?"

I looked to Uncle Press, who answered the tough question.

"Osa is dead," he said solemnly.

Kalaloo looked genuinely hurt. "She had a daughter," he said.

"Her name is Loor," I said. "And she's everything her mother wanted her to be."

"I am saddened to hear of Osa's passing," said Kalaloo. "She will be missed."

There was a silent moment of respect for Osa, then Kalaloo said, "We should go. They're waiting for you at The Council Circle."

"Who is?" asked Uncle Press.

"The Council of Faar," he answered. "They are anxious to hear from you."

The three of us exchanged looks. They were waiting for *us*? This was all very strange, but there was no reason not to play along, so we followed Kalaloo toward the light.

As we walked I noticed that the ground was now completely dry. When we rounded the corner of the tunnel we stepped into an area that looked like a locker room—Faar-style. There were several people there, all pulling off their green fish skins. They must have been the swimmers we saw outside. They all had the same look as Kalaloo: light skin, bald, no eyebrows, and bluish eyes. It was kinda freaky, but I was already getting used to them. What should I call them? I wondered. Faarites? Faarmers? Faarbarians? I soon learned to refer to the people there as "Faarians."

They hung their swim skins on hooks and then put on these soft, white tunics that had a little bit of an ancient Roman feel. These gowns pulled down over their heads and went to above their knees. They tied them tightly at the waist with pieces of cloth that varied in color from rich green to deep red. Nobody wore shoes, not even sandals.

As Kalaloo led us past them, many of the people smiled and welcomed us.

I said "hi" back as many times as I could. I wanted to show them that I was cool too. It got to the point where I was walking backward to keep eye contact with them. I kept walking backward until I walked right into Uncle Press.

"Oops, sorry, didn't mean to—" I turned around and froze. The words caught in my throat. That's because I had just gotten my first glimpse of the Lost City of Faar. Or maybe I should call it the Found City of Faar. Maybe I'll just call it Faar. Or maybe I'll just call it . . . phenomenal.

Where should I start? Yet again, I was about to enter an entirely new and amazing place. I had to keep telling myself that according to legend it once existed on the surface. If that were true, then this city would be plenty cool. But when you factor in that we were sitting hundreds of feet below the ocean—well, then it became unbelievable.

As strange as this may sound, I was looking out at a rocky mountain. I know, that's impossible, but that's what it was. The city was built into and around the craggy ledges of a small mountain. The mouth of the tunnel was closer to the top than the bottom so we were actually looking down at most of Faar.

The city had an ancient feel to it. There were no modern buildings, no cars, and no sign of technology anywhere. But there were plenty of birds. Can you believe it? Birds were flying in this underwater cavern!

The buildings had an ancient Greek look with marble staircases that led up to the columned entryways of domed structures. They were perched all over this craggy mountain and ranged in size from huge, impressive monuments like you'd see in Washington, D.C., to small simple stone houses made of whitewashed stucco. I saw many Faarians strolling along gentle pathways that snaked in and around and up and down and everywhere in between. There were beautiful, hanging vines draped over most of the city and several waterfalls cascaded from springs hidden deep in the mountain.

Far below, at the base of the mountain, I saw lush, green

fields. There were some larger buildings down there that didn't seem as elaborate as the ones that dotted the mountain. I made a mental note to ask what they were later.

Remember, we were underwater. A major detail that I've left out is that the whole place was protected by a glittering dome. There was no sky, only a vast dome that allowed filtered light to make this city as bright as day. I now understood what the upside-down smile on Spader's father's map was. It represented the dome that protected Faar.

Kalaloo let us stand there for a while to soak in this wondrous sight. He must have known how amazed we were. Finally he asked Spader, "Is it what you imagined?"

"Hobey," Spader said in awe. "It's like someone reached into my mind and pulled out everything I ever thought about Faar and made this."

"I have to admit," said Uncle Press, "I'm not familiar with the legend."

"Let's walk," said Kalaloo.

He led us along a gently winding path made of soft sand. That was good, since none of us wore shoes.

"I think the myths have grown larger with time," he began. "But I can give you the simple story. In the beginning Faar was the only dry land on Cloral. The myths say that it sank after a cataclysmic event, but that isn't exactly what happened. The simple truth was that the waters of Cloral rose. Luckily it took a very long time to happen. The Council of Faar knew the water was coming and had time to prepare. A giant dome was erected over the center of the city. What you see here was only a small part of Faar. It wasn't possible to save it all. The waters began to rise even as the dome was being constructed. It was a race. By the time Faar was completely sealed and safe, the water was nearly to the top."

I thought back to our swim to get here and realized that while we were skimming across the shallow reef, the city of Faar was down below us, hidden by a skin that looked like coral.

"Why does the dome look like coral from up above?" I asked.

"Because it is," Kalaloo answered. "At first the dome was crystal clear, but over time the coral grew and enveloped it. For the longest time it was kept clear, but eventually the Council of Faar thought it best to allow the coral to hide us. However, we keep the covering thin so that light can find its way through."

We continued to walk through this amazing city. People strolled by us and always gave a friendly wave. They were all pretty mellow. I heard soft music coming from one of the buildings we passed. It sounded like that New Age stuff you hear in the dentist's office that's supposed to calm you down before they drill into your head. Not exactly my taste.

"Why did you decide to hide?" asked Uncle Press.

"Faar was the beginning of life on Cloral. It grew into an advanced civilization that used water for power and created building materials from the silt under the seabed. But people eventually grew restless. Long before the water rose, adventurers built ships and left to explore the rest of our world. They went in search of other dry land, but there was none to be found. Those people lived with many hardships as they struggled to survive on the ocean. Generations passed and because Faar was the only civilized place on all of Cloral, it became a target. The sons of Faar who left in search of adventure now returned as enemies in a desperate search of food. Faar was in danger of being destroyed. So when it was discovered that Faar was going to be swallowed by the sea, it was considered a miracle that gave us our only hope of salvation."

"So when the city sank, you stayed hidden underwater to protect the city from the descendents of people who were born here?" I asked.

"Exactly. The people in the ships above had to create an entirely new world from nothing. Many died to pave the way for the mighty habitats you see today. The fact that they've come as far as they have is due to their undying spirit to survive, and because of the people of Faar."

"What do you mean?" asked Spader.

"From the time the Council of Faar decided that we would remain hidden, it was declared that we would do all we could, secretly, to help those who remained living on the surface of the water. How could we not? They were our brothers. It became the principal goal of all Faarians. The Clorans, which we call the people above, needed all the help they could get to help them. We would secretly tend their underwater farms. We led them to mines which held material for building. We even saved many from drowning as they struggled to build the habitats."

"Just for the record," I interrupted, "you keep saying *we* like you were there. You're not like, ancient, are you?"

Kalaloo laughed and said, "No, not at all. Most of what I am telling you was passed down to me by my ancestors. There are at least two hundred generations separating me from the Faarians who built the dome."

"Okay, cool, just wondering."

"Make no mistake," Kalaloo continued. "If not for the people of Faar, the Clorans would not have survived to become the great society they are today. We are all very proud of this, and still do all we can to help our brothers above."

Uncle Press asked, "What do you know of the trouble that's facing them right now?"

"This brings us to the meeting we must attend at the Council Circle," said Kalaloo. He suddenly became serious.

"We first heard of the problem from Spader's father. It is a very rare occasion that a Cloran stumbles upon Faar, but your father was not a typical Cloran. It was like he had a much greater sense of . . . purpose."

I knew exactly what Kalaloo meant. Spader's father was a Traveler. He totally had a greater sense of purpose.

"And I sense that you three are much the same," he added.

Right again, fish-man.

"What did he tell you?" asked Uncle Press.

"He said he feared a great plague would soon come to Cloral that would endanger every living person."

I shot a look to Uncle Press and Spader. It seemed as though Spader's dad saw Saint Dane's plan coming. The horrible thing was that he became a victim before he could stop it.

"Did he know exactly what was going to happen?" Uncle Press asked.

"He was afraid that something might damage the crops," answered Kalaloo. "From what we have seen, he was right. We are receiving word from all over Cloral that underwater farms are now producing poisonous crops."

"It's the fertilizer," I said. "It makes plants grow faster, but they become poisonous."

"Why did my father come to you?" asked Spader. "Was he trying to warn you?"

"Yes," Kalaloo answered quickly. "But he also came looking for help. Our knowledge of the life cycle is far greater than the Clorans'. He wanted to know if we could do anything to help prevent such a disaster."

Kalaloo fell silent. The big question hung in the air. Was Spader's father right? Could the answer to battling the deadly chain reaction be found right here in Faar?

"Well?" Uncle Press finally asked. "Can you help?"

"Absolutely," answered Kalaloo with a smile.

He pointed down to the bottom of the mountain of Faar and to the large buildings I described before.

"Those buildings contain the life of Cloral," he explained. "For hundreds of generations we have studied every variety of plant that exists here. To put it simply, we know how Cloral works."

"So, what about the poisonous plants?" I asked.

"We have already analyzed samples of the mutated plants. We found that their cell structure was changed and their chemistry corrupted. This new fertilizer created a very complex problem, but we have the means to undo it. Even now we are preparing to send hundreds of Faarians out to the underwater farms of Cloral with a simple chemical compound that will reverse the damage. It is a large task, but we have the means. But the Clorans must stop using the fertilizer."

"That's already happening," said Uncle Press. "They know the damage they've done and they're going to stop."

Kalaloo broke out in a big smile.

"Then you are giving me wonderful news!" he said happily. "Once the Faarians reverse the damage, the crops will be safe again!"

Kalaloo was thrilled that everything was well on the way to being put right.

But we knew differently.

Uncle Press looked worried. So did Spader. An absolute feeling of certainty came over me that made me shiver. I knew what the final act of this conflict was going to be.

These brilliant, ancient people held the key to saving all of Cloral. There was no doubt about what that meant. Saint Dane was going to attack Faar to prevent them from saving the territory.

The people of Faar had been protected for centuries by the waters of Cloral, but they couldn't hide any longer.

Saint Dane knew where they were, and he was coming.

I had no idea if these brave people were capable of defending themselves, but we were going to find out. I'm going to end this journal here, guys, because, whatever is going to happen, I'm sure will happen soon. This journal was written and sent to you from Faar, an amazing city of guardian angels that is hidden hundreds of feet below the waters of Cloral.

Unfortunately, it won't be safe much longer.

END OF JOURNAL #7

☯ SECOND EARTH ☯

Mark finished reading the journal before Courtney and sat down on the floor with his back leaning against his desk. Of course he feared for Bobby and Press and Spader and for the battle that was soon to erupt on Cloral. Actually, he wondered if the battle had already taken place. Was Bobby on Cloral in the past? Or was it the distant future? Or was everything happening at the same time as events here on Second Earth? The whole relative timeline thing was one of the many great mysteries of Bobby's adventures as a Traveler.

It was also tough to read about Bobby's troubles without being able to do anything about them. Not that he had any ideas. And even if he did he wasn't allowed to interfere. Not after what happened on Denduron. His entire job here was to be a librarian for Bobby's journals.

Which was the other thing that was upsetting him. As a keeper of the journals, he was doing a lousy job. He kept glancing at his watch, hoping that Courtney would hurry up and finish and get out of there before Andy Mitchell called back to ask about reading them.

Finally Courtney finished the journal and looked up at Mark.

"Those people can't defend themselves," she said somberly. "From what Bobby described, they're totally peaceful."

Mark stood up and gathered the stray pages together. "Yeah, well, we'll see."

"Aren't you worried?" Courtney asked.

"Of course I'm worried, but what can we do?"

Courtney dropped her head. Mark was right. There was nothing they could possibly do to help.

"It's getting late," he added. "I got stuff to do."

He wanted her out of there because the phone was going to ring any second. She took the hint.

"Right," said Courtney. "The algebra guy."

"Huh?" Mark didn't know what she was talking about. But a second later he remembered his lie and tried to cover.

"Right," he said quickly. "Algebra. Gotta help m-my friend."

There it was again. The stutter. Mark tried not to wince.

"You okay?" she asked curiously. "You're acting all nervous."

"I-I'm just afraid for Bobby.

Mark hated to lie to Courtney, but he didn't know what else to do. Besides, it wasn't a total lie. He *was* afraid for Bobby.

Then the phone rang. Mark shot a look to it as if he wanted it to explode. Courtney caught this look, but didn't react.

"I'm out of here," she said, getting up to leave. "You'll call me when—"

"Soon as the next journal shows up."

Ring. The phone sounded like thunder to Mark.

"See ya," said Courtney, and left Mark alone in his room.

Mark answered the phone before the horrible bell could stab at him anymore. "Hello?"

"Well?" came the dreaded voice from the other end of the line.

"Hang on," Mark said. He glanced out of his window to make

sure Courtney was gone. Moments later he saw her walking down the sidewalk, away from the house. His gut rumbled. He felt like a traitor.

"Let's meet on the Ave," Mark then said into the phone. "That pocket park below Garden Poultry."

"Fifteen minutes," snorted Mitchell.

"Could you make it a little later—"

Click.

"Guess not," said Mark to himself as he put the phone down. He was trapped. He had to bring Journal #6 to Mitchell. Or Mitchell would tell the police about Bobby. There was no way out of this.

So Mark went upstairs to his attic and opened the old desk that was his safe place for keeping Bobby's journals. He took out Journal #6 and replaced it with the one they had just finished reading—Journal #7. He had a brief thought that he should probably just take *all* the journals to Mitchell so he could read them at once and get this torture over with. But he didn't even like carrying around one journal. What if he got hit by a bus? Putting them all together would give him a nervous breakdown.

No, he had to play this out slowly. Hopefully Mitchell would lose interest and just leave him alone. That was his best and only hope. So he slid the drawer closed, made sure it was locked, placed Journal #6 in his backpack and started on his way to Stony Brook Avenue.

It was late Saturday afternoon by the time Mark arrived at "the Ave," as all the kids called it. It was a busy street, full of shops and restaurants and people strolling the sidewalks in search of bargains and their next latte. But it was just past six o'clock, closing time for most stores. The crowds were getting thin.

Mark hurried along the sidewalk, past his favorite shop, a

deli called Garden Poultry. They made the best French fries in history. The smell of hot cooking oil always hovered around the place like a delicious, salty cloud. Normally Mark couldn't resist the temptation and would always go in for a box of fries. (They always came in boxes, like Chinese food.) But not today. Today he had other things on his mind.

He got to the pocket park that was a few doors down from Garden Poultry. They called it a pocket park because it was nothing more than a space between two buildings, like a pocket. At one time there was probably another building there, but Mark couldn't remember seeing one. The town had turned the space into a miniature park with grass, a stone walkway, flowering trees, and several wooden benches where people could eat their boxes of French fries from Garden Poultry.

It was a pretty little place except for one thing: Andy Mitchell was sitting on one of the park benches, waiting for him. Actually, he was sitting on the back of the park bench with his feet on the seat.

"You're late!" shouted Mitchell the instant he saw Mark.

"You didn't give me much time," answered Mark.

"You got the—" He didn't finish his own sentence. Instead he grabbed Mark's knapsack away from him and dug inside to get the journal.

"Take it easy!" scolded Mark. "You gotta treat these with respect."

"Yeah, yeah, whatever."

Mitchell unrolled Journal #6 and began to read. Mark sat down on the bench next to Mitchell's feet, settling himself in for a long wait. He knew Mitchell was about the slowest reader in history.

As with the last journal he read, Mitchell had to ask Mark the meaning of several words. Mark still couldn't believe that a guy could live to the age of fourteen and still not know the meaning of words like "manipulate" and "elaborate." What a loser. It killed Mark to watch Mitchell clutch the valuable pages with his greasy, nicotine-stained fingers like a week-old newspaper. It also turned his stomach every time Mitchell pulled in one of his signature snorts and hawked it out on the sidewalk. Didn't this guy ever hear about Kleenex?

Finally, after what felt like forever, Mitchell was done.

"Jeez," he said with a touch of awe.

Mark's first sarcastic thought was *Could you be any less articulate?* But he wouldn't dare say it for fear of getting pummeled.

"You think this is all really happening?" Mitchell asked.

"I do," was Mark's simple, honest answer. He wanted to be home.

"Did you get the next one yet?"

Mark thought of how to answer this question, but came to the conclusion that it wasn't worth lying. He was tired of lying.

"Yes."

"Well, I don't want to read it," Mitchell said.

Huh? Mark suddenly perked up. Could it be true? Was Mitchell actually losing interest? Maybe reading the journals was too hard for him. Maybe all the big words were taxing that raisin-size brain of his beyond capacity. Or maybe he was getting freaked out by what the journals meant and wanted to pretend like he had never seen them, like the ostrich who sticks his head in the sand. Whatever the reason, it didn't matter so long as Andy Mitchell left Mark alone and never asked to see another journal again.

"I don't want to read it until I see journals one through five. I feel like I'm picking up a story in the middle. I want to know how it all started."

Mark was crushed. The little bit of hope he had that Mitchell would go away, just went away.

"And I want to read 'em all at once," added Mitchell.

"No way!" shouted Mark. "I am not going to bring all the journals out at the same time. I can't let anything happen to them. The best I can do is show you one at a—"

Mitchell tossed the pages of Journal #6 into the air.

"Hey!" shouted Mark in horror as he dove for the pages that scattered across the park.

Mitchell laughed as Mark frantically chased the pages now blowing around in the wind. Finally Mark got them all together and brushed off the bits of dirt.

"You don't get it," said Mitchell. "You only got two choices— do what I tell you, or I go to the police."

This was going from bad to worse to total disaster. Andy Mitchell wasn't going to go away. That much was clear now. He had gotten a taste of Bobby's adventure and he wanted more. All Mark could do now was try to control the situation as best as he could.

"Okay," Mark said. "But I don't care what you say, I'm not taking all those journals out at the same time. The best I can do is have you come over to my house to read them."

The idea of Andy Mitchell setting foot in his house made Mark feel like termites were digging into his flesh. It was a nightmare of untold magnitude. But he couldn't think of any other solution.

Mitchell smiled. "Okay," he said. "I can live with that. When?"

"I don't know," answered Mark. "It's gotta be when my parents are out. I'll let you know."

Mitchell walked over and stuck his nose in Mark's face. Mark could smell his stale cigarette breath and nearly gagged.

"I like this," he chuckled. "We're becoming regular partners."

Mitchell then snorted, wheeled, and walked away. Mark couldn't take it anymore. The snort put him over the edge. He gagged a couple of dry heaves. He then sat down on the park bench and looked at the rumpled pages of Journal #6. *I'm a failure.*

The next week in school Mark did everything in his power to avoid Mitchell. He went to school late because Mitchell knew he usually went early. He went in a different door every time, just to avoid following any patterns. He carried all his books with him so he wouldn't have to go to his locker. He didn't even go close to the Dumpster area behind the school where so many kids went to smoke. That part wasn't so hard; he never went back there anyway—unless of course it was to jump in the garbage and search for a lost page of a journal sent to him by his best friend who was on the other side of the universe. He didn't like remembering that little adventure.

With all of his planning, Mark had actually gotten through an entire week without seeing Andy Mitchell. But the stress was crushing him. His schoolwork was going south, too. Something was going to have to give soon.

On Saturday it did. Mark's parents had both left for the day and he was looking forward to a long morning of cartoons. It was a guilty ritual he was sure most of the kids at school still practiced, but would never admit to. He had just settled down into the couch, ready for anything Bugs Bunny, when the doorbell rang. For a second he considered not answering it, but if it were a Federal Express delivery for his father, then he'd be in trouble. So he went to the door and opened it. It wasn't FedEx.

"I'm getting sick of you ditching me," Andy Mitchell said as he backed Mark into the house. "What is your problem?"

Mark knew exactly what his problem was. It was Mitchell.

"M-My parents have been around all week," stuttered Mark nervously. "There w-wasn't any g-good time."

"Where are they now?" asked Mitchell.

Mark considered telling Mitchell that they were both upstairs, but he realized he couldn't take another week of dodging Mitchell.

"They're out," said Mark.

"Good! Where are the journals?"

"W-Wait in the living room," Mark said. "I'll get them."

There was no way he was going to show Andy Mitchell his secret hiding place in the attic. Having him know the journals were in his house was bad enough. So while Mitchell sat in front of the TV laughing at Pepe Le Pew, (Who laughed at Pepe Le Pew? Nobody thought Pepe Le Pew was funny!), Mark went to get the journals.

He tried to be as quiet as possible so Mitchell wouldn't know where he was going. Mitchell was the kind of guy who was a step away from juvi. Mark wouldn't put it past him to break into the house and steal the journals. But there was no way he would do it if he didn't know where they were. So Mark quietly went up into the attic, opened the desk drawer, took out the four brown scrolls that were Bobby's first journals, and quickly went back downstairs. He got as far as the second-floor hallway near his bedroom when—

"You got a bathroom?" Mark jumped and yelped in surprise. Mitchell was upstairs, in his face.

"Of course we got a bathroom," answered Mark. "Downstairs, near the—"

Mark felt his ring twitch. Oh, no. He couldn't believe it was happening now, in front of Mitchell. Again.

"What's the matter?" asked Mitchell. "You look sick. You gotta use the can too?"

Mark had to think fast. He didn't want Mitchell to see the next journal arrive. The less this creep knew, the better.

"Use the bathroom in my room," Mark ordered. "It's closer."

Mark would sooner drink acid than let Andy Mitchell go into his room, but it was the only thing he could think of quickly.

"Lemme read the journals while I'm sittin' on the can," snorted Mitchell.

Mark didn't need that image. But then he felt his ring move again. It was starting to grow. There wasn't any time so he handed the four precious journals over to Mitchell and pushed him into his room.

"Let me know when you're done," said Mark, and pulled his bedroom door closed.

Mark had pulled it off. Mitchell would be occupied long enough for Bobby's next journal to arrive. Mark ran down the hallway, yanking the ring from his finger. It had already grown to its largest size and was getting hot. Mark ducked into his parents' bedroom so that when the light show started, there would be no chance of Mitchell hearing or seeing anything.

Mark closed his parents' door, placed the ring on the floor, and backed away. Instantly the glowing lights told him the doorway to Cloral was opening up. With a quick tumble of the familiar musical notes and a final, blinding flash, the delivery had been made.

Mark looked at the floor to see the ring had returned to normal and another roll of green paper had been deposited next to it. For a moment the excitement of getting Bobby's next journal made Mark forget about his problems with Mitchell. He knew that the pages on the floor were going to tell them about the battle for the Lost City of Faar. He wanted to grab the pages, pull them open, and start reading right away. But he couldn't do that for two very good reasons. One was that Courtney wasn't here. They never read the journals without each other. He had messed up a lot recently, but that was one thing he wouldn't fail on. The other was that Andy Mitchell was sitting on his toilet, reading the journals from Denduron. The thought made him shiver.

He didn't want to risk going up to the attic to hide the newest journal, so he ditched it under his parents' bed. The journal would be safe there until Mitchell left. Of course, at the speed that Mitchell read, it might take a week to get him out of there. But that was a risk Mark would have to take.

After stashing the journal under the bed, Mark went back to his room to begin the long ordeal of explaining every other word of the first four journals to Mitchell. He opened his bedroom door and saw that the bathroom door was closed. That was good. He didn't want to catch a glimpse of Andy Mitchell sitting there with his pants around his ankles. Gross.

"Do me a favor, Andy," Mark called out. "Finish what you're doing and read the journals out here, okay?"

Mark didn't want to risk getting the journals wet, with water or anything else.

"All right?" Mark called out.

Mitchell didn't answer. Mark went to the bathroom door and knocked.

"You okay in there?" he asked.

Still no answer. Mark began to panic. Could Mitchell have fallen down and hurt himself? Could he have gotten sick? How would he explain any of this? He had no choice, he was going to have to go inside. But then he feared Mitchell was just being Mitchell and choosing not to answer. The last thing he wanted to do was open the door and catch him sitting on the toilet. But still, he had to make sure nothing was wrong. So he opened the door.

"Are you all—"

The bathroom was empty.

"Andy?" Mark called out in confusion. "Mitchell!"

Mark backed out of the bathroom, totally confused. What had happened? He looked around his bedroom, trying to see any tell-tale clue that would explain what was going on.

That's when he saw it. His window was open. With rising panic he ran to it and looked out. The roof of the first-floor porch was just below the window. There were many times when Mark and Bobby used this route as a secret way to get in and out of the house. The roof led to a rose trellis on the far side of the house. Climbing down the trellis was like climbing down a ladder.

Mark went into brain lock. The evidence was all before him. He didn't want to accept it, but he had to.

Andy Mitchell had just stolen Bobby's journals.

CLORAL

It's over.

I guess I don't have to tell you guys that I made it, since I'm writing this journal. I'm back on Grallion now, where I'm feeling safe for the first time in a long time. But the sad truth is that not everybody was as lucky as I was.

As I sit here in my apartment reliving the events of the last few days, I'm feeling a little numb. Maybe this is what they mean when they say somebody is in shock. Everything that happened seems like it was a dream. Maybe that's a good thing. When you feel as horrible as I do, then pretending it was all a dream makes it a little easier to handle.

Many people acted bravely, even in the face of death. I think that's what I'll remember most about the ordeal I've just been through. I have met some special people here on Cloral. I hope they think the same of me.

This is what happened.

Kalaloo led Uncle Press, Spader, and me along a winding path that brought us higher up on the mountain. The path ended at a giant outdoor shelter that was perched on a plateau near the peak. We walked up several marble steps to a large, round platform that had all sorts of tile work on the floor. We're talking intricate stuff here. There were elaborate scenes of people building ships and swimming with schools of colorful fish, and even one scene that showed the dome being built over Faar mountain. I guessed this incredible mosaic showed the history of Faar. I hated to walk on it. It was like walking on art.

Around the perimeter of this platform were massive round columns that supported a giant, marble dome. It felt like we had just arrived on Mount Olympus! Above the stairs that led to the platform, attached to the dome was a large, marble symbol. It was the familiar symbol of Faar that Spader's father had drawn for him.

In the center of the platform was a circle of bleachers that were also made out of marble. People were sitting there, gibbering with animation. I counted twelve in all. Men and women, all wearing the same tunic-looking outfits that everyone else on Faar wore. Of course, they were all bald, too. Even the women. Weird. I figured this was the Council of Faar that was waiting to meet with us. Kalaloo led us into the circle and everyone immediately fell silent. It was kind of creepy. We stood at the dead center, surrounded by all these bald people who looked at us with sour expressions, as if we were strangers intruding on their perfect world. The fact is, we were.

We stood there like dopes, not sure of what to say. Finally Kalaloo took the lead.

"We have news," he announced to the group. "Not all of it is good. These brave voyagers are continuing the work of our good friend Spader, who died so tragically."

He walked behind Spader and put a hand on his shoulder. "In fact," he continued, "this is the son of Spader. We must welcome them all."

The twelve members of the council applauded politely, but they didn't have a whole lot of enthusiasm. It was all so stiff and formal. I really wanted to start screaming, "Wake up, people! Saint Dane is coming to kick your teeth in! Hel-lo! You gotta get ready!" But that wouldn't have been cool.

Uncle Press then brought the council up to speed. He told them of the tragic mistake the Clorans made by creating a fertilizer that turned the underwater crops into deadly poison. He told them how thrilled we were to hear that the good people of Faar had the means to undo the harm and make the crops safe again. I have to admit, he was good. He strode around the circle like a lawyer presenting his case. Nobody could take their eyes off him.

Uncle Press then gave them the bad news. He told them that a raider had discovered the location of Faar, and was probably headed this way to attack them at this very moment.

This caused a big hubbub. *Finally,* the council was showing some life.

"How did this happen?" one woman demanded. "How could a raider learn of Faar?"

Uncle Press didn't back away from the truth.

"I'm afraid he learned of Faar's location at the same time we did," he answered. "The elder Spader had a map to guide us here, and the raider pilot saw it."

Spader dropped his head in shame, but I gave him a shove. He had nothing to feel bad about. He didn't have any choice but to show the map to Saint Dane.

"Trusting the elder Spader was a mistake," shouted one man angrily. "We should never have let him leave!"

This caused another uproar. The crowd was getting hostile. It was true, we were the ones who were bringing the boogeyman to their doorstep. I couldn't blame them for being angry, but I was beginning to like them better when they sat there like boring, bald statues.

"Please!" shouted Uncle Press, trying to restore order. "There is a larger issue here!"

"Larger than the safety of Faar?" yelled a councilwoman.

"Yes!"

The crowd grumbled, but they wanted to hear what Uncle Press had to say.

"The man who is coming to attack Faar is the same man who poisoned the crops," Uncle Press said. "He wants nothing less than the destruction of Cloral. Spader's father realized that. If he didn't come here, you wouldn't have learned about the disaster until it was too late. Now there's a chance to stop it."

"But he brought the shark to our very door!" a man yelled angrily.

"The shark was already at your door!" Uncle Press shot back. "Did you think the people of Faar would be immune? You eat from the underwater farms, don't you? How many of you would already be dead if you hadn't been warned?"

No one said anything because Uncle Press was right. If Spader's father hadn't gone to Faar and sounded the alarm, there would be many more dead than the people of Magorran.

I saw the council members exchange worried glances. Their perfect world was looking a little bit shaky right about now.

"I beg you," said Uncle Press with passion. "You must send out the Faarians to begin the process of saving the farms as soon as possible. That's what this man is coming for. He wants to prevent you from saving Cloral."

"And who will save Faar?" one woman demanded to know. "We are not warriors. Our sole defense has been secrecy. We have no weapons to fight with, no shields to protect us."

Good question. Nobody had a good answer.

Finally someone spoke up. "Maybe there is a way," Spader said to the group. "Right now floating above us is an aquaneer from Grallion. I can swim up in a jiff and tell her the score. It wouldn't take long for her to get back to Grallion, gather a force of aquaneers, and return to stop the raiders. It would be a real natty-do, but I trust my aquaneers against a band of raiders any day!"

"That will never do," said Kalaloo. "You would have to reveal the existence and location of Faar. Think of what we would be giving up in exchange for their protection."

"Think of what you'd be giving up if you don't get any protection," Uncle Press countered.

It was a tough choice. Nobody was quick to offer an opinion. The decision that would be made in the next few moments, no matter what it was, would change the future of Faar and of Cloral forever.

That's when an elderly man who had been quiet up until now, stood up. This must have been out of the ordinary, because every one of the council members seemed to snap to attention. It was clear that this guy had their respect. I got the feeling that he didn't speak much, but when he did, the others listened. In other words, he was the *man*. He spoke slowly and with a soft rasp.

"We have been preparing for this day since the waters closed over our city," he began. "No one, not even the builders of the dome, expected us to hide until the end of time. Cloral is a changed world. Mostly, for the better. I believe it is time for us to rejoin it."

This caused some quiet murmuring among the council members. Finally a woman stood and said, "Are you suggesting we transpire?"

I'm not sure what "transpire" meant, but the woman said it with such horror that I'm guessing it was a pretty dramatic thing.

"No," the elderly man answered. "Nothing that drastic. I am suggesting we move slowly and reintroduce ourselves to our brothers above."

"Can I remind you?" interrupted Uncle Press. "We have to move quickly to save the underwater farms. If we don't you may not have any brothers left up there to reintroduce yourselves to."

The council members shared troubled looks. They were about to make the most important decision in the history of this city since they discovered the waters were going to rise up and swallow them. It was pretty intense.

I finally got the guts up to say something.

"You've been helping the Clorans forever," I said, trying not to let my voice shake. "Maybe it's time you let them help *you*."

The elderly man locked eyes with me. He may have been old and frail, but those fierce eyes told me he was a force that shouldn't be taken lightly.

"What is your name?" he asked me.

"Pendragon."

He seemed to be sizing me up, and it was giving me the creeps. I suddenly wished I had kept my mouth shut. But then he gave me a small smile.

"Much has been said before this council today, all of it well-intentioned. But the words of the youngest ring the clearest."

He then turned to the council and continued with conviction. "It is time to accept help from those we have helped for so long. All in agreement with sending young Spader to return with his aquaneers, say 'ho.'"

The responses didn't come all at once. Nobody wanted to go first. But eventually each council member responded with a "ho," and with every response, they became louder and more assured.

"All against, say 'no.'"

There wasn't a single "no" to be heard. The elderly man then turned to us and said, "We have set a new course. Young Spader, please go now. We must act swiftly."

Spader looked to Uncle Press and me. His eyes were alive with excitement. He was born for this moment.

"Will Yenza do this?" Uncle Press asked him quietly.

"You know that answer," Spader said with absolute conviction.

"Then what are you still doing here?" Uncle Press said with a smile.

"Hobey-ho!" I said, and gave him a reassuring clap on the shoulder.

"Don't start the do without me, mates!" he said, then turned and bounded off the platform.

I could only hope that he got to Yenza fast, and that her help wouldn't be too little, too late.

"Now," said the elderly man. "There is the matter of the underwater farms. Kalaloo, are we prepared?"

"I believe so," he answered. "The crafts are being loaded."

"Then off you go," the man commanded.

Kalaloo said to us, "Come. You'll want to see this."

We definitely wanted to see how the Faarians were going to save the underwater farms. It seemed pretty impossible to me, but as I've learned, nothing is impossible.

After a respectful bow to the council members, we started off the platform.

"Pendragon!" called the elderly man.

I stopped and turned back to him.

"This fellow who wants to harm us . . . should we truly fear him?"

Now *there* was a question. What he was really asking me was if Saint Dane were capable of destroying Faar. I had to answer this question as truthfully as possible. I didn't want the council to second-guess their decision. I held the old man's gaze so he knew how serious I was.

"I could just say yes," I began. "But the absolute truth is that he is evil beyond your imagination. You can't back down from him. The biggest mistake you could make would be to not fear him enough."

The old man nodded in understanding. He looked tired. He raised his hand to me in thanks and to tell me to get going.

Kalaloo hurried us off the council platform, along a different path down the mountain and into a tunnel that brought us into Faar's mountain. We walked along a narrow hallway that brought us deep inside the city. I was amazed to see wonderful works of art hanging on the walls. Most were posed portraits of stern-looking men and women. I figured they were past council members, but didn't bother to ask. We had more important things to do than study art history.

"We must go to the base of the mountain," explained Kalaloo. "That is the staging area."

"It's a long way down," said Uncle Press.

"Not the way we're going," answered Kalaloo.

We arrived at a big tube. It came down through the ceiling and disappeared into the floor. There was a door in the tube right in front of us, and I imagined there were more doors if you walked around. Kalaloo led us through the door into a small room that was no bigger than an elevator. As it turned out, that's exactly what it was. The big tube held four elevators.

Kalaloo grabbed a lever on the side of the room and pushed it forward. I heard a *whoosh* of air, and a moment later we were on our way down. We were hauling, too. There wasn't any door on this thing and seeing the floors fly by made it seem even faster. I held on to the side of the car nervously. Kalaloo laughed.

"Do not worry, Pendragon. You are floating on a cushion of air. That is how we power so much of Faar, with air that is compressed through channels built into the mountain."

That was cool. But until we were on firm ground again, I had to hope this aerovator wouldn't spring a leak. We descended so fast my ears popped. Kalaloo then eased up on the throttle and we began to slow. A moment later we gently touched down.

"Like floating on a cloud," I said, trying to sound casual, but my voice cracked.

Uncle Press laughed. He knew I was freaked out.

Kalaloo led us out through another long corridor that soon brought us back into daylight. As soon as we stepped outside I looked up to see that we were at the base of Faar's mountain. It was a pretty majestic sight, this mountain city with the glittering dome covering it.

We hurried along a pathway that led to the large buildings I described to you before. We passed many other Faarians along the way. I couldn't help but notice that the people down here were moving a little more quickly. Where everyone else was kind of strolling around, enjoying the weird music, these guys down here had jobs to do.

"The mutated crops may be deadly," Kalaloo explained, "but the cellular change that occurred was a fairly simple one. We have prepared a chemical compound that when spread over the living plants will quickly reverse the process."

That sounded good, but we weren't talking about sprinkling plant food on a rose bush. We were talking about thousands upon thousands of acres of farmland. I didn't care how advanced these guys were, that was a big job.

"How can you possibly spread the chemical over such a vast area?" Uncle Press asked. Great minds think alike. He didn't believe it was possible either.

"That is the easy part," answered Kalaloo with a proud smile.

We were now at the door to the large building. Unlike the ancient, marble structures farther up on Faar's mountain, this building seemed a bit more modern. It reminded me of a big airplane hangar.

When we stepped inside, I saw that my first impression wasn't far off. It wasn't an airplane hangar, but it could have been. The space inside was vast. The ceiling was high and there were no walls or partitions to divide up the space. It was just one big garagelike room. But the building itself wasn't the impressive part. What my eye first went to was every science fiction geek's fantasy. Since I thought it was pretty cool, maybe that means I'm a science fiction geek too.

Lined up in front of us side by side was a fleet of small submarines. I counted twenty in all. My first thought was that they looked like those helicopters where the pilots sit in big, clear bubbles. They were about the same size and the fronts had similar-looking bubbles. Inside one bubble, I saw seats for two pilots, surrounded by the vehicle's controls. Attached in front was a long mechanical arm that I guessed must be used for grabbing things, kind of like what they have on the space shuttle. Behind the bubble the body of the submarine was light green, which I figured made it tough to see underwater.

Each sub floated in its own individual pen. I looked below

the waterline and saw two large cylinders attached to the bottom of the sub that could only be the engines. Each sub pen had its own big door that I was sure would open when it came time to launch.

The place was pretty busy. Faarians were swarming over the submarines, preparing them for their mission. It looked like they were being fueled up because many of the vehicles had thick hoses attached to the back. These hoses came down from giant bins that were up near the ceiling. But I knew they didn't need fueling, since they used water for power. I wondered what these snaky tubes were for, but waited for Kalaloo to explain. In all, it was a pretty impressive operation.

"We call them haulers," Kalaloo said proudly. "They may not look like it, but at full speed they move so quickly they are nearly impossible to see."

If that were true, then "haulers" was the perfect name because it sounded like they could really haul.

Kalaloo motioned for me to get inside one of the subs. I thought that was cool. The bubble had a door on top that was open, so I slipped down into the pilot's seat. I felt like I was at the controls of a jet fighter, especially since the main control was a stick near my right hand, just like a jet.

"One pilot drives the hauler," he continued. "The other navigates, controls the arm, and delivers the cargo."

"Cargo?" asked Uncle Press.

Kalaloo pointed to the tube that ran from the bins in the ceiling down to the haulers.

"That is the main purpose of the haulers. We have used them to secretly tend Cloral's underwater farms for generations. The back is a cargo area where we carry seed, or fertilizer, or minerals, or anything else that is needed. Right now we are loading the chemical that will save the mutated crops."

Now it made sense. The hoses weren't loading fuel, they were filling up on the chemical that would save the farms. These haulers were like underwater crop dusters.

"How far can they travel?" asked Uncle Press.

"With these twenty vehicles, we can cover all of Cloral," answered Kalaloo.

That was pretty impressive. These guys knew exactly what they were doing. I was beginning to think they were going to pull this off. If their counteracting chemical actually worked, and I had to believe it would, then they were going to bring Cloral back from the brink of disaster. I couldn't wait to see these haulers pulling out of their pens and getting on their way.

"When will you be ready to launch?" asked Uncle Press.

"Soon. They are nearly loaded and final repairs are—"

"Press!"

We all looked up to see Spader running toward us. Uh-oh. He was supposed to be on his way to Grallion with Yenza. What was he doing back here? He ran up to us all out of breath and wild-eyed.

"She's gone," he said, gulping for air.

"What do you mean gone?" asked Uncle Press calmly. "Is Yenza headed back to Grallion?"

"No. I mean she wasn't there when I surfaced. Something's happened to her."

This was bad. My mind already jumped to the worst possible conclusion. Could Saint Dane have gotten to her? She was tough, but she had been alone up there. She would have been no match for a team of armed raiders. I pulled myself out of the hauler and jumped down between Uncle Press and Spader.

"Do you think Saint Dane got to her?" I asked.

A second later I had my answer, but it didn't come from

Uncle Press. There was a low, far-off rumble. It sounded like an explosion. We all exchanged looks, then Uncle Press turned to Kalaloo.

"Get the haulers out *now*!" he shouted.

Kalaloo turned to his team and started barking orders. "Don't load them all! We have to launch!"

Uncle Press ran for the door. We followed right behind him. The three of us blasted outside just as two more explosions sounded. They were coming from outside the dome. They sounded close, too.

Several Faarians stood still, looking around in confusion. They had never experienced anything like this before. As I looked at their faces, my heart went out to them because I knew it was only going to get worse from here.

"He's here, isn't he?" I asked.

"I'm afraid the party just started," said Uncle Press.

CLORAL

The booming explosions were coming closer. There were more of them now, and it was getting scary. The ground began to shake under our feet with each new blast.

"What is Saint Dane doing?" I asked nervously. "Does he have some kind of depth charges or bombs or something?"

Uncle Press said to Spader, "Did you see anything on the surface? Any ships?"

"No, mate," Spader answered quickly. "Nothing!"

More explosions followed. Saint Dane was trying to rip Faar apart.

"Bobby," Uncle Press said. "The Faarians have to get out now."

"Excuse me?" I said, not sure if I believed what I was hearing.

"They've got to get out of Faar. If they stay here, they could die."

"But . . . where are they going to go?" I asked. "There's nothing but water out there."

"You've seen them in the water, you think they'll have any trouble?"

He was right. These Faarians were part fish.

"They've got a better chance out in the water," he added. "If they stay here, they're targets."

"Why are you telling me this?" I asked.

"Go back to the council. Convince them to . . . to . . ." He was having trouble finding the words.

"To abandon ship?" I finished the thought for him.

"Yes, abandon ship," he said sadly. "Spader and I will do what we can to help them launch the haulers."

This was getting intense. He wanted me to tell these people to leave Faar . . . to leave their home. It was a city that for centuries had battled back everything that man and nature had to throw at it. But now they were being threatened by something far more dangerous than people desperate for food, or rising floodwaters. They were now being attacked by pure evil. Even as we stood there, the explosions were getting louder. Uncle Press was right. The Faarians had to get out.

I started to run off but—

"Bobby!" Uncle Press called. "Get your air globe first."

At first I wasn't sure why he was telling me this. About a second later, it hit me. We were stuck in here just like the Faarians. If we had to abandon ship, we didn't have any of those spiffy fish suits with the built-in breathers. We needed our air globes if we wanted to survive . . . and we definitely wanted to survive.

"What about you guys?" I asked.

"We'll do what we can down here then meet you up at the tunnel we entered through. Understand?"

I nodded.

Spader gave me a nervous smile. "We're in a tum-tigger now, Pendragon."

"Yeah. Let's not stay long, all right?"

The two of them headed back for the hauler hangar as I ran for the tunnel that led to the aerovator. Using this elevator didn't thrill me. I always thought you weren't supposed to take an elevator if there was an emergency like a fire or an earthquake. Being attacked by raiders probably qualified as an emergency, but I didn't have time to run all the way up the mountain's paths. I'd probably get lost anyway. So I had to take my chances on the elevator.

I had to circle the big elevator tube until I found a car. When I jumped inside, I realized I wasn't sure of how it worked. I only saw Kalaloo do it once. I grabbed the handle, pulled it toward me and—whoa! I rocketed off the ground so fast my knees buckled. I nearly got knocked to the floor from the force! I was afraid this aerovator was going to launch off the mountain like a missile, so I quickly backed off on the handle and slowed down. Whew!

The next challenge was to figure out which floor to stop on. I first had to get my air globe, then climb back up to the Council Circle.

After rising up for a few minutes, I took a wild guess and stopped the elevator on one of the floors. When I ran out, I passed a lot of Faarians who looked stunned. There were women gathering their kids together and pressing against the rock walls of the mountain. A few people ran past, pulling on their green swimskins. I guess they figured out for themselves that it would be safer outside in the water. But mostly people just stood around, looking confused, and scared. I thought about screaming, "Get out! Get out! Abandon the city!" but figured they'd think I was a nut job. No, if there was going to be an official evacuation order given, it would have to come from the council.

When I got out of the corridor into the open air, I saw that

I was only one level below the rocky entrance to the tunnel we had used. I had made a great guess! So I sprinted up the winding pathway toward the entrance.

That's when another huge explosion hit Faar. This was the closest yet, and it nearly knocked me off my feet. A few Faarians screamed. They had never experienced anything like this before. Hey, neither had I, but at least I knew where it was coming from, sort of. I'm not sure which was worse, being clueless, or knowing that someone totally evil was out there who wanted to destroy Faar.

Back in the submarine hangar, Uncle Press and Spader were doing all they could to help Kalaloo and the Faarians launch the haulers. Obviously I wasn't there to see what I'm about to write. It was explained to me afterward.

The Faarian submariners scrambled into their ships. They all pulled on their green swimskins and lowered themselves into the clear cockpit domes. There were two submariners in each hauler. The whole time explosions rocked the hangar, but they couldn't speed up the process for fear of damaging a hauler.

Finally the first hauler was ready for launching. The airlock door opened behind it and the small craft eased out. Once the hauler was beyond the door, the outer compartment flooded and the ship floated free.

The first hauler was on its way to save the underwater farms of Cloral.

As I ran for the tunnel where we left our gear, the explosions started coming faster. It was like Saint Dane had found his target and was zeroing in. I had no idea what his weapon was, but it was pretty powerful. I could only hope that the

Faarians had built this place tough so it could withstand the attack.

I found our gear right where we had left it and grabbed my air globe. For a second I thought I should bring the other two down to Uncle Press and to Spader, but that wasn't my mission. I had to get to the Council Circle and convince them to abandon Faar. That was the plan; I had to stick to it.

I ran back through the tunnel and made my way out into the light. I quickly debated about the best way to get up to the Council Circle. Should I take the aerovator or just run? Since the aerovator scared me and I had already traveled the paths to the platform once before, I decided to run. It wasn't easy though. Every time an explosion rocked the place, I was nearly knocked off my feet. Once I almost stumbled off the path and would have fallen down the steep, craggy mountain if a Faarian hadn't grabbed me. He saved my life. But I didn't stop to give him more than a quick "thanks." I had to get to the council.

I retraced the route we took before and was soon running up the marble steps that led to the fancy platform and the Council of Faar. I didn't know what I'd find there. For all I knew these people had already left. But when I got to the top of the steps, I saw that they were all still sitting on the round bleachers. They seemed to be in heated debate. I didn't want to step into the middle of it, but I had to. I had to somehow convince these people that the best thing they could do was announce to all of Faar that it was time to leave.

Down in the submarine hangar, the second hauler was ready for launching. The cargo hold was loaded with the precious chemical and the submariners were at the controls, ready to go. Slowly the door at the rear of their pen began to rise. In a few moments the second hauler would be out and on its way The other eighteen haulers wouldn't be far behind. Things were looking good . . .

. . . and then there was an explosion. A big one. It was a direct hit to the air lock behind the hauler that was on its way out. A wave of water blasted in that rocked the hauler forward. The submariners were bounced around like they were in a washing machine. Worse, the half-open door to the sea stopped moving. Several Faarians desperately tried to work the controls to get it moving again, but it was no use. The door was jammed.

Then they discovered something even more ominous. The explosion had done more harm than they first realized. The Faarians discovered that *none* of the doors behind the haulers would open! This last explosion had done some major damage. If they couldn't repair it, then the rest of the haulers would be stuck in their pens, unable to be launched.

While the Faarians frantically tried to repair the damaged controls, Uncle Press told Spader to get out of there and bring back their air globes. Spader refused. He didn't want to leave Uncle Press. But Uncle Press insisted. He reminded Spader that the Faarians had breathers in their suits. If they had to abandon Faar, they would be fine. But as for he and Spader, the Travelers wouldn't be doing much more traveling.

Spader got the point. He didn't want to leave, especially when things were looking the bleakest, but he knew he had to go. So, reluctantly he left the hauler hangar and started up toward the tunnel where the last two air globes were waiting.

At the Council Circle I approached the bleachers and heard some of the arguments that were being made.

"We must protect Faar at all costs!" one woman yelled.

"Cloral cannot afford to lose our knowledge and support."

"It was a breakdown in security," another man jumped in. "We should never again allow an outsider to enter Faar."

Another woman yelled at this man, "Wake up! The secret is out. They know we're here."

"We can recover from this," another argued. "We can lock down. We are impenetrable!"

They were arguing in all different directions and getting nowhere. More important, they were missing the big point. Faar was in mortal danger now. I was about to step into the circle, when I felt a hand on my shoulder. I turned quickly and saw that it was the old man who everyone listened to before.

"What is happening below?" he asked.

"They're starting to launch the haulers," I answered.

"This . . . demon who is attacking Faar," he continued. "What is his goal?"

"That's a tough one to answer," I said truthfully. "But right now, he wants to send Cloral into chaos. That's why he poisoned the crops. The only thing stopping his plan from working is Faar."

"What kind of person would destroy a city so that he can destroy an entire world?" he asked with pain.

"You said it yourself. He's a demon. And he's capable of a lot worse, trust me."

The old man closed his eyes. I guessed he was processing the information. He seemed hurt by the fact that such hatred and evil could exist. For all of his wisdom, the evil that Saint Dane brought to his doorstep was beyond anything he could imagine.

"This is going to sound horrible," I continued, "but you have to abandon Faar."

His eyes snapped open and he shot a look at me like I had just slapped him across the face.

"I don't think he's going to stop until this place is rubble," I added.

"This is our home," he said defiantly. "It is the home of our ancestors. We will not leave our home."

I knew exactly what it was like to be asked to leave home, but I didn't want to go down that road with him.

"I know, it's a horrible thing," I said, trying to sound reasonable. "But if your people stay here, they might die."

"And what if this attack is unsuccessful?" he asked.

"Then they come back," I answered quickly. "Simple as that."

Two more explosions rocked the dome. The old man lost his balance, but I grabbed his arm and held him up before he could spill. The council members fell silent. That last jolt was pretty hairy.

"I don't think there's much time," I said.

The old man looked at me. I saw the pain in his eyes. He had made his decision. He stood tall and walked back into the council meeting. All eyes were on him. No one said a word. He walked directly to the center of the circle and addressed the crowd.

"It is time to act," he said.

He then knelt down to the floor and lifted up a piece of tile. He reached into the space that the tile had covered, and he must have turned a switch or pushed a button or something because the floor began to move. A two-foot-round section of floor rose up and up and up until it became a podium in front of the old man.

The council members watched in awe. Some whispered to each other, but most just stared. I had no idea what was going on.

The podium looked like some kind of control panel. There were four chunks of crystal on top that were about the size of baseballs. One was clear, another green, a third yellow, and the fourth was reddish.

"We have been prepared for such a disaster," the old man announced to the council. "We must not ignore the inevitable."

"No!" a man shouted. "You cannot transpire!"

There was that word again. What was transpire? It sounded like some kind of last resort.

"We will not transpire, at least not yet," the old man responded. "Faar is strong. We may still withstand this attack. But I am ordering the evacuation."

With that, the old man put the palm of his hand over the yellow crystal, and pushed it down. Immediately, it began to glow yellow, and an alarm sounded. At least I think it was an alarm. It was a loud horn sound that I guarantee was heard everywhere on Faar. From what I could tell, this was a signal. It was telling everyone that it was time to abandon Faar.

The council members hung their heads in defeat.

"Go," said the old man with compassion. "Join your families. Be sure they get out. If you hear the safe command, then return. But if you do not, my love is with you all."

Slowly the council members started to file off the bleachers.

One woman called out to the old man, "Come with us. My family will care for you."

The old man just shook his head. "My place is here," he said. "There is still the chance we may need to transpire."

The old guy was going to stay at his post, no matter what. It felt kind of like the sad resolve of a captain going down with his ship. Moments later the council had left the platform and the old man and I were alone.

"What's your name?" I asked him.

"I am Abador," he said proudly. "Senior to the Council of Faar." The guy shuffled over to the bleachers and sat down. He looked tired.

"What is this transpire thing you keep talking about?" I asked.

The old man looked at me with a sly smile. "You have learned much about our world here, Pendragon," he said. "But there are some secrets that are best kept that way. I will tell you this much: The grand city of Faar is a wonderful miracle. Since we were hidden below the sea, we were never attacked by enemies, we never sought to expand our land, we never wanted more than to better ourselves and be the guardians of Cloral. I truly believe this was possible because we were hidden. We did not face the same difficulties or temptations that control the lives of so many above."

He took a deep, tired breath and continued, "There have been preparations. We knew the day would come when our existence would be revealed. It was inevitable. Now that the day is here, I face a dilemma. Should we reveal ourselves fully and become part of Cloral once again? Should we allow this perfect world to be infiltrated and corrupted by the petty concerns of the Clorans? Or is it better to cherish what we once had and not allow the dream to be corrupted?"

"I'm not sure I get the problem," I said. "You're saying you've got a choice between joining the rest of Cloral or being destroyed?"

"That puts it simply," he answered.

"Then if you're asking me, I say it's a no-brainer. You may think the people of Cloral are these horrible boneheads who aren't as advanced as you guys, but from what I've seen it's a great place. People live in peace. They work hard, they have fun, they respect one another, and compared to where I come from, they pretty much have it all figured out."

A few distant booming explosions erupted. Abador looked up.

"And what of this . . . attack?" he asked. "Is this what we have to look forward to?"

"No," I said as strongly as I could. "This is a different enemy. This attack isn't just about destroying Faar. It's about destroying the Cloral I just described to you. And if you call yourselves guardians then you won't roll over and let it happen. Look at it this way, if you give up now, then you've failed all those generations of Faarians who helped Cloral become the place it is."

Abador looked right into my eyes with that same powerful stare that I had seen before. I hoped I hadn't pushed the guy too far. But I felt strongly about what I had said. Here he was thinking Faar was such a special place that he wouldn't want to become part of Cloral. But I didn't think he truly appreciated what a great place the rest of Cloral was. And now that Cloral was in deep trouble, it wasn't time for the Faarians to give up. I didn't know what this transpire thing was, but it sounded to me like it was a self-destruct plan. It sounded like he wanted to destroy Faar rather than let it become part of Cloral. That was dead wrong.

"You must go," Abador said. "I will think about what you have said."

"So . . . you're not going to transpire or anything dumb like that, right?"

Abador glanced over at the control podium with the four crystals. The yellow alarm crystal was still glowing. He chuckled and looked back to me.

"You are very wise for someone so young," he said. "But

do not make the mistake of thinking you know all there is to know."

What did that mean? Before I had the chance to ask him, another explosion hit that made all the others seem like minor fireworks. It was deep, it was loud, and it knocked me off my feet. The marble bleachers shifted and Abador was thrown to the platform as well. I got up and helped the old man to his feet, but he pulled away from me and shouted, "Go! Now!"

"You can't stay here! Let me take you out."

"Pendragon, my place is here," he said with absolute authority. "If the worst comes to pass, and Faar is in danger of being destroyed, I must be here to transpire."

He glanced back at the podium. I now understood, sort of. That podium was the last resort. He said how they had planned for this day, and if all else failed, he needed to be at those controls. I still feared what "transpire" would do, but if this was his destiny, it wasn't my place to challenge him. No, I had said all I could and now it was time to go.

"Good luck, Abador," I said. "I know you'll do the right thing."

"Thank you, Pendragon. You have helped an old man see things more clearly."

There was nothing else to say, so I turned and ran off the platform. When I got to the edge I looked down on Faar and saw what the alarm had set in motion. Hundreds of Faarians were streaming along the paths, flowing out of the mountain like ants from their hill. They were all pulling on their green swimskins, ready to hit the ocean. There were men and women of all ages. Many helped the elderly and the very young to pull on their skins. There was no panic; there were no fights. I wondered if they had practiced this before, like a fire drill.

They were going to get out in an orderly manner, and that was good.

Then something happened that wasn't good. It was a very small thing that didn't mean much to me at first. But a few seconds later the horrible reality hit me like a shot to the gut. It was something that I felt on my arm. It was a little tickle that I scratched without giving it a second thought at first. But then I lifted my arm up and saw it for what it really was, and my heart sank.

It was a drop of water. Nothing more, just a single drop of water. But then, another drop fell on my arm. Just a drop. No biggie, right? Wrong. I slowly looked up and realized with horror that this single, innocent drop of water came from the dome overhead. That could mean only one thing.

The dome that had protected Faar for hundreds of generations was starting to crack.

CLORAL

As I stood on the steps of the council platform I looked up at the glittering dome that had kept the oceans of Cloral away from Faar for hundreds of generations. What I saw looked like rain. The droplets glistened in the light as they fell. Believe it or not it looked beautiful, like thousands of small, glittering diamonds falling from the sky.

But these beautiful gems brought some seriously bad news. If the dome were cracked and letting in water, where would it stop? Could the pounding that Saint Dane was delivering weaken the dome? If that was the case, then the pressure from the millions upon millions of pounds of water might eventually crack it—like an eggshell. That image was too horrifying to even imagine. I could only hope that the alarm was sounded early enough so that Faar would be evacuated.

And the explosions continued. Saint Dane's attack was relentless. The entire mountain shuddered with each new blast. I couldn't imagine what kind of weapon he had that could destroy something that had been rock solid for centuries.

Then I thought of Spader and Uncle Press. I didn't yet know of the disaster that had happened in the hauler hangar. The only thing I could do was stick to the plan. So I ran for the tunnel that would lead us out of Faar and to my rendezvous with Uncle Press and Spader.

It was getting treacherous. Enough water was now falling from the dome that the pathways were getting slippery. Since many of these paths were right on the edge of humongous cliffs, I had to be careful or a simple slip would mean *splat*. So I moved quickly, but carefully. Soon I joined the flow of Faarians headed for the tunnel, and safety. It was still orderly, but people kept looking up at the falling water and I could tell they were on the edge of panic. Still, they held it together and kept moving toward the tunnel.

Then, just as I was about to enter the tunnel, I saw something that totally lifted my spirits.

"Hey!" I yelled.

Spader was coming out of the tunnel, carrying the other two air globes. It was a struggle for him because he was working against the tide of people flowing in the other direction. I stepped to the side of the path, out of the stream, and waited for him. When he finally got to me, he was all out of breath and excited.

"Where's Uncle Press?" I asked.

"It's a tum-tigger down there, Pendragon," he blurted out. "They launched one hauler and then there was an explosion. They can't open the doors to launch the rest."

Oh, yeah, things were getting worse. Faar was on the verge of collapse, and the haulers weren't on their way. Saint Dane was winning.

"Press is still down there," he said. "I think we've got to get him out."

We both looked up at the dome. The water was coming down harder now. Whatever cracks were made by the explosions were getting bigger.

"Let's go get him," I said, and we both ran along the path back into the mountain to get to the aerovator.

It wasn't easy. There were hundreds of Faarians moving in the other direction. We tried to be respectful, but ended up having to push our way through. Now was not the time to be polite. When we finally got into the mountain and to the tube with the aerovators, we saw a pretty huge Faarian guy directing traffic. He was making sure that as each aerovator arrived, everyone got off quickly and kept moving toward the escape tunnel.

Another aerovator arrived and people flooded out. As soon as it was empty, we tried to jump into the car. But this big guy grabbed us both and pulled us back.

"No passengers," he said firmly.

"But we've got to get down to the hauler hangar!" I shouted.

"Don't you hear the alarm?" the man said. "This is an emergency. These lifts can only be used for the evacuation."

This guy was big and he wasn't kidding around. There was no way Spader and I could push past him and force our way onto the aerovator. But we also couldn't take the time to run all the way down to the bottom of the mountain. We were stuck. I had to make this guy understand how important it was that we get down there, so I grabbed him by the arm and forced him to look right at me. When I spoke, I tried to do it slowly and calmly.

"Listen to me," I said. "There are people down there who are in danger. It's really important that we get to them. We have to use this lift. Please let us pass." I didn't act all frantic or threaten the guy or anything. I just tried to get across how important this was. At first, I thought he was going to shove me out of the way, but a strange thing happened. He kept looking at me and I sensed that he was relaxing. It was totally weird. He went from being a brick wall in our way to a puppy dog. He then stepped out of the way, leaving the path open for us to enter the aerovator.

"I understand," he said softly. "Good luck."

Spader and I walked past him, not sure what had just happened. But we weren't about to question it. We got on the aerovator, I grabbed the controls, and we headed down.

"What was that about, mate?" Spader asked. "It's like you hypnotized him or something."

"I have no idea," was all I could answer. I was just as confused as he was. The only thing I could think of was the way Uncle Press had done the same thing to Wu Yenza back on Grallion. She was all ready to throw us out of her office, until Uncle Press talked her out of it. I was thinking now more than ever that the ability to get through people's toughest defenses might be a special Traveler ability, like understanding all languages. This was something I was going to have to learn more about, no doubt about it.

But that would have to wait, for we were almost at the base of Faar's mountain.

"We've got to get them out of there," I said. "This place is going to get very wet, very fast."

"They're all working on the water doors," Spader said. "I'll bet they don't even know what's going on out here."

The aerovator hadn't even stopped moving when the two of us jumped out and ran through the tunnel to get out of the mountain and reach the hauler hangar. One thing I noticed right away was that there were no more Faarians evacuating down here. That was good. Maybe it meant that the city was nearly empty. I could only imagine what it looked like outside of Faar, in the ocean with thousands of green swimmers in the water. I knew they would be okay out there, but if the dome over Faar continued to crack, they wouldn't have a home to come back to.

It was a sad thought, but there were bigger problems to deal with right now. Spader and I ran out into the open to find that it was pouring rain. Water was now flooding through the cracks in the dome.

I looked up at Faar's mountain and was relieved to see that the paths weren't clogged with people anymore. That meant everyone was getting out. From the looks of things, it was none too soon.

We continued running toward the hauler hangar. Spader held the two air globes, and I had mine. I hoped that when we got inside we would find that they had fixed the damage and that the haulers were all on their way. Once that was done, we could get the heck out of Faar and deal with Saint Dane. That wasn't a happy thought.

We were about twenty yards away from the entrance to the hangar, when we heard it.

It sounded like thunder. It was different than the explosion sounds. The explosions were a low rumble. This new sound was like the sharp peal that comes right after a nasty bolt of lightning strikes. But it wasn't short and sweet. No, this sound continued as if it were the longest crack of thunder in history. Unfortunately crack was the perfect word to describe it.

Spader and I froze and looked up to see a sight so horrifying, I hate to even remember it long enough to write about it. The dome that protected Faar from the ocean above was beginning to crack. I saw long slits of light starting to spiderweb their way across the coral-covered surface. In seconds the force of the water would smash through and flood the rest of Faar.

"Uncle Press!" I shouted, and started to run for the hangar.

"No!" yelled Spader, and pulled me back.

It was a good thing, too, because an instant later, a section of dome caved in. It wasn't the whole dome, just one section, but it was directly over us. If I had kept going, I would have been crushed by the torrent of water that was on its way down.

"We gotta get out of here!" Spader shouted.

I couldn't move. I looked up at the broken pieces of dome and the tidal wave of water that was now plummeting toward us. I then looked to the hangar. Uncle Press was in there.

"Pendragon, move!" shouted Spader, and pulled me back toward the mountain. We had maybe ten seconds before the water would hit. Would it be enough time to get to the aerovator? The two of us booked back toward the mountain tunnel on a dead run. We got inside, but we weren't safe yet. As soon as the water hit, it would flood the tunnel and keep coming. This was the beginning of the end of Faar.

I heard a deafening *boom* outside behind us as the pieces of dome and water crashed down. Immediately the water came surging through the tunnel, headed for us. All we could do was run and stay ahead of the torrent that was quickly shooting through the tunnel to get us.

We made it to the tube and saw that our lift was still there. That was huge, because if it hadn't been, we'd be dead. We both dove in and turned back to see the flood of water was rushing toward us. I grabbed the control stick and slammed it all the way forward. The aerovator blasted off so quickly that the two of us were thrown to the floor. I had a death grip on the control lever. There was no way we were stopping. Now our biggest concern was if the rising water would destroy the aerovator tube before we got out. I held my breath, expecting the speeding car to suddenly stop. But it didn't. We kept rising. Moments later we were back to the escape-tunnel level.

The Faarian guy who was guarding the lift a few minutes before was gone. No other Faarians were around. Spader and I ran through the empty corridor. I feared what we would find outside of there. Would the dome have totally collapsed? If that had happened, we might as well stop running because it would be over for us. The weight of the water would be too much. The whole mountain would probably be crushed.

As we got closer to the end of the tunnel that led out of the mountain, the sound of rushing water was deafening. It sounded like Niagara Falls out there. This gave me hope. It meant that the whole dome hadn't collapsed, just the one section that we saw crumble. If that were the case then we still had a shot at getting out. The two of us reached the entrance and cautiously looked outside.

What we saw was both horrifying and wondrous. So far the dome was holding. But there was a huge, jagged hole that must have been thirty yards wide. Water was pouring down so hard, it looked like it was coming from a powerful hose. Imagine a hole thirty yards wide with a solid stream of water powering through. It was awesome, and frightening.

"Pendragon, look," said Spader.

He was pointing down. What I saw made me catch my breath. The water was rising inside Faar. It was only a matter of time before the entire city would be underwater. But that's not what hit me. Spader was pointing to the hauler hangar. The water was rapidly rising and would soon cover the huge building. If this weren't bad enough, the sight that really made my heart sink was near the door where we had been only a few minutes before. There was a pile of rubble that must have been pieces of the collapsed section of dome. It had fallen right in front of the hangar, blocking the entrance. I had hoped that Uncle Press and the Faarians would be protected inside the hangar. Their only hope would be to wait until Faar was submerged, then swim out. Uncle Press could even buddy breathe with one of the Faarians in their swimskins. They would make something work.

But now that the entrance was blocked under a ton of rubble, there was no way they'd get out of there. Now their only hope would be if they could repair the pen doors and escape that way.

"This is bad, Pendragon," Spader said solemnly. "If they don't get those hauler doors open—"

"Yeah, I get it," I said.

The two of us stood there in a daze. There was every probability that the hauler hangar was going to be a tomb for those brave Faarians, and for my Uncle Press.

"We gotta go," Spader then said.

I looked up toward the tunnel that led out of Faar and saw that we had actually caught a break. The rush of water that was powering down from the dome was on a free fall to the bottom. If it had hit any of the paths, it would have wiped them out. But as it was, the paths weren't being hit and we could still make it up to the escape tunnel. There was some rubble from the crumbled dome lying around, but nothing we couldn't jump over or run around. But we had to do it fast. The water level was rising.

There wasn't a single Faarian left. They had all made it out. We got to the tunnel safely, but before ducking inside I remembered something and stopped. I turned around and looked up toward the Council Circle where I had left Abador. I briefly wondered what he was going to do. It was clear now, Faar was doomed. Did that mean he was going to transpire . . . whatever that meant?

One look up at the distant platform told me that whatever transpire meant, it wasn't going to happen. That's because the white marble roof that had protected the Council Circle was gone. It must have been knocked over by pieces of the falling dome. That could only mean one thing—Abador was dead. If he had stayed at the podium, which I was pretty sure he had, then the crashing marble would surely have killed him. And since nothing else dramatic had happened to Faar, I could only assume that it had gotten him before he had the chance to transpire. My heart went out to the old man. His love for Faar and all that it stood for was huge. He had saved his people from a horrible death, but he failed in his last important act. After seeing the dome collapse, he would surely have begun to transpire but he never got the chance. I felt sad for the man who wasn't able to help Faar through to the final destiny that his ancestors had so carefully planned for.

"Uh, Pendragon, can we leave now?" asked Spader.

I turned away from Faar for what was sure to be the last time and followed my friend into the tunnel. We ran past the empty locker room and right to the spot where we had left our gear. Spader put Uncle Press's air globe down next to his water sled.

"You never know, right?" he said.

Yeah. You never know. But you usually have a pretty good idea. I didn't think Uncle Press would be needing his air globe anymore. For a moment time stood still. Seeing that air globe did it. It didn't matter to me that Faar was crashing down, or that Saint Dane was about to destroy Cloral. All I could think about for those few seconds was that I had lost my Uncle Press. After telling everybody else how they had to be strong and do the right thing and make tough choices, all I wanted to do was stand there and cry.

Spader must have realized what I was going through, because he put a hand on my shoulder, and said, "Time for that later, mate. We have to go."

Right. We were outta there. We both grabbed our water sleds and headed back through the tunnel. We soon hit the water. It quickly got deep, first covering our ankles, then our knees, our hips, and then finally became so deep that we had to start swimming. We popped on our air globes, triggered our water sleds and submerged into the waters of the tunnel.

Luckily the lights were still on so we could see where we were going. It would have been tough trying to find our way in the pitch black. We sped along, back through the tunnel, without saying a word. I can't speak for Spader, but I knew where my thoughts were. Though it looked as if we were about to escape the destruction of Faar alive, we were about to enter another mess. No doubt waiting for us in the ocean outside were Saint Dane and his raiders. I only then realized that once the dome cracked, the explosions had stopped. I guess Saint Dane had done all the damage he needed. He had destroyed Faar and kept the haulers from saving the underwater farms. His mission was complete.

The sad truth was that we had failed Cloral. Saint Dane's plan for pushing the territory into chaos was about to succeed. Food would grow scarce, people would fight to get whatever safe supply was left, and who knew how many thousands would die from either starvation or poisoning.

And still, we had to face Saint Dane. He was out there,

waiting for us, I was sure. All we could hope to do now was escape to fight another day.

We swam back to the large rock door that led to the open ocean. The door was wide open, and why not? This wonderful city was history. Why bother to close it? Spader and I shot out into open water, not really sure what we would find.

"Gotta be careful, mate," said Spader. "Don't want to get sucked back into that hole in the dome."

Good point. There were millions of tons of water flooding into that hole. It was like a giant, open drain. It would be easy to get sucked in. I hoped that the Faarians realized this and were keeping their distance.

As we rode our water sleds away from the tunnel to get away from the dome, I actually felt a slight tug, as if we were swimming against a strong current. I knew it was the pull of the water being sucked into the hole in the dome. Luckily we were far enough away that our water sleds kept us moving forward and safe. Did I say safe? Yeah, right. Real safe. I looked ahead and began to see shapes. They were hard to see at first because they weren't much different than the color of the water, but the closer we got, the more distinct they became. In a few moments I realized what they were.

It was the people of Faar. There were thousands of them, all floating in the water, looking back at the coral reef dome that had protected their city and kept it hidden. It was gut wrenching. These people were now all homeless and stranded in the middle of the ocean.

And we were stranded right along with them. I began thinking about how we could find the closest habitat and get the word out to the aquaneers to start picking up these people, when something caught my eye.

At first I thought it was a shadow. But it was really big,

like a shadow from a cloud when it crosses the sun. It was far away and blurry, so I couldn't tell what it really was. What I could tell for certain was: It was coming toward us.

"You see that?" I asked Spader, and pointed toward the moving shadow.

Spader spun around and looked.

"Never seen any fish that big," he said.

"Maybe it's a school of fish, or a whale . . . or . . ."

The words stuck in my throat. As the shadow drew closer, it became very clear how Saint Dane had attacked Faar. I also knew why Spader hadn't seen it coming when he was on the surface.

Saint Dane was in a submarine. It was a huge, black, monstrous-looking craft with a flat bottom and rounded body. My guess was that it fired underwater missiles, just like the battleship he used to attack Grallion. There was no doubt about it, this was a weapon of war, and it was at Saint Dane's command.

"About time you two showed up!" came a voice from behind us.

Spader and I both spun around to see four raiders floating there, each with a water sled and holding spearguns on us.

"Looks like you were the last to leave the party," one laughed. "There's somebody wants to see you."

Two of the raiders moved to either side of us, while the other two trailed from behind, guarding us with their spearguns. They motioned for us to swim along with them. There was nothing we could do. We were trapped and on our way to Saint Dane's submarine.

◉ SECOND EARTH ◉

The phone rang next to Mark's bed.

"Don't answer it," ordered Courtney. She was too involved in Bobby's adventure to stop reading, even for a moment.

"I have to," answered Mark. Though he didn't want to. He was afraid of who might be calling.

"Hello?" Mark answered tentatively.

"Mark Dimond?" came a familiar man's voice over the phone.

"Yes," Mark answered. He wasn't giving up any more information than necessary.

"This is Captain Hirsch, Mark. Stony Brook Police."

Mark's heart instantly started beating faster. This was it. This was the call he was dreading.

"Hi, Captain, how are you?" Mark asked, trying to sound more together than he felt.

At the sound of the word "captain," Courtney's ears pricked up.

"Mark, you're aware that there's a reward out for any information that would lead us to finding the Pendragons, right?"

"Yeah. Twenty-five thousand dollars."

"That's right. Do you know where Courtney Chetwynde is?

I called her home but her parents said she was out."

"Well, yeah. She's here with me."

He looked at Courtney. Courtney raised her eyebrows as if to say, "He's asking about me?"

"That's good," Hirsch said. "I wonder if you two would mind coming down to the station. There's something here I'd like to show you."

Uh-oh. Mark thought he knew exactly what Captain Hirsch wanted to show him.

"Uhh . . . I guess. We're kind of in the middle of something now though."

"How about an hour?" asked Hirsch. "We could send a car for you."

"An hour? Uh . . . y-yeah, okay. I guess we could be finished in an hour. You have my address?"

"Yes, I do," answered Hirsch. "Oh, Mark, one more thing. Do you know a guy named Andy Mitchell?"

That was it. The door holding back Mark's fears was blown wide open. Andy Mitchell had stolen Bobby's journals and it took him all of one day to take them to the police, figuring he'd collect the reward money. The only thing that truly surprised Mark about it was that he'd thought it would take Mitchell a week to read those first four journals.

"Mark, you still there?"

"Y-Yeah, I'm here."

"Do you know Andy Mitchell? Is he a friend of yours?"

Two completely different questions. Mark wondered what Mitchell had said to the police about their relationship. He wondered if Mitchell admitted that he was a bully who had blackmailed Mark into showing him the journals, only to steal them and turn them in for a reward. No, Mitchell probably didn't go into that kind of detail.

"Yes, I know him. But he's not exactly a friend of mine."

"Okay then, we'll see you in an hour."

"Bye." He hung up the phone.

"That was Hirsch? What did he want?" asked Courtney.

"He wants us to come down to the station to show us something."

"Did he say what it was?"

"No," answered Mark. "He's sending a car here in an hour. I figured we'd be finished reading by then."

Mark's mind raced. The drama with Andy Mitchell was going to end in an hour, one way or another. But as anxious as that made him, it didn't even come close to the drama that was playing out on the pages of Bobby's journal.

Courtney said, "I don't want to think about the police until we finish. My mind's not there. That okay?"

That was *more* than okay with Mark. His mind wasn't there either. He didn't want to have to discuss Andy Mitchell or the missing journals or his being an idiot who got blackmailed until they found out what happened to Bobby and Spader and Uncle Press.

"Yeah," Mark answered. "We gotta read."

Mark got back on the bed. He and Courtney stretched out on their stomachs, side by side, with the journal in front of them, ready to discover what happened on that dark day under the oceans of Cloral.

CLORAL

You'd think things couldn't have gotten any worse than they were at this moment: Faar was destroyed. Its entire population was now homeless and floating in the ocean. All but one of the haulers were stuck under tons of water and rubble, unable to save the underwater farms of Cloral. Uncle Press, Kalaloo, and several Faarians were trapped down there as well. If they weren't dead already, they would be soon.

And now Spader and I were being escorted into an ominous-looking submarine full of killer raiders that was commanded by Saint Dane.

As the raiders brought us toward the hovering sub, I said to Spader, "I didn't know they had these on Cloral."

"Same as with the battle cruiser," answered Spader. "Warships were built long ago in case there was a territory war between the habitats. They never had to use them, and a few were hijacked by raiders."

"Quiet!" shouted one of our guards.

It now made sense. Saint Dane was able to fire under-water missiles at Faar. He just kept pounding away at the dome until it couldn't take it anymore.

We were now directly underneath this war machine. I wasn't sure where we were going until I saw a large door slide open in the bottom of the hull. It led up to a large, flooded chamber. It was probably big enough to bring a truck inside. The raiders directed us to swim up and in. I looked into the black chamber above me and stopped. I didn't want to board this evil boat. But a sharp jab in my ribs from a raider's speargun told me we didn't have a choice. So Spader and I swam up inside Saint Dane's city-killing submarine.

We floated in this dark chamber while the hull door slid closed below us. We were now inside, in pitch darkness. A hiss of air told me that they were pumping the water out of the chamber. It didn't take long. Soon we were standing on the hull door that had just closed. The water level kept going down until the chamber was dry. That's when the lights kicked on and I saw something that made this horrible situation even worse.

Sitting next to us in this large chamber was the one and only hauler that had been launched from Faar. Saint Dane must have captured it the instant it left the underwater city. This was totally depressing. Now there was no chance for any of the underwater farms. Saint Dane had won a complete victory. He didn't leave any loose ends.

I looked to Spader, who seemed as deflated as I was.

"Drop your gear!" ordered one of the raiders.

We took off our air globes and dropped our water sleds.

"Let's go. He's waiting for you," commanded the same raider.

With another jab in the side from his speargun, Spader and I were escorted out of this chamber and through the submarine to meet Saint Dane. I had never been in a submarine at home. I had only seen pictures and movies. But compared to the high-tech subs from Second Earth, this vehicle looked pretty simple. I expected to see all sorts of tubes and pipes and valves all over the place, but there were none. It was cramped and the walkways were narrow, just like you'd imagine, but there were very few signs of the technology that ran the thing. It was just like walking down a narrow corridor, with rooms off to either side. I guess that made sense. The Clorans definitely had water technology down cold.

Suddenly there was a jolt. The submarine shuddered and we all nearly lost our balance.

"What was that?" I asked.

"We're surfacing," answered one of the raiders. "Keep moving."

We got to a ladder that led up. Two raiders went up first, followed by us, followed by the other two. They were taking no chances with us. I wasn't exactly sure why. It wasn't like we were going anywhere.

The ladder led us up to what looked like the control room of the sub. Again, it wasn't as high-tech looking as the submarines we know. There were two raiders sitting at dual steering wheels forward. Three other raiders manned various control stations. I'm sure one of them controlled the weapons that were fired at the city of Faar. There was only one other person there, and I'm sure you can figure out who that was.

It was Roder, the pirate pilot. Of course, we knew that it was really Saint Dane. He stood between the two guys steering, looking out of a narrow window at the underwater seascape.

"We found only two," said one of the raiders to him.

Saint Dane turned to us.

"Welcome aboard, my friends," he said with a warm smile. "I just love the toys they've got here on Cloral, don't you?"

We didn't say anything. What was the point? I glanced at Spader and saw that he was grinding his teeth in anger. His hatred for Saint Dane because of what he did to Spader's father had come flooding back. I really hoped he wouldn't do anything stupid.

"And where is my friend, Press?" he asked. "Not still on Faar, I hope."

I didn't answer. But Saint Dane walked up to me and looked me right in the eye. I didn't want him to think that he scared me, so I looked right back at him. It was like he was searching my mind. After a few seconds he shook his head slowly.

"It's all in your eyes, Pendragon," he said. "Press is dead. I am sorry. He was a worthy adversary, but as I've told you before, I cannot be beaten. This is the way it was meant to be."

"No, it isn't," I shot back at him. I couldn't stand hearing those words. "Cloral isn't done yet."

Saint Dane chuckled like I was some kind of stupid kid who didn't know what he was talking about. I hated that. Mostly because he was right.

"Is that what you think?" he asked. "Let me show you something."

He pointed forward and I now saw light outside through the window. We were no longer underwater.

"All clear," announced one of the raiders at the controls.

A raider who had been guarding us stepped to the rear of the control room to a round door in the wall. There was a wheel on the door that he spun to disengage the locking mechanism. He then pulled the door in on its hinges and sunlight flooded into the submarine.

"Please," said Saint Dane, gesturing for us to go outside.

I walked to the door and stepped out, followed by Spader.

The control room was inside the tower above the main body of the sub, so when we went outside, we stepped right onto the top of the hull. The sub was big. I'm guessing from the bow to the tail it was about fifty yards long. The control tower was about two-thirds of the way forward. I also noticed that there were long guns jutting from the control tower. They weren't as big as the battle cruiser's, but I'm sure they were just as deadly.

Saint Dane walked past us and strode toward the bow of the ship.

"Come," he ordered.

Spader and I had no choice but to follow. Saint Dane walked almost to the bow of the ship and the three of us stood there, alone.

"Do you see that?" he asked.

We looked ahead and I didn't see anything at first, but once our eyes adjusted to the light, we saw what he was talking about. It was a giant whirlpool. And I mean, giant. There was no question as to what was causing it. This was the spot directly above the shattered dome of Faar. The swirling water was pouring into the doomed city, creating this monstrous whirlpool. Saint Dane stood there with his arms folded in front of him, smiling, enjoying his handiwork.

Spader said, "Where are—" but Saint Dane held up his hand to quiet him.

"Please, a moment more," he said.

We all looked back to the swirling water to see that he was right. A few moments later the whirlpool stopped. The water was still for a moment, and then a giant bubble of air erupted on the surface.

"That's it," Spader said softly. "Good-bye, Faar."

It was heart-wrenching. That bubble of air was Faar's last

gasp. The city was now completely underwater. The ocean surface was once again still.

Saint Dane then turned to us.

"Now, what were you saying?" he asked Spader politely.

"Where are the pilots from the hauler?"

Saint Dane waved his hand as if this were an insignificant detail.

"We threw them back in the sea," he said. "Two small little fish of no consequence. But they did help us quite a bit."

"How's that?" I asked.

"The moment we saw them launch from Faar, we knew the exact spot to target our missles and cripple their fleet. No more bubble boats emerged," he added with a laugh. "So we must have been successful!"

"You trapped a dozen men down there!" Spader spat out in anger.

"And destroyed the heart and soul of Cloral," Saint Dane replied calmly. "Not bad for an afternoon's work, don't you think?"

I could feel Spader's tension. He was out of his mind nuts with hatred for Saint Dane and was a hair away from lunging at him. But that would have been a huge mistake. So I put a hand on his shoulder. Spader jumped. He really was a raw nerve.

"Calm down," I said as softly as possible.

Spader forced himself to take a breath and seemed to relax a bit.

"Pendragon, I am impressed," said Saint Dane. "You've grown wiser since our adventure on Denduron."

"I beat you on Denduron," I shot back.

"So you think," Saint Dane said. "Honestly, do you really

think I care which territory is my first domino? Cloral will do just as nicely as Denduron. As I told you before, once the first falls, the rest will tumble in turn."

"Cloral hasn't fallen," Spader spat out.

"But it will," Saint Dane replied smugly. "Eventually they will find a way to purify the crops, but not before thousands have died and thousands more go to war. It was a delicate balance here, with all the habitats existing together. But now with Faar gone, the scale just tipped."

Saint Dane then walked over to me and leaned down. Our eyes were on the same level and he was so close I could smell his breath. It was sour. I wasn't surprised. But I wouldn't back off. No way.

"It is all happening exactly as I planned," he said softly. "Even if you managed to stop me here, I would simply move on to another territory. You have no idea what is waiting for you, Pendragon. If you continue to fight me, you will certainly go the way of all the pitiful Travelers who came before. Is that what you want? Do you want to die in futility like Spader's father? Or Osa? Or Press?"

This last comment stung, but I wouldn't let him know it.

"The offer still stands, Pendragon," he said with a tempting smile. "When Halla is mine, there will be grand rewards for those who helped me. You seem to enjoy splashing around Cloral. I'll give it to you. Do what you want with it. Restore their farms, make Spader an admiral, be their hero, make them love you. Whatever you want. It would be so easy and the fight would be over. What do you think?"

This is going to be hard to explain, but at that moment something changed for me. Yes, I was still afraid of Saint Dane. I still didn't know much about being a Traveler or even why I was chosen to be one. There was still a ton for me to learn, but at that moment, something became very clear and it filled me with a sense of confidence that I hadn't felt since, well, since I was on the basketball court at Stony Brook.

"You want to know what I think?" I asked Saint Dane. "I think if you truly knew what was going to happen, if you really believed this was all part of your plan and that you couldn't be beaten, then you wouldn't keep begging me to join you."

Saint Dane blinked. I saw it. I had hit a nerve.

"What do I think?" I added. "It might not be here, it might not be today or even on this territory, but for the first time since I met you on Second Earth, I think that when this is all over, I'll be the one who's beaten *you* . . . because *that* is the way it's supposed to be."

Something clicked in Saint Dane's eyes. It wasn't huge. He didn't gasp or shout or anything like that, but I saw it: Saint Dane was afraid of me. I was sure of it.

The two of us stood there for a moment, not knowing who would make the next move. And that's when I heard it. It was a far-off sound and hard to make out. But it was definitely a sound I had heard before. It was a faint whistling sound. It was coming closer, too. Fast. Where had I heard it before? It took me exactly two seconds to remember.

I turned to Spader and shouted, "Incoming!"

I grabbed him and dove down onto the deck. An instant later the submarine was rocked by an explosion. The control tower was hit by a water missile—just like the ones that Saint Dane had launched on Grallion. The sound I heard was that of an incoming bomb.

Boom, boom! Two more missiles hit the control tower and the submarine rocked in the water. But where was this attack coming from?

"Look!" shouted Spader, pointing off the port side of the sub.

I looked and saw such a wonderful sight, for a moment I thought I was dreaming. But it was no dream. It was a fleet of speeder boats full of aquaneers, and they were attacking.

"Hobey, Pendragon! It's Yenza," Spader laughed. "She was a step ahead of us."

That had to be the answer. When we didn't resurface, Wu Yenza must have gone to get her rescue team. And they were coming in full force. Some of the speeders looked more like gun ships. They weren't as big as the battle cruiser, but they would definitely stand up to this submarine.

There was frantic activity on the deck of the submarine.

"Dive!" shouted Saint Dane. "Get us below!"

A raider shouted, "Sir, we can't!" He pointed to the control tower and sure enough, the first few missiles from Yenza's aquaneers had blown a hole in the skin of the tower. If they tried to dive, they'd sink. Saint Dane looked at the damage, then spun to look back at the approaching fleet. He looked angry. I liked that. When he got angry, it meant things weren't going his way, and that didn't happen too often.

"The guns!" he commanded. "We'll fight them off."

He then ran along the deck and disappeared into the control tower. Spader and I were left flat out on the deck. Saint Dane no longer cared about us. And why should he? We were targets too.

"Time to go, mate," said Spader. "Let's slip over the side and we'll swim for it."

Three more missiles struck near the sub, sending up waves of water that splashed over us. The raiders were now on the guns and firing back. This was going to be a fierce battle—a natty-do, as Spader would put it—and I didn't want to be floating in the water in the middle of it.

"I have a better idea," I said.

I got up and ran back toward the control tower. Two more shots hit the hull, rocking the sub and nearly knocking me off. But Spader caught me and kept me going.

"No place to run, Pendragon," he said.

"Sure there is," I answered.

I ran inside the control tower. Spader was right after me.

We had to push past a bunch of raiders who were scrambling to get to their battle stations. They didn't care about us anymore. Remember, they were raiders. They knew nothing of Saint Dane's grand plan to conquer all the territories and control Halla. All they knew was that they were being attacked.

Even Saint Dane wanted a fight. He stood at his station, barking orders, turning the submarine so it wouldn't be such a wide target. If there were ever a time to get out of there, it was now.

I led Spader back the way we came, down the ladder into the hull of the ship and back toward the water tank we arrived in. I figured there was only one way we could get off this sub and survive in open water. We had to get to the hijacked hauler.

As we ran through the submarine we kept getting knocked around by the force of the missiles that were hitting the hull. Yenza was really pouring it on. That was cool, as long as Spader and I were off by the time she sent it to the bottom the same way she had the battle cruiser.

Luckily it's kind of hard to get lost in a submarine, so we found the tank chamber pretty easily. When I threw the door open and we saw the hauler, Spader smiled.

"Why didn't I think of this?" he laughed with surprise.

"You know how it works?" I asked.

"Pendragon, if it moves in the water, I can drive it."

"Okay," I said. "But can you get it out of here?"

Spader gave me a "don't ask dumb questions" look, and ran for the hauler.

"Get our gear, then go over to those levers," he instructed as he climbed up onto the bubble.

As Spader lowered himself into the bubble, I ran to get our air globes and water sleds. I grabbed them all, then threw each up to Spader, who stood with half of his body out of the top of the bubble.

"Now what?" I asked.

"Four levers," he said. "One floods the chamber, another empties it, third opens the hatch, fourth closes the hatch. We don't have to flood the chamber because we're already on top of water. The pressure keeps the water out. All we have to do is open the hatch, and we're gone."

"Okay, which lever opens the hatch?"

"Hobey, Pendragon. I don't know *everything*!"

He then slipped into the bubble and started powering up. This was the old Spader, the one I knew before his father was killed. It felt good.

I went to the four levers. None of them were marked. There was only one way to figure out which was the right one. I had to call upon all my Traveler experience and special powers to figure it out. It's called . . .

"Eenie, meenie, miney . . . *mo*! I pulled on "mo" and with a grinding screech, the floor began to move. The hatch door was sliding open! Go, mo! Unfortunately, as soon as the hatch began to open, it set off an alarm. A shrill, blaring horn blew, which said only one thing: "Someone is trying to escape in the hauler." My guess was at least one of the raiders would come to find out who it was.

"Better hop in," Spader shouted.

I ran across the moving floor and leaped on to the bubble

craft. I dangled my legs down into the cockpit and was just about to drop in when Spader said, "Hold on, mate. We gotta release first."

He was right. The floor hatch was now all the way open, but the hauler wasn't free. The craft was suspended from two hooks that kept us dangling over the water below.

"So how do we release?" I asked.

"I'd say you should swing that lever right there."

Sure enough, there was a lever right over my head. I grabbed it, pulled it toward me and—whoa! The hauler fell free and splashed down in the water. I lost my balance and fell into the globe, right in Spader's lap.

"Thanks for droppin' in, mate," Spader said. "Close 'er up, please."

I stood up and pulled the bubble closed over us. With Spader in the left pilot's seat and me in the right, we were ready to go.

That's when the door to the chamber flew open and two raiders jumped in with guns.

"Dive, please," I said.

"Right!"

Spader hit four toggle switches, air bubbles hissed through the water around us and we began to sink. The raiders shouldered their rifles and took aim. All I could hope was that the bubble on this hauler was strong enough to take a direct shot from a water rifle. I didn't have long to wonder. The raiders opened fire on us. I ducked, expecting the bubble to shatter to pieces. But it didn't. Their water bullets splattered against the clear shield without leaving so much as a scratch. Score another one for the genius of the people from Faar.

We were now almost submerged. The raiders had stopped firing and watched us helplessly as we sank below the surface.

Then, just before the water closed over us, someone else entered the tank room. It was Saint Dane. For an instant I actually thought I saw a look of worry on his face. That's the last image I saw of him, then we slipped underwater.

Spader took control of the vehicle like he had been a hauler pilot his whole life. We descended well below the submarine, then he hit the throttle and we left the dark shadow behind.

"What about the big guns?" I asked. "The ones they used on Faar. They can blow Yenza's boats out of the water."

"They can, but they won't," Spader answered. "They only fire when it's submerged. Yenza knows what she's doing, all right. She nailed that control tower so they can't submerge again. Saint Dane made a big mistake. On the surface, he's no match for my mates. There's only one problem."

"What's that?"

"It's going to be over too fast. I want to join up with them and take a couple of shots at Saint Dane myself before the natty-do's all done!"

I looked back at the dark submarine. If Spader was right, the battle above was as good as over. Yenza would handle the raiders, and with a little luck, Saint Dane would go down with his ship. I was no longer worried about what was happening up there. My thoughts were elsewhere entirely. So I reached forward and killed the engines.

"Hobey, mate, what're you doing?"

"You really know how to pilot this thing?" I asked seriously. "Don't get all macho aquaneer on me. I want the truth."

"This is a fine piece of machinery," he said, looking around. "It's way more advanced than anything I've ever seen. But that just makes it easier. All modesty aside, I can move this little beauty through a mile of kelp and not break a single leaf."

My mind was working hard, figuring the possibilities.

"What are you thinking, Pendragon?" Spader asked. "You think we should start dumping this cargo over some of the farms?"

"Good idea, but no," I said. "We can do that later. Right now, I got something else in mind."

"What?"

"I want to go after Uncle Press."

Spader's eyes opened wide with surprise. He hadn't expected me to say that.

"Hobey, mate!" he said in awe. "Do you know how dangerous that would be? You're talking about finding our way down through that submerged city; poking through who knows what that's floating around in there waiting to get us all tangled up and trapped. Then if we're lucky enough to make it to the bottom we'd have to dig through the pile of rubble that's covering the door with a mechanical arm we've never used before and for all we know can't even lift that kind of weight. And it's all on the chance that Press and the others are still alive down there. Do you know that's what you're asking?"

"Uh . . . yeah, that pretty much sums it up."

"You're crazy!" he said. A moment later, he smiled. "I like that."

"Then why are we still here?"

Spader fired the engines back up, banked hard to the right, dipped the nose, and we were on our way back toward the coral reef for one last visit to the city of Faar.

CLORAL

Descending into Faar wasn't exactly like diving into the unknown. We had just come from there. But to say that things had changed a little would be a major understatement. We sort of knew the geography of the place, but now that it was underwater it would be like traveling through the dangerous insides of a giant sunken ship. The whole space would be filled with water and that meant stuff would be floating all around.

Still, I didn't think we had a choice. There were a dozen Faarians down there who could still be alive, and Uncle Press was with them. We had to give it a try.

Spader drove the hauler back toward the coral reef that was the dome over Faar. He kept making slight maneuvers he didn't need to so he could get used to the controls of the hauler. Smart idea. Better to get totally familiar with the craft out here in open water than down in the murky depths.

As we approached the coral reef, I looked for the hole that Saint Dane had blown open. It would be our doorway into Faar. It wasn't hard to find. There were long, parallel lines dug into the reef that must have been caused by the huge volume of water that was pulled across it as it was sucked toward the hole. It was like a road map. All we had to do was follow it.

A few moments later we both saw our goal. The huge, jagged hole stood out like a black scar on the reef. It looked even bigger up close than it had from down below. Spader stopped the hauler just shy of the edge and we hovered there, looking at the damage in silence. A moment later something floated up from down below. It was a white tunic, the kind the people of Faar always wore. The piece of clothing rippled and moved in the current. It looked like a lonely spirit leaving the city forever.

"Pendragon, I want to get 'em out as bad as you do," Spader said. "But we have to be smart. If it's a tum-tigger down there, we'll have to pull out."

"I understand," I said.

Spader then pushed the little sub forward and soon we were hovering directly over the middle of the black hole. He looked to me. I nodded.

"Let's give it a go," he said.

He toggled a switch on the control panel and we began to sink straight down. We passed the jagged edge of the hole, dropping from the bright blue-green of the ocean into the dark tomb of the sunken city. We first traveled through a debris field of clothes, books, and memories. Everything on Faar that wasn't attached was free to float around. There were constant bangs and thumps against the bubble of the hauler as we knocked into all this lost junk. I hate to call it junk though, because not long ago these were important possessions. We passed lots of clothing and dishes and we even saw a small doll that a child must have left behind. That one was tough. It made me think of my little sister, Shannon.

Soon it got so dark I lost all sense of direction. I couldn't tell up from down or if we were even moving.

"Must be some lights on this beauty," Spader said.

That was important. We had to descend quite a ways before we reached the peak of Faar's mountain, but before we got there we needed some kind of light to guide us or we'd surely crash into it. Spader scanned the control panel and chose a switch.

"Let's try this one."

He toggled the switch and instantly a series of lights sprang to life below the bubble. They weren't headlights, but they sent out a bright cocoon that allowed us to see a few yards in every direction. It wasn't much, but at least now we would know if we were about to hit something. I looked to my right and—

"Ahhh!" I screamed, and nearly jumped into Spader's lap.

It was one of the portraits from the corridor leading to the Council Circle of Faar. I was staring out at a stern-looking guy who gazed right back at me with a sour puss.

"It's like diving through an underwater junkyard," Spader said.

"Or *graveyard*," I added.

The portrait floated away and I got my nerves back under control. Spader tried another switch and this time another light kicked on. This one was attached outside of the bubble on my side. It was the headlight we were looking for. Excellent.

"Try that knob there," Spader instructed.

Next to my right arm were two controllers that looked like video game joysticks. I grabbed the smaller of the two and moved it. Sure enough, the searchlight outside moved too. We had found our eyes!

"Let's see where we're going, then," instructed Spader.

We could only see what the headlight was shining on. Everything beyond fell off into darkness. I directed the light forward and we got our first view of the top of Faar's mountain. It appeared out of the distance like a ghost. It was an incredibly eerie sight. Luckily the water was pretty clear. I expected there to be sand kicked up and floating around, but it wasn't too bad. Also, the layer of junk seemed to have thinned out. Most everything that could float was headed to the surface. We were now traveling below the debris field.

"Let's get moving," said Spader, and we plunged deeper.

The best thing about having the lights was that we could navigate. Spader dropped the nose of the hauler so we weren't sinking blindly anymore. We had to descend in circles, like a corkscrew, so that we could drop as straight down as possible.

"I want to see something," I said and pointed to our left.

Spader directed the hauler to where I pointed and soon our headlight was moving across the platform that had held the Council Circle. As I described before, the marble roof had been knocked off when the water began to flood through the dome. It was on its side now, half covering the platform. The round symbol of Faar had broken off and it lay on the platform, cracked in two pieces. How's that for symbolism? Most of the marble pillars still ringed the platform, but they no longer had anything to hold up. A few had tumbled over, and now crisscrossed on top of one another.

"Closer," I asked, and Spader dropped us in for a better look.

We were now hovering only a few feet above the platform. I played the light over the wrecked surface until I saw exactly what I was looking for, but hoped I wouldn't find. The podium that held the four crystal controls had been knocked over. It was still functioning because the yellow crystal continued to blink. Even now it was sounding the alarm to evacuate Faar. But that's not what I was looking for.

"Oh, no," Spader said sadly. He had just seen it too.

From beneath the toppled ceiling, an arm was reaching out. There was no doubt in my mind that it was Abador. He had stayed at his post until the end and was killed when the marble dome crashed down. It seemed as though in his last moments he was reaching for the control podium in the desperate attempt to transpire. He had failed. Of course it was tragedy enough that this brave man had died, but I hated to think that he died knowing he had failed. I could only hope that he knew that Faar had been safely evacuated.

"Let's move on," Spader said with respect.

I nodded and he steered the hauler away so we could continue our descent into Faar. All the way down I kept the headlight trained in front of us, looking for any danger in our way. We passed by some familiar sights. We saw the pathways we had walked along. We saw the entrance to our escape tunnel and all the smaller entrances that led deep into Faar's mountain. As of now the crushing water hadn't done any major damage to the city. The buildings seemed intact and the paths weren't washed away. This was great news because if some of these big marble buildings had fallen down and piled on top of the hauler hangar, this rescue would be over before it got going.

I had a brief feeling like we were inside one of those snow globes that you shook to create a storm. I wondered how long it would take for erosion to start doing its worst. Eventually the city would turn to sand, but for now it was intact. It was hard to believe that only a short time ago it had been completely dry and busy with people.

"There we go!" announced Spader.

We were nearing the hauler hangar. I was thrilled to see that it looked pretty much the same as when we saw it last. The building hadn't collapsed under the weight of the water. There was the pile of dome rubble in front of the entrance, but other than that nothing new had fallen down that would stop us from getting through. Now the question was whether the mechanical arm could move the stuff away.

Spader put the hauler down on the same path we had run along just a while ago. We landed so gently that only a small cloud of sand was kicked up.

"Give it a go, mate," he said.

He meant the mechanical arm. I grabbed the other joystick that was at my right arm and twisted it. The mechanical sound around us proved the arm was activated and working. The long, white tube of an arm had about four joints so it could move in pretty much any direction. On the end was a large, white mechanical hand. It had three fingers and a thumb, like Fred Flintstone. Swiveling the joystick made the arm move easily. It took me all of thirty seconds to figure out how to move it. Finally I discovered that pulling the trigger on the joystick made the hand close shut. I maneuvered the arm out in front of the hauler, brought the hand back, and right in front of Spader, released the trigger so the hand opened wide—and waved at him.

Spader laughed.

"I guess you've got it figured out," he said.

I was totally ready to begin the excavation.

Spader gently lifted the hauler off the bottom and got us in position over the pile of rubble in front of the hangar entrance.

"Go slow," he said. "Once you grab on to a piece, I'll pull

us back. I gotta be careful though, I don't want to start kicking up sand or we'll be blind down here."

I rubbed my hands together, grabbed the joystick, and made my first attempt. I reached the long arm out and found a small piece of rubble. This was just a test. I maneuvered the hand over the chunk, squeezed the trigger, and the hand clamped on. I then lifted the piece away and dropped it off to the side.

"That was spiff," said Spader, as if he expected it to be harder.

"Let's try something a little bigger," I said with confidence.

I saw a chunk of coral sticking out of the pile. It looked perfect to grab on to. Spader didn't even have to move the hauler. I eased the arm over toward it and latched on with no trouble. But as I tried to pull back, there was some serious resistance.

"It's not moving," I said.

"Let's use hauler power," said Spader.

He started to ease the hauler backward, but the piece still wouldn't budge. Spader hit the throttle, the engines whined, but still the piece wouldn't budge.

Spader said, "Maybe you should try a smaller—"

Suddenly the piece broke free, and so did the pile of rubble. It seemed as if half the pile had been leaning against this one little piece and when we pulled it loose, it was like pulling a card out from the bottom of a house of cards. Huge pieces of dome tumbled toward us and hit the bubble of the hauler. The impact knocked us back and we twisted over on our side. Then another piece hit us from the other side and spun us back the other way. Sand was swirling everywhere. It was impossible to see. Then with a jolt, we hit the bottom on our side and two more heavy pieces fell down on us. There was nothing we could do but hold our breath and hope we wouldn't spring a leak. We finally ended up on our side with a bunch of broken dome all over us.

"Wrong piece," said Spader.

"Yeah, no kidding."

We didn't move for a while and let the sand settle so we could see what the deal was. I was convinced we were now pinned here on the bottom of Faar and was already making plans to put on our air globes and abandon ship, when Spader gently gunned the engine. I was thrilled to see we could move. He slowly backed us away from the pile of rubble and let it fall down in front of us. We were completely free now, so Spader righted us and we were hovering once again.

"Let's pick our pieces a bit more scientifically this time, right?" Spader said.

I gave him a sideways "give me a break" look, then started scanning the pile of rubble to choose my next victim. After what had just happened, it was obvious that this wasn't going to be a quick task. We were going to have to start at the top and only move pieces that were completely clear. We couldn't afford to have another collapse. This was going to be like playing a game of Jenga . . . a really *dangerous* game of Jenga.

So we went about the painstaking task of moving the pile. Of course the little pieces were easy. The bigger pieces took a lot more power. One good thing was that because we were underwater, they were a lot lighter than they would have been on land. Many of these pieces were wide, thick chunks of material that withstood centuries of pressure. We pulled off a few pieces that were bigger than a car. I was afraid those pieces would be too much for the hauler, but the little vehicle proved time and again that it was up to the task.

I don't know how long we were digging. It could have been hours. I tried to focus on the job and not think about the worst, which was that we were too late for Uncle Press and the Faarians.

Finally, with one final tug from the hauler, we pulled over a huge chunk of dome and revealed the doorway to the hangar.

"Yeah!" I shouted.

"Hobey!" added Spader.

It was unbelievable that we had gotten this far. But our victory celebration was short-lived because almost immediately our thoughts went on to the next step. We had no idea what we were going to find beyond that door.

"Uh-oh," said Spader ominously.

I hated "uh-oh." Nothing good ever happened after "uh-oh."

He pointed to a gash that was cut in the wall that must have been made by a falling piece of dome. The gash was so big, it went right through the wall. That meant that as soon as the rising water got high enough, it would have flooded the hangar. We could only hope that the Faarians had their swimskins, and that they could buddy-breathe with Uncle Press. If not, the hauler hangar was now a tomb.

Spader gently touched the throttle and the hauler eased closer to the door. I shone the headlight on it so we could see exactly what we had to deal with. The door itself was bent. I hoped that didn't mean it was jammed or anything.

I reached for the joystick of the mechanical arm and was about to go after the door handle, when something caught my eye. It was a flicker of movement. I quickly looked to see that it had come from the gash in the wall. Something was moving in there!

"Don't stop now," said Spader with excitement. He'd seen it too.

I had to force myself to keep calm. We were too close now for me to blow it by doing something dumb. So I slowly moved the mechanical arm over to the handle and grabbed on. I tried to tug it open using just the arm, but it wouldn't budge.

"Back it up," I said to Spader.

The engines of the hauler began to whine. But the door still wouldn't budge. Spader throttled up. I could hear the engines strain, but the door wouldn't move.

"I'm going to really gun it," said Spader. "If the door pops, release it quick or—"

Crack!

The door gave way. I instantly released the trigger and we went sailing backward. Spader threw on the water brakes and stopped us before we slammed into anything from behind.

"Go back, go back!" I shouted.

Spader reversed the engines and we moved right back to the hangar and to the now open door. I shone the light on it, hoping that whoever was inside would see it and know that this was the way out. We hovered there, and waited.

"C'mon," I begged. "C'mon!"

"We saw something move in there, right?" Spader asked.

"Yeah, I thought that—look!"

Something moved inside the open door! I held my breath. Was someone still alive in there, or was it a floating corpse?

Then a Faarian in a green swimskin poked his head out of the doorway. He was alive! He held his hand up to shield his eyes from our bright light and looked around the sunken city in wonder. He then gave a wave, and with a kick, began swimming to the surface.

I couldn't stop smiling. We had saved at least one of the

Faarians, but were there more? And what about Uncle Press?

One by one, more Faarians in swimskins began to float out of the door and swim to the surface. It was kind of eerie. They were like green ghosts floating up and out of a grave. Then again, this wasn't a grave. This building had saved them from being crushed and drowned—or drowned and crushed. It wasn't a tomb at all; it was their lifeboat.

I kept waiting to see Uncle Press. Since he didn't have his air globe, I expected to see him emerge from the doorway while buddy-breathing with one of the Faarians. But after counting fourteen swimmers, there was no Uncle Press. I started to get nervous again. Could all the Faarians have survived because they had swimskins, but Uncle Press have died because he didn't have the right gear? That wasn't fair. But still, nobody else was coming out! I was all set to put on my air globe and figure out a way to get out of this hauler to go look for him, when a knock came on the outside of the bubble. I turned to my right and came face-to-face with a Faarian in a swimskin. "Ahhh!" I jumped again.

Since the skins completely covered their heads, they were kind of creepy looking. Imagine Spider-man as a frog, and you'd pretty much have a Faarian in a swimskin.

This guy clung to the bubble of the hauler and was pointing at something.

"What does he want?" Spader asked.

"He's trying to tell us something," I said.

The Faarian was pointing to something inside the hauler, behind my head. I spun around and saw that perched on a hook behind my seat was a pair of headphones. Spader had a pair behind him as well. I pointed to the headphones and looked at the Faarian. He nodded.

Spader and I both shrugged and put the headphones on.

We then looked back to the Faarian and heard a familiar voice say, "What took you so long?"

It was Uncle Press!

"Yeah! All right! Hobey-ho!" we shouted. Spader and I were over the moon. I guess the Faarians had an extra skinsuit in the hangar.

"How did you end up with this hauler?" Uncle Press asked.

"Long story," I answered.

"How bad is it?" he asked.

"Faar is underwater," I said. "Saint Dane blew a hole in the dome. But the entire city was evacuated. As far as I know there was only one casualty—the old man from the Council of Faar. What about the other haulers? Were they launched?"

"No, they're all still in there," Uncle Press said. "The outside doors were buried."

That was horrible news. The underwater farms of Cloral couldn't be saved. Saint Dane was still going to win.

"We should get out of here, mates," said Spader. "Find something to hang on to, Press. We'll give you a ride."

Uncle Press couldn't get inside the hauler because we were watertight. He would have to hitch a ride to the surface. He found a spot behind the bubble and grabbed on.

"Watch out," I said. "There's a lot of junk floating around."

Spader pushed the throttle, lifted the nose and we began our final ascent from Faar. We had to go slowly because we didn't want Uncle Press to get swept off. Besides, we weren't in any hurry. It gave me time to fill him in on all that had happened since we split up. The hard truth hit him the same as it did me. We had totally failed. The underwater farms were still producing poison crops, Faar was destroyed, and Cloral was on the verge of chaos. Even if Yenza had a complete victory over Saint Dane topside, it wouldn't matter. The damage was done.

The three of us fell silent during our final stage of the ascent. I wanted to take one last look around at the city that died trying to be the salvation of Cloral. The last chapter in the legend of the Lost City of Faar was a tragic one. And no figure was more tragic than poor Abador, Senior to the Council of Faar, who died trying to fulfill his destiny. Whatever transpire was, it would never happen. Instead it would be just one more unexplained mystery in the myth.

That's when a thought came to me.

"Stop," I commanded.

"What?"

"Stop right here," I said.

Spader stopped our ascent and we hovered in midwater.

"What's up, Bobby?" asked Uncle Press.

"Faar is dead. There's nothing we can do to save it. And there's nothing we can do to bring the rest of the haulers up to save the crops, right?"

"Yeah, that's about how the day has gone," said Spader. "What's your point?"

"My point is there's nothing else to lose."

"You getting philosophical on us, or is this leading somewhere?" Uncle Press asked from outside the hauler.

"I think we should take it all the way. We should complete Faar's destiny."

"Which is . . . ?"

"Transpire," I said sharply. "I say we finish what Abador couldn't."

Uncle Press said, "But we don't even know what that is. You said yourself it might be a self-destruct mechanism."

"So what?" I shot back. "If that's the way the Faarians

wanted it, then I think they deserve to end things the way they planned. It can't make things any worse for Cloral, right? Abador said they had been preparing for this moment for generations. Who are we to deny them?"

I looked to Spader for an opinion. He only shrugged.

"Why not?" he added.

I looked outside the bubble to Uncle Press, but it was impossible to read any expression on his face since it was covered by a green swimskin.

"Do you know how to do it?" he asked.

"I think so."

"Then you're right. There's nothing to lose," he said. "Let's do it."

"Get us back to the Council Circle," I said to Spader.

Spader took control and we started moving again. In a few minutes we were once again hovering over the platform and looking down at Abador's hand that, tragically, had fallen only a few feet short.

"You have no way of knowing this, old man," I said to Abador. "But we'll finish it for you."

"What do I do?" asked Uncle Press.

"You see that blinking yellow light?" I asked.

"Yeah."

"There are three other crystal switches. One of them must be the control to transpire."

"Okay, which one?"

"Beats me," I answered. "If in doubt, eenie, meenie, miney, mo. I'm partial to mo."

"Great," scoffed Uncle Press, and swam off toward the panel.

He looked at the three other switches: green, red, and white. He first reached forward and pushed the green one. All that happened was that the green crystal started to glow, and the yellow light stopped blinking.

"That must be to turn off the evacuation alarm," I said.

There were two choices left. From where I sat, the white crystal looked as if it had already been pushed down.

"I think the white crystal raises and lowers the podium," I said. "It must be the red one."

"Red it is," said Uncle Press.

He reached forward, touched the red crystal, and glanced back to me. I gave him a nod, and he pushed it down.

And that's when the party *really* started.

First, the red crystal flashed brightly. That much I expected. The next thing we knew we were surrounded by sound. It started as a low whine, but then grew in volume. It sounded like giant engines were powering to life. Then the mountain rumbled. The waves it sent out from its movement started to buffet the hauler.

Uncle Press shot back to us and grabbed on.

"I think now's a good time to be someplace else," he said.

"Hang on!" shouted Spader.

He hit the throttle and we began rising again. The monstrous sound grew louder. The hauler was being buffeted so hard that it was making my teeth chatter.

"You okay, Press?" called Spader.

"Get us outta here!" he shouted back.

Then I heard something new. It sounded like cracking, but it was immense.

"Uh-oh," said Spader.

There it was again. "Uh-oh." I *hated* "uh-oh."

Spader was looking up. I looked up too and saw that we were getting closer to the hole in the dome, and safety. But that's not what the "uh-oh" was about. The trouble was, the rest of the dome was cracking! The rumble was sending shock waves through the water that were so strong, we could actually see cracks traveling across the surface of the dome. But unlike the last time the dome cracked, this wasn't in one single place. Now, the entire dome was beginning to shatter!

"It's breaking up," shouted Spader.

"Get under the hole!" I shouted back. I figured that if it all came down, humpty-dumpty-style, then our only chance of not being crushed would be if we were under the hole.

"I gotta pick up speed!" shouted Spader.

"I'm okay," answered Uncle Press. "Go!"

Spader pushed us faster. It was a race to make it out of that hole before the whole world came crashing down on us.

"Come on, come on!" Spader coaxed the hauler on.

I killed the lights because we didn't need them anymore and could use every last bit of power for speed. We then hit the field of floating debris. Pieces of everything hit the bubble. I wasn't worried about the glass breaking. If the raiders' waterguns couldn't shatter it, then I didn't think a chunk of floating junk could. I was more afraid that something would hit Uncle Press.

"We got it!" Spader yelled.

And a second later we shot up out of the hole and into the light of open ocean. Unbelievably, the dome had held. But we weren't safe yet. The sound of the roaring engines was even louder outside of the dome. The water was still vibrating like crazy, and there was something new. All around us were massive jets of air bubbles shooting up from around the perimeter of the dome.

"Keep moving!" shouted Uncle Press.

Spader hit the throttle and we sped away. It didn't matter where we went so long as we didn't stay here. The jets of air shot up all around us, like fissures opening up somewhere deep below and letting off pressure. There was no way to avoid them. They kept hitting us and knocking us around. This was probably the closest I will ever come to being inside a washing machine.

"Press?" called Spader.

"Don't talk, drive!" shouted Uncle Press.

Finally we got past the fissure jets and Spader was able to put us right. The water just beyond them was absolutely calm. In seconds we had gone from being tossed in heavy seas to floating as calmly as if we were in a bathtub. It was a strange feeling. I wasn't complaining.

"Now *that* was a tum-tigger," said Spader.

But it wasn't over yet. The roar of the engines, or whatever they were, was still growing louder even though we were out of the turbulent zone. The air fissures had suddenly stopped erupting, and as soon as the bubbles stopped shooting up, the engines whined louder.

Then we heard another cracking sound.

"The dome's collapsing!" Spader shouted.

We all looked back at the coral reef, expecting the dome to collapse in. But that's not what happened. It erupted. Yes, it started to expand upward.

"I don't believe it," Spader whispered in awe.

Believe it.

A moment later we saw. Something was pushing the dome up from below. It was the top of Faar's mountain! In that one amazing moment, it all came clear to me what transpire meant. When Abador and the council debated about whether to reveal themselves to Cloral or remain hidden, they weren't talking about self-destruction. They were talking about rejoining their world, literally. The preparations that had been going on for centuries were all about pushing the Lost City of Faar back to the surface. The three of us watched in shock as the top of Faar's mountain broke through the weakened dome and continued to rise toward the surface.

Luckily one of us had the smarts to do a little mental calculation.

"Faar is a big place, gentlemen," said Uncle Press. "We are still in the wrong spot."

Good thinking. If Faar was coming up, we were still too close.

"Outta here!" shouted Spader, and hit the throttle once again.

As we sped away I looked back around at the spectacle. The mountain continued its impossible rise up through the shattered dome. In a few moments, the peak would break the surface of the sea. It was awesome . . . but we weren't home-free just yet.

"Slight problem," Spader said while scanning the instruments.

"What?"

"We're not moving."

Whatever force was being used to power this city's ascent had gotten hold of us. It felt as if we were fighting a wicked current coming right at us.

"More power!" I shouted to Spader.

"I'm trying! It's pulling us back."

Spader pressed the throttle to full power, but it didn't help. We were being sucked back toward the mountain. It was like being sucked into a rip-current. But then, suddenly, everything reversed. I didn't know if the force of the mountain rising was now stronger than the pull of the engines that were forcing it up, but in an instant we went from being pulled back to being pushed forward by a tidal-wave force of water. Our hauler suddenly shot forward faster than it was ever designed to go.

This underwater wave ride lasted a full minute. Finally Spader was able to get control and slow us down.

"I'm taking us up," he announced, and we shot topside.

A few moments later we broke the water's surface. I quickly opened the bubble top and pulled myself out to get to Uncle Press. He was exhausted, but okay. He pulled the swimskin off his face and looked up at me.

"Are you sure it was the red button?" he said with a smile.

I had to laugh. Man, this guy was cool.

We then heard something that sounded like a giant whale breaching the surface. But it wasn't a whale, of course. It was Faar's mountain. Spader joined us on the top of the bubble and the three of us watched in wonder.

The mountain rose slowly from the water. It was impossible, yet there it was. We were far enough away now that we were safe, but close enough to see detail on the mountain. As it rose higher the marble buildings were revealed along with the paths that wandered between them. Bit by bit the city that had been hidden for hundreds of years was once again feeling sunlight.

"Look!" shouted Spader.

We looked around us and saw green heads popping up in the water everywhere. The Faarians were coming up to witness the rebirth of their home. There were hundreds of them stretched out on either side of us. They all pulled off their swimskin hoods so they could see this miracle through clear eyes.

Faar's mountain continued to rise. Of course the higher it got, the larger it became. I was beginning to think that maybe we were still a little bit too close. If this thing kept getting bigger, pretty soon we'd be lifted up with it. The mountain now towered over us. What emerged next from below was the hauler hangar that was the lifeboat for Uncle Press and the brave Faarians.

It suddenly hit me that with Faar rising, the haulers came up with it. They could now be pulled from the hangar and sent on their mission after all. This was incredible! There was still a chance to save the underwater farms.

With a final shudder, Faar's mountain stopped moving. One last wave of water hit us—we rode up and over it, and then settled. The three of us sat there on the floating hauler, in complete awe. We were now looking at a huge island, and a city.

All around us the Faarians began to cheer. They screamed and laughed and hugged each other and they cried. They had gone from losing everything to starting an incredible new life on Cloral. This was their destiny and they welcomed it.

I couldn't help but think of Abador. I hoped he somehow knew what had happened. It may not have been his hand that brought Faar back to life, but it was definitely his spirit.

There was one other amazing fact. We were now looking at the only dry land on the entire territory of Cloral. As Saint Dane had said to us earlier: "Not bad for an afternoon's work, don't you think?"

CLORAL

The sea was now calm. The three of us sat on the bubble of the floating hauler, staring at the reborn city of Faar. None of us could say anything for the longest time. There were no words that could truly describe the spectacular sight we had just witnessed. Well, maybe there was one.

"That was . . . cool," I said, knowing it was the biggest understatement of all time.

The three of us exchanged glances and started to laugh. It was an incredible moment. We helped the city of Faar complete its destiny and probably saved Cloral at the same time. If there was a lesson here it would have to be that you should never, ever lose hope. We had given up. Thrown in the towel. The fat lady had not only sung, she had left the stage. Saint Dane was already doing his victory lap. But we pulled it out. Unbelievable. The only way we could show our disbelief was to laugh. It felt great.

We watched as the Faarians swam toward their city and tentatively crawled up on the shore. One by one they emerged from the water, gathered together, and stood looking up in awe at their mountain city. It was the first time the sun had touched their buildings in centuries. Water still poured from the beehive of tunnel openings that dotted the mountain. The transpire was complete.

As we sat, watching this wondrous sight, we heard the sound of waves slapping against a hull. All three of us turned to see that the black submarine was cruising toward us. My first thought was to jump back in the hauler and get the heck out of there, but a closer look told us there was no reason to be afraid. The deck of the submarine was lined with aquaneers. They were all staring at Faar with the same look of wonder. Just as Spader had predicted, his mates had won. They now commanded the raiders' sub.

Stepping from out of the control tower was Wu Yenza. She walked out into the sun and stood with her hands on her hips confidently, watching as they drew closer to us. She was very much in charge.

"She's good," Uncle Press said.

"She's better than good," I added. "If not for her . . ."

I didn't have to finish the sentence. We all knew where we'd be right now if Yenza hadn't gone for help. I turned to Spader and said, "Maybe you'll get a promotion for this."

An odd thing happened. Spader didn't smile and make a clever comeback. He just watched the approaching submarine intently. His mind was somewhere else. Even though we had just pulled out an incredible victory, there was now a dark frown on his face. Without a word, he dropped back down into the hauler and powered up so we could rendezvous with the sub. I looked at Uncle Press. All he could do was shrug.

As Uncle Press pulled off his swimskin, Spader guided our hauler right up alongside the sub. An aquaneer tossed us a rope so we could tie on. Spader handed me the two air globes and water sleds and I tossed them up to the aquaneer. We then all climbed aboard the sub and were reunited with Yenza.

"I guess you found Faar," she said with a wry smile. Another understatement.

"What made you leave?" asked Uncle Press.

"A hunch," she said. "When you didn't surface, I assumed you had found the city. And if Zy Roder was right behind us, I didn't want to take him on myself. I'm good, but not *that* good."

"Where is he?" asked Spader with no emotion.

Uh-oh. Now I knew what was in Spader's head. The sight of the sub approaching had reminded him of Saint Dane. I was afraid that he would still be looking for revenge.

"He's in the brig down below," answered Yenza. "I won't let him get away again."

Spader walked past us toward the control tower.

"Spader, let it go," I called.

But Spader kept walking. What was he going to do? Uncle Press and I followed him.

Spader entered the control tower. He grabbed an aquaneer by the shirt and demanded, "Where is the brig?"

"Below, halfway to the stern," answered the aquaneer, a little intimidated.

Spader pushed him aside and headed for the ladder.

Uncle Press called, "Spader, stop. Take a breath."

Spader wasn't listening. He slid down the ladder. We were right behind him. We hit the main deck and had only taken a few steps when we heard a scream come from the back of the sub. It was a horrible, pained howl. Without a word we all began running toward the sound. Spader was a few feet ahead of us and glancing into each doorway as he passed, looking for the source. Finally he saw something and entered a doorway. We followed right behind.

This was the right place. The room was split in half. We had just entered the front half. The back half was closed off by prison bars. On the floor in front of us was an aquaneer. Another aquaneer was behind the bars of the cell. Roder/Saint Dane was nowhere to be seen.

"He killed him!" shouted the aquaneer behind the bars. He was all sorts of excited and out of breath.

Uncle Press immediately went to the fallen aquaneer.

"Who did?" demanded Spader.

"Zy Roder! We were putting him in the cell when he suddenly turned on us. The guy is strong! He threw me in here and closed the door, then grabbed him and choked him and—I think he's dead." The guy was out of his mind with panic.

Uncle Press checked the aquaneer's pulse.

"He's not dead, but he needs help," said Uncle Press. "I'll get Yenza." He blasted out of the door and turned left to get back to the control room.

"Where's Roder?" asked Spader.

"I don't know! He ran out. Let me out of here. We've got to find him!"

I pulled a set of keys from the belt of the fallen aquaneer and threw them to Spader. Spader unlocked the door to the cell and the other aquaneer ran out.

"I've got to report this to Yenza!" he shouted, then ran out and turned to the right.

"Help me," I said to Spader, and the two of us moved the aquaneer into a sitting position so he was more comfortable. His eyes opened slowly and focused on me.

"Are you all right?" I asked.

"Roder . . ." the guy gasped. "I got too close to the cell. He grabbed me."

"We know," I said. "Your friend told us."

The aquaneer focused on me and frowned. "What friend?"

"Roder locked the other aquaneer in the cell after he attacked you."

The aquaneer shook his head and said, "Roder was already in the cell. He reached out and grabbed me. Nobody else was here."

Spader looked at me with confusion, but I knew instantly what had happened. Saint Dane had transformed himself again. That wasn't an aquaneer in the cell, it was Saint Dane, and we had just freed him.

"He took a right," I said. "The control room is to the left."

"He's going for the launch chamber," shouted Spader.

"Let him go," I begged.

Spader wasn't listening. He bolted from the room, hot after Saint Dane.

"You okay?" I asked the aquaneer.

He nodded and waved for me to get going.

"Spader!" I shouted. "Spader, stop!"

I ran after my friend, but there was no stopping him.

Moments later we both got to the door of the launch chamber that had once held the hauler. Spader pushed on the door, but something was keeping it closed from inside. He pushed harder and the door finally gave way. Someone had put a barrel against it. We both jumped into the room in time to see Saint Dane about to make his escape.

He had transformed back into his normal self. His steely blue eyes flashed at us as we tumbled into the room. He was on a skimmer, like the underwater skimmers we used to sabotage his battle cruiser. We saw him a second before his head went under the water. His long, gray hair billowed out, like a spiderweb in the water around him. Our roles had reversed.

This is how Saint Dane had seen us as we made our escape on the hauler.

Saint Dane shot us a look of such hatred that I thought my hair would ignite. Then his head sank below the surface. Spader made a move as if to dive for him, but I held him back.

"Let him go," I begged Spader. "You'll get another chance."

Spader threw me aside and ran back out into the corridor. I followed, but had trouble keeping up because he was running flat out.

He got to the ladder, scrambled up into the tower, then jumped outside, onto the hull. As I was climbing up the ladder after him I kept yelling, "Stop him! Somebody stop Spader!"

Things were happening so quickly no one had time to react. Spader ran across the hull and headed right for the hauler we had arrived on. Before anyone could stop him, he cast off the line, jumped on board, and dove into the bubble.

Uncle Press and Yenza came running.

"What is he doing?" Yenza asked.

"Saint Dane, I mean Roder, escaped. He's got a skimmer."

Spader was already submerging in the hauler. Uncle Press watched him sink below the surface, his mind turning. He then looked to the deck, grabbed an air globe, and threw it to me. We were going after him.

"I know where he's going," he said.

"How? Where?" asked Yenza.

I wanted to ask the same thing, but I figured Uncle Press would tell me on the way. He grabbed his own air globe and one of the water sleds. I grabbed the other.

Yenza said, "I'll send a team of aquaneers with you."

"No!" commanded Uncle Press quickly. "We can handle it."

Something about the way Uncle Press snapped at Yenza made me realize where we were going. It all made sense. I should have figured it out myself. We were headed for the gate. Saint Dane was going to try and escape through the flume. It was the only option left to him. The aquaneers didn't need to see this. It was a Traveler thing.

"Ready?" asked Uncle Press.

"Close enough," I answered.

We both splashed down and plunged below the surface.

"You know which way?" I asked.

Uncle Press looked around and said, "There!"

I looked and saw a thin trail of bubbles left by the hauler. We both triggered our water sleds and followed the trail like breadcrumbs in the forest.

"This could take hours," I said to Uncle Press as we shot along side by side.

"Maybe," he answered. "Or maybe Saint Dane knows about another gate."

I hadn't thought of that. On Denduron there were two gates. Who's to say Cloral had only one? But neither of us knew for certain, so all we could do was follow the trail of bubbles.

"Spader is going to be an important ally to you, Bobby," Uncle Press said. "But he's got to learn how to control his emotions."

"Yeah, no kidding," I said.

"Killing Saint Dane isn't the answer," he continued. "I wish it were that simple, but it's not."

"You mean . . . he can't die?" I asked.

"His body can die," Uncle Press explained. "But he would just come back in another form."

"What is he? Some kind of . . . ghost?"

"Not like you're thinking. His spirit is evil, Bobby. Killing his body won't stop him from his quest."

"Okay," I said, not really understanding. "What *will* stop his quest?"

Uncle Press didn't answer at first. I wasn't sure if he didn't want to tell me, or he didn't know. Finally he said:

"It won't end until he thinks he's won. That's when he'll fail."

O-kay. That meant almost nothing to me. But I was used to that. The truth was, things were actually getting less confusing . . . sort of. When I thought back to how clueless I was the first time I hit the flume, I was amazed at how far I had come. But there was still a long way to go and much to learn. I had to accept that. So I didn't push Uncle Press anymore. Besides, getting too much information just freaked me out.

We traveled for a long time and my arms were getting tired from holding the water sled out in front of me. I kept having to change my grip, sometimes holding on with only one hand to rest my other arm. I didn't think it was going to be possible to keep going at this pace and hang on for the hours it would take to get back to the flume near Grallion.

And that's when my ring started to twitch. We were nowhere near the rock shelf where we had first arrived, so that could only mean one thing: There was another gate.

The bubble trail from Spader's hauler led us deeper. It was getting darker too. And cold. Up ahead I saw a rock formation rising up from the bottom. It looked kind of like a mesa you'd see in a Western movie, but of course it was underwater. It rose up to a flat top, with steep cliffs on either side. My glowing ring told me the gate must be hidden in this formation somewhere.

Something else made me think we were almost there. On

the far side of the rock formation I saw a fat stream of air bubbles rising toward the surface. Whatever was causing this was on the other side of the formation, out of our sight. It could have been Spader's hauler, but I didn't know why it would be spewing so much air. Uncle Press and I directed our water sleds toward the bubbles, and as soon as we passed over the top of the formation, we had the answer.

It was Spader's hauler all right, but Spader wasn't in it. The hatch was open and it was now filled with water. Jets of air spewed up from inside. But that wasn't the most dramatic part. There had been an accident. Okay, maybe accident wasn't the right word because it looked like Spader had meant to do what he did.

It was an unbelievable sight. Jammed between the bubble of the hauler and the rock wall was a dead quig. It wasn't as big as the others, but it looked plenty nasty just the same. Spader had no weapons to protect himself, so he rammed it with the hauler. The shark had fallen onto a ledge, with the hauler right on top of it.

"Nice shot," said Uncle Press.

The quig's tail twitched. Maybe it wasn't dead after all. We kept our distance.

"So where's the gate?" I asked.

We had to be in the right place. Not only was my ring going nuts, but the quig was a dead giveaway. I hoped that it was close because Spader didn't have an air globe. Once he got out of the hauler, he was going to have to hold his breath. The two of us scanned the steep wall of the rock formation, but saw no opening.

Then I caught something out of the corner of my eye. It was a bubble no bigger than a golfball that rose up near one section of the wall.

"There!" I announced, and drove my water sled toward it.

When we got close to the wall I saw that the whole rocky face was draped with a curtain of red sea kelp. I tried to remember the exact spot where I saw the bubble rising and started pushing the kelp aside, looking for an opening. But there was nothing behind the kelp but rock. No opening, no tunnel, no gate. The whole time I was looking, I kept glancing over at the quig that was pinned by Spader's hauler. If that thing suddenly sprang to life, I was out of there.

Finally I grabbed a handful of kelp and pushed it aside to reveal a star dug into the rock.

"Got it!" I shouted.

Uncle Press joined me and we dug through the vines until we found a narrow opening. It wasn't much wider than a human body, but it had to be the gate. I don't know why I was feeling so brave all of a sudden, but I went first. I entered the dark crevice and pulled myself along by grabbing on to the rock walls. It only took a few seconds before I saw a shaft of light streaking down through the water ahead of me. A second later I surfaced into another underwater cavern. Uncle Press surfaced right behind me and we both pulled off our air globes.

I didn't know what to expect. What I really hoped was to find Spader there alone and safe, with no Saint Dane to deal with.

The cavern itself was much smaller than the one near Grallion. The pool of water that we now floated in was barely big enough for the two of us. Directly across from us was the flume. We were definitely in the right place. None of this was a surprise. What was hard to believe were the two people inside the cavern.

One was Spader. He was sitting on the rocky floor to our left, crying. And it was pretty obvious why. The other person in the cavern . . . was his father. I had only seen the guy once, and he was dead at the time, but I remembered him. Dead guys tend to leave an impression. The question was, how could he possibly be here? Alive?

When Uncle Press and I threw off our air globes, Spader's father turned to us and said, "Look, your friends have arrived."

The two sat together looking like they were having a quiet, father-son heart-to-heart. There must have been a hundred emotions fighting for Spader's brain time.

He looked at us through his tears and cried, "Hobey, Pendragon! He's alive! Saint Dane kept him here, like a prisoner! Can you believe it?"

The truth was, I couldn't. But my mind wasn't firing on all cylinders at that point either. It was Uncle Press who kept a clear head and gave Spader the bad news.

"It's not him, Spader," he said. "Your father is dead. You saw him on Magorran. He was poisoned."

Spader looked at Uncle Press in confusion. If he had been thinking clearly, he would have realized the truth on his own. But seeing his father alive again had done a number on his head. It sure messed with me for a second, but I soon understood the truth as well. It made me hate Saint Dane even more, if that were possible. He was truly an evil being to have done this to Spader.

"Oh, Press, you are such a killjoy," Spader's father said. "And I thought you were dead."

He turned to Spader and said with a sigh, "Your daddy *is* dead, Spader. And you will be too if you don't back off."

Spader's brain wasn't computing. He watched with wide eyes as his father stood up, walked to the mouth of the flume, and announced, "*Veelox!*"

Instantly the flume sprang to life with light and sound.

Spader's father then looked back to Spader and said, "Who knows? Maybe I'll find your mother along the way and kill her, too!"

Spader fell back against the wall like he had just been punched in the stomach. Spader's father then made a quick transformation back into Saint Dane. He then looked right at me and stared into my brain with such an intense look, I wanted to sink back under the water to escape it.

"Until next time . . . ," he said with an evil grin. Then with a slight bow, he was enveloped by the light and sucked into the flume. I looked at Spader. His eyes were huge. He was only now starting to realize what had happened.

Uncle Press and I pulled ourselves out of the pool of water and went to him.

"His evil reaches out in a lot of ways," said Uncle Press. "He takes as much pleasure in causing you this kind of anguish as wiping out a territory or murdering hundreds of people. It's all the same to him."

I could see Spader's anger growing. His look went from one of confusion, to realization, to rage.

"I'll kill him," he seethed, and went toward the flume.

Uncle Press held him back. "Don't," he said firmly. "This isn't about your own vendetta. This is about protecting the territories, and Halla."

Spader shoved Uncle Press aside. He pushed him with such force that Uncle Press slammed into the rock wall and fell to the ground.

"I don't care about the territories, or Halla, or whatever it is you say I'm supposed to be fighting for. He killed my father and he will die for that."

He strode toward the flume. That's when I heard the faint sound of the musical notes coming back.

"*Veelox!*" called Spader.

The light began glowing from the flume and the notes got louder. But something was wrong. I had heard them coming *before* he said "Veelox." The flume had already been activated. Something was coming our way.

Uh-oh. I thought back to the mine tunnel on Denduron when Saint Dane had sent back a quig shark through the flume that nearly ate Loor and me. Spader stood in the mouth of the flume, expecting to be taken away, oblivious to the danger. The musical notes grew louder and light blew out from deep inside.

"No!" I shouted. "Something's coming back!"

I started to run for Spader, but Uncle Press grabbed me from behind and pulled me back so hard I tripped and fell on my butt.

"Spader, get out of there!" he yelled, and ran for the flume.

Spader wasn't moving. There was only one thing on his mind, and that was revenge. I scrambled back to my feet in time to see Uncle Press headed for Spader. The light was so bright now that whatever was coming would be here in a second. Spader stood at the mouth of the flume, waiting for a ride that wasn't coming.

What happened next took only a few seconds, but they were the longest seconds of my life. I will never forget them. They were seared into my brain forever. Uncle Press dove at Spader and knocked him out of the way. Spader crashed against the far wall, out of the light, away from the flume, and safe from whatever was coming back. But now Uncle Press stood there alone. He had saved Spader, but whatever was coming through the flume was going to hit him.

I heard a whistling sound, then a scream, and an instant later the rock wall opposite the tunnel exploded. At first I thought it was some kind of bomb that had come through, but there wasn't one big boom; there were several smaller, sharp cracks. Bits of rock were blasted off the wall and rained down on me. There was no mistaking what it was—these were bullets. It was like someone had fired a machine gun into the flume and the bullets traveled all the way through, only to be spit out here.

Another second went by and it was over. The lights stopped, the musical notes stopped, and the storm of bullets ended.

"Uncle Press!"

He was lying on the ground, right at the mouth of the flume. I ran to him to see if he had been hit, but I already knew the worst. There was no way that many bullets could come flying out of the flume and miss him completely. It would have to be a miracle. But since my life had been one miracle after another lately, that's what I was hoping for.

When I knelt down next to my uncle, I saw that my miracles had run out. Uncle Press had been hit. More than once. His eyes were unfocused, but they still had life. I looked quickly to Spader, who was crouched in the corner where he had fallen. He, too, looked at Uncle Press in shock. He had no idea what could have happened.

"Get the hauler," I screamed at him. "We've got to get him back to Grallion."

"Bobby, no," Uncle Press said, grabbing my arm.

"You are *not* going to die!" I shouted. My uncle was lying in front of me, mortally wounded. My invincible uncle. The uncle I loved and who took me on more adventures than any kid deserved . . . and that was *before* I became a Traveler.

"Listen, Bobby——," he said weakly.

"No! You are not going to tell me this is the way it's supposed to be! Not like this. Not you!"

Spader crawled over to us and listened. He was in even more emotional agony than before. I knew what he was going through. Uncle Press was going to die because he saved Spader's life, the same as Osa died saving mine.

"You've asked me a lot of questions, Bobby," Uncle Press whispered. "But there's one you never asked."

"What?" I said, tears streaming down my cheeks.

"I've told you there is only one Traveler from each territory," he said. "You never asked why there were two from Second Earth."

He was right. I never did. I don't know why, but the thought never crossed my mind. It was so obvious, but I never thought about it. Or maybe I didn't want to.

"Are you going to tell me?"

"The answer is, there *can't* be two Travelers from Second Earth. I knew my time was short. That's why I brought you from home. It was your time. It was Loor's time, and Spader's, too. You are the next Travelers."

I couldn't think straight. I didn't care about Traveler rules or Halla or Saint Dane or anything else, only that my uncle was lying here, dying.

"I'll tell you something else," he said. "You are the last. All that has gone before is prelude. The fight is yours. You will take it to the end. You are the last Travelers."

He was growing weaker by the second. He looked to Spader and said, "Spader, I know this is hard to believe, but you will see your father again. Your mother, too."

He then slipped his hand down my arm and held my hand. "And I promise you, Bobby Pendragon, you will see your family again. And when you do, I'll be there. Remember that and don't be sad . . . because this is the way it was meant to be."

He then closed his eyes, and he was gone.

CLORAL

The ceremony was everything it should have been.

The Council Circle was loaded with people. The marble bleachers held the entire Council of Faar. Seated next to them was a group of aquaneers in full dress uniform. Among them was Quinnick, the pilot from Grallion, and Wu Yenza, the chief aquaneer.

The rest of the bleachers held an assortment of others. Some were from Faar. Others were from the Agronomy Society and had made the trip from Panger City. Seated with them was Ty Manoo, the agronomer from Grallion. There were also dignitaries from other habitats. Word was spreading quickly about the reemergence of the city of Faar. It had only been two days since the city rose, but the haulers had already been lifted from their hangar and sent across the territory to rescue the farms.

Cloral had reached its turning point—and survived.

Of course, no one seated in that circle had any clue about the bigger picture. They had no idea that Cloral was only one territory of many that Saint Dane was trying to spin into chaos. To them, victory was having ducked a huge ecological disaster. Nothing more, nothing less. And there was an added bonus in that this near-catastrophe had triggered the discovery of their own ancient roots. The raising of the city of Faar was an amazing event. Imagine if Atlantis had suddenly appeared back at home. How cool would that be? Well, this colossal discovery was all the people of Cloral could focus on now. They didn't know about the larger evil that had almost destroyed their world.

But I did. So did Spader.

I had mixed feelings about Spader after what happened to Uncle Press. I knew it wasn't his fault. If he thought his actions would have put Uncle Press in danger, he would have backed off. I'm sure of that. Still, I couldn't stop thinking that if Spader had listened to us, Uncle Press would still be alive. Spader *had* to learn to control his emotions. He and I were very much in the same place right now. I still feel guilty because Osa died while protecting me. And now I knew what it was like to lose a loved one to death, and Saint Dane. But if we were going to work together as Travelers, we had to move past this. As I stood on the council platform waiting for the ceremony to begin I wasn't sure if that was possible. I would always remember how Spader ignored our warnings and because of it, Uncle Press was dead.

I hadn't seen Spader since we got back to Faar. Maybe that was a good thing. It gave us both a chance to chill out and get our heads together. But I was beginning to worry. He should be here for this ceremony. He was the Traveler from Cloral now. I really hoped that he hadn't bailed.

I stood alone on the edge of the platform, outside of the Council Circle. The marble ceiling had been repaired and hoisted back onto the pillars right away. The round symbol of Faar was rejoined and placed back in its prominent spot. The rest of Faar was still pretty much a mess, but I think restoring the Council Circle was important because it represented the heart of Faar. From here, decisions about the future of Cloral would be made.

The sun was setting on the ocean. Sunsets are always beautiful and this one was no different. There were a few long clouds on the horizon. The warm sun lit them up like blazing arrows shooting across the water. The amber light washed over the marble buildings of Faar, making the city look like a painting. As I looked down on Faar's mountain I saw that there were hundreds of people standing on the paths, watching the beautiful sunset. For them it must have been extraordinary. Faar had not seen sunsets in hundreds of years.

Kalaloo had explained to me how the transpire had been planned for generations. The scientists of Faar had devised an ingenious mechanism that when triggered would pump air into vast chambers below the city. The pressure built up in the chambers and lifted the city high enough to allow the sea to rush in and force the city even higher. The chain reaction continued until the surrounding seabed collapsed into the chambers, creating a base. It was like a controlled earthquake, where all the force was funneled upward.

It may have been physics that brought Faar to the surface, but to me it was pure magic. Seeing the people of Faar enjoying this sunset made it seem even more so. In spite of how horrible I felt right now, something good had come out of this adventure.

"Pendragon?"

I turned to see Spader standing there. He was dressed in his full aquaneer uniform, the same as on the day he thought he was going to meet his father. What a relief. Though it was going to be tricky working through what happened, at least I knew he understood that his place was here.

"I've thought a lot about what to say to you," he said quietly. "But there's nothing I can think of to tell you how sorry I am for what happened."

I said, "How about 'I'm sorry for what happened'?"

He dropped his head.

"I wish I could change what I did."

I just nodded and said, "If I told you it was cool and to not worry about it, I'd be lying. But the thing is, now I know how you felt when your father died. Saint Dane killed Uncle Press, just like he killed your father. I want him stopped now more than ever. But there's something you gotta understand. Getting revenge on him isn't the answer. If you understand that, we're cool. If not, then I'm going to have to go forward alone."

"He understands, Pendragon," said a familiar voice.

Walking up to us was Loor. I was stunned. Seeing her here, on Faar, was totally out of context. She was wearing a light green Cloral suit that really showed off her athletic body. She looked more beautiful than ever. I wanted to throw my arms around her and give her a hug, but that wasn't Loor's style. She stepped up to me and put a hand on my shoulder. That's about as warm as Loor got.

"Spader came for me. He was confused, and afraid to speak with you," she said.

I could understand that. If he needed help, the last person he could go to was someone who blamed him for getting his uncle killed.

Loor continued, "We have all lost the ones we loved most. Press always said how this is the way it was meant to be. I believe him. Spader was no more responsible for Press's death than you were for the death of my mother. When she died, I hated you, Pendragon. But I came to see how this is the course we were destined to follow. It will often be a tragic one, but there is a greater purpose. I understand that. I believe Spader does too."

I looked at Spader, who finally looked back to me, waiting for a reaction. I could see how genuinely pained he was.

"I can't tell you that I don't want revenge on Saint Dane," he said. "But I believe the only way to do that is to complete our mission. I'm with you, Pendragon."

We shared eye contact for a moment. I could tell that he was aching for me to say something to make him feel better.

I didn't say anything at first. That's because there was something I had to do. I had thought long and hard about it, and after all that had happened, I wasn't sure if I could go through with it. But now, with Loor's help, I realized that it was the absolute right thing to do. So I reached into my pocket and pulled something out that I had been holding on to for weeks.

"You're a Traveler now," I said to Spader. "This was your father's. Now it belongs to you."

It was the ring that Uncle Press had taken from Spader's father. The Traveler ring. Uncle Press told me I would know the right time to give it to Spader. This was it. I reached out and dropped it into Spader's outstretched hand.

Spader looked at the large ring and I could tell he was holding back tears.

I then smiled and said, "You realize it's going to be a tumtigger."

Spader smiled. "Hobey-ho," he said.

The two of us hugged. Our friendship was going to survive this, as it should. I looked at Loor, who winked at me. I always thought that I'd have to call on her for help with some kind of nasty battle. When you needed a warrior to bail your butt out of the fire, call Loor. As it turned out, the first time she came to my rescue, it was to help me work through an emotional crisis. Funny thing, this Traveler business.

Kalaloo then walked up to us and said softly, "We're ready to begin."

I saw that now standing on the edge of the platform were two small groups of people. One group was made up of six Faarians, the other six aquaneers. Each group carried a long, yellow container on their shoulders. These were the bodies of Abador, and my Uncle Press. At home you'd call them coffins, but they didn't look like anything I'd seen on Second Earth. They were more like oval-shaped tubes made out of yellow plastic. The coffin held up by the Faarians had the words *"Ti Abador"* written in black letters on one end. The coffin carried by the aquaneers had my uncle's name *"Press Tilton."* (Did I ever tell you that Uncle Press's last name was Tilton?)

The two groups of pallbearers stood with the coffins up on their shoulders. They each walked slowly toward the Council Circle. Abador's coffin was first, followed by Kalaloo. Then came Uncle Press's, followed by Spader, Loor, and me. As we walked slowly into the circle everyone stood up. Soft music was playing too. It wasn't all sad like the church music you hear at funerals. No, this was nicer than that. It kind of reminded me of the mellow New Age music I wrote about before, but somehow it felt right to me now.

The pallbearers placed the two coffins next to each other on pedestals that were in the center of the circle. Kalaloo stood by them while the three of us walked to seats in the marble bleachers. When we had gotten to our places, Kalaloo raised his hands. The music stopped and everyone sat.

"Today is a sad and glorious day," Kalaloo began, addressing the group. "Here, amid the splendor of a Faar that has been reborn, we must also face the realities of death."

He went on to give a very nice speech about Abador. He spoke about how he had dedicated his life to serving Faar and its people. He was often the voice of reason when others had trouble finding the truth. And finally, it was his vision and bravery that saved Faar from destruction. He finished by saying that not only was Faar reborn, but for generations to come, people would remember Abador as the father of the new Cloral.

When he was finished, he turned and raised his hand for me to join him. This was going to be tough. I had to say a few words about Uncle Press. I had never done anything like this before. It wasn't that I didn't know what to say. Far from it. The problem was, I was afraid that I wouldn't be able to get through it without crying. Uncle Press deserved better than that.

I walked up next to Uncle Press's coffin as Kalaloo stepped back. I stood there and looked around at the group. Only a few of them even knew Uncle Press. Most had simply heard about how he helped save Faar and Cloral. To them he was a faceless hero. But he was more than that and I wanted them to understand.

"People have called my uncle brave," I began. "And he was. But that can be said of many people. Many of you here today have shown incredible bravery. But that's not what made Press Tilton special. The thing is, Uncle Press cared. Where most people can't see past their own personal problems, Uncle Press always looked beyond. He helped many people in times of trouble in ways you will never know. Even I don't know most, and that's the way he wanted it. He didn't do it for glory or for riches or to be honored at a wonderful ceremony like this. He did it because he cared. It's what helped save Cloral, and Faar, and why he's not with us today. But you know, that's not really true. He *is* with us today. I know he's with me. And I know that as long as I keep his vision alive, he will never truly be gone. As I say good-bye to him, there's one thing I hope for above all else. I hope that when the time comes that I see him again, he'll be half as proud of me as I am of him today."

That was it. I couldn't say anymore. I touched Uncle Press's coffin and walked back to my place. As I walked everyone stood up. It was time to pay their last respects. I stood between Loor and Spader, trying to be brave. Loor actually reached over and held my hand.

The music began playing again. It was soft and soothing, but began to feel very sad. The two groups of pallbearers gathered around the coffins and lifted them up as the pedestal lowered away. Each group walked their coffins over to a different section of the platform and gently placed them down on the tile. The groups then stepped away, leaving the coffins on the floor of the platform. A moment later the coffins began to sink below. There were panels beneath them in the platform that acted like elevators to gently lower them down.

Kalaloo had come to me the day before and asked if I would honor them by allowing Uncle Press to be buried in the Grand Mausoleum of Faar. This was a place where only the most revered people in Faar's history were laid to rest. It was right under the ornate, mosaic platform we had been standing on. Of course Abador would be buried there. Having Uncle Press there as well was proof of the Faarians' gratitude for all he had done for them.

As much as I knew this was a great honor, my first thought was that he should be brought back home, to Second Earth. But if he were on Second Earth, he would be alone. My family was gone. There would be no one to visit his grave or even remember who he was. But on Faar, he was a hero. I remembered his first words to me after he made that perfect swan dive into the pool of water below the flume. He told me that this was his favorite territory. What better place to stay forever?

I humbly accepted Kalaloo's offer. Uncle Press would stay here on Faar. He'd be remembered as a hero, though the people here wouldn't even come close to knowing how great a guy he really was.

Shortly after the ceremony we returned to Grallion. Loor came with us and we showed her around the amazing farm habitat. We even raised a glass of sniggers to Uncle Press at Grolo's.

I was happy that Cloral was out of danger. We had done our job. But I still felt kind of numb. Of course, most of that was because of Uncle Press. Not having him around was . . . strange. That's the best word I can use. Of course I missed him and the sadness was like a heavy weight on my chest, but there was more. The sadness was about looking back. Losing him was also losing the final link to my family and my life on Second Earth.

The strange part came when I thought about the future. Uncle Press had been my guide. Though I wasn't freaking out twenty-four-seven anymore, I still didn't know much more about being a Traveler than when I started. Up until now, if I was confused about something, I could turn to Uncle Press. He wouldn't always give me the answer, but I always felt as if he was pointing us in the right direction.

Now I was on my own. The biggest question now was, what next? I seriously thought about getting back to Second

Earth and hiding under your bed, Mark. You could feed me leftover mac and cheese, nobody would know where I was, and I'd never have to think about anyone named Saint or Dane again.

But that wasn't going to happen. The real question was, should I chase Saint Dane to Veelox? That's the last territory he flumed to. I wasn't sure if it was the right step or not, but if it was, I didn't want to go alone. Loor was gone. After spending a few days on Grallion, she returned to Zadaa. Tensions there were growing worse, and she feared that something nasty could happen anytime. She wanted to be there and I didn't blame her.

That left Spader. He would be a great partner. We had become friends before things went south and now that things were calm again, we rekindled our friendship. I knew he would go with me, but I was still nervous about how he would handle Saint Dane. I didn't want him getting all out-of-control crazy again. I figured the best way to deal with my worries was to put them on the table. So one evening after dinner, Spader and I took a walk through the farm.

"I have to leave," I said. "Cloral is past the turning point. There's no reason to stay here."

"Even for the great fishing?" asked Spader with a laugh. He was kidding. I knew it. He then said, "Where will you go?"

"Veelox, I guess," was my answer. "That's where Saint Dane went." Of course, I'd rather go someplace where Saint Dane *wasn't*, but that's not how it works.

"Ever been there?" he asked.

"Nope. Don't have a clue about the place. Uncle Press was always my tour guide but now, well . . ." I didn't have to finish my sentence.

We walked along in silence for a while. I wasn't sure how to ask him if he wanted to go with me. More important, I didn't know how to ask him if he was going to be a loose cannon and get us both killed.

"I want to go with you," Spader said. That took care of that problem. "I'm a Traveler, right? That's what Travelers do. If Cloral is safe now, there's no reason for me to be here either."

"Spader, I—"

"You don't have to worry about me, Pendragon," he said sincerely. "I'm with the program. I meant what I said before. It's not about getting revenge on Saint Dane. It's about stopping him from hurting the territories. Look, mate, it was a rough time. I was out of my head. But I'm back now, and I want to go with you."

That pretty much covered all the points I didn't know how to bring up with him. That was easy. The question was, did I believe him?

"You need me, Pendragon," Spader added.

That brings me to where I am right now, sitting in my quarters on Grallion, writing this journal. Tomorrow, Spader and I are going to leave. Our destination: Veelox. Whatever *that* is.

Writing this all down was hard, but believe it or not, it's made me feel a little better. Looking back on the events that led to the salvation of Cloral made me realize how important our mission is. Uncle Press always told me this, but it took seeing it for myself, again, to understand. I have no idea what we'll find on Veelox, or how we should begin hunting for Saint Dane. I guarantee he won't be walking around with a sign saying: HI, BOBBY, HERE I AM! I'm sure he'll take on some disguise and be working his evil magic just as he did with Denduron and Cloral. The biggest difference will be that I won't have

Uncle Press to rely on. Welcome to Traveler life . . . chapter three.

As I finish writing this journal, I have to say how Uncle Press's last words are really helping keep my head together. He said, no, he *promised* that we would be together again. I'm not sure how that's possible, besides meeting up in heaven or something. But I don't think that's what he meant. The more I think about it, the more I realize he was talking about actually being together again. For real. In this lifetime.

Of course, that raises the biggest question of all. Where exactly is here? For that matter, when is now? That all depends on what territory you happen to be on. For the first time I'm beginning to see some amazing possibilities. I wonder how many territories there are? Are they all like the ones we've been on so far, or is it possible to flume into a whole 'nother plane of existence? The potential is incredibly exciting, and makes my head hurt.

This is where I will end it, guys. I'll send this off to you and then get some sleep. Please know that I miss you both. I hope I can get back there soon. Thank you again for reading my journals and keeping them safe. You are the light of reality in my otherwise dark and confused new life.

Hobey-ho.

Bobby.

END OF JOURNAL #8

◉ SECOND EARTH ◉

Mark and Courtney rode in the back of a black-and-white police cruiser on their way to the Stony Brook Police Station. They had been picked up at Mark's house by a nice cop named Officer Wilson. When he showed up at the door, Mark half expected him to say: "You're under arrest, slimeball!" and slap the cuffs on him. But that didn't happen. He was all friendly and as they rode along he even offered to put the siren on for them. Mark had to fight back the urge to say: "Yeah, go for it!" The kid in him thought it would be cool, but this was serious business, not time for fun. It also didn't help that Courtney gave him a sharp look that said: "If you say yes to the siren, I'll clock you." They rode in silence.

Both were a little bit stunned. They had finished reading Bobby's last journal and had just learned that Press was dead. They had met Press a few times and gotten to know him better through Bobby's journals. Hearing about his tragic death was a shock. Of course it helped that Bobby and company had kicked some serious butt on Cloral. It took some of the sting away. They were already anticipating what they would hear from the territory of Veelox.

But riding above these thoughts was the reality they faced in their own world, here and now.

Mark had a pretty good idea why Captain Hirsch had called them. It was about the journals Andy Mitchell had stolen. He was sure that Mitchell had turned them in to the police to get the reward. Why else would Captain Hirsch want them to come in?

Mark and Courtney had met the captain months before. They were the first ones to alert the police that Bobby and his family were missing. But since that meeting, they learned the truth about what had happened to Bobby through his journals. Though they didn't have any idea where the Pendragons had gone, they knew now *why* they had disappeared. They were here to raise Bobby to become a Traveler, and their job was complete. That's why they left to go . . . somewhere.

Mark and Courtney never told the police what they knew. It was just too unbelievable. They were afraid they would be locked up in some hospital for the mentally deranged, or become suspects in the investigation they started themselves. Worse, they were afraid if people found out about the truth, it would make it harder for the Travelers to complete their mission—especially when it brought them here to Second Earth. So after lots of discussion and thought, Mark and Courtney decided to keep the truth a secret.

But now, with Andy Mitchell bringing the journals to the police, it was possible this whole thing could blow up in their faces.

Those were the worries going through Mark's mind as Officer Wilson pulled into the parking lot of the Stony Brook Police Station. Both he and Courtney tried to act all casual, as if nothing were wrong. They had to be very careful about what they said to the police, or they could find themselves in deep trouble.

Officer Wilson led them through the precinct and had them

wait in the same conference room where they first met with Captain Hirsch months before.

The room was empty except for two thick file folders sitting on the end of the long conference table. Both Mark and Courtney had a pretty good idea of what was in those folders. It was the reason they were here. They gave each other a look, but didn't say a word. There was no way to know if they were being watched and listened to from behind the two-way mirror that ran the length of one wall. Mark wondered what was going through Courtney's mind. She looked pretty calm. That was good. She would have to be calm for both of them, because Mark wanted to hurl.

"Hi, guys. Thanks for coming in," said Captain Hirsch as he walked quickly into the room. "Sit down, please."

Mark and Courtney took seats next to each other on one side of the conference table. Captain Hirsch sat down at the far end, in front of the two file folders. He was dressed in his usual gray business suit, with his tie loose around his neck. Mark wondered if he slept in that suit. Hirsch looked to Mark, then to Courtney, as if he wanted them to say something. They didn't.

"So, you both know Andy Mitchell?"

"Yes," they both said.

"What do you think of him?"

Mark wanted to say he thought Mitchell was an obnoxious slug, but he didn't want Hirsch to think he had a negative attitude.

Courtney said, "He's an obnoxious slug."

Obviously, Courtney couldn't care less about what other people thought of her attitude.

Hirsch nodded. He then reached for one of the file folders.

"This look familiar?" he asked, as he pulled something out and held it up for them to see. It was the first page of Bobby's first journal. It looked *very* familiar. Courtney shot a look to Mark. Mark had to stay cool, even though his worst fear had come true. It was official. Mitchell had turned the journals in. Mark had kept the journals rolled up and tied with a cord, the way Bobby had sent them. Mitchell must've flattened them out and stacked them up so they could fit in a folder. Mark hated Mitchell all the more for being so disrespectful.

"Yeah, it's familiar," said Mark, trying not to appear angry.

"It sure is," added Courtney, sounding a little bit more upset than Mark would have liked. He was afraid Courtney would go ballistic when she saw the journals, but thankfully, she didn't.

Captain Hirsch put the page back in the folder.

"Andy Mitchell brought this in about an hour ago," he said. "He's still here. I'd like to have him join us."

"He's here?" said Mark with surprise. "Now?"

"Yeah. Is it okay?" Hirsch asked.

"Sure," said Courtney. "Bring the slime in."

Captain Hirsch nodded to the mirror, which meant they were being watched. That was a totally creepy feeling. A few seconds later the door opened and Andy Mitchell strode in looking like a guy who had just won the lottery. He walked all cocky and had a smug smile on his face. When he saw Mark and Courtney, the smile fell off. But he got his act back together quickly.

"Man, that was fast," he said with a sneer. He then said to Mark and Courtney, "You guys feeling the heat yet?" He snorted and gave an obnoxious laugh.

"Sit down please, Andy," said Hirsch.

Mitchell threw one leg over a chair and sat on the far end of the table. Mark half expected him to spit on the floor.

"Why's this taking so long?" Mitchell asked. "You guys gonna buy me lunch or what?"

Hirsch didn't respond. He turned to Mark and Courtney,

saying, "Andy brought these pages to our attention. He tells us they're proof of what happened to Bobby Pendragon. If it's true, he's going to get a large reward."

"You got that right!" snorted Mitchell. "Twenty-five big ones."

Mark saw Courtney's hand clench. He knew she was fighting the urge to jump over the table and pummel this weasel. Or maybe she wanted to pummel Mark. He wasn't sure which.

"Andy," Hirsch said with a friendly smile. "Could you tell me how you gained possession of these papers?"

"I told you," Mitchell answered, pointing to Mark. "He had 'em! The two of 'em were keeping them secret so nobody would know what was really going on. I figured it was my civic duty to bring 'em in."

Mark closed his eyes. This was horrible. *Civic duty, yeah right.*

"That's not what I asked you, Mr. Mitchell," said Hirsch politely. "I asked how you gained possession of these pages."

"You mean . . . how did I get 'em?" Mitchell asked. Clearly he wasn't sure of the meaning of the word "gained." *What a tool.*

"Yes," answered Hirsch patiently.

Mitchell began to squirm. He started to answer a few times, but stopped himself as if he wasn't sure he was saying the right thing. Finally, he just blurted out:

"I took 'em, okay? I just took 'em. But so what, man? You would have done the same thing! This kinda stuff shouldn't be secret! People gotta know!"

Hirsch continued calmly, "So you're telling me you stole them from Mark Dimond?"

It was clear that Mitchell didn't like where this was going. "Yeah, I stole 'em. But that's not the point!"

Hirsch nodded. He then reached for the second file folder on the table. Mark and Courtney watched without saying a word or showing any emotion. Hirsch opened the second folder to reveal a thick stack of white paper with lines of typing on it. The lines were single spaced and traveled neatly from margin to margin.

"I'm going to read something to you, Mr. Mitchell," said Hirsch. "I want you to tell me if it sounds familiar."

"Knock yourself out," responded Mitchell.

The police officer looked down at the top page, and began to read aloud.

"'I hope you're reading this, Mark.

"'Heck, I hope anybody's reading this because the only thing that's keeping me from going totally off my nut right now is getting this all down on paper so that—'"

"'That's from the journal," said Mitchell, a little confused. "The first one. That's how it starts. What are you reading that from?"

Hirsch held the thick stack of clean printed pages up for Mitchell to see. "Mark and Courtney brought me this story last week," he said.

"What?" gasped Mitchell, stunned. "I don't get it."

Hirsch put the pages down and chuckled. "Yeah, that's pretty obvious."

"What's goin' on?" demanded Mitchell in confusion.

"This is a story they wrote," said Hirsch, trying to hold back a smile. "A story. It's fiction. Do you know what that means? They made it up."

Mitchell shot a stunned look at Mark and Courtney. The two sat there looking like innocent angels.

"No. No they didn't!" shouted Mitchell. "Pendragon wrote it! It's all true!"

Courtney shook her head and spoke to Hirsch, saying, "Like we told you, it may be childish, but it was our way of dealing with Bobby's disappearance."

"Yeah," added Mark quickly. "I even wrote it out in long hand on those brown pages, as if Bobby wrote it himself. It makes the whole thing seem more real that way."

"But we also typed it on the computer, so it was easier to work on," said Courtney. "It's just a fantasy, but it felt good to pretend that Bobby was on some big adventure instead of, well, instead of being wherever he really is. Now that we're sitting here talking about it, it's kind of . . . embarrassing."

"Don't be embarrassed," said Hirsch kindly. "People deal with loss in a lot of ways. You two were very creative about it."

"You gotta be kidding me!" screamed Mitchell as he jumped up from his chair. "They are lying! Ly-ing! I . . . I saw pages appear from nowhere in a big flash of light through . . . through his ring. Look at his ring!"

Mark shrugged and held up his fingers. He had no rings.

Mitchell was in full-on panic mode. Mark could see that he had gone from thinking he had twenty-five thousand dollars in his pocket to being treated like an idiot thief who believes in fairy tales. He desperately tried to turn it around.

"Okay, okay," he stammered. "Answer me this: Why did they bring you those printed-out pages? Huh? I'll tell you. They were trying to beat me here and get themselves off the hook, that's why."

"No," said Hirsch patiently. "They came here to report their handwritten pages had been stolen. They brought the typed pages to prove the story was theirs. Quite frankly, I never thought the stolen pages would turn up, but then you walked in out of the blue. How very convenient!"

"No!" shouted Mitchell in anguish. He was losing badly.

Hirsch looked at Mark and Courtney and said, "Do you want to press charges against Mr. Mitchell?"

Mark and Courtney looked at each other, then Courtney said, "No, just getting the pages back is enough."

"Yeah, in a way we feel kind of bad for him," said Mark sympathetically. "We never thought somebody would believe our story was good enough to be true!"

"Really!" added Courtney with a laugh.

"But it *is* true!" shouted Mitchell, on the verge of tears. "Isn't it?"

"You're free to go, Mr. Mitchell," said Hirsch. "But I first want you to apologize to these two for what you did."

Mitchell flashed a look of anger and hatred at Mark that rocked him back in his chair. It didn't seem to bother Courtney, though. Mitchell didn't scare her. Mitchell got all red in the face, like he was in horrible pain, then he squeezed out a weak, "I'm . . . sorry."

"It's okay, Andy," Courtney said sympathetically. "Let's forget this ever happened."

"Yeah," added Mark.

"Thank you, Mr. Mitchell. Now go away," ordered Hirsch.

Mitchell stood there for a second, desperately thinking of something he could say to turn this around. But he wasn't smart enough to do that. He looked at Courtney. Courtney gave him a tiny little smile and a wink. That was it. Mitchell couldn't take it anymore.

"Ahhhh!" he shouted, and stormed out of the conference room.

Hirsch said, "You're right. He *is* an obnoxious slug."

"Thank you, Captain," said Courtney in her most polite voice. "I knew you would be the right person to come to for help."

"No problem, that's my job. I do have a favor to ask though."

"Anything," said Courtney quickly.

"Would you let me read this story? It's really pretty good!"

Mark and Courtney exchanged glances, then Mark said, "Sure, but could you read the printed pages? We'd like to hold on to the handwritten ones."

Hirsch quickly slid the folder with Bobby's journals over to Mark.

"Of course, here you go," he said. "That Mitchell guy's a piece of work. Did he really think this story was true?"

All Mark and Courtney could do was shrug innocently.

A few minutes later Mark and Courtney were out of the police station and walking down the Ave. Bobby's first journals were safely tucked into Mark's backpack. They had politely turned down a ride home from Officer Wilson, saying they'd like to walk. They said the whole ordeal was pretty stressful and they needed to cool down.

They went right to Garden Poultry and bought two boxes of French fries, along with a Coke and a Mountain Dew. Mark did the Dew. They brought the food to the pocket park and sat on a bench to enjoy their feast. Neither one had said anything from the time they left the police station. They just kind of drifted toward Garden Poultry without even discussing it.

Finally, as he finished his last crispy golden fry, Mark said, "I'm sorry, Courtney."

Courtney gulped down the rest of her Coke, then said, "Losing that page from the journal was an accident. It was as much my fault as yours. But not telling me right away that Mitchell found out about the journals . . . Mark, that was bad."

"I know, I know," was all Mark could say. "I thought I could handle the guy. I . . . I was embarrassed to tell you how bad I screwed up. But man, when he wanted to see all the journals and started talking about how we were going to be famous when we showed the whole world what we had—I didn't know what to do."

"You should have come to me before it got that bad," said Courtney. Mark could tell she was angry.

"Yeah," said Mark guiltily. "But your plan was awesome." He

thought back to the moment when he finally fessed up to Courtney about what had happened. It was right after Mitchell demanded to see all of the journals. Courtney didn't get angry. Instead she came up with the idea to turn the tables on Mitchell. She knew he would tell the police about the journals to claim the reward. That was a no-brainer. But they figured they could beat him to the punch by pretending they wrote the story themselves. It took Courtney three late nights of grueling typing to get Bobby's first journals into her computer. Then they printed out the pages and took them right to Captain Hirsch. That's when they told him the bogus story about their handwritten version being stolen. The key to the whole thing was showing the story to the police *before* Mitchell did. Neither of them liked to lie, but the situation was desperate. Mitchell had to be stopped from exposing Bobby's story to the world.

As it turned out, it became only half a lie when Mitchell came to Mark's house and ended up stealing the journals after all. Still, if Mitchell had just read the journals and returned them, that would have been the end. But they knew Mitchell wouldn't do that. He was too greedy. They knew he'd take the journals to the police—and walk right into their trap. The sting worked beautifully. They got Bobby's journals back and Mitchell couldn't demand to see them anymore by threatening to go to the police.

It was a beautiful thing, but Mark still felt bad for not having been totally honest with Courtney.

"You brought me into this when you showed me the first journal," Courtney said. "If you want me to stay in, you've got to be honest with me, always."

"I will, I promise," Mark whined.

The two were silent for a second, then slowly, Courtney smiled a devilish smile. "But it sure was sweet seeing Mitchell squirm!"

Mark laughed too and they slapped high-fives. Mark then reached around his neck and pulled out the chain that held the key to his secret desk. Dangling next to it was Mark's ring. He took it off and put it right back on his finger, where it belonged.

There was nothing left to do now but go home. They walked together until Courtney reached her street.

"So, you'll call me?" asked Courtney.

"Soon as the next journal shows," answered Mark, as he always did.

The two then gave each other a hug and separated.

They wouldn't get back together for another five months.

Both went back to their normal lives at home and at school. Since the only friend they had in common was Bobby, that meant neither of them saw much of each other. Occasionally they'd pass in the hallway. Courtney would look at him as if to ask: "Well?" Mark would just shake his head. Nothing yet.

Courtney played softball for the Stony Brook team. It was fast-pitch and she was the pitcher. The team went undefeated that spring, and Courtney was MVP of course.

Mark's big project was to build a battling robot for a county science fair. He had a real knack for mechanics and physics. The robot was killer. It destroyed the competition with a combination hook, buzz saw, sledgehammer package. He took first prize and started to investigate how to get on the TV with his battling robotic baby.

Courtney had a birthday on March 6. She turned fifteen. Mark sent her a card with the greeting: "Happy Birthday, Hobey-ho!"

The two did get together once, on March 11. Bobby's birthday. They went back to Garden Poultry on the Ave, got some fries, and toasted Bobby in the pocket park with Coke and Dew.

Both wondered if Bobby had any idea that he had just turned fifteen.

The next big event was graduation from Stony Brook Junior High in June. Mark was valedictorian and was supposed to give a speech. But he was too nervous and let the runner-up take his place on the podium. He was still the valedictorian, though, and got a huge dictionary as a prize. The next stop for these two was high school—a big, scary step. They would soon be going to Davis Gregory High, the big public high school in Stony Brook. Nobody knew who Davis Gregory was, but they figured he must have been somebody important. Mark wondered if someday there'd be a school called Bobby Pendragon High.

The summer went along lazily. Courtney played baseball and got her junior lifeguard certification. Mark tinkered with his killer robot, getting ready for the big state competition. He had gotten an invitation and everything. His reputation was getting around.

Mark always wore the ring, waiting for the day when the next journal would arrive. The truth was, both Mark and Courtney tried not to think about Bobby, because the longer it went without getting a journal, the more they feared that something nasty had happened to him. That was something they didn't even want to consider, so it was easier to put Bobby out of their minds entirely.

Then, on August 21, two things happened. First, it was Mark's fifteenth birthday. He celebrated in his usual way: getting some creepy new clothes from his mother and a gift certificate from his father that would be spent wisely at the local electronics store.

The other thing that happened was Mark got a strange phone call at home.

An official-sounding woman's voice said, "May I speak to a Mr. Mark Dimond, please?"

"That's me."

"This is Ms. Jane Jansen, vice-president of the National Bank of Stony Brook. Are you familiar with us?"

The woman sounded like somebody's idea of a pruny old schoolteacher.

"Uh . . . sure," he said. "You're on the Ave . . . uh . . . Stony Brook Avenue."

"Correct," she answered. "Do you know a Ms. Courtney Chetwynde?"

"Yes, what's this about?"

"Mr. Dimond, would you and Ms. Chetwynde please come down to our branch as soon as possible? With some identification? I believe this may be an issue of some importance."

This really threw Mark. He didn't even have a bank account. What could they possibly want with him and Courtney? He was just about to tell this wacky woman that he wanted to call his parents first, when she dropped the bomb.

"It has to do with a Mr. Robert Pendragon."

Those were the magic words.

"We'll be right there," Mark said, and hung up the phone before she had the chance to say good-bye.

Mark immediately called Courtney and was relieved to find her home. Half an hour later, the two of them were standing outside the large, gray cement building with the big brass letters that read: NATIONAL BANK OF STONY BROOK.

Mark never understood how Stony Brook could have a national bank, but it had been around forever so he figured they must know what they were doing. The bank itself was old-fashioned. There was a huge lobby with a high ceiling capped by a glass dome. This was not like the modern banks that Mark had been in with his mother. This looked like the bank from Mary Poppins. There was lots of dark polished wood, brass hardware, and leather furniture. There were a lot of customers, too, and they all whispered when they spoke. It was like a library. Mark thought this bank probably looked exactly the same as it did the year it was built. Based on the cornerstone he saw outside, that year was 1933.

Mark and Courtney told the receptionist they were there to see a Ms. Jansen. They were asked to have a seat in the waiting area, so the two of them sank into the cushy leather chairs to wait for this mysterious woman who had some news about Bobby.

"You have any clue what this is about?" Courtney asked Mark.

"None, zero, nada," Mark answered.

A second later they both saw a rail-thin woman walking toward them. She wore a gray suit and had her hair up in a bun. Her glasses were black with perfectly round lenses. Mark knew immediately that this must be Ms. Jane Jansen. She looked exactly like her voice sounded. She was old, too. Mark wondered if she had been working here since the bank opened.

The woman walked up to the receptionist and asked her a question that Mark couldn't hear. The receptionist pointed to Mark and Courtney. Ms. Jansen looked at them and frowned.

"I guess we're not what she was expecting," Courtney whispered.

Ms. Jansen walked over to them quickly. She had perfect posture and a stiff neck that didn't turn. Whenever she looked in a different direction, she moved her whole body.

"Mr. Dimond? Ms. Chetwynde?" she asked with a snippy tone.

"That's us," answered Mark.

"Do you have some form of identification?" she added suspiciously.

Courtney and Mark gave the woman their student ID cards. Jansen looked at them over her glasses and then frowned again.

"You two are quite young," she said.

"You needed our ID's to figure that out?" Courtney asked.

Mark winced. Courtney was being a wise-ass, again.

Ms. Jansen shot Courtney a sour look and handed them back their ID's. "Is this the way young people dress today to attend a meeting?" she asked, sounding all superior.

Mark and Courtney looked at each other. They were both wearing shorts, T-shirts, and hiking boots. What was wrong with that?

"We're fifteen, ma'am, what did you expect?" said Courtney. "We don't have snappy outfits like you're wearing."

Jansen knew this was a cut, but let it go.

"Please follow me," she said, then turned and walked toward the back of the bank.

Courtney rolled her eyes at Mark. Mark shrugged and the two of them followed the stiff, skinny little woman. A minute later they were sitting across from her at a large oak desk.

"We have been holding an envelope for the two of you," she explained. "We assume it must be some sort of inheritance from a relative of your. Are either of you related to Mr. Robert Pendragon?"

That was a tough one to answer. Mark was about to say that they were just friends, but Courtney jumped in first saying, "Yeah, he's a distant relative."

Jansen continued, "Well, it doesn't matter actually. The instructions are quite clear."

She then handed the envelope to Mark. It was an old, yellowed letter that had two names written on it: "Mark Dimond" and "Courtney Chetwynde." It was Bobby's handwriting. Both Mark and Courtney had to force themselves to keep from smiling.

Jansen continued, "We were instructed to deliver this

envelope to you on this date. We were also instructed to have you open it right away."

Mark shrugged and opened the letter. He pulled out a sheet of paper that was folded in half. It was old and yellow too, like the envelope. There was a header engraved on top that read: "National Bank of Stony Brook" in fancy lettering. Below it were the words: "Safety Deposit Box #15-224."

There was one other thing in the envelope: a small key.

Mark and Courtney had no idea what to make of this, so they showed it to Ms. Jansen. She looked at the note and the key, then said quickly, "Follow me, please."

She got up and walked off again. They followed her.

"This is freaky," whispered Courtney.

This time Ms. Jansen led them into a place Mark had always wanted to go—the huge bank vault. Since the bank was open for business, so was the vault. There was a giant, round door that looked like something you'd see in Fort Knox. When this baby closed, there was nobody getting in. Or out, for that matter.

Mark wondered if inside they would see big bags of money with dollar signs on them. Or stacks of clean crisp bills. Or maybe even bars of gold.

But there was none of that. Ms. Jansen led them to a room full of brass lockers. Some were as big as the lockers at school, others were no larger than a few inches wide. These were the safe deposit boxes of the National Bank of Stony Brook.

Ms. Jansen walked along one row of doors, scanning the numbers inscribed on each. She finally arrived at the one marked: 15-224. She stopped and handed the key to Mark.

"You both are now the owners of the contents of safe deposit box number 15-224. I will leave you alone to inspect the contents. When you are finished, please relock the box and return the key to me. Any questions?"

"I'm kind of confused," said Mark. "Who set this up?"

"I told you, a Mr. Robert Pendragon."

Courtney asked, "He came in here? Did you see him?"

The look on Ms. Jansen's face got even more pinched, if that were possible.

"I know you consider me to be a fossil, Ms. Chetwynde, but I assure you, this account was opened long before I was employed here at National Bank."

"So when was that?" asked Mark.

"I'll have to double check the exact date, but I believe it was sometime in May."

"He was here three months ago?" shouted Courtney in surprise.

"Please, Ms. Chetwynde," said Jansen testily. "I'm not a fool, so do not try to play me for one. This account was opened in May of 1937."

Mark and Courtney went into stunned brain lock.

"Do you have any more questions?"

Both Mark and Courtney could only shake their heads.

"Then I'll be at my desk."

Jansen gave them a last annoyed look and hurried off.

Mark and Courtney couldn't move. They both tried desperately to get their minds around the incredible information.

"Is it possible?" Courtney finally asked.

"There's one way to find out," answered Mark.

He inserted the key into the deposit box marked 15-224. This was one of the larger boxes compared to the others. It looked to be about two feet high. The door hinged outward, revealing a handle attached to a steel box. While Mark held the door open, Courtney pulled on the handle. The steel box slid out easily. It was roughly the size of two shoe boxes.

"Take it over there," said Mark.

Built into one wall was a row of four desks set up with partitions between them, kind of like the study carrels in the library at school. These wooden desks looked ancient, just like everything else at this bank. Courtney put the box down on one of the old desks and they each pulled up a chair. Mark was happy nobody else was here.

The two looked at the steel box. The lid was still closed so they couldn't see what was inside. Mark's heart was racing. He knew Courtney's was too.

"I can't breathe," Mark said finally.

"Then open it. This is killing me!"

Mark reached for the lid, hesitated a moment, then lifted it up.

They saw that the deep box was mostly empty. But lying on the bottom was a stack of four books, each bound in dark red leather. They were about the size of a piece of computer paper: 8x10 inches. Each looked to be about a half-inch thick. The weird thing was that they didn't have any titles. There were no markings on the covers whatsoever.

There was something else in the box too. Sandwiched next to the stack of books was an envelope. Mark's hands were shaking as he pulled it out. It was a business-size envelope with a printed return address in the upper left corner. It was the name and address of the bank. Whoever wrote this letter wrote it here in the bank. There was something else on the envelope. In Bobby's handwriting were the words: "Mark and Courtney."

"That's us," said Courtney with a weak smile.

Mark nervously opened the envelope and pulled out the single page inside. He unfolded it to reveal a letter written on National Bank of Stony Brook stationery. The words were written in Bobby's handwriting.

Dear Mark and Courtney,

I gotta make this fast. I don't have much time. Here's the deal. I lost my ring. I haven't had it for months now. That's why you haven't been getting my journals. I've been writing though. Every thing that's happened I put down on paper, just like always. But it's been making me crazy. I hate having all the journals together. They're not safe with me. I can't believe it took me as long as it did to come up with a solution.

I came to Stony Brook. I knew the National Bank was around forever and sure enough, here it is. What a rush. The Ave is a totally different place, though. I was kind of hoping Garden Poultry was here to grab a quick box of fries, but no such luck. You know what's there instead? A barbershop. Same building, different business. Weird.

I could go on forever about how strange this is, but I don't have time. If my plan works, and I can't think of why it won't, you'll be sitting in the same spot where I am right now, reading this letter.

I've put all four journals in the safe deposit box. The whole adventure is contained here. Hopefully, the next time you hear from me it will be through the rings. I think I might know where mine is now, and that's where I'm headed.

Thank you, guys. I miss you.
Bobby
May 31, 1937

P.S. If they still have these wooden desks in the vault, look under the one to the far right.

Courtney and Mark both read the letter a few times to make sure they understood. Somehow Bobby got here in 1937 and left his journals. It made sense. Bobby knew the National Bank would still be here in the present, so there was no reason why it wouldn't work. The bigger question was, how the heck did he get to 1937? It began to raise all sorts of questions about the flumes sending Travelers through time as well as territories.

They both turned their attention to the desk they were sitting at. They looked pretty old and were probably the same desks that Bobby had sat at. They both got down on their knees to look under the desk on the far right. They had no idea what they should be looking for until—

"Oh, man, look!" Courtney said.

She pointed to a spot underneath the desk. Something was carved into the woodwork. The only way you could see it was to be down on the floor, looking straight up. The words said: "Happy Birthday, Mark."

As they lay on their backs, looking up, Mark and Courtney started to laugh. This was so perfectly Bobby. Mark wished he had a camera with him so he could take a shot and keep it with the journals. He planned on coming back and doing just that.

The two then pulled themselves out from under the desk and stood up. They stared at the open safety deposit box and the four journals inside.

"I can't believe there's a whole story here," said Courtney.

"We should bring them home," Mark said.

"Yeah," agreed Courtney, "but this is killing me. Let's just look at the first page."

Mark couldn't think of a reason not to, so he reached inside and took the first journal off the pile. It was nicely bound, like a book that had never been opened.

"Not exactly old parchment papers," Mark said.

He then carefully opened the cover to the first page.

Unlike the stories from Denduron and Cloral, Bobby had typed this journal. The pages were the size of regular computer printer paper, but they were heavier and cream colored. Also, the typing looked all messy. This wasn't like a clean page from a printer. This had actually been typed on an old-fashioned type-writer. Neither of them had ever seen something like this—it was like looking at a piece of history. In a way, that's exactly what it was.

"Let's at least see where he was," said Courtney.

"Okay," agreed Mark.

The two sat down at the desk and began to read.

to be continued

Where will Bobby Pendragon's adventures take him next? Here is a look at Pendragon: Book Three: THE NEVER WAR

FIRST EARTH

That's where I am. First Earth. Veelox was a misdirection. Spader and I flumed to Veelox, but found the action wasn't there. It was here on First Earth.

Where is First Earth? The better question is, *when* is First Earth? I'm in New York City and it's 1937. March of 1937 to be exact. To be *really* exact, it's March 11 of 1937. I'm writing this on my birthday. Here's a weird thought: If I'm in 1937 and it's my birthday, did I still turn fifteen? Kind of freaky, no?

I'll begin this new journal by telling you I stumbled into the most bizarro, confusing, dangerous situation yet. But then again, haven't I said that before? Let me give you a little taste of what happened in only the first few minutes since I got here. . . .

Spader and I were nearly killed. Three times. We were also robbed and witnessed a gruesome murder. Happy birthday to me! The way things are going, I know what I want for my fifteenth birthday . . . the chance to have a sixteenth.

When Spader and I flumed in from Veelox, I had no idea of what "First Earth" meant. Since I'm from Second Earth, I could only guess that First Earth was sometime in the Earth's past. But how far past? For all I knew we were fluming back to a time when quigs were dinosaurs and we'd be on the run from hungry, yellow-eyed raptors.

I was totally relieved to find that when we landed at the gate, it was the exact same rocky room that I had been through many times before. Yes, we had arrived at the gate off the subway tunnel in the Bronx, New York. Phew. At least there were no T-rexes or Neanderthals waiting for us. That was the good news.

Bad news was that we weren't alone. As soon as the flume dropped us off, I saw two guys standing there, facing us. They wore old-fashioned gray suits, like Clark Kent wears in the old *Superman* show on TV Land. Actually, a better analogy is that these guys were dressed like the *bad guys* from that old show, because that's what they were. Bad guys. *Very* bad guys. They wore wide-brimmed hats that were pulled down low and had white handkerchiefs around their noses and mouths like banditos. There's only one word to describe these dudes.

Gangsters.

Their eyes looked wide and scared. No big surprise. They had just seen Spader and me drop out of nowhere in an explosion of light and music. They seemed totally stunned, which was good because there was one other detail I haven't mentioned. . . .

They were both holding machine guns that were aimed at the flume—and at us.

"Down!" I yelled at Spader.

The two of us jumped to opposite sides of the flume just as the gangsters started shooting. I crouched in a ball, totally unprotected as the deadly clatter from their rapid-fire guns echoed off the rocky walls. I thought for sure I'd get hit, but after a few seconds the shooting stopped, and I was still intact. I was afraid to move and even more afraid to look over and see if Spader was okay. The sharp explosions fell off to a distant echo that bounced around the cavelike room. My ears were ringing and the chemical smell of gunpowder burned my nose. I figured this was what it must be like to be in a war.

"Get up!" one of the gangsters ordered. "Hands in the air!"

I cautiously looked over to Spader and saw that he was okay. We stood slowly and raised our hands. The gangsters held their guns on us. I didn't know why. It wasn't like we had weapons of our own. The second gangster kept glancing nervously between the two of us. He looked almost as scared as we were. Almost.

"Th-They from Mars?" he asked his buddy nervously.

Under less terrifying circumstances, I would have laughed. It must have looked like we had just landed from outer space. Not only did we flash in through a storm of light, we were still dressed in our bright blue swimskins from Cloral. For a second I thought about pulling a huge bluff and chanting: "Drop your weapons or we will vaporize you with our mind-heat," or something equally sci-fi, but I didn't get the chance.

"Don't matter," barked the other gangster. He was definitely the one in charge, but I could tell from his voice that he was a little shaky too.

"We done our job," he added.

"S-So what about th-them?" the nervous gangster asked.

The guy in charge looked us over. I could almost hear the wheels turning in his brain. He didn't exactly seem like a rocket scientist, so they must have been very small wheels. I wondered if they hurt when they turned.

"You!" the guy barked at me. "Gimme that ring!"

I couldn't believe it. He wanted my Traveler ring! This was serious. You guys know how badly I need that ring. It shows me where the flumes are, and it's the only way I can get my journals to you. Without this ring, I'm lost.

"It's not worth anything," I said in a feeble attempt to talk him out of it.

"Don't matter," the gangster snapped back at me. "All I want is proof to show you two are real."

"Then take us with you, mates!" said Spader, trying to be friendly. "We're all the proof you need, in the flesh!"

"Those ain't my orders," he snarled.

"Really? What *are* your orders?" I asked.

"Just hand over the ring," the boss commanded. He raised his machine gun to prove he meant business. What could I do? I took off my ring and tossed it to him. He caught it and jammed it into his pocket.

"Let's step outside, nice and easy," the guy said.

This was good. It meant they weren't going to gun us down right that moment. Maybe there was a way out of this after all. The nervous gangster threw the wooden door open, then both stepped aside and motioned with their weapons for us to go through. I looked at Spader. Spader shrugged. We had to play along. With our hands up, we both stepped out of the gate and into the dark subway tunnel.

Everything was familiar, so I made a sharp right, knowing it was the way to the abandoned subway station.

But the gangster had other things in mind. "No, you don't," he ordered. "Keep walking."

We had to walk straight ahead, away from the door. Three steps later we stepped over the rail of the subway track. This was beginning to look bad again.

"Stop! Turn around."

Oh yeah, this was bad. We were both now standing on the train tracks.

"You move, you die," said the first gangster.

Yeah, right. We move, we die. If a train comes along, we *don't* move, we die. Not a lot of wiggle room here.

"Where are we, Pendragon?" whispered Spader.

His answer came in the form of a far off whistle. We both looked to our right and saw the headlight of a subway train rounding the bend, headed our way, on our track.

"What is that thing?" asked Spader nervously. Being from a territory that was covered entirely with water, he had never seen anything like a train before.

"That," I said, trying not to let my voice show the fear that was tearing at my gut, "is a pretty big tum-tigger."

"Hobey," said Spader in awe. "We just got here and we've already lost."

We had been on First Earth for all of two minutes, and we were staring death right in the eye.

Welcome home, Bobby Pendragon.

That's a taste of how our adventure on First Earth began. I don't want to get too far ahead because there was a whole lot that happened between the time I finished my last journal, and when we landed here. But I wanted to explain to you how I lost my ring. This is serious because as I write this journal to you, Mark and Courtney, I'm not really sure if you're ever going to read it. If I don't get that ring back, I'll never be able to send this to you. The only thing I can do is keep writing, hang on to the journals, and hope that I get the ring back soon.

Now, let me rewind to where I finished my last journal and get you guys back up to speed.

I spent my last few days on the territory of Cloral in a haze. We'd defeated Saint Dane, but I didn't feel much like celebrating. That's because Uncle Press was gone, and I kept replaying his last moments over and over in my head. Saint Dane had escaped through a flume and Spader tried to chase him. But a storm of bullets came back at him. Uncle Press realized what was happening, knocked Spader out of the way . . . and took the bullets himself.

He died in my arms. It was the absolute worst moment of my life. The only thing that kept me from totally losing it was that just before he died, he promised me we'd be together again. I know this sounds pretty loopy, but I believe him. If being a Traveler has taught me anything, it's that nothing is impossible. My eyes have been opened to so many new worlds and levels of existence that the idea of hooking up with Uncle Press again doesn't seem all that far-fetched.

Of course, I have no clue how it might happen. That's because I've only scratched the surface of knowing all there is to know about being a Traveler. I wish there were an instruction manual I could buy through Amazon.com that would spell out all the rules and regulations. Unfortunately, it's not that easy. I've got to learn things as I go along. And now I've got to do it without Uncle Press.

Welcome to my life as a Traveler, phase two.

In those last days on Cloral, I knew what my next move had to be, but I was putting it off because, well, I was scared. Things were different now. I was alone. It was a whole new ballgame and I wasn't sure if I was good enough to play in it.

When Saint Dane flumed out of Cloral, he was headed for a territory called Veelox. I knew I had to follow him, but the idea of going after him alone was about as appealing as setting my hair on fire. All things being equal, I think I'd rather have set my hair on fire. So I made a decision that I hope I don't regret.

I asked Vo Spader to go with me.

Don't get me wrong, Spader is a great guy. He's the Traveler from Cloral, after all. He saved my life more than once; he's an incredible athlete; he's about as brave as can be; and most importantly, he's my friend. So why should I be worried about asking him to come with me?

It's because his total, blind hatred of Saint Dane is dangerous. Saint Dane caused the death of his father and for that, Spader wants revenge. Big time. Hey, I don't blame him. But there were a few times on Cloral where Spader got so completely wrapped up in Saint Dane—hating that he nearly got us all killed. Truth be told, Spader's anger toward Saint Dane is one of the reasons Uncle Press is dead.

Since then, Spader promised me he would control himself, and his anger. I can only hope that when we come face-to-face with the demon again, and I guarantee we will, Spader won't do anything stupid. These were some of the conflicted thoughts that were banging around inside my head as I finished my last journal.

"Hobey-ho, Pendragon," Spader said as he strode into my apartment the morning of our departure.

Spader had almond-shaped eyes that looked sort of Asian. They turned up slightly and made him look as if he were always smiling. The truth was, most of the time he *was* smiling . . . when he wasn't obsessing over Saint Dane, that is. His long black hair was still wet, which meant he had been in the water. Spader spent a lot of time in the water, playing traffic cop with the boats and barges that came and went from Grallion. He loved his job, and his life there. At least he loved it before he found out he was a Traveler. Things had changed a little since then.

"It's time," I said.

"For what?" was his quick response.

"Cloral is safe. Uncle Press is gone. And I'm as ready as I'll ever be to go after Saint Dane."

Spader gave me a devilish smile. "Now you're talking, mate! I've been waiting to hear those words for weeks! What if the trail's gone cold?"

"I don't think that's possible," I answered. "Uncle Press always said that time between territories isn't relative."

Spader frowned. "You lost me."

I had to laugh. This didn't make a whole lot of sense to me either, but I had to trust Uncle Press.

"Look at it this way," I explained. "Saint Dane flumed to Veelox a few weeks ago, but since then he may have spent five years there. Or a minute."

"Now I'm totally lost," Spader said in frustration.

"Bottom line is, we're not too late," I said. "It doesn't matter when we go after him, because the flume will put us where we need to be, *when* we need to be there."

"O-kay," said Spader tentatively. "I'll trust you on that."

I'd already said good-bye to our friends on Grallion, and I'd sent my last journal to you. I had explained the importance of journals to Spader and he had already started his own. The person he chose to send them to on Cloral for safekeeping was Wu Yenza. She was the chief aquaneer and Spader's boss. He couldn't have picked a better person.

I took a last look around my apartment. Then we went down to the docks, loaded our air globes and water sleds onto a skimmer boat, and left Grallion for the flume. Spader was the expert, so he drove. As we shot across the water I looked back at the giant, floating farm habitat of Grallion, wondering if I'd ever see it again. I liked Cloral. There were times when I actually had fun on that territory. It gave me hope that being a Traveler didn't mean I always had to live in a state of fear and confusion.

Now the question was, what lay ahead of us? Pretty much a state of fear and confusion. Great. Here we go again.

The trip to the flume was cake. We anchored the skimmer near the reef, popped on the air globes that allowed us to breathe underwater, triggered the water sleds, and quickly sank below the surface. We didn't run into any shark quigs either. I think that once Saint Dane is finished with a territory, the quigs no longer patrol the gates. Still, I wasn't taking any chances. As we sped through the water being pulled by the sleds, I kept glancing back to make sure nothing nasty was sneaking up on us to try and get a nibble.

I didn't relax until we shot under the shelf of rock that led to the gate. Following the glow from my ring, we quickly found the wide circle of light that led up and into the cavern that held the flume. Moments later we were standing together in the cavern, staring up at the dark flume tunnel that was cut into the rock wall high over our heads.

This was it. The last few seconds of calm.

Spader looked at me and smiled. "My heart's thumpin'."

So was mine. We were standing at the starting line and the gun was about to go off. Spader loved adventure. Me? I'd just as soon be home watching toons. Knowing Spader was nervous made me feel like I wasn't such a weenie after all.

He added, "We're in for another natty-do, aren't we, mate?"

"Yeah," I answered. "Pretty much."

"No use in wasting time here then," he said, sounding a lot braver than I felt.

"Yeah," I said. "We're on the wrong territory."

I stood straight, looked up to the dark hole of the flume, and shouted, *"Veelox!"*

The tunnel sprang to life. Shafts of bright light shot from deep inside. The familiar jumble of musical notes could be heard faintly at first, but quickly grew louder. They were coming to get us.

Spader turned to me and smiled. "Hobey-ho, Pendragon."

"Hobey-ho, Spader," I answered. "Let's go get him."

A second later we were swept up by the light and sound and pulled into the flume.

Next stop . . . Veelox.

◉ SECOND EARTH ◉

Mark Dimond and Courtney Chetwynde huddled together in the vault of the National Bank of Stony Brook, reading Bobby's journal from First Earth. It was a journal unlike any of the others Bobby had sent.

First off, the pages weren't loose. They were bound nicely into a book with a deep red cover. And the pages weren't hand-written. They were typed . . . on an old-fashioned typewriter. They knew it was a typewriter because the letters weren't all perfectly lined up and there were a ton of mistakes. Besides, they didn't have computers or printers back in 1937. This new journal was definitely a far cry from the pieces of rolled up parchment paper Bobby had written his first journals on.

The other difference was that Bobby usually sent only one journal at a time. When he finished writing one he'd send it, through his Traveler ring, to Mark's ring. But this time, sitting in front of Mark and Courtney were four journals. After reading what happened with the gangsters on First Earth, Mark and Courtney knew why.

Bobby's ring had been stolen.

The mysterious manner in which the journals arrived was further proof of that. Earlier that day, Mark had gotten a strange phone call from a lady at the National Bank of Stony Brook. She asked for Mark and Courtney to meet her at the bank to discuss something about a Mr. Robert Pendragon. That was all Mark needed to hear. He and Courtney were at that bank in half an hour.

When they arrived, they discovered that Bobby had rented a safe-deposit box at the bank in 1937. Bobby had left explicit instructions that the bank should contact Mark Dimond on this very date—August 21, Mark's fifteenth birthday.

When Mark and Courtney opened up the safe-deposit box, they found the four journals. They had been lying in that box for over sixty years.

This whole episode was another bizarre twist in an already incredible situation. Bobby Pendragon had mysteriously left their hometown of Stony Brook, Connecticut, with his Uncle Press almost nine months before. Since then his family had disappeared, and the journals began showing up. The only people who knew the truth were his best friends, Mark and Courtney. Bobby trusted them to take care of his journals in case he might need them again someday.

But more important, it seemed to both Mark and Courtney that writing these journals helped keep Bobby sane. He was now smack in the middle of an incredible adventure that had nothing less than the future of everything at stake. Writing the journals seemed like a perfect way for Bobby to help keep his head on straight, while everything around him was so twisted. Both knew that one day Bobby's adventure would take him home. But until then, the only thing they could do to help him on his quest was to read his journals, try to understand what he was going through, and keep them safe.

"We're closing," snapped Ms. Jane Jansen, the bank manager, making Mark and Courtney jump.

Ms. Jane Jansen had only just met the two, but she didn't seem to like them. She didn't seem to like much of anything. Her face was in a permanent state of pucker, like she had a lemon in her pocket that she was constantly sucking on.

"Oh, sorry," said Mark, as if he had been caught doing something wrong. "We were reading. Can we come back tomorrow?"

"Tomorrow's Sunday," snapped Ms. Jane Jansen. "And this isn't a library. You children have spent far too much time here already."

Courtney didn't like Ms. Jane Jansen's attitude. And she definitely didn't like being called a child, especially by such a prune.

"So if we can't read here, what are we supposed to do?" asked Courtney politely, trying not to let her distaste for the woman show through.

"The content of that box belongs to you," Ms. Jane Jansen said. "Do whatever you want with it."

"You mean, we can take it all home?" asked Mark.

"I said, whatever you want," said Ms. Jane Jansen impatiently.

"Why didn't you say that in the first place?" asked Courtney. "Or do you always provide such lousy service?"

Mark winced. He hated it when Courtney clicked into wiseass mode.

Ms. Jane Jansen's eyes popped open wide. "Miss Chetwynde, I have been an employee of the National Bank of Stony Brook for over twenty years and I have always provided thorough and professional service."

"I'll be sure to include that in our report to your president," Courtney said. "That's what this is all about, you know. To test how bank employees deal with unusual situations. So far, you haven't exactly rolled with the punches, now have you, Ms. Jane Jansen?"

Ms. Jane Jansen's eyes grew wide. She suddenly turned all friendly and polite. "Well, uh, if you have any complaints I'd be more than happy to personally ensure your complete satisfaction."

"There *is* something," Courtney said. "If you'd be so kind, would you return the empty drawer to our safe-deposit box? We'll be taking the contents with us."

Ms. Jane Jansen clenched her teeth. It wasn't her job to clean up after people. But she sucked it up.

"Of course," she said with a big, phony smile. "I'd be happy to."

Mark quickly scooped up the four journals and stashed them in his backpack. He wanted to get out of there before Courtney got them into trouble.

"Th-Thanks," he said with sincere courtesy. "We'll get out of your hair now." He went for the door, pulling Courtney along with him.

"Thanks for all your help, ma'am," said Courtney sweetly. "You really put the *ass* in *ass*-istance."

Mark yanked Courtney out of the vault, leaving Ms. Jane Jansen with a twisted smile that actually looked painful. A minute later they rushed out of the gray bank building onto Stony Brook Avenue. Courtney was all smiles. Mark was angry.

"Are you crazy?" he yelled. "What if she threw us out of there? We could have lost the journals!"

"No way," assured Courtney. "You heard her. They belong to us. Besides, she deserved it. She treated us like a couple of turds."

"Yeah, well, some things are more important than your bruised ego," Mark muttered.

"You're right, Mark," Courtney said sincerely. "I'm sorry."

Mark nodded, then looked at Courtney and smiled. "She *did* deserve it."

The two burst out laughing. Now that their bank adventure

was behind them, their thoughts turned to the n.
After waiting for months, they had another journal fro.
Better, they had *four* journals. In Mark's pack was an entire ..
adventure. They wouldn't have to wait impatiently for new journals to show up. They had a full story in their hands.

"I don't know about you," said Mark, "but once I start reading
again, I'm not going to want to stop."

"Agreed," said Courtney.

"Here's what I'm thinking. It's getting late. How about if we
wait till tomorrow?"

"You're kidding!" protested Courtney.

"I'm serious. Tomorrow's Sunday. I'll come over to your house
real early, like eight A.M. We'll go down to your father's workshop
and won't come out until we're finished."

Courtney gave this some thought. "You promise not to read
anything tonight?" she asked.

"Promise," Mark said, crossing his heart.

"Okay, cool," she said. "I'll make some sandwiches. You bring
chips. We'll make it a marathon."

"Excellent. I'll bring the Dew, too," Mark said with excitement.

"Whatever." Courtney didn't do the Dew.

"This is gonna be great!" Mark shouted.

The next day at 8 A.M. sharp, Courtney's doorbell rang.
Courtney's dad opened the door to see Mark standing there with
a loaded grocery bag.

"Morning, Mark," he said through sleepy eyes. "Going on a
picnic?"

"Uh . . . no," answered Mark. "Courtney and I are working on
a school project in your basement. It's gonna take all day so we
need provisions."

"Really?" said Mr. Chetwynde. "It's August."

"Right," said Mark, thinking fast. "Summer school."

"Courtney doesn't go to summer school."

"I know," Mark said, mentally kicking himself for being such a lousy, uncreative liar. "I do."

Mr. Chetwynde looked at Mark. Mark smiled innocently.

Mr. Chetwynde shrugged and yawned. "Whatever, c'mon in." He stepped aside and Mark rushed in.

Mark knew exactly where to go. He and Courtney had used Mr. Chetwynde's basement workshop as a private place to read Bobby's journals many times before. Mr. Chetwynde had set up an entire workshop down there and never used it. He was a lousy do-it-yourself type guy. Mark and Courtney could be there all day, even on a Sunday, and never worry about anybody coming down.

Mark settled into the big, dusty couch as Courtney ran down the stairs. "Sandwiches are in the fridge," she announced. "Ready when we need 'em."

She sat next to Mark on the couch as he pulled the four red-leather journals from his backpack. He put them down reverently on the low table in front of them. The two sat there, staring at the precious stack. Neither made a move to pick one up.

"This is kind of weird," Mark finally said.

"Really," agreed Courtney. "I'm excited and afraid at the same time. I'm dying to know what happened to Bobby, but what if it's bad?"

The two fell silent, staring at the books.

"There's something else," added Mark thoughtfully. "This whole *First* Earth thing makes me nervous."

"Why?" Courtney asked.

"It's like Saint Dane is coming closer. To us."

"You don't know that," Courtney said quickly.

"No, but Second Earth is a territory like all the others. One

day Saint Dane is going to come here, too. And whe.
we're going to be doing more than just reading about it."

"Unless Bobby and the Travelers stop him first, right?"
Courtney asked hopefully.

Mark didn't answer. He looked at the journals thoughtfully,
then reached for the top one. "Let's just read, okay?"

Courtney took a breath to calm down, then said, "Let's try
something different this time. We'll read out loud to each other."

Mark was secretly relieved. He was a faster reader than
Courtney and always had to wait for her to catch up. This was the
perfect solution.

"Yeah, that sounds good," he said, and handed her the journal. "You first."

Courtney took the journal and cracked open the cover. "We
left off where Bobby and Spader flumed to Veelox, right?" she
asked.

"Right," answered Mark. He sank back into the couch, put a
hand behind his head, got comfortable and said, "Go for it."

Courtney turned to the page where they had left off the day
before, and began to read out loud.

"*A second later we were swept up by the light and sound and
pulled into the flume. Next stop . . . Veelox.*"

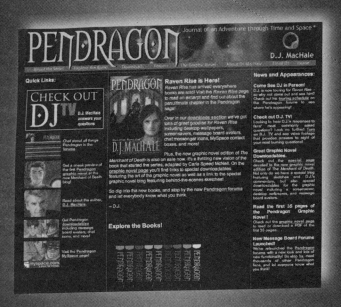

"Imagination runs wild in *Fablehaven*.
It is a lucky book that can hold this kind of story."

—OBERT SKYE, Author of *Leven Thumps and the Gateway to Foo*

Gather your courage,
collect your wits, and
join Kendra and Seth as
they discover a hidden
refuge for mythical and
magical creatures.

Shadow Mountain
Book one, Hardcover, 368 pages
ISBN: 978-1-59038-581-4

Book two, Hardcover, 448 pages
ISBN: 978-1-59038-742-9

Simon & Schuster/Aladdin
Book one, Trade Paperback,
 368 pages
ISBN: 978-1-4169-4720-2

Ages: 9 and up

VISIT FABLEHAVEN.COM

DON'T MISS THIS UNFOOGETTABLE ADVENTURE!

Fourteen-year-old Leven Thumps is in for the journey of a lifetime when he learns about a secret gateway that bridges two worlds: the real world and Foo. A place created at the beginning of time in the folds of the mind, Foo makes it possible for mankind to dream and hope, aspire and imagine . . . and it's up to Leven to save it.

Available from Aladdin Paperbacks

PLAY!
Live the Game
Read the Adventure

Imagine the Unimagined

Log on to **ThePendragonAdventure.com**.
Answer the clue to unlock the secret
code! How good are you?

**What was the name of
Zy Roder's raider cruiser?**

There will be a game for each
book and a code to match. Be sure
to use the answer to this clue as
the code to Game #2!

Keep reading Pendragon books
for more codes!